A LADY NEVER LIES

Juliana Gray

BERKLEY SENSATION, NEW YORK

THE BERKLEY PUBLISHING GROUP
Published by the Penguin Group
Penguin Group (USA) Inc.
375 Hudson Street, New York, New York 10014, USA
Penguin Group (Canada), 90 Eglinton Avenue East, Suite 700, Toronto, Ontario M4P 2Y3, Canada
(a division of Pearson Penguin Canada Inc.) • Penguin Books Ltd., 80 Strand, London WC2R 0RL,
England • Penguin Group Ireland, 25 St. Stephen's Green, Dublin 2, Ireland (a division of Penguin
Books Ltd.) • Penguin Group (Australia), 250 Camberwell Road, Camberwell, Victoria 3124, Australia
(a division of Pearson Australia Group Pty. Ltd.) • Penguin Books India Pvt. Ltd., 11 Community
Centre, Panchsheel Park, New Delhi—110 017, India • Penguin Group (NZ), 67 Apollo Drive,
Rosedale, Auckland 0632, New Zealand (a division of Pearson New Zealand Ltd.) • Penguin Books
(South Africa) (Pty.) Ltd., 24 Sturdee Avenue, Rosebank, Johannesburg 2196, South Africa

Penguin Books Ltd., Registered Offices: 80 Strand, London WC2R 0RL, England

This is a work of fiction. Names, characters, places, and incidents either are the product of the author's
imagination or are used fictitiously, and any resemblance to actual persons, living or dead, business
establishments, events, or locales is entirely coincidental. The publisher does not have any control over
and does not assume any responsibility for author or third-party websites or their content.

A LADY NEVER LIES

A Berkley Sensation Book / published by arrangement with the author

PUBLISHING HISTORY
Berkley Sensation mass-market edition / August 2012

Copyright © 2012 by Juliana Gray.
Excerpt from *A Gentleman Never Tells* by Juliana Gray copyright © 2012 by Juliana Gray.
Cover art by Gregg Gulbronson.
Cover design by George Long. Hand lettering by Ron Zinn.
Interior text design by Laura K. Corless.

ISBN: 978-0-425-25092-1

BERKLEY SENSATION®
Berkley Sensation Books are published by The Berkley Publishing Group,
a division of Penguin Group (USA) Inc.,
375 Hudson Street, New York, New York 10014.
BERKLEY SENSATION® is a registered trademark of Penguin Group (USA) Inc.
The "B" design is a trademark of Penguin Group (USA) Inc.

PRINTED IN THE UNITED STATES OF AMERICA

10 9 8 7 6 5 4 3 2 1

ALWAYS LEARNING   **PEARSON**

To the incomparable ladies of the Romance Book Club,
I raise my glass of pink champagne:
Alexandra, Liz the First, Liz the Second, and Abigail.
(Emily and Stefanie, you're next.)

ACKNOWLEDGMENTS

As a Clandestine Author, I am obliged to keep certain identifying details secret to Protect the Innocent. I do, however, deliver my most heartfelt thanks to the following:

The divine Alexandra Machinist, agent extraordinaire, dear friend and tireless advocate, from whose scheming brain this madness first sprang, and whose enthusiasm sees me through my Blackest Moments. All of this is your fault.

Kate Seaver, my brilliant editor, who took a Grand Leap of Faith on this unusual proposal from an unknown writer, and whose keen perception improved the book beyond measure.

The team at Berkley who brought it all together, including Katherine Pelz, who performs daily miracles and deserves a Very Large Bonus; my copyeditor, whose attention to detail has saved me from Great Public Embarrassment; the fabulous art department, which produced this sumptuous cover; and the unsung heroes of marketing and publicity who make sure that every book finds its reader.

All the writers who have offered their support and advice with such generosity, including (but not limited to) Lauren Willig, Chris Farnsworth, Jenny Bernard, Darynda Jones, Karen White, Eloisa James, Elizabeth Kerri Mahon, Stacey Agdern, Sarah MacLean, Elizabeth Hoyt, and Julia London. There are no words to describe your loveliness. I offer my most tasteful *mwa-mwa* kisses to all your dear cheeks.

My seventh-grade English teacher, Fran Ennis, who devoured High Literature and Kathleen Woodiwiss with equal appetite, and who first predicted I would write romance when I Grew Up.

Mr. Gray and all the Gray family, in whose love and loyalty I am blessed to Bask Daily.

Finally . . .

William Shakespeare, who gave me both the initial concept for the trilogy and a world of comic inspiration with which to write it; and Giuseppe Verdi, who gave me the Horrid Curse of the Castel sant'Agata and its accompanying music.

PROLOGUE

The Duke of Wallingford was not at home, said the butler, with an upward tilt of his chin.

"Nonsense," said Finn. "We both know very well he's at home. I left him here last night, in the sort of condition that would render impossible his departure by"—he flipped open the case of his battered gold pocket watch—"eight o'clock the following morning. Except, I suppose, in a coffin."

The butler cleared his throat. "The Duke of Wallingford is not receiving."

"Ah, that's better. We deal so much better, Wallis, when we speak the truth to each other. Where might I find the old chap, then?" Finn looked past the butler's head to the wide, high-ceilinged entrance hall beyond, with its floor of checkerboard marble and its profusion of acanthus-leaf plasterwork. Just the sort of entrance a duke's London town house ought to sport, Finn supposed, which made him jolly well grateful (and not for the first time) that he wasn't in line to a dukedom.

"Mr. Burke." The butler straightened to his full height, which was not great in the best of circumstances, and certainly not when interposed against the tall, loose-limbed figure of Mr. Phineas Fitzwilliam Burke, R.S. "I am deeply aggrieved to discover that I have not, perhaps, *quite* made myself clear. His Grace, sir, is not receiving."

"Oh, rot," Finn said amiably. "He'll receive *me*. Besides, we've a breakfast appointment, or hadn't you been told? If you'll excuse me . . ." He executed a cunning side step, agile, really, except that it ended in his chest bumping Wallis's well-oiled forelock and his foot landing squarely on the butler's equally well-oiled shoe.

To his credit, Wallis didn't even wince. "I fear I have been misunderstood once more," he said, voice quavering into the ceiling. His ancient breast strained outward against its natural concavity. "His Grace"—heave, gasp—"the duke"—heave, gasp—"is *not receiving*."

"Now look here, my good man," Finn protested, attempting another dodge. "I realize breakfast appointments aren't the usual thing in this house, but I assure you . . ."

"Bloody hell, Wallis!" The Duke of Wallingford's voice roared down the profligate curve of the main staircase. "Let the poor fellow in the breakfast room, for God's sake. I'll be down in five minutes."

Wallis narrowed his eyes and issued a faint sniff from his sharpened nose. "As you wish, Your Grace," he said, and stepped to one side.

Finn removed each glove in a single decisive tug. "The trouble with you, Wallis, is that you're a dreadful snob. We can't all be lords, you see. The trade wouldn't bear it."

"Don't harass my butler, Burke," called the duke.

Finn cast an eye up the stairs and then looked back down, not without sympathy, at Wallis's defeated shoulders. He handed over his hat and gloves in a kind of conciliatory gesture. "I'll show myself in, shall I?" he said, and strode across the entrance hall toward the breakfast room at the back of the house.

"Damned sodding ginger-haired scientist," the butler muttered, just loudly enough for Finn to overhear. "No sodding respect."

The Duke of Wallingford's breakfast room was a remarkably pleasant spot, for a house without a presiding female. Spacious, south-facing, it overlooked the high-walled back garden at such an angle as to block the sight of the neighboring houses and create the misleading impression of having been transported to the countryside, or at least as far as Hampstead. The room's only flaw was its unmistakable air of disuse. The duke and his brother seldom arose before noon, the natural consequence of seldom retiring before dawn.

Not the case today, however, Finn observed, as he crossed the stately threshold. The sideboard overflowed with all the necessary elements of a proper English breakfast—kidneys, bacon, kippers, toast, eggs without number—and on the chair at the end of the table lay the shipwreck of Lord Roland Penhallow, the duke's younger brother.

"Good God, Penhallow," Finn said, tossing his newspaper on a nearby chair. "To what do we owe the honor?"

"Haven't a clue," Lord Roland mumbled. "Told to make myself ready by eight sharp, or I should have my estates foreclosed. Though now that I recollect"—he rubbed his forehead meditatively—"I paid off those mortgages years ago."

Finn moved to the sideboard and claimed a plate of bone china, so fine it was almost translucent. "Shabby of Wallingford. Still, it's your own jolly fault, drinking yourself insensible. I've explained to the two of you on any number of occasions . . ."

"Sod yourself, you damned saint," Lord Roland said. "You workaday scientists have no notion of what's expected of idle aristocrats. I'm scarcely keeping up as it is." He hid his beautiful face behind a cup of thick black coffee and drank in gulps.

"Then your luck rides high this morning, old man. I've brought the solution to your dilemma into this very room." Finn folded his long frame into a shield-backed Hepplewhite chair, acquired in a fit of modernization several decades earlier by the present duke's grandmother, and pointed his fork at yesterday's evening edition of the *Times* on the cushion next to him. "Your salvation, m'lord, and your brother's."

Lord Roland stabbed at his kidneys. "And if I prefer damnation?"

"No one asked your preference," barked the Duke of Wallingford, entering the room in a ruckus of booted heels. "Nobody asked mine, to be perfectly honest. But here I am, Burke, your obedient servant. I trust you're enjoying your breakfast?"

"Very well, thank you. I find a brisk morning walk sets one up perfectly for a substantial breakfast like this. Your kitchen is to be commended."

"Sod yourself, Burke," said Wallingford. He made his way to the sideboard, an impressive figure in his morning tweeds, tall and broad shouldered, his hair unfashionably long and his chin unfashionably clean-shaven. Only the most familiar observer would detect the signs of last night's revelry on his face: the trace of puffiness in his eyelids, the slackening about the corners of his mouth.

"You raise an interesting point," said Finn, "and, in a round-about way, sodding oneself may have some bearing on the proposal I bring to you this morning."

Wallingford heaped an odd dozen or so kippers onto his plate and dropped the serving fork back into its dish with a significant crash. "I'm panting to hear it."

"I'm damned if I don't detect a note of sarcasm in your words, Your Grace. And yet you were more than curious last night. Curious enough, I'm compelled to point out, to arrange this morning meeting, at vast inconvenience to yourself and"— a glance at Lord Roland's bowed head—"your suffering brother."

"Last night I was blazing drunk." Wallingford dropped himself into a chair at the head of the table. "This morning I'm in my proper senses."

"Shall I cut to the point, then?"

"Do." The single syllable echoed through the room.

Finn reached for his newspaper. "Gentlemen, have either of you two been to Italy?"

"Italy!" Wallingford barked out a laugh. "My good man, I daresay I bedded half the women in Venice whilst you were fiddling around with those damned gadgets in that laboratory of yours, making your sordid millions. What of it?"

Lord Roland raised his head into a shaft of morning sunlight. "Rot. You had that lovely little mistress, the Marquesa Whatsit. Charming gel, jealous as the devil. I should think less than half a dozen genuine notches in the old bedpost, and those only when the little bird was shut up in her confinement."

"Not mine," the duke said swiftly.

Lord Roland squinted one eye and touched his fingers, one by one, against his thumb. The sunlight formed an incongruous halo about his golden brown head. "No. No, you're right. Couldn't have been yours. All the same," he went on, looking at Finn, "he isn't half such a devil as he makes out."

"I should hope not," said Finn. "God save us from an Italy

populated by miniature Wallingfords. In any case, the Italy I have in mind for us lies at a far remove, a far remove indeed, from the sort of Italy with which I suspect you're familiar." He unfolded the pages of the newspaper, one by one, until he came to the item of interest. "Here," he said, thrusting it toward Wallingford. "See what you make of that."

Wallingford raised one heavy black eyebrow. "My good man. One of my most inflexible rules is the avoidance of all reading before luncheon."

"Again, rot," Lord Roland said, his spirits visibly reviving. He began cutting into his sausage. "Let's have it, then, Burke. You've quite awakened my interest."

Finn sighed deeply and cleared his throat. "An advertisement. *English lords and ladies, and gentlemen of discerning taste*—I expect that's why you missed it, Wallingford—*may take note of a singular opportunity to lease a most magnificent Castle and Surrounding Estate in the idyllic hills of Tuscany, the Land of Unending Sunshine.*"

"Dear me," said the duke, "does the earth's rotation fail to affect the fair fields of Tuscany? I am amazed."

Lord Roland pointed his knife at the newspaper. "Not much chance of a proper sleep, without you have at least a few hours of darkness."

"*The Land of Unending Sunshine,*" Finn continued, in a loud voice. "*The Owner, a man of impeccable lineage, whose ancestors have kept the Castle safe against intrusion since the days of the Medici princes . . .*"

"Look here," Lord Roland said, with a thoughtful frown, "I thought all your Tuscan fortifications were in the nature of city-states, eh what? A single castle by itself . . ."

"It's not meant to be a damned geography course," Finn said in exasperation. "It's an advertisement. Oh, blast. Now you've lost me. Impeccable lineage . . . Medici princes . . . Here we are. *The Owner, et cetera, et cetera, is called away by urgent business, and offers a year's lease of this unmatched Property at rates extremely favorable for the discerning traveler.* Again, Wallingford, I shall undertake negotiations myself, so he won't smoke you out, ha-ha. *Applicants should inquire through the Owner's London agent . . .* I say, Wallingford, are you quite all right?"

Wallingford, sputtering into his coffee, had been overtaken by a fit of violent coughing.

"I daresay he's a trifle flummoxed." Lord Roland shrugged.

"By what?"

"Presumably by the suggestion that you're taking out a year's lease on an Italian castle, on his behalf."

"Oh no. No, indeed. You've quite misunderstood me. Only a dash of humor, you see." Finn put the newspaper to one side and set to work on his eggs.

Wallingford, coughs subsiding, dabbed at his watering eyes. "Humor?" he gasped out, clearing his throat with a rough hack. "You call that *humor*, Burke? My God, you might have killed me."

"Really, Wallingford. I should never take out a lease on your behalf. I've well enough sordid millions of my own, as you yourself observed." Finn cast a benevolent smile across the table and reached for his toast. "No, the lease will be entirely in my name. You two shall be my guests, nothing more. Penhallow, the marmalade, if you will."

Lord Roland passed him the pot of marmalade as if in a dream.

Really, it was all proving even more amusing than Finn had imagined. The look of dazed confusion on Penhallow's face. The slow purpling of the duke's expression, the whitening of knuckles clenched about two-hundred-year-old silver cutlery.

Who would speak first?

Wallingford, of course. "I'm certain, my dear Burke," he said, biting out the *dear Burke* in discrete chunks, "I must have misheard you."

"I assure you, you haven't." Finn spread his marmalade over his toast with neat precision. "My dear fellows, I shall lay my cards upon the table, as they say. I've been concerned about the two of you for some time."

Wallingford's expression grew even blacker. "I can't imagine why. Our poverty, perhaps? Our lack of female companionship?"

"There it is! There's your trouble, right there. You don't even recognize how frivolous your lives have become. You've no purpose, no driving force. You drink yourselves into oblivion, night after night . . ."

Lord Roland set down his fork with a clink. "Now look here. As if I haven't seen you positively legless, on more than one occasion."

Finn flicked that away with a brusque movement of his hand. "Once or twice, of course. One's allowed a bit of high spirits, now and again. But you've made a career of it, you two. 'Wine, women, and song,' as the saying goes."

"I object to that. There's been very little song at all," said Lord Roland.

"And that of very poor quality indeed," Wallingford added. "Hardly worth noting."

Finn leaned forward and placed his elbows squarely on each side of his plate. "Three days ago," he said, in a quiet voice, "I came across an old acquaintance of ours, from Cambridge days. Callahan. You'll remember him?"

"Callahan, of course. Jolly chap. A bit thick, but good company on a lark." Lord Roland's brow puckered inward. "What of him?"

"He was dead. Choked on his own vomit in his mistress's parlor in Camden."

In the silence that followed, Finn fancied he could detect the tiny scratches of the ancient ormolu clock above the mantel, counting out the passing of each second into eternity.

"Good God," said Wallingford at last.

"Camden," muttered Lord Roland, as he might mutter *Antarctica*.

Finn removed his elbows and picked up his fork and knife. "I came across his funeral procession, you see. They'd taken his body back to the old family place, in Manchester, not far from a machine works of which I've been contemplating purchase. An only son, did you know? His mother looked quite destroyed."

"There, you see?" Wallingford shrugged. "Our mother's been gone these ten years. Nothing at all to worry about."

Finn went on. "I'm told the body was not even viewable. The mistress discovered him in the morning and fled with her cook-maid. Poor fellow wasn't found for a week."

Wallingford sat back in his chair and regarded Finn with a speculative expression. He crossed two solid arms against his chest. "Very well, Burke. A fine point. The dissipated life ends in ignoble tragedy and whatnot. Women are not to be trusted.

Forewarned is forearmed. I shall retire instantly to the country, call for my steward, and endeavor to live a life of sobriety and virtue."

Finn had expected resistance, of course. One didn't go about telling dukes to mend their ways without anticipating a certain bristling of the old hackles, after all. He smiled kindly and said, "I have a proposition for you."

"I daresay you do. I daresay it has something to do with castles in Italy."

"I have been corresponding for some time with a man near Rome, who's approaching the same project as I am, only with rather a different plan."

"Do you mean these damned horseless carriages of yours?" the duke asked.

"Damned rubbishy machines," put in Lord Roland.

Finn's gaze rose to the ceiling. "Luddites, the pair of you. In any case, a few weeks ago, my colleague in Rome, Delmonico's his name, proposed to me the idea of holding a . . . well, I suppose you might call it a competition, a contest, in which the best examples of the machines might be displayed and judged. If enough working engines are brought to the exhibition, he expects to hold a race."

"A race!" Lord Roland began to laugh. "A race! What earthly use is that? I daresay I could walk faster than any of your contraptions."

"The exhibition," Finn said, ignoring him, "is to be held in the summer, on the outskirts of Rome."

"I begin to see your scheme, old man," Wallingford said darkly.

"I shall need the most absolute calm, in order to concentrate on the project without any distractions. And it occurred to me, you see, that a year spent in the peace and tranquility of the countryside, far away from your own circle of degenerates and wastrels, devoting yourself to scholarly pursuits and absolutely proscribing the company of women . . ."

"Wait. Stop. Do you mean to say," Lord Roland responded, in incredulous tones, "you intend for us to embark on a year of . . . of . . ." He struggled.

"*Chastity?*" the duke supplied, as he might say *disemboweling*.

"Why not? There are solutions to hand, so to speak, should one's urges become uncomfortable. Though I suspect, in the manner of monks, we shall soon be grateful for the serenity and find our own physical needs diminish in response."

"You're mad," said the duke.

"I pose it as a challenge," Finn said. "If I can contemplate it, surely you can. You're a man of considerable self-control, Wallingford, when you choose to exercise it. And as for you, Penhallow, I can remember distinctly a time when you adopted a far more virtuous approach to living . . ."

"That was long ago," Lord Roland said sharply, "and best forgotten."

"All the same, you were capable then of restraint." Finn paused and looked back and forth between the two men, heads hanging toward their plates, forks picking away at the remains of the noble breakfast. "Think, my friends. Think what we can accomplish in a year, if we forgo idle pleasure. A temporary exile, no more. A few months. Study a new subject, learn a new talent. Sunshine and olives and whatnot. The local wine, perhaps; I'm sure we can make allowance for a glass or two, as we establish the rules of our little society."

Wallingford looked up. "Absolutely *not*. The most absurd scheme I've ever heard."

"You're mad even to suggest it," said Lord Roland.

Finn shifted his gaze to the window. The heavy January sky had begun to shed bits of snow into the yellow air, though it wasn't quite cold enough to stick. London in winter: how he hated it, all brown and tired and slushy, the atmosphere so thick with coal smoke it seemed to burn the lining from his lungs. "The land of unending sunshine," he said, in a low voice, and turned back to Wallingford. "At least think on it."

"Out of the question," said Wallingford.

"Quite impossible," agreed Lord Roland.

Finn picked up the paper and folded it with care, flattening the creases just so. "A year away from the miseries of London. A year free of vice and obligation, devoted to study, devoid of the distractions of the fairer sex." He rose, tucked the paper under his arm, and smiled broadly.

"What could possibly go wrong?"

ONE

She had always maintained high standards. While other young ladies dreamed of finding Mr. Right, Alexandra set her sights on the Duke of Right.

In the end, she had accepted a marquis, but as Lord Morley had been both extremely rich and extremely old, she still considered her marriage a success. Ask and ye shall receive, went her motto. (It *was* in the Bible, after all; she was almost certain.) And never, ever settle for second-rate.

Not even when fleeing from one's creditors.

This room was decidedly second-rate. No, not even that. It was little more than a cupboard, hardly larger than the wardrobe in which she stored her summer nightgowns during the off-season. A narrow cot, wedged against the wall, left no space for even a hatbox; the single coarse wool blanket looked a perfect paradise for fleas. It was fourth-rate, even fifth. It simply wouldn't do.

Alexandra turned to the landlord. "It simply won't do, I'm afraid. *Non possiblo.* Understand? *Comprendo?* It is too small. *Troppo*, er, *petito*. There are three of us. *Trio*. And the boy."

The innkeeper frowned. Perhaps he had not quite understood her Italian phraseology. "The inn, she is full, milady. I make beds in the commons, very warm, very comfort."

"Sleep in the commons! Three English ladies! You can't

possibly be serious." Alexandra produced a chuckle to empha-
size the idea's absurdity.

"But milady, it rains, the bridge is . . . is flood. The rooms,
they are all take!"

"By whom?" she demanded, straightening her spine to an
impressive length.

"Is a duke, milady," said the innkeeper, hushed and reverent.
"An English duke. His brother, his friend."

"The devil you say! Show me their rooms, if you please. Er,
chamberos. You see, my good man," she explained kindly, as
she herded him down the narrow creaking corridor, "we have,
in my country, a darling little custom by which gentlemen are
obliged, absolutely *obliged*, to relinquish any present comforts
for the benefit of ladies in need. It imposes such a perfect civilized order upon the world, wouldn't you agree, without which
we should descend into mere barbarism, like those poor chaps
the Romans. This duke of yours, I'm sure, will quite understand. Oh yes!"

She stopped in the doorway and cast her eyes about the
room. This was much more the thing. Large, commodious. A
plump double bed in the exact center of the opposite wall, with
a wardrobe to one side; a fireplace on the other wall, being
tended at that moment by an apple-cheeked young miss with
that rippling dark Italian hair one couldn't help envying, in
one's wilder moments.

It was plain, of course. The inn formed a remote outpost
along an obscure Tuscan road, far from the civilized refinement
of Milan or even Florence, but Alexandra was willing to make
allowances for the rustic furniture and lack of proper trim work
and so on. And after all, the rain lashed harrowingly against the
small many-paned window, and the wind howled down the
chimney flue. Really, one couldn't afford to be too particular.

"It's ideal," she said, turning to the landlord. "We'll take it.
And the connecting room as well." She gestured to the door
standing ajar next to the wardrobe.

The landlord's face had clearly suffered through a long and
rainy winter. It hardly seemed possible those hollow cheeks
could lose any further color, and yet, before her eyes, every last
remaining atom of pigment drained from the face of her host.
"But milady," he said feebly, "the room, she is already take! The

duke have her! A very big duke! Very *strong* duke! And his brother, his friend! All very big!"

"Yes, isn't it extraordinary? I often find that large-framed men tend to befriend other large-framed men, and vice versa. One imagines it must arise from one of those clever little laws of nature one reads about from time to time. Indeed, I should very much like to discover why. A large duke, you say?" She cocked her head and turned to walk back to the staircase. "It can't be Wallingford, do you think? Wallingford in Italy? *I* never heard anything about it."

"Wallingford! Yes!" the landlord exclaimed, trotting behind her. "Is Wallingford! He will not like!"

"Oh, rubbish. Wallingford has a sharp bark, I grant you, but really he's as gentle as a lamb. Or perhaps . . . perhaps a sort of youngish ram." She poised at the top of the staircase, nearly flattened by the mingled scents of woodsmoke and wet wool and roasting meat, rising up in a fug from the bustle of the common room below, and went on with renewed determination. "In any case, quite manageable. Just leave everything to me, my good fellow. I shall have it all sorted out in short order."

"Milady, please, is not so bad, the commons . . ."

"It isn't at all acceptable, *non possiblo*, do you hear me?" she said, more loudly, just to be sure he understood. "We are English, *anglese*. We can't possibly . . ." She paused about half-way down the stairs and turned to scan the noisy wood-beamed room, with its long tables and bowed hungry heads. She had little trouble finding the one she sought. "Oh! Your Grace!" she called, infusing her voice with just the proper balance of surprise and gratification.

The Duke of Wallingford seemed to have been expecting her. His lean face wore an expression of deep resignation, and he muttered something to his companions before he tossed his napkin on the table and stretched his limbs to their full forbidding height. "Lady Morley. Good evening. I trust you're well." He seemed, to Alexandra's ears, to growl rather than speak.

She drew in a fortifying breath and continued down the stairs. "Darling Wallingford, you're just the man I was hoping for. I can't seem to make these Italian fellows understand that English ladies, however sturdy and liberal minded, simply *cannot* be expected to sleep in a room with strangers. *Male* strangers. *Foreign* male strangers." She stood before him now, smiling her winning smile, the one that had laid waste to haughty noblemen beyond number. "Don't you agree, Your Grace?" she finished softly, looking up at him beneath her eyelashes, delivering the coup de grâce.

His face remained hard. "Are there no rooms available upstairs, madam?"

She made a helpless shrug. "A small room, a very small room. Hardly large enough for Lady Somerton's boy to sleep in, let alone the three of us." She glanced aside to his companion. His brother, she remembered the landlord telling her, and everyone knew Wallingford's brother was . . .

"Lord Roland!" The enormity of it exploded in her brain. Her thoughts fled outside, to the sodden innyard where she'd left her sister and her cousin to see to the disposition of the baggage, not a quarter hour before. "I'd no idea! Have you . . . my cousin . . . Lady Somerton . . . good God!"

Lord Roland bowed. Thank goodness, Alexandra thought, thank *goodness* he was a charming, well-bred rascal, nothing like his arctic brother. Society had decreed the younger man the handsomer of the two, though in fact their features were clearly cast from the same symmetrical mold. Perhaps it was his coloring, which was lighter than Wallingford's, his eyes a friendly hazel next to the blackened orbs of his brother, and his golden brown hair giving him the air of a particularly enthusiastic retriever. He spoke, however, with subdued formality. "I had the great honor of meeting her ladyship outside on the . . . the portico, a moment ago. And her charming son, of course."

Something caught in Alexandra's throat; she wasn't quite sure if it was a laugh or a groan. Lord Roland and Lilibet stumbling into each other on the portico, after all these years! Good God!

"Charming! Yes, quite," she got out at last. She felt hideously wrong-footed, with several pairs of fascinated male eyes witnessing her confusion. It was intolerable. She rallied and cleared her throat, hoping the motion would cause something more rational to tumble out into the thickening silence.

Nothing did, however, and she was forced to turn back to the duke. "Look here, Wallingford, I really must throw myself on your mercy. Surely you can see our little dilemma. Your rooms are ever so much larger—palatial, really— and *two* of them! You can't possibly, in all conscience . . ." A thought occurred to her. She turned back to Lord Roland and fixed him with a beseeching smile. "My dear Penhallow. Think of poor Lilibet, sleeping in . . . in a *chair*, quite possibly. With all these strangers."

Lord Roland's expression turned stricken. She opened her mouth to pursue her advantage, but before she could speak, a voice intruded to thwart her.

"Did it not, perhaps, occur to you, Lady Morley, to reserve rooms in advance?"

For an instant, she was confused. That resonant timbre could only come from a singularly spacious chest, and the clipped tones and rumbling impatience could only come from an Englishman. But it was not Wallingford, nor was it Lord Roland.

Oh, of course. The third man.

She knew better than to acknowledge him at once. She was not the Dowager Marchioness of Morley for nothing. She counted off one second . . . two . . . three . . . and then turned in the direction of the voice.

He was not at all what she expected.

Wallingford's friend. Who the devil was he? He was tall, of course—extraordinarily tall, topping even the duke by a good three or four inches—and broad shouldered. She'd known that already, Wallingford and his pack of goons. But a voice that dark, that silky, that *weighty* ought to belong to one of your saturnine characters, your brooders: all black hair and eyes, like Wallingford himself. This fellow was ginger haired, with lawn-green eyes and *freckles*, actual freckles, an unmistakable dusting of them around the bridge of his nose, descending across the strong, wide wedge of his cheekbones. A damned leprechaun, if leprechauns had blunt bones and stern eyes and ran to nearly six and a half deuced feet in their curly toed stockings.

Surely she was equal to an overgrown leprechaun.

"As a matter of fact, it did, Mr. . . . ." She dropped a devastating pause, a pause that might have brought lesser souls to their knees. "I'm so terribly sorry, sir. I don't *quite* believe I caught your name."

His expression didn't change, not by so much as an ironically elevated eyebrow.

"I beg your pardon, Lady Morley," said the Duke of Walling-

ford. "How remiss of me. I have the great honor to present to
you—perhaps you may have come across his name, in your
philosophical studies—Mr. Phineas Fitzwilliam Burke, of the
Royal Society."

"Your servant, madam," Mr. Burke said, with a slight inclination of his head.

Alexandra's brain took a moment or two to absorb this information. "Burke," she said numbly, and then, with effort: "Phineas
Burke. Of course. The Royal Society. Yes, of course. Everyone
knows of Mr. Burke. I found . . . the *Times*, last month . . . your
remarks on electrical . . . that new sort of . . ." She found herself
stammering again. Bloody Wallingford. Bloody Wallingford, to
be traveling in the Italian countryside with a man of exalted
genius and near-divine eminence. How on earth had he come to
know Phineas Burke?

She recovered herself and attempted a smile, a friendly
smile, to make amends for her earlier haughtiness. "That is to
say, of course we reserved rooms. I sent the wire days ago, if
memory serves. But we were delayed in Milan. The boy's nursemaid took ill, you see, and I expect our message did not reach
our host in time." She flashed the bemused landlord, who stood
a few deferential feet away, a shaming expression.

"Look here," said Lord Roland, unexpectedly, "enough of
this rubbish. We shouldn't dream of causing any inconvenience
to you and your friends, Lady Morley. Not for an instant. Should
we, Wallingford?"

The duke folded his arms. "No, damn it."

"Burke?"

The scientist made a noise of agreement.

Lord Roland grinned his dazzling grin. "You see, Lady Morley? All quite willing and happy and so on. I daresay Burke can
take the little room upstairs, as he's such a tiresome, misanthropic old chap, and my brother and I shall be quite happy to
make ourselves comfortable downstairs. Will that suit?"

Relief flooded through her. Good old Penhallow. She could
have kissed him, except for propriety and Lilibet, which were
almost the same thing. As it was, she pressed her hands together
in an elegant kidskin knot. "Darling Penhallow. I knew you'd
oblige us. Thanks so *awfully*, my dear; you can't imagine how

thankful I am for your generosity." She said it with gushing gratitude, really *quite* sincere, and yet she became uncomfortably aware of Mr. Burke's assessing gaze along the periphery of her vision.

Why *had* Wallingford brought along a scientific gentleman? Really, it was intolerable, having the man look at one with such thorough eyes, as if one were a *subject* of some sort. As if he understood all one's secrets.

She returned to the landlord, steeling her voice back into its usual tone of brusque efficiency: "Do you understand? *Comprendo?* You may remove His Grace's luggage from the rooms upstairs and bring up our trunks at once."

The landlord made a sullen bow and hurried off, just as the thick wooden door swung open and two bundled figures hunkered through, sodden and dripping.

Alexandra turned to the entrance and felt a warm glow of mischief evaporate her discomfort. "Ah! Cousin Lilibet! There you are at last. Have you sorted out the trunks?"

Lord Roland reacted with near-instantaneous haste. He wheeled about to the doorway and stepped in Lilibet's direction, before he remembered himself and froze on the spot.

Most satisfactory.

Even more satisfactory, Lilibet gave no sign of noticing him. All her cousin's attention focused on the little boy before her: She had already knelt down and was helping young Philip with the buttons on his wet woolen coat, the picture of concerned motherhood. "Yes, they've all been unloaded," she said. "The fellow's coming in the back." She glanced past the three men to Alexandra, as though they didn't exist at all; not an easy thing to do, when the gentlemen in question might have made up a side of rugby without bothering to recruit another player.

Almost *too* unconscious, Alexandra thought, but then who needed wiles with a face like Lilibet's? Her cousin straightened and began to unbutton her own coat, and Lord Roland seemed even more transfixed than before.

"Oh, for God's sake," someone muttered behind her. Wallingford, from the tone.

"I take it they know each other?" the other—Burke—asked dryly.

It was better than a play.

Alas, just as Lilibet reached the bottom of her coat, and Alexandra held her breath to see what would happen next, Miss Abigail Harewood swept through the door and ruined the scene.

She shook the droplets from her hat like a careless young spaniel and rushed up to her sister. "Alex, darling," she said, shattering the silence, "you won't believe what I've found in the stables!"

Alexandra heaved a disappointed sigh and wrinkled her nose. "What on earth were you doing in the stables, darling? Oh, do leave off that gesticulating and remove your coat. You're showering me, for goodness' sake. Here. Your buttons." She unfastened Abigail's wet coat with efficient fingers. "Now come along with me to the fire and warm yourself. We've a lovely hot dinner waiting for us at the table next to the fireplace. You can tell me all about what you've discovered in the stables."

She slung the coat over her right arm, grasped Abigail's hand with her left, and steered a course directly to the massive hearth, where Lilibet hovered, hands outstretched: a sight to enrapture the heart of any English gentleman, and particularly one that had belonged to her for years.

Alexandra would have to keep a close eye indeed on Lord Roland Penhallow tonight.

As she passed the gentlemen, however, those eyes did a vexing and unexpected thing. They observed not Lord Roland's lovestruck gaze, nor even Wallingford's thundering scowl.

They lingered, instead, on the way the warm ginger hair of Mr. Phineas Burke kindled into red gold flame in the light from the fire.

TWO

Alexandra knew she should have left after dinner. The men expected it, expected her to follow Lilibet and Abigail when they went upstairs to put the yawning boy to bed. It was what Englishwomen did, leaving the men to brandy and cigars and politics, even in a rustic crowded hostelry in the middle of Italy.

But tonight she didn't. She'd always longed to stay and discuss politics, and after all, she *was* a widow now, far away from England's drawing rooms, grappa at the ready. Even more importantly, halfway through her generous hunk of roasted Tuscan goose, as Abigail leaned toward her and revealed what she'd discovered in the stables, Alexandra had remembered exactly where Mr. Phineas Burke was said to be investing his brilliant mind these days. And, not incidentally, his capital.

Horseless carriages.

As if God had sent him to her, in her hour of need.

So tonight she sat firmly in her place, and when Lilibet's skirt had disappeared around the upstairs landing she turned to Mr. Phineas Burke and said, with a provocative smile, "Tell me, Mr. Burke, what on earth brings you to this remote wilderness? I can understand Wallingford and Penhallow going in for such eccentricities, but you seem a rational sort of chap."

He stared at her across the table, with that probing gaze of his, as if peeling back the layers of her mind. "I might perhaps ask the same of you, Lady Morley."

"Oh no. Not at all. We ladies are allowed our secrets, I'm afraid. It's the privilege of our sex." She forced herself to keep her gaze on his, to meet the onslaught of his expression. "You poor fellows, on the other hand, must reveal everything, without reserve. Now do go on. I'm quite panting to hear it. A grand tour? Searching for a lost Renaissance painting? Or has Wallingford perhaps got an Italian contessa with child?"

"I'm insulted," drawled the duke, "you think me capable of such carelessness."

Alexandra shifted her eyes to Wallingford with relief. Most women found the duke intimidating, but she'd lost that telltale nervous flutter around his large, laconic figure a long time ago. Once one knew what a man was really made of, he became as ordinary as the earth, and about as appealing.

She now settled back in her chair and fingered the dull pewter base of her cup, which held the last sediment-clouded dregs of the landlord's stock of wine. It was rough and tannic and fought her palate with tooth and nail, and she meant to make it last as long as she could. "One hears such stories, Wallingford. One hardly knows what to credit."

"I assure you, Lady Morley, it's nothing so exciting. A course of study, nothing more."

She laughed. "A course of study! What rot. I can well believe that of Mr. Burke, but the two of *you*?" She took in Lord Roland with a swift glance. "A course of study in what, Your Grace? Whist, perhaps? Roman orgies?"

"Of course not." Wallingford brushed at his sleeve. "If we were planning any sort of orgy, Lady Morley, we would certainly have invited you along."

Alexandra felt a surge of warmth spread across her cheekbones and throughout her face, and she cursed herself. She'd thought herself above blushing, at her age, and at such a crude and unjust swipe.

"For God's sake, Wallingford," muttered Mr. Burke, bringing down his wineglass with a little crash.

"Dashed coarse of you, brother," Lord Roland said, looking up as if from a reverie.

The duke shrugged. "My apologies."

Alexandra gathered herself. "You won't convince me it's some sort of academic endeavor. Why, the tales I heard, only a few weeks ago . . ."

"True, I'm sure. All true."

She leaned forward. "Do you expect me to believe that you've shrugged off the accumulated dissipation of some ten or twelve years, in order to pursue philosophical study? In Italy?"

"Improbable, of course," Wallingford said, "but true."

Mr. Burke's voice was low and sure. "We have devised a rigorous schedule of study and exercise, free from the vices of metropolitan life."

Alexandra looked back and forth between him and the duke. How different they looked, the one so dark and cynical, the other so subtle and many colored. "I suppose it has something to do with this engine exhibition in Rome this summer, hasn't it? Your particular field of inquiry, Mr. Burke."

He made a startled movement, lawn green eyes widening at last. "What on earth do you know about it?"

She shrugged. "An idle interest of mine. And you, Wallingford? Will you be assisting in Mr. Burke's workshop?"

"God, no," said the duke, looking horrified. "I shall be undertaking far more cerebral activity, I assure you."

"Oh really?" She smiled kindly. "Are you planning to purchase a cerebrum outright, or simply lease it month-to-month?"

"Very amusing, your ladyship."

"Or perhaps you plan to economize and share one between you and Penhallow."

Lord Roland looked up and twinkled at her. "Perish the thought. Awkward, beastly things, brains. Look what it's done to my poor old friend Burke, here."

She laughed. "Indeed. He's only the most worthy man among you."

As soon as the words came out of her mouth, she wished them back. All three of them arrested movement and stared at her: Mr. Burke with his wineglass glued to his lips, Wallingford with his eyebrows arching into his hairline.

Oh, brilliant. Now what the devil had made her say that?

She cleared her throat. "But don't give up hope, Penhallow. Perhaps Wallingford can be persuaded to let you borrow the organ on alternate Thursdays, in exchange for your charm and good humor, of which he stands in even deeper need. Tell me, how long a period have you established for your little sabbatical?"

"A year," barked Wallingford.

A year.

She stiffened in her chair. "A year, did you say?"

"I did."

She looked from one face to another; all wore masks of perfect sincerity. A chill feeling gathered at the top of her spine; she tried to ignore it. "Oh, well played," she said brightly. "You nearly had me convinced."

"My dear Lady Morley, I wasn't trying to be funny. I haven't any humor, after all, as you yourself pointed out."

"Ha. Did you speak with Miss Harewood? Lady Somerton?"

"I haven't the slightest idea what you're talking about," Wallingford said, in a bored voice.

Her pulse throbbed in her throat, like a warning signal. It couldn't be coincidence. Could it? Had someone told Wallingford of their plans? Who? Who else could possibly know?

With effort, she kept her voice even. "A year, you said. A year of philosophical study. Jolly odd."

"Odd?" asked Lord Roland. "Why *odd*? I agree that the whole scheme's quite mad. Half-lunatic, in my opinion; really, I'm only along to see for myself how spectacularly it will crash. But *odd*?"

Alexandra picked up her spoon and toyed with her marscapone. How much should she tell them? "As it happens, Penhallow, the reason I find your excursion so *odd* is that my companions and I find ourselves embarked on a similar one. I beg your pardon; does anyone quite understand what this . . . this pudding is, before us?"

"Forgive me," said the duke. "I don't quite understand you."

"This. This bowl of . . . Dear me, I don't know how to describe it . . ."

"Not the damned pudding. This project of yours."

"Oh, of course. I mean," she said, leaning forward and fixing him with a frigid smile, "that we—Lady Somerton and Miss Harewood and I—have traveled to Italy on a sort of scholarly retreat of our own."

Wallingford stared at her, incredulous, as if unable to tell if she were mocking or serious. "A scholarly retreat? To study . . . what?"

"We have prepared an extensive list of subjects."

"No doubt. With a change of dress for each one, I'm sure."

She shot him a murderous glare. "We are quite serious about this, Wallingford."

"Oh, come. What about Lord Somerton? Does he look kindly on his wife's absence? And your poor sister, languishing away in study when she should be finding a husband." Wallingford crossed his tweed arms and grinned. "It's madness."

Her blood began to rise. As if her duty to Lilibet and Abigail weren't what brought her here in the first place! "No more so than *your* plan."

"I'll wager you don't last out a month."

"I'll wager you've packed your trunks within a week, Wallingford. You, without a skirt to chase? Penhallow, bending his brain to Greek philosophers?" She tilted her head in Mr. Burke's direction, not daring to look him full in the face. "Poor Mr. Burke will be left quite to himself, though I daresay it will suit him very well."

"Rubbish," said Wallingford. "Ladies have their virtues; indeed, no one admires the sex more than I do, I assure you. But the ability to conduct protracted philosophical study, away from the charms of social life, is not, I'm afraid, among them."

"Quite the opposite," Alexandra said. "Men, as your own life amply demonstrates, cannot easily control their baser impulses. Women would make far better scholars, if allowed the opportunity."

Wallingford leaned toward her. "Name your stakes, then."

"My stakes?"

"You mentioned a wager, Lady Morley."

"Are you quite serious?" she demanded.

Lord Roland broke in. "Oh, I say. Hardly cricket, old man, wagering with a lady."

She made a brushing movement with her hand. "Don't bother, my dear. We've left all that civilized rubbish back in England, haven't we? No, I like Wallingford's proposal immensely. It makes things matter."

"My sentiments exactly," said Wallingford. "As I said, what are your stakes?"

Alexandra ran her thumb along the length of her spoon. She had the sudden and deeply vexing impression that she'd been baited, and expertly. "To the party that remains at study the longest: a forfeit"—she hesitated—"to be determined later."

"A lady's trick." The duke rolled his black eyes. "Naming the forfeit after the wager's won. It should *mean* something, Lady Morley."

Oh, damn. What had she done? Wagers had a fatal habit of becoming public knowledge, and public knowledge was the last thing she needed just now. She'd gone to great lengths to keep their departure from England, and their destination, a secret. "You don't think pride's a sufficient motivation?" she asked, trying to edge herself back from the brink. "Must there be money involved?"

Mr. Burke's voice intruded, with quiet authority, hardly more than a whisper. "Nobody said anything about money, Lady Morley."

Her heart gave a thud. She fixed him with her gaze. "What's that, Mr. Burke? Do you have a *personal* interest in this disagreement? Do you, too, feel men to be superior scholars to women?"

He shrugged. "It seems to me to be a scientific question, which can be settled in a scientific manner. We have three members of each sex, attempting roughly the same project. A rather well-designed experiment, I should think."

"And you think your side will win, of course."

He made a little bow of his head. "I'm a scientist, Lady Morley. I'm only interested in outcomes. But since the issue has been raised, I don't see the harm in allowing a forfeit of some sort to the winner."

"And what," she said, leaning forward, letting a feline smile curl the edges of her mouth, because she really couldn't resist the challenge in his eyes, "do you propose?"

He leaned back in his chair and reached for the dish of walnuts at the end of the table. "I've always believed that the results of important scientific studies are of essential interest to humanity at large," he said, placing a walnut between his thumb and forefinger. "I see, therefore, no reason why the loser should not publish in the *Times* an advertisement of no less than, say, a half sheet, acknowledging the superiority of the winning side."

He cracked the walnut solidly, straight down the middle, and picked out the flesh with an expert curl of his finger.

A silence settled in the middle of the table, intruded upon only by the tuneless roar of an inebriated man by the fire, attempting the drinking chorus of *Otello*.

"You," Alexandra said at last, "are a vastly overconfident man. I look very much forward to proving you wrong."

Mr. Burke rose and tossed down the last of his wine. A bright flush stained the skin beneath his freckles. "If you'll excuse me," he said, eyes glittering, and strode from the room.

The trouble with rustic Italian inns, thought Phineas Burke, much later, hurrying through the rain-soaked midnight toward the inn's ramshackle stableyard, was not the lack of general creature comforts, of which he took little notice. He'd lived in student rooms at Cambridge and hide tents in the Siberian steppes and his godfather's mansion on Park Lane, and all were more or less equal to his abstemious taste.

No, the real trouble was the lack of space. From childhood, he'd made a habit of securing himself a retreat, wherever he was: an unused cupboard, a hollow tree, a shed. A place to flee, when the pressure of company became too much, or when an idea flashed into his brain and took over all his conscious thought.

Or when a talkative and damnably alluring woman invited herself to dinner.

Well, to be fair, she hadn't quite invited herself. A precise observer would have to admit that Lord Roland, the lovesick puppy, had actually issued the fatal request. And perhaps it would have been, according to the rules of so-called polite behavior, rather rude to ignore the ladies when they sat at the adjacent table, not three feet away in a room crowded with foreigners.

But Lady Morley had accepted with far too much eagerness. She had fairly dragged her companions into their company, when it was obvious even to Finn—no expert on feminine behavior—that the beautiful Lady Somerton, for one, had no wish to join them.

To make matters worse, she had gone on in that lilting,

self-assured voice of hers, practically forcing everybody to converse, raising daring subjects and flashing witty remarks; asking questions he should have thought impertinent, except that Lady Morley had the irritating trick of making it all seem clever and confidential and sophisticated instead. Even Wallingford had been moved to laugh, once or twice. It was intolerable. Hadn't the three of them left England *expressly* to avoid such distractions?

When Lady Somerton and Miss . . . what the devil was her name, Lady Morley's sister . . . Miss Harewood, that was it; when the two of them had taken the little boy upstairs, Finn had drawn a deep sigh, expecting Lady Morley to rise as well and leave them in masculine peace. But she hadn't. She'd stayed, damn it all, and now he'd revealed far more than he'd intended, and committed an unspeakably rash act as well.

A wager.

Why on earth had he done it? He must have been mad, he thought angrily, tucking the brim of his hat more firmly against his forehead and quickening his steps. The rain had eased since the afternoon's deluge, but it still coursed coldly against the back of his unprotected neck and inside the collar of his coat, doing little to improve his mood. Unbidden, her image rose again in his brain: Lady Morley, with her gleaming brown eyes and the faint blush coloring her high, wide cheekbones, leaning forward until her neatly wrapped bosom had hovered, with excruciating promise, just above her dish of marscapone. The rise of her eyebrows as he cracked that damned walnut, as if she could divine the nervousness of the gesture.

A wager implied further contact, made further contact necessary. That, of course, was why he'd done it. He'd lost the wager simply by making it.

Finn darted through the doorway into the stables. "Hallo!" he called, the word echoing faintly off the old stones. He heard the rustle of animals moving about and smelled the earthy scents of horse and hay and manure through the dank air. It wasn't much warmer here, despite the presence of God knew how many beasts, and certainly not much lighter, with a pair of dark lanterns providing the only illumination. Finn stood still, allowing his eyes to adjust, to pick through the shadows until they resolved into shapes and details. No point stumbling about aimlessly, after all.

He'd watched the hostlers unload the wagon this afternoon, and he knew exactly where his machine had been placed. He'd supervised everything, down to the plain wool blanket thrown over the top and tucked into the corners. He had no reason at all to be here, no reason for concern, other than the same watchfulness a father might bear for his child, wanting to check its sleeping head one last time before retiring, to be sure of the slow steady pulse of its breathing.

When at last he could make out the contours of the building around him, Finn walked with soft feet in the direction of the remote corner into which he'd directed his man earlier, past the inquisitive heads of several horses, noses reaching forward for treats; past rusting bits of farm equipment in winter storage; past various stacks of wooden boxes and crates, wine perhaps, waiting for transport elsewhere.

Until the last moment, he wasn't aware of the other presence at all. A scent, a warmth flashed across his senses, just before he reached his destination.

"Who's there?" he snapped out, bracing himself.

A faint rustle in the shadows. He listened a moment, and then moved forward: one step, another, the floorboards sighing under each foot.

Another rustle. "Look here," he said, softening his voice, "I know you're there. You might as well come out."

He thought he heard a sigh slipping through the darkness, and then a voice spoke out, just above a whisper: "I beg your pardon, Mr. Burke. You quite startled me."

Lady Morley. He saw her shape emerge from the shadowed corner, straight and queenly, features indistinguishable and yet as clear as day in his mind.

"What the *devil*?" he demanded, without thinking. "Lady Morley?"

Her hesitation filled the air. "Yes, I only . . . a bit of fresh . . ." She paused and seemed to compose herself. "You'll think me foolish, of course. I must have got myself turned around, you see, in the night. I thought I'd reached the inn, and realized I hadn't, and then the rain started up again. I beg your pardon if I gave you a fright."

He felt her warmth, the vibration of her nerves a few feet away. He could reach out and touch her, if he wanted.

"I must say," she went on, after her pause went uninterrupted, "you gave me something of a fright yourself! I thought you were one of the stableboys, come to ravish me." She laughed, a light, musical laugh, redolent of Belgravian drawing rooms and entirely out of place in the Italian countryside.

"And if I were?" he heard himself ask, in a dark voice he hardly recognized as his own.

Another laugh. "Well, then I should be obliged to smite you over the head, of course. Though you're so fearfully tall, I don't suppose I should manage it very well. I should have to climb upon a stepladder to do the job properly."

Her words fell away. In the silence, Finn heard the drum of rain against the roof tiles, harder now, the storm regaining strength as if determined to hold the two of them in place. A horse whuffled behind him, whether in encouragement or disapproval he couldn't say.

"Lady Morley," he said, "what the devil are you doing here?"

Her body shifted. "I told you. I was out for a walk to clear my head and wound up losing myself in the stables."

The falsity of it seemed to rattle against the walls around them. She was lying, and he knew she was lying, and of course she must know he knew it. But what could he say? He couldn't accuse her of falsehood. It would be tantamount to accusing her of murder: no, worse. And so they stood there, the lie squatting between them, like an incontinent lapdog that must be politely ignored. Finn let out his breath, long and heavy with the realization that he might never know exactly what Alexandra, Lady Morley was doing at midnight in a Tuscan stable, hovering over the physical representation of his life's work.

"Mr. Burke? Have I offended you in some way?" Her voice was low and subdued, conscious of the debt she owed to his delicacy.

Damn it all. It was too much; *she* was too much: her cleverness and beauty and incandescence, the faint scent of lilies that seemed to rise from her skin and drift through his mind like the headiest wine. He never could speak properly around women, never could feel like himself; they were an alien species, a code to which he had no key. He felt a stammer rise in his throat and forced it back down.

"Mr. Burke?" she asked again, very close, and he thought he could feel her breath settle into the hollow of his throat.

"No. No, of course not."

"Will you, then, be so kind as to escort me back to the inn?"

He hesitated, for a fraction of an instant, because as much as her company unsettled him, he couldn't quite bring himself to leave it. "Certainly. But . . ."

"*But*, Mr. Burke?"

He lowered his voice. "But not before you satisfy my curiosity on a single point, madam."

She made a slight intake of breath. "Curiosity isn't considered polite, Mr. Burke."

"I rarely bother with such considerations." Something about her answer, about its faint frisson of uneasiness, gave him confidence. He leaned his head down, until his lips nearly brushed her temple. "Tell me, Lady Morley, the real reason you're here in Italy."

She didn't back away. "I told you, Mr. Burke. We're embarking on a year of study, just as you are."

"Devil of a coincidence."

"Yes, isn't it?"

"And so unexpected of you. After all, you're a leading figure in London society." He closed his eyes and drew in her scent, the warmth of her skin so near his own. Without looking down, he knew the tips of her breasts just brushed the wool of his greatcoat.

"You're well-informed."

"Why, I ask myself, would such a woman give up her life's work, the adulation of friends, in order to steal away for a year of rustic living?" He dropped his voice almost to a whisper, in order to keep her close.

"Perhaps I'm bored of London life," she breathed back. Was it his imagination, or did she sound unsteady? Surely not. Surely not the Dowager Marchioness of Morley, standing in a hay-strewn Italian stable, next to him.

God, it was tantalizing.

"Are you? Bored of London life?"

"Among other things, yes."

"Nothing to hide, then? No secrets to disclose? I am, I assure you, the most discreet of men."

Something wavered in the air, some current of expectation, and then it was gone. "Nothing so thrilling, I'm afraid. Three dull ladies, embarked on a dull mission."

"Ah." He moved his hand, just grazing the gloved tips of her fingers. The small contact streaked through his body with unexpected force. "In that case, I suppose we should return to the inn."

She sighed. "Yes, of course."

Her arm slipped through his, resting with extraordinary lightness on the curve of his forearm, her kidskin fingers just touching the back of his wrist. His bones stiffened beneath the pressure. He led her through the stables and out the door, where the cold shock of spitting rain dashed away the last remnants of the spell between them.

On the portico, as he reached for the door, she turned to him.

"Mr. Burke, it occurs to me that . . ." She hesitated.

"Yes?"

Her hand, still resting on his arm, fell away to fist at her side. "Well, as I said, we've no secrets. But all the same, I'd be rather grateful if you forbear mentioning our presence here to . . . to any mutual acquaintance, back in England."

The inn was dark; the night was dark. He looked hard at her face but couldn't read her expression. "Of course not, if you'd rather."

"Thank you." She made a dry little laugh. "I should hate to have all London come galloping down to join us, after all."

He didn't answer, only opened the door and allowed her through, to scamper up the stairs to the room he'd vacated for her.

Thank God, Finn thought, as he settled into his meager room. Thank God he'd be leaving at daybreak for a remote castle hidden in the rugged Tuscan hills.

Thank God he'd spend the next year far away from whatever corner of the world the maddening Lady Alexandra Morley planned to occupy.

THREE

The baggage would have to be unloaded, the driver told
them, shaking his head in sorrow. There was no other way.

"What does he mean, *no other way*?" demanded Alexandra.
"It will take hours, to say nothing of the mud ruining all that
beautiful leather." She ran her eyes over the neat rows of trunks
in the cart, covered with a thick sheet of the best sailcloth to
ward off the lingering damp.

"The mud's the difficulty," Abigail said. "He says it's too"—
she rubbed her first and middle fingers against her thumb,
searching for a word—"too sticky, too heavy, for the horses to
move. Unless the weight is removed from the back, of course."

"For the amount of money he's charged us," said Alexandra,
"he ought to have been more careful. The road is perfectly dry
on the other side. Or . . . or at least rather less muddy." She knew
she was being petulant and didn't much care. She had drunk a
little too much wine last night, which was not her usual habit,
and her head felt as if several dancing elves were presently
becoming sick between the folds of her gray matter.

It was all that Mr. Burke's fault, of course. He'd examined
her from across the dinner table, silent and lion eyed, shoulders
squared beneath the plain dark wool of his jacket. She'd felt his
brain turn over her words, analyze her expressions, judge her
character. It was impertinent! A mere scientific gentleman, no

matter how celebrated. Irish, probably, with that name and that coloring and that outrageous self-assurance.

And then to find her in the stables, inspecting his machine, when she'd been quite certain the inn was quiet and somnolent! Stupid, stupid, to go for a look. What had she hoped to gain from it? She put one gloved hand to her temple and rubbed furiously, as if that would erase the image of those long, blunt-tipped fingers cracking a walnut in half.

"It was bound to happen," said Lilibet, lowering herself onto a large rock and drawing Philip into her lap. "The road's impossible; we were mad to have left the inn at all." Her voice held just the faintest trace of annoyance.

"Rubbish," Alexandra snapped. "We'd be mad to linger in a public inn. No, we've got to reach that castle tonight, and the earlier the better. Come along, ladies." She stepped toward the cart and gave the broad canvas cloth an angry jerk. It rippled along the lumps and ridges of the baggage but did not quite come loose. "Abigail, come along the other side of the cart and help me. At this rate we shan't push off until midnight." She said the last words loudly, so that even the Italian driver would understand her.

"Oh, look!" Abigail said.

Alexandra turned. Her sister stood tall and straight, looking down the pitted road behind them, holding her hand above her eyes, though there wasn't any sun to speak of. "Aren't those the gentlemen from last night?" she asked, her voice high and eager against a gust of breeze.

"Oh, the devil take them," Alexandra muttered under her breath. "It would be, wouldn't it?"

She rose on her toes and stretched her considerable neck, trying to peer through the dank air. Sure enough, that unmistakable ginger hair popped into view, pale red gold against the grayness of rock and road and sky, before disappearing again under the blackness of his hat. They were all riding horses, presumably far ahead of whatever vehicle was conveying their baggage, and Alexandra cursed rather more picturesquely. She ought to have ridden, too, on these roads. If it weren't for the little boy . . . but she quashed that thought instantly. They could never have left Philip behind.

For one wild instant, Alexandra imagined hiding between the massive rocks by the roadside. Or, more romantically, throwing the sailcloth over her head and pretending to be a peasant woman. She looked at the cart, at the shabby brown horses, at the driver, at the mud: Anything at all to escape the unfolding horror.

"Come, ladies," she said, because she'd be damned if she'd accept imminent humiliation like a dumbstruck peasant awaiting the emperor's arrival. "Let's sort out the trunks, shall we?"

The driver had already climbed down from his seat, pulling back the rest of the sailcloth with the languorous movements of a man who saw no reason to rush any of life's adventures. Abigail skipped up next to her and reached inside for one handle of her single leather-bound trunk. Alexandra took the other and heaved.

It was heavy. Much heavier than she'd expected, and firmly wedged against its neighbors. "What the devil did you pack, my dear?" she asked, breathless, pulling again, to no effect.

"Only clothes. And . . . well, and perhaps a few books. A *very* few."

"Books! I *expressly* forbade books!" The words came out in a puff of lost breath that lacked the weight Alexandra intended.

"Only a few, Alex! Not more than a dozen, I promise! I knew"—she huffed and tugged   "I knew this castle of yours wouldn't have anything *recent . . .*"

"Novels! You've brought *novels!*" Alexandra accused, and then, quite by coincidence, the sisters managed to heave at the same time, and the trunk gave way into Alexandra's chest, knocking her into a particularly sloppy patch of mud.

Cold, sloppy mud.

Abigail dropped to her knees. "Oh, Alex! I'm so awfully sorry! Are you all right?"

"Quite all right, thank you," Alexandra gasped, "if you'll perhaps be so good as to remove this damned *crate of novels* from my chest."

"Oh yes, of course." Abigail tugged the trunk from her sister's wool-covered torso and into the mud beside her.

Alexandra struggled to sit upright. "After I gave express instructions that only academic subjects are to be considered . . ."

"Alex," said her sister, in a strange voice, "you might . . ."

"If you don't *mind*, Abigail. These damned useless *skirts . . .*" She struggled to plant her feet in the slick layer of mud.

Lilibet interrupted. "Er, Alexandra, my dear . . ."

"Aren't either of you going to *help* me? Those damned gentlemen will be here in a matter of minutes . . ."

"Lady Morley."

The words moved low and quiet through the sodden air.

With a lurch of her innards, Alexandra looked up into the face of Mr. Phineas Burke, bent toward her with grave care, his black-gloved hand outstretched. "May I be of assistance?" he inquired.

As if she had a choice.

She let out a little sigh and placed her hand in his.

His walnut-cracking fingers closed around hers, large and capable, and she found herself rising weightlessly from the Tuscan mud to stand before him, entirely too close to that formidable chest. She stared at the plain horn button a few inches from her nose and realized again how disturbingly tall he was, up close. She wanted to take a step back, but found that she could not.

Not from reluctance, thank God, but because the mud had already closed around her trim ankle boots, holding them fast.

"Lady Morley?" Mr. Burke's voice rumbled next to her ear.

"My boots," she said feebly, looking down. "It appears they're stuck."

"A curious species of mud," he observed, bending in a sinuous motion and grasping at her ankle. "Extraordinarily viscous." He pulled firmly, freeing one foot and then, as she was forced to lean against him, the other.

Then he lifted her, actually lifted her—her breasts pressing against the ridge of his shoulder, his broad arm lying firmly against the backs of her legs—and placed her on a rock. She felt the round eyes of her companions, staring.

"Thank you," she said primly, shaking free the folds of her mud-slicked coat.

"Not at all." He had evidently ridden on ahead. She could hear the sound of hoofbeats to her left, Wallingford and Penhallow drawing near, but she could not, for a few vital seconds, bring herself to look away from Phineas Burke's green eyes. Their color had muted, out here in the chill gray Italian morning, more lichen now than grass, rimmed with lashes a few shades darker than his hair. They regarded her with sober warmth, completely absent of any sort of invitation or flirtation, scattering her wits.

Such a particular stare, a knowing stare, teeming with the memory of last night's encounter in the stables. Alexandra could hear the beat of her heart thumping against her eardrum. Surely his curiosity hadn't been piqued; surely he hadn't discovered her secrets already?

No, it was impossible. He could have no knowledge of her personal affairs, no idea of the straits to which she'd been reduced. All the world knew that Lord Morley's widow must be a wealthy woman.

"Look here, Burke," came Wallingford's voice, making a sharp crack through the charged air. "You're supposed to be leading us wretched sinners down the path of scholarly virtue, not seducing the first willing woman to cross your path."

Mr. Burke's head snapped up, as if someone had nudged him with a cattle prod. He stumbled backward, his boots slipping in the mud, and turned to the brothers. "For God's sake, I was only offering my assistance."

The duke pulled up a few yards away, his wide mouth turned upward with amusement. "What an unseemly predicament you've gotten yourself into, Lady Morley. Typically impulsive behavior, to set out in carts with the roads knee-deep in mud."

"We're in a hurry," she said, preparing to rise in full haughty splendor and shatter the duke's disdain. She was brought up short, however, by the realization that she wasn't wearing any boots. Those, she saw in horror, still dangled absently from Mr. Burke's right hand.

She closed her eyes and cleared her throat.

"Mr. Burke, if you would be so kind as to return my boots."

He gave a start and looked down at his hand. "Good God. I'm so terribly sorry. Here you are . . . If you'll allow me . . ." He made a motion as if to put them back on her himself.

"Quite all right," she said swiftly, snatching them from his hand. She could feel her face erupt in a blush. "You needn't bother."

Her words seemed to startle Abigail out of her shocked immobility. "Oh, Alex, let me," she said, darting forward contritely and taking the left boot.

"Tell me, Wallingford," gasped out Alexandra, since she could not quite bring herself to address Mr. Burke's green eyes, "what hideous mischance brings you along the same road this morning? Are you headed for Siena?"

"No," he answered, and then, after a brief pause: "Are you?"

"No." Her heel slid down at last and she began to relace the boot. "Are you determined to watch the entire process, Your Grace? Perhaps you're unfamiliar with the proper lacing of a lady's boot."

"Oh no," he said. "Quite familiar. I was only hoping for a glimpse of your stocking, but I see such privileges are allowed only for my fortunate friend Burke."

She heard Mr. Burke grumble something, under his breath. "The other one, if you please," she said to Abigail, fuming inwardly at Wallingford, the ass. She spoke without thinking. "I don't allow such privileges to anyone. Least of all Mr. Burke."

An icy silence descended. Alexandra glanced up in time to see Mr. Burke turn away, walking back to his horse. He had apparently tossed the reins in haste to the driver of the cart, and he retrieved them now, swinging aboard the animal with a single lithe movement, not scholarly at all.

"That is to say," she said helplessly, "since we have only just met."

"Excellent," drawled Wallingford. "For I should hate to see you lose our wager so easily. No sport in it at all."

"I have no intention of losing the wager, Wallingford," Alexandra snapped. "And certainly not in *that* manner."

Mr. Burke's horse shifted about impatiently, its hooves making deep sucking noises in the mud.

Lord Roland cleared his throat. "I say," he chirped out, "that's hard luck, about your cart. How exactly are you expecting to go on?"

Alexandra rose. "We're unloading the baggage," she said, with dignity, "in order to push the cart out of the mud."

Wallingford gave a low whistle. "Do you know, I should almost like to see you do it."

"You're a beast, Wallingford." Lord Roland swung from his horse, looped the reins about one of the slats on the cart, and reached inside for a trunk.

"Oh, I say," Alexandra said gratefully, "that's awfully kind of you." She picked a path back to the cart between the stickier patches of mud and fell in beside Lord Roland. "Come along, then, Abigail," she called, over her shoulder.

"Oh, bugger it," Wallingford muttered, and dismounted in resignation.

Four hours later, trudging along a winding narrow track into a fogbank, his left boot rubbing a blister the size of a guinea on the knuckle of his fourth toe, Finn found himself cursing the name of Alexandra, Lady Morley.

"Just how far along is this inn of hers?" he grumbled to Wallingford.

"My dear man," sighed Wallingford, "you don't suppose it actually *exists*, do you?"

Finn drew in his breath. "She wouldn't!"

"The thing is, she used to be a nice sort of girl," Wallingford said, kicking viciously at a stone, until it tumbled over the ledge and fell in long dramatic plunges to the switchback below. "I believe I first met her in Lady Pembroke's ballroom, directly after she came out. Fetching creature. Round cheeks, glossy hair, fresh from the country. Bit of a sharp wit, of course, but charming enough, all told. If I'm not mistaken, I kissed her once, on someone's terrace, moonlight and all that. And then . . ." He paused to kick another stone.

"And then?" Finn prodded, a little too eagerly.

"What's that? Oh, I suppose I got distracted. I was chasing after Diana at the time, and . . . oh, gad, yes. Now I remember. Diana caught me at it, you see, on the terrace, and . . . well, Burke, old fellow, if you ever want to get a particular woman in bed—which I daresay even *you* must, from time to time—the thing to do is to get caught kissing another one." He chortled mirthlessly and sent another stone flying off the ledge. "Bloody hell, yes. The desk in the library, it was. I had to borrow her handkerchief, as my own was . . ."

"Look here," Finn broke in, "about that inn. Do you really think she made that up?" He narrowed his eyes to peer some twenty or so yards ahead, where the graceful figure of Lady Morley floated along the road atop his own horse, her black skirts gathered cunningly to accommodate the saddle. In the shrouding mist, the two beasts blurred together like a kind of female centaur, only with rather more clothing.

Wallingford shrugged. "It don't matter, Burke. Not a whit. Don't you see? We're all at her mercy. Look at the three of them. Well rested, riding our horses, the damned baggage cart miles behind, no end in sight." He stopped walking and placed his hands on his hips, scanning the rocky hillside and the befogged valley below. He flung out an arm. "Behold your land of endless sunshine, Burke. *Endless . . . bloody . . . sunshine*. So you see," he continued, resuming the track, "it don't matter whether the inn exists or whether it's her own damned invention. We simply walk, Burke, until she tells us to stop."

Finn looked down at the damp speckled stones sliding past, at the pattern of his booted feet going *crunch crunch* into the track. "Reason, of course, tells us there must be an end to it. The castle itself can't be more than a few miles farther. When we reach the access road . . ."

"Ah, Burke. You and your rational brain. Don't you see? Even if we should reach your castle before Lady Morley's mythical inn, it won't be the end of it. Oh no. We'll be obliged to take them in, offer them shelter until the baggage cart catches up, and then, my good fellow"—his voice rose into a bark, almost frantic—"then we'll *never see them leave!*"

"Nonsense," Finn said pragmatically. "They've leased their own lodgings, after all. And there's the wager, which, practically speaking, requires a complete cessation of contact with the opposite sex . . ."

A high peal of laughter wafted down to them from the mist ahead, followed by the rumble of Lord Roland's genial chuckle.

"The sister," Wallingford said darkly. "Mark my words, Burke. She'll be the most trouble of all."

Finn opened his mouth to question why, but Lady Morley's voice carried down the road, clipped with excitement, and cut him off.

"Why, here it is!"

Finn turned to the duke. "You see?" he said triumphantly. "The inn."

Lady Morley had brought her horse to a halt a short distance away and overheard him. "No, not the inn, of course," she said, waving the map in her gloved hand. "The inn is . . . well, never

mind about the inn. Look there, near the bend up ahead. There
are our lodgings! Or at least the access road, you see."

"The access road," Finn repeated numbly.

"It can't be above two miles from here," said Lady Morley
cheerfully, "and then we can send you quite on your way, with
our deepest appreciation. Although if you'd be so kind as to find
the fellow with our baggage and direct him properly, we'd be
most abjectly grateful."

"Now see here, Lady Morley," Finn burst out. "This has gone
on far enough."

"Really, Burke," said Lord Roland, visible now, standing
next to Miss Abigail Harewood's horse. Or rather his own horse,
which she was riding. "You can't possibly be proposing that we
leave the ladies here and trot off on our merry way. Anything
might happen. Brigands, even."

Finn glowered. "Brigands have been unknown in these parts
for at least a century, Penhallow. And I should think that ladies
so sturdy and self-sufficient would be grateful for the exercise."

"Ah, Burke," Wallingford said placidly. "It's pointless to
argue, merely a waste of valuable energy. Lady Morley wishes
us to follow her to her lodgings, and as she's got our horses, I
don't see we have any means of stopping her."

Finn crossed his arms and cast a speculative look at Lady
Morley. The map dangled from her long fingers, coated with
clear wax against the damp, and a rather disturbing idea insinu-
ated its way into his brain. "Lady Morley," he said, "would you
perhaps be so good as to show me your map?"

She eyed him, her elegant brow arched with suspicion.
"Haven't you a map of your own, Mr. Burke?" she inquired
coolly.

He returned her look and reached into the inner pocket of his
jacket. His map, which was unwaxed, damn it all, had grown
damp next to his perspiring body. He unfolded it gingerly and
ran his eyes along the erratic squiggles of railway line and road
until he came, roughly, to their present location. His chest
heaved with relief. By his own best estimate, they were at least
a few miles away from their own turnoff from the main road.

In any case, he had the owner's letter of confirmation still in
his pocket, warm and wilting against his chest.

There was nothing to worry about.

"Very well," he said, turning away from Lady Morley. "I suppose we can spare another hour, since we'll soon have our horses back."

"That's ever so kind," she replied, and wheeled the horse about, urging it into a trot up the drive. Finn began to walk in her wake. The duke paced along beside him, shielding him from the small signpost at the crossroads that read CASTEL SANT'AGATA 2 KM and pointed up the path Lady Morley had taken.

My dear," said Lady Somerton, ranging up next to Alexandra, "are you quite sure about all of this?"

Alexandra tilted her chin and replied briskly, "All of *what*, Lilibet? Really, it's rather late to be asking those sorts of questions. We've made our decision, haven't we? We've left England behind."

"I don't mean that," her cousin said. "I mean all this business with the duke. This wager of yours, and making them give up their beds, and now the horses." She spoke, as she always did, in that smooth mellifluous voice of hers, as if nothing on earth could annoy her. Even now she rode Wallingford's horse with ease, though she'd probably never attempted to ride astride in her life, and certainly not with a five-year-old boy wriggling before her in the saddle.

"I don't see what you mean," Alexandra said. "They were quite happy to offer us assistance. We should have done them a disservice if we'd refused; just think of all that offended chivalry. I don't know about you, darling, but I shouldn't have been able to live with the guilt."

Philip made a sudden grab for the reins, and the horse tossed his head at the intrusion. Lilibet's body shifted, adjusting, and it occurred to Alexandra that her cousin was a much better horsewoman than she'd imagined. "All the same," Lilibet was saying, as she pried the boy's fingers away and recalled the horse to its duty, "Wallingford and . . . and the others know where we're staying, and what we're doing. They may mention it to their friends, or . . ."

"I assure you," Alexandra said, a trifle haughty, "they will not. Mention it to whom, anyway? The birds? The rocks?"

"Don't be tedious, Alex. They'll write letters, send wires.

They won't cut themselves off completely. They're men of the world."

"But that's the point. They're supposed to be cutting themselves off, aren't they? Scholarly seclusion." Her horse, feeling her rising tension, began to mince his steps.

"But there's a chance, isn't there? A chance that word will reach home . . ."

"And then what?" Alexandra asked impatiently. "You're afraid your husband will come galloping after you? Really, Lilibet."

"Not for me," she said, glancing down at the fine light brown hair bobbing along below her chin.

Alexandra spoke in a low voice. "We're more than a match for Lord Somerton, I assure you. I shall turn him away with a shotgun, if I must."

"But don't you see," Lilibet pleaded, "it's better, far better, if word never reaches him."

"If you must know, I've already spoken to Mr. Burke," Alexandra said. "He may be a cad, but I'm confident he's discreet."

"Have you, now?" Lilibet said, in a different tone. "That may explain a great deal."

"What on earth do you mean?"

"You know exactly what I mean. That business with the boots. I should almost have said you were flustered."

"I was not flustered," Alexandra insisted. "Mr. Burke is a man of no standing . . "

"No standing?" Lilibet let out a peal of laughter. "Really, Alex. You've just given yourself away. No standing, indeed! Even *I've* heard of him. That speech he gave to the Royal Society last autumn; why, the *Times* carried it verbatim, with the most breathless introduction. And I suppose he's made millions from those inventions of his."

"Millions indeed!" Alexandra sniffed. "One or two, at most. No more."

"Oh, no more than two million pounds, then." Lilibet laughed. "A pittance."

"*Money* does not concern me in the least, Lilibet." Her voice was sharp.

"They're sure to knight him, at least. Or perhaps a baronetcy," Lilibet went on.

"How charming for him. Though I don't see that it's any concern of ours; we, after all, have sworn off all that, and I've no intention of giving Wallingford the satisfaction of winning . . . Oh, look ahead! Do you see it?" Alexandra shifted the reins to one hand and pointed ahead with her riding crop.

Beyond, in the clearing mist, a dun-colored bristle of medieval towers jutted into the heavy sky, surrounded by tall, unkempt cypress and overgrown with rampant vegetation. It rested, or appeared to rest, on a ridge of some sort, for Alexandra could see nothing behind it but thick, impenetrable gray.

"Good God." Lilibet shifted her son's weight and strained to see more. "It looks as though it hasn't been lived in for years."

Alexandra urged her horse forward. "Nonsense. It's just the Italian style. Rustic, you see. It's all a carefully cultivated wilderness."

"Look here, Lady Morley!" Mr. Burke's voice lashed out from behind them. "What sort of game is this?"

Alexandra turned in her saddle and slowed the horse, allowing him to catch up. He came forward in long, angry strides, his face deeply flushed, the sprinkling of freckles almost jumping from the bridge of his nose.

"Game, sir? You have me at a loss."

"This is the Castel sant'Agata! You can't deny it!"

"Why, so it is," she replied, running her thumb around the rim of the riding crop, quite slowly, so the gesture wouldn't betray her anxiety. "The Castel sant'Agata. You've heard of it?"

"Of course I bloody well have!"

"Such language, Mr. Burke!"

"You know very well," he went on, his voice constrained, as if he were leashing his words tightly, "what the Castel sant'Agata means to us. How, I imagine, did you find out? Did you rifle through our belongings, perhaps? Bribe our driver?"

"Really, Burke!" Lord Roland's words snapped out with unaccustomed sharpness.

Mr. Burke turned in his direction. "I suppose you think it's all a dreadful misunderstanding, do you, Penhallow?"

Alexandra felt a pressure begin to collect between her eyes, a gathering sense of foreboding. "I don't understand you at all, sir. What's the castle to you?"

He returned to her, arms folded across his chest, eyes glinting narrowly. His ginger hair seemed to have stiffened about his head, the way a dog's might, when faced by an unexpected threat. "It's only our home, Lady Morley, for the next year. Only that."

She let out a relieved laugh. "Your home! Oh, you're quite mistaken, sir. The Castel sant'Agata is *our* home. We've taken it for a year from the owner, a very nice fellow named . . . oh, Rossini. Or Paganini. Something like that."

"Rosseti," said Abigail, in a low voice.

"Yes! Rosseti! That's it exactly." She patted her coat pocket. "I have his letter and directions right here. A very nice fellow indeed, most accommodating. Though his command of English is not perhaps as exact as one could wish."

Mr. Burke reached into his inside coat pocket. "The same Signore Rosseti, I suppose," he said grimly, drawing out a folded paper, "who sent me this letter, confirming receipt of payment for a year's lease of the Castel sant'Agata, in the district of Arezzo, in the province of Toscana, Italy?"

Alexandra's breath sucked into her body. "No! It's not possible! I demand to see your letter!"

"I demand to see yours!"

Wallingford's voice intruded in a thunderous ducal boom, amplified by four centuries of blood authority. "Look here, the two of you! Enough of this squabbling. Give your letters to me."

There was no question of disobeying him. Alexandra, with a subdued flourish, delivered the paper into his outstretched hand; Burke handed his over in a defiant slap.

Wallingford unfolded both papers and held them before him, side by side, studying each one by turns.

As if sensing the tension in the air, the horses began to step about, mouths straining against bridles, leather creaking and metal clinking. A cold breeze rolled against them from the north, ruffling the papers in the duke's hands before continuing on to beat against the castle walls, a quarter mile ahead. Alexandra turned her head to watch the line of cypress shiver in the wind, and it seemed to her that the trees were laughing at her. She looked back at Wallingford, just as his own gaze lifted and met hers.

He began with a ritual clearing of his throat, which didn't bode well. "Well. Rather awkward. It appears Signore Rosseti is either a senile fool or . . . well, or a scoundrel." He held up both papers with his two hands. "The letters are nearly identical, except that the ladies appear to have negotiated a better price for the year's lease than you have, Burke."

"I was told," Burke said tightly, "there was no room for negotiation."

Alexandra laughed. "Oh, rubbish, Mr. Burke. Merely tactics, as anyone knows."

He shot her an angry look. "We have paid for a year's lease on the castle, and we intend to take it."

Alexandra returned his look squarely, and then glanced at Wallingford, who was frowning in deep lines, rearranging his face into his best magistrate's scowl and girding himself for a lengthy battle of legalities and technicalities.

God, no. Anything but that.

Not after a week of hellish heaving seas in the Bay of Biscay, of long days rattling along in damp provincial train carriages, of hours trudging along the unkempt Italian roads.

Not after all the rain and mud and discomfort, the constant fear of discovery by Somerton or one of his lackeys, the precious coins spent irretrievably away.

Not now, with the damned castle, the long-sought haven, in sight at last.

There was only one thing to do. She wheeled her horse about—Burke's horse, of course, what beautiful irony—and galloped down the drive toward the castle, hearing with pleasure the outraged masculine shouts chasing her along.

Possession, after all, was nine-tenths of the law.

FOUR

She might have saved herself the trouble of knocking. Urgent seconds ticked along and the door remained immobile, as heavy and silent as the castle itself.

"Is anyone there?" called Abigail, trotting up the drive behind her, as eager as she.

Alexandra could hear the voices and footfalls growing in strength behind her. "I don't know." She tossed the reins to her sister, leaned her shoulder into the ancient wood, and pushed.

It swung open easily, too easily: She staggered through the doorway like a drunkard, only just saving herself from falling to her knees.

"Are you all right?" demanded Abigail. "What's there?"

Alexandra forced herself upright. "Yes, quite all right," she said, with an unconscious brush at her coat, which was still crusted with mud. She looked about in bemusement. What had she expected? Well, a castle: a great hall lined with medieval statuary; an imposing staircase leading to a minstrel's gallery; tapestries hanging about, rampant with unicorns and whatnot. That sort of thing.

Apparently the Italians had a different notion of castles.

She stood in a narrow, low-ceilinged hallway, lined with bare stone walls so cold and damp she could have sworn she felt an arctic draught wafting off them against her cheeks. Or perhaps it came from the rather forbidding metal grating a few yards ahead, which effectively blocked her passage and no doubt accounted for the lack of any lock on the outer door.

Alexandra walked a few steps forward and wrapped her fingers around the flat metal bars. "Hello! *Buon* . . . er . . . *giorno!*" she called out, craning her neck to see within. It seemed to be some sort of paved courtyard, with a dry stone fountain in the middle and a patch of heavy sky above, and no sign whatsoever of human habitation, other than the faintest trace of woodsmoke in the air.

"What's there?" Abigail's words echoed from the walls.

"Nothing at all," said Alexandra, and at that instant the metal grate gave way with a groan of its elderly hinges. "Hello!" she called again. The sound bounced uselessly about the courtyard.

Mr. Burke's voice exploded in the air behind her. "Look here, you can't possibly try to *charm* your way into *our* legally leased house . . ."

She stepped forward and looked about the courtyard. "It doesn't matter. There's nobody here."

She heard him ranging up behind her. His boots clacked decisively on the paving stones, the murmurings and footfalls of the others blurring together in the distant background, beyond the gate. "What's that? Nobody's here?"

He came to a stop just behind her left shoulder, in a little gust of wet wool and clean rain-washed skin and laundry starch. She thought she could feel his warm breath just reaching the tip of her ear. "It's deserted," she said, and walked briskly to the fountain and peered into the bowl, making a great show of studying it, like a detective in a play. "Lichen. Hasn't been used in ages, I think."

He didn't reply.

She looked up just in time to catch his gaze, before he turned away in a swish of black coat to study the courtyard walls. In the shadowed light, his hair lost its vividness, a low bronze fringe beneath the weight of his hat. "Perhaps the owner's a hermit," he said offhandedly.

"I suppose you know all about that," she said. "Being a hermit, I mean." Strange, that with the others so near, just the other side of the wall, she should feel so alone with him. The cool still air in the courtyard seemed to hold them in place, to enclose them, the rest of the world going on behind an invisible curtain.

He began to walk the perimeter, eyes scanning the stone as if searching for weakness. "I see you know all about me."

"Aren't you, though? A hermit?" she pressed. Where was everybody? Wallingford should have come storming in by now, demanding answers, shattering this odd, unbearable tautness in the space between them.

He turned to her at last. "I am not. Where's the owner, do you think? Shall I go in and have a look?" He nodded to the doorway on the opposite wall.

"Oh no you don't," she said quickly, moving in that direction. "I won't have you reaching him first and prejudicing him. We have just as fair a claim as you do."

"And neither will I allow you to . . ."

Wallingford's boots crashed down the entryway at last. "What the devil are you about, Lady Morley? And you, Burke. Christ, the pair of you." He stopped and cast about, hands secured to his hips. "Well? Where's the owner, then?"

Mr. Burke started off in the direction of the doorway. "I don't know, but I mean to find out."

"I'll go with you," Alexandra said, making a move to follow him.

Wallingford threw up his hands. "I might as well be talking to the trees! Burke, what's the damned situation here? What did the agent say, back in London?"

Burke turned to face them both, his hand on the large iron ring on the door. "He said nothing at all. Only forwarded the executed lease with a note."

"What did the note say?"

"Oh, the usual rubbish. Very happy and so on. That the owner was quite pleased, and that he was certain . . . let me see . . . that he was certain the castle was exactly what we needed."

Alexandra felt an odd wobble at the base of her spine, a wobble she had felt only once before, at the reading of her husband's will. She heard her own voice in the air, thin and wavering. "Those were his exact words?"

"Yes, more or less." He paused. "Are you quite all right, Lady Morley?"

She smiled wanly. "Quite all right. Only, if I'm not mistaken, those were the man's exact words to me."

What a splendid adventure," Abigail said cheerfully, as she brushed aside a mildewed curtain and peered out the window. "Such delicious grime! I daresay it hasn't been washed in years. Do you suppose there's ghosts?"

"Of course not," Alexandra snapped. "The very idea."

"I expect there's dozens of them," said Abigail. "An old pile like this. And Italians! Always poisoning one another and so on. I shall be very much disappointed if I don't discover a ghost in every corridor."

Alexandra sighed. "Really, it's the wonder of the world you haven't found a husband yet."

"I never wanted one. Come, let's explore." She reached for Philip's little hand and strode across the great hall, her long legs eating up the flagstones with unladylike greed.

"Slow! Slow!" said Philip, laughing.

"Hurry, hurry!" Abigail tugged on his hand, and he moved into a spirited trot, his sturdy legs churning next to hers.

"Oh, wait!" called Lilibet, preparing to dash after them, but before she'd taken more than a few steps she was brought to a skidding halt by the appearance of a figure in the opposite door-way. "Abigail!"

Abigail looked up and stopped. "Hello there!"

The figure stepped forward: a woman, wearing a long woolen dress, a neat white apron at her waist, and a white headscarf over her hair. "*Buon giorno*," she said warily.

Alexandra stepped up. "*Buon giorno*. Are you the owner?"

The woman smiled and shook her head. "No, no. I am the . . . what is the word? I keep the house. You are the English party?"

"Yes," Alexandra said. "Yes, we are. You're expecting us?"

"Oh yes. We have much pleasure to see you. Though I think you are a day before? We are expecting you tomorrow. You like the castle?" She spread her arm with pride across the barren length of the great hall, free of any such inconvenient encumbrances as furniture, its tall windows set deep into hard-seated alcoves.

"Who could resist such an inviting scene?" said Alexandra. She received a sharp elbow from Lilibet at her side.

The woman shrugged. "Is so long when the family is live here. Is only me to keep the house."

"Haven't you any help?" Alexandra asked, astonished.

"Oh, the maids, they stay in the village. They are not staying here, when there is no master. Is so lonely. Giacomo, he keeps the . . ." Her forehead wrinkled with thought. "The earth?"

"The grounds. He's the groundskeeper. Very well. And what is your name, my good woman?" Alexandra pressed.

"I am called Signorina Morini." The woman made a little curtsy. She spoke well, neither too timid nor too forward, friendly but not familiar. A handsome woman, not far past forty and carrying the years gracefully, her cheeks still round and her jaw firm. Her hair, where it slipped out behind the headscarf, was full and black, without a single gray strand.

"Oh, what a lovely name. I do so like Italian names," Abigail said. "I'm Miss Harewood, signorina, and I think your castle is perfectly magnificent. Could you perhaps show us about?" She made a little wave toward the staircase at the far side of the hall. "Are our rooms upstairs?"

"But yes, they are upstairs." She seemed to hesitate and looked around the hall. "But . . . the gentlemen? Where are the gentlemen?"

"The gentlemen? What about them?" asked Alexandra coolly.

"Do you mean you were expecting us both?" demanded Abigail. "Signore Rosseti did it on purpose?"

Signorina Morini spread her hands before her. "I only know there come three ladies, three gentlemen. They are not your husbands?"

"I should say not!" Alexandra's hands went to her hips.

"Your brothers?"

Abigail laughed. "Oh no. Not at all."

Morini's eyebrows lifted.

"No, no," said Lilibet in haste. "It was all a great mistake. We understood . . . we thought we had taken out a year's lease, but it appears the three gentlemen made a similar arrangement, and . . . perhaps you can find Signore Rosseti, and he can explain . . ."

"I see, I see." Morini cocked her head to one side, the thoughtful frown returning. "Is very strange. The master, he is very careful, very particular. Is very strange mistake." She straightened and clapped her hands. "But is good! Six English is very good! We have talk, laughter. The castle will be . . . transform. *Buon.* I will find your rooms."

Alexandra stared in astonishment as the woman turned, a brusque, cheerful movement, and motioned them along behind her. "But, my good woman! What about servants? Has the place been readied for our arrival? Is there dinner?"

Signorina Morini turned her head and spoke over her shoulder. "We are expecting you tomorrow. The servants, they arrive in the morning, from the village."

"In the morning? Do you mean there's no dinner? Is nothing ready?" asked Alexandra, chasing after the woman, who moved with singularly nimble speed across the hall.

"Where is Rosseti?" said Abigail.

"He is not here. I make all arrange. Come, come. Is growing late!"

The woman hurried up the stairs, without bothering to look back and make sure they were following.

The man appeared almost out of nowhere, blocking the entrance to the stables with his hands planted forbiddingly on his hips.

"Oh, I say!" Lord Roland's voice rang out with its customary cheer. "Signs of life at last!"

The man let loose a torrent of Italian.

"See here," Finn said, "we're looking for a chap named Rosseti. Your master, I daresay. Can you tell me where to find him?"

"Rosseti!" The word spat from the man's lips. "Rosseti! Always he make the trouble! Now English!"

Finn had had enough. "Yes, English. Three of us, to be precise . . ."

"Six," said Lord Roland.

". . . and we shall need stabling for our horses at once. Our baggage should be along shortly, if it hasn't got stuck in the mud again, and . . ."

"Enough!" The man held up a weather-beaten hand. "I am not with the horses. I keep the grounds. Horses, I do not know."

"Summon a stableboy, then," Finn said, feeling his impatience rise.

"Is none, signore."

"Good God," exploded Wallingford, "is no one expecting us at all? I've a good mind to find this fool Rosseti and show him exactly where he can put his damned unending sunshine . . ."

Finn was about to add his own objections, but Lord Roland made a quelling movement with his hand. "Look here, my good man," he said kindly, "what's your name?"

The man's mouth formed a surly curl. "Giacomo, I am called."

"Giacomo, then. Are you not expecting us? Has no one told you of our arrival?"

"No one." Giacomo's eyes shifted to the castle behind them and narrowed into a malicious squint. "No one tells me. She make arrange, and the visitors, they appear, and it is all begin again . . ." He threw up his hands and looked back at the three Englishmen. "Is not your fault," he said, voice softening.

"Thanks very much," Finn grumbled.

"Who's *she*?" asked Lord Roland.

Giacomo ignored him. "And the women?" he went on, behind a resigned sigh. "They are in the castle now?"

"The women?" Finn demanded. "How did you know about them?"

"The women, they are always there." Giacomo nodded his head at the horses. "We have the hay and the oats. Come, I show you." He turned and ducked back inside the stable doorway.

"Wait just a moment!" Finn darted forward to follow him. "Do you mean to say we're to fodder our own horses? What about the damned baggage carts?"

"The boys from the village, they arrive in the morning," came Giacomo's doleful voice, echoing through a haze of dust motes. "Is always so."

"And what the devil," muttered Wallingford, following Finn into the stable, "does he mean by that?"

By the time Finn trooped back inside the castle with his friends, the dark-skied afternoon had already lowered into evening, and the rooms were hardly visible in the shadows.

"Hello!" he called out, hoping that by some miracle nobody would answer, that the whole disastrous episode of damned Lady Alexandra Morley and her damned party of female dilettantes had been nothing more than a particularly vivid hallucination. The morning's events certainly *seemed* like a dream by now. He'd done the bulk of the labor in settling in the horses, as neither Wallingford nor Penhallow had touched a bucket in their lives, and no sooner had the three animals been safely stowed for the night than the baggage carts had arrived at last, requiring endless hauling and supervision and tedious repetition of orders in his inexpert Italian.

To their credit, the brothers Penhallow had pitched in without much complaint. They'd unloaded chests and carried machinery like a pair of overdressed drovers, cursing with cheerful specificity and offering a catalogue of incisive remarks on topics as far ranging as the excellence of Italian spring weather and the probable nature of Signore Rosseti's parentage.

In fact, they were decidedly more talkative than Finn himself, whose mood grew blacker and blacker as he envisioned what was likely taking place in the Castel sant'Agata while he and his friends labored away in the stableyard—barricades going up, no doubt, and the entrances blocked. At the very least, the women would have claimed all the best bedrooms, leaving the men to shiver through the night on bare pallets down some wretched hallway until they crawled, defeated, out the door and down the mountain.

Ruthless creatures, ladies.

"I daresay they're all abed by now," said Wallingford, planting his feet on the flagstones and taking in the darkened hall. The baggage lay in a scrambled heap at the bottom of the staircase, almost indistinguishable in the shadows, and Finn contemplated with misery the prospect of hauling it all up to their quarters. Wherever those might be.

"D'you suppose there's any dinner to be had?" asked Lord Roland, with unconscionable cheerfulness. "I don't mean to raise any false hopes, but I believe I caught a whiff of something, an instant ago. Something edible," he added quickly, since the scents they'd encountered during the past few hours had been of the sort to put one off one's dinner entirely.

Wallingford started off down the opposite end of the hall, away from the courtyard entrance. "Kitchen's likely at the back, though I expect the ladies have eaten anything lying about by now. Licked the damned crumbs off the floor, too, by God."

Lord Roland set off after him, but Finn, after a few steps, paused and looked back at the chests. "Go along," he called. "I'll catch up in a moment."

"Don't be too long," Wallingford tossed over his shoulder. "I shan't be saving anything for you."

Lord Roland's voice echoed amicably from the end of the hall, "You're an ass, Wallingford . . ."

Finn shook his head and turned to the chests. The very thought of food made his belly howl in desperation; his last meal had consisted of a hard lump of Parma cheese and an even harder husk of bread, wolfed down in haste along the rainy trek up the hillside. But he'd seen the cavalier way in which the baggage men had tossed the chests and trunks about, and if any of his instruments and gadgets had been broken, it might mean weeks of wasted work, waiting for replacements to arrive from London, or else finding a suitable machinist nearby.

No, he had to satisfy himself before dinner, before bed, or else he wouldn't be able to sleep.

In the settling dark, he could hardly distinguish one box from another; they had been stacked against one another in reckless disorder, reeking of mildew and damp air. He stumbled about, running his hands along the various textures of leather and metal and canvas, searching for the familiar shapes of his own custom-made chests, designed to absorb the shocks of travel and weather and careless foreign drovers.

He found them at the back of the pile, larger and plainer than the rest. They'd been battered about, the leather a bit scuffed. Probably stained with rain, too, though the light was too dim to tell. He reached into his jacket pocket, pulled out a little ring of keys, and felt through them until his fingers encountered the shape he sought.

With a twist of his wrist, he slipped the key into the lock of the first chest. The tumblers clicked into place with a satisfyingly efficient clink, undamaged by the damp, and Finn opened the lid. The familiar mingled smell of metal and leather and oil rose up to greet him like an old friend, faithful and unchanged, endless blissful memories of tinkering and experimentation distilled into this clean musky scent he'd known since childhood. He ran his fingers over the bumps and ridges within. All tight and snug, the close-fitting felt wrappers undisturbed, the delicate bits of engine and instrumentation safe and sound at last.

A deep sigh of relief heaved under his ribs.

"Is that you, Mr. Burke?"

Finn jumped and whirled. His knee knocked over the chest and spilled the contents onto the floor with a god-awful metallic crash, followed by an equally catastrophic secondary crash, followed by a few solid clinks and then the lonely ring of a single machine part revolving to infinity on the stone floor.

"Oh dear," Lady Morley said faintly. "I'm so terribly sorry."

Ordinarily Phineas Burke was a solid man in a crisis. Kept his wits, reacted with cool efficiency, started putting things to rights almost before the disaster had finished unfolding. And in fact, as soon as the chest had struck the flagstones, Finn's brain told him he ought to be dropping to his knees, attempting to recover the lost machinery and assess the damage.

His body did not obey, however. He stood frozen, contemplating the figure before him, wrapped in a dazed sense of déjà vu, as if the events of the previous night had returned like a recurring nightmare. This time she was holding a candle, and the light wavered between them, turning her skin to gold. "Lady Morley," he said stupidly, "what the devil are you doing here?"

"Your . . . your things . . ." she said, equally dazed. "Let me . . . let me help you . . ." She sank to the floor and set her candle next to the dark pool of her skirts.

"No . . . quite all right . . . it's nothing," he said, and dropped down next to her to run his hands along the cold stone. "You've done enough already." The words fell from his lips before he could think.

She straightened, still on her knees, and her voice turned hard. "I beg your pardon, Mr. Burke. I shouldn't have startled you like that. I only came to tell you about the arrangements."

"The arrangements."

"For the . . ." She rose and made a motion with her arm. "For all this."

He felt himself stiffening for battle. Damn it all, where was Wallingford? Finn hadn't the faintest idea how to deal with women like this, imperious women who carried all before them. Always taking offense, always saying one thing and meaning another, always looking at one as if one's nose were protruding through a garden hedge. "Yes, of course. And what do you propose?"

"The housekeeper tells me that the castle is divided rather neatly into . . ."

"The housekeeper?" Finn asked witlessly, because he had just discovered that at some point in the past few hours, Lady Morley had removed her jacket, and she stood now before him in her plain white shirtwaist, unbuttoned at the neck.

"Yes, a woman named Morini; she appeared directly after you left for the stables. She showed us about, and it seems that, for the time being, that is to say until Signore Rosseti can be found to set things right, our respective parties can take up residence in the castle's two wings with very little . . . I say, Mr. Burke, are you attending me?"

"Yes, quite."

"As I said, then, very little need for interaction between our two parties. Except at mealtimes, as I regret to say there is only one room suitable for dining."

He realized she'd stopped talking. "Very well. I suppose that will do."

"How generous of you," she said. "I expect you'll be equally grateful to hear we've been slaving like charwomen for hours, setting up the beds and finding your dinner."

He cast about for something to say. "Are there no other servants, then?" he asked finally, trying not to let his eyes stray farther downward, to discover just how far the unbuttoning of her shirtwaist had progressed.

"What astonishing powers of deduction you have, Mr. Burke. I can well imagine how you lay those chaps at the Royal Society absolutely flat with your logic."

He opened his mouth to form some suitably cutting riposte (*When faced with a roomful of reasonable men, Lady Morley, instead of a single housekeeping shrew . . .*), but then his eyes broke discipline at last and caught fatally in the center of her chest.

It was worse than he'd dreamed. The unbuttoning continued unabated down her bosom, forming a daring gap in the white starched fabric, and her skin glowed lusciously beneath in the flickering candlelight. Worse, one panel—probably in the midst of her bed-making exertions, God help him—had pulled aside to reveal the curve of a gloriously generous breast, etched by the delicate lace of her snug-fitting corset.

Finn's eyes shot back to Lady Morley's face. "I . . . that is . . ." *My dear Lady Morley, I beg to inform you that your left breast is quite nearly hanging out of your shirtwaist* . . .

"Oh yes," she said scornfully. "Most impressive."

. . . *That is to say, your* right *breast, since it is adjacent to my left hand, and we are naturally facing each other* . . .

"Have you nothing to say at all, Mr. Burke?"

. . . *You're welcome, of course, to tuck your splendid mammary back in its rightful place, or else I should be more than happy to assist you with the adjustment* . . .

She shifted the candle to her other hand, and as the light passed before her face he saw the drawn paleness of her skin, the violet smudges beneath her eyes.

"Well then," she said, into his silence, "since your grateful thanks don't appear to be forthcoming, I'll lead the way into the dining room, such as it is." She turned with a broad sweep of her skirts. "I do hope I don't step on any of your things, Mr. Burke. If I detect any crunching beneath my feet, I'll be sure to inform you at once."

"You're too kind, Lady Morley," he choked out, following the bouncing motion of the candle as if it were a beacon. "And Lady Morley," he ventured, as they passed from the great hall toward the mirthful sounds of a well-attended dinner table, "may I suggest that you attend to . . . that is . . . a very slight stain upon the fabric of your collar."

He was going to murder Rosseti, he decided. If the man ever bothered to show up.

FIVE

Alexandra, about to launch a discussion of Aristophanes, found herself interrupted by a goat.

"Oh, I'm awfully sorry!" exclaimed Abigail, jumping from her chair to snatch at the scruffy beast's leather collar. "No, no, dear. Not the *curtain*, if you please."

"Most unappetizing," sighed Alexandra.

Abigail looked up with an apologetic expression. "It's milking time, you see. You've come to find me, haven't you, you clever thing? Ouch," she added, as the goat butted its granite head against her chin.

"Abigail, my dear." Alexandra placed her finger in the crease of her book and closed the pages together. "I don't mean to dampen your enthusiasm, but we did *not* travel a thousand miles to this . . . to this delightfully rustic outpost in order for you to milk goats. We came to study, to elevate our minds."

"But the poor thing needs milking. Don't you, darling? Yes? Oh, look, I say, that's my *petticoat . . .*"

"I'm sure there are any number of . . . of goat . . . people . . . to perform the task. Or at least one or two." Alexandra frowned at her sister, who circled about the goat in an awkward pas de deux, attempting to recover her petticoat from the creature's surly jaws.

"But there aren't, really. The men are all out sowing the

vegetable fields, and poor Morini's got her hands full with the cheese-making, and Maria and Francesca are turning the rooms out before the priest arrives tomorrow for the Easter blessing . . ."

Alexandra held up her hand. "Enough! I fail to see why . . ."

"Besides," Abigail went on, freeing her petticoat at last and grasping the goat's collar with authority, "I like milking goats."

"But Aristophanes . . ."

"I've read the man already. Twice," Abigail said, over her shoulder. "In the original Greek."

Alexandra rose to her feet and called after her. "In which case you can perhaps lead our discussion . . ."

But Abigail was already gone, through the gap in the plastered wall by which the goat had exited a moment ago. A fresh gust of breeze filled the room in her wake, smelling of damp new grass and tilled earth, and Alexandra dropped to her seat with a sigh. "*You* weren't much help," she said, turning to where Lady Somerton occupied a rush-seated chair, her book lying open and forgotten in her lap.

"What's that?" Her cousin raised her dark head.

Alexandra's eyes rolled upward. "Exactly. Why is it," she asked nobody in particular, "I'm the only one of us who takes this endeavor at all seriously?"

"I beg your pardon," Lilibet said, rearranging her book. "I take it all very seriously. Where were we? Why, where's Abigail gone?"

"Abigail's busy with her damned goats and cheeses and whatnot, and *you're* mooning over Penhallow, and . . ."

"Mooning! Over Penhallow!"

". . . and we're reduced to this . . . this ramshackle little room for our discussions . . ." Alexandra waved her hand to encompass the groaning wooden beams, the yellowed plaster crumbling from the walls, the tendril of wisteria curling luxuriously downward from a wide crack in the ceiling.

"It's a lovely room," said Lilibet. "It catches all the daytime sun."

"That's because there are *holes* in the roof!" Alexandra thrust a finger in the direction of one particularly offensive example. "And the walls!"

"The holes hardly matter, now that the weather's turned."

"That's not the point!"

Lilibet shrugged her white cotton shoulders. "Would you rather we meet in the hall? Or the dining room?"

Alexandra tossed her book atop the small wooden table next to her chair. "I don't see why the men were allowed the library. There are no holes in the library walls."

"But it's dark and faces north. And it's in their wing." Lilibet closed her book, with a little too much eagerness. "That was your idea, don't you recall? Separate wings."

"I thought they'd be gone in a fortnight." She rose from her chair and strode to the entirely superfluous window. The hillside rolled away before her, ancient terraced fields shooting up with the eager new green of cornstalks and grapevines, down to the red-roofed village nestled in the valley below. To her left, she could see the local men in the vegetable gardens, bending and straightening as they tucked the seeds into the newly turned soil; to her right loomed the opposite wing of the castle, where Wallingford and Penhallow and Burke had entrenched their belongings in the few habitable rooms, stubbornly refusing to admit defeat.

"Of course it was an excellent idea," Lilibet said. "Reasonable and equitable, and saves us the awkwardness of meeting them, except at mealtimes."

Alexandra turned from the window with a little smile. "Oh, terribly awkward, isn't it? Terribly awkward that poor old Penhallow is as desperately in love with you as before."

A blush rose up in Lilibet's elegant cheeks. "That's not true. He hardly speaks to me at all."

"Could there be more damning proof than that? Oh, come now." Alexandra crossed her arms, enjoying the sight of Lilibet's confusion. "Don't be maidenly."

Lilibet rose to her feet, book clutched between her fingers. "You shouldn't speak of such things. You shouldn't accuse me like that."

"Accuse you?" Alexandra started. "Accuse you of what?"

"He's nothing to me. I'd never . . . I have a *husband*, Alex!"

"Good God! Darling, of course I didn't mean . . ." Alexandra stepped forward and took Lilibet's shoulders. "I only meant that he admires you. Of course he does. You're frightfully admirable."

"I am not." Lilibet returned Alexandra's gaze with serene blue eyes. "I am not admirable. If I were admirable, I'd have stayed in England."

"He's a beast, Lilibet. A beast."

Lilibet spoke quietly. "Yes, he is. But he's also the father of my child."

She stepped away, the book still clasped in her hands, and left the room.

Alexandra made a movement to follow her, but then some force seemed to press against her limbs, stilling the impulse. She turned again to the window.

A cloud, scudding past the sun, cast the broad panorama in shadow. The men in the garden had stopped work and were passing around a large brown jug, from which each took a long and thirsty draw. Alexandra watched them idly, their easy movements and familiar gestures, and it occurred to her that they'd probably known one another since childhood. Had tilled these fields as their fathers had, and their grandfathers. Had eked existence from this dramatic patch of landscape all their lives, with hard work and simple reward, knowing nothing of rates of return and company shares and the bitter shock of retrenchment.

A movement caught her eye, from the other side of the scene before her: a figure striking forth across the crest of the vineyard terrace with giant, purposeful strides. She knew who it was, of course, even before the sun, slipping at last from behind the covering cloud, lit his bare head in an explosion of burnished red gold.

Without realizing it, she leaned forward against the windowsill, bumping her nose against the mottled glass. For such a tall man, he moved with surprising grace. His long legs ate the ground and his arms swung alongside in perfect cadence, and though she couldn't see his face from this angle, she knew exactly how it would look: forehead creased in thought, lawn green eyes narrowed, gaze ravaging the ground directly ahead.

"*Molto bello*, no?" came a voice at her shoulder.

Alexandra jumped away from the window and spun around.

Signorina Morini's dark eyes sparkled. "You do not think so?" She nodded at the window. "The young English. So tall, so *bellissimo.* Such eyes, like the young grass, the first green of the spring."

"I . . . I really don't know." Alexandra folded her arms and glanced outside. "He doesn't speak to me."

Signorina Morini made a broad shrug. "Ah, that is nothing. This gentleman, he says not much. But he feels"—she pressed her fist against her breast—"he feels much."

"How do you know that?"

"Gentlemen, I understand. The one who speaks little, feels much." Her face opened into a smile. "You like him? Signore Burke?"

"Me? I . . . I hardly know him. He's a scientist," Alexandra added, as if that might explain everything.

"He is very clever, this Signore Burke. He works all the day in the . . . what is the word? The little . . . house? For the carriages? The one near the lake, in the valley."

"Does he? How lovely for him." Alexandra glanced quickly through the window and back again.

Signorina Morini was still smiling. "You like, perhaps, I tell you where to find this little house?"

"I haven't the slightest interest, I assure you."

Signorina Morini moved past her to the gap in the wall, in a rush of air that smelled tantalizingly of fresh bread. She stood in the sunshine and pointed her long, sturdy arm down the terraced slope to the valley. "Is down the terraces, so. To the left. You see the trees at the bottom, by the lake. And there is the little house." She turned back to Alexandra. "Is one time the house of the—oh, these English words—he watches the carriages, the coaches." Her fingers rubbed helplessly against her thumbs.

"The coachman?"

"Yes! The *coach man.*" She said it slowly, as two separate words, as if her tongue were testing out the sounds.

"And doesn't he live there anymore?"

Signorina Morini flicked her fingers. "Is no *coach man* now. Is only Giacomo. I come to tell you the post is arrive this morning from the village. You have letter, newspaper." She nodded at the wooden table, where a small pile of correspondence lay next to Aristophanes.

Alexandra squinted at the topmost letter. "Thank you."

"Is no trouble," said Signorina Morini. She turned to leave, and then looked back over her shoulder at Alexandra, eyes crinkled with good nature. "There is also letter for Signore Burke, I think. Is a shame the girls are so busy with the cheese and the clean."

"A dreadful shame. He shan't receive his letter until he returns."

Signorina Morini nodded to the gap in the wall. "Down the terraces, to the left. The trees, the lake. No one goes there. Is very quiet."

"How peaceful for him. Thank you ever so much, signorina."

"Is nothing, milady." The housekeeper winked and disappeared through the doorway, leaving the faint scent of baking bread hanging in the air behind her.

Alexandra stared for a moment at the small stack of envelopes on the table. In her earlier life, her married life, the ritual of the twice-daily post had brought her much joy. Letters, invitations, newspapers; even the bills from her dressmaker and her milliner gave her a certain amount of satisfaction, since they were easily settled and reminded her of the comforting material abundance that surrounded her.

No longer.

Buck up, Morley, she told herself. You might as well look. Bad news won't improve by ignoring it.

A breeze floated in from the garden, verdant and delicate, and Alexandra let it carry her toward the table and the envelopes. A newspaper lay beneath, the *Times*, which Wallingford had instructed his London solicitor to forward weekly. She picked it up first, sliding it out from under the letters, and scanned the headlines. The usual rubbish, Parliament and Ireland and whatnot. The sort of thing she used to care about, when her own world, her personal world, had been properly secure. Oh, the hours she'd spent arguing cabinet appointments and Commons votes with her political friends, in her well-appointed drawing room, with champagne and dainty sandwiches of thinly sliced ham or watercress or Stilton cheese, delivered on polished salvers by a fleet of tall footmen! Her salons had been legendary. She'd been the queen of them all, the darling, her place assured and her future serene.

Once.

She let the newspaper fall from her fingertips and reached for the topmost letter. She recognized the stationery at once, even the handwriting in which her name and address had been neatly inscribed. She slipped her finger beneath the seal, opened the envelope, and pulled out the paper within.

The bank presented its compliments, and requested a further deposit of funds before additional payments could be honored. It respectfully referred her attention to the size of the overdraft, and remained her obedient servant.

She folded the paper with trembling fingers, tucked it back inside the envelope, and picked up the next letter.

This one was longer and less personal, addressed to the shareholders of the Manchester Machine Works Company, Limited, and describing in woeful detail the Company's inability to produce a workable prototype this quarter due to an unexpected failure of its patented propulsion device and lack of capital at reasonable rates. The Company enjoined the patience of shareholders, as the Board, headed by its chairman, Mr. William Hartley, had a number of proposals in which it was actively engaged, and high hopes that an investor might be found to fund further development.

The Company thanked her for her faith in the future of mechanized personal transportation, and remained her obedient servant.

This time Alexandra stuffed the paper back in its envelope with considerably more venom. Oh, no doubt William Hartley had any amount of high hopes. He always had, the little fool, her husband's well-meaning and deeply impractical nephew. How on earth had she been persuaded to allow him trusteeship over the investment of her jointure? She must have been mad!

She slapped the envelope back down on the table. Well, not mad, of course. Simply young and unseasoned and newly engaged to a wealthy man, without a thought in the world that invested money might actually disappear if one weren't careful. If one paid no attention to business letters and allowed one's well-intentioned step-nephew to invest almost the entirety of one's jointure in his newly formed limited liability corporation. The Manchester Machine Works Company! It sounded so stable, so reliable, the sort of enterprise that turned out practical items like sewing machines and . . . and that sort of thing.

Not horseless carriages.

Now she had nothing, or nearly nothing. No more salons, no more elegant house in town, no endless stream of friends who worshipped her every word. She had her title and her twenty-odd thousand useless Manchester Machine Works shares; she had a sister entirely dependent on her, for upkeep and for dowry; she had debts and shame and perhaps fifty more years of life ahead of her, with no idea how to live them.

She had to get her old life back. Because if she wasn't Lady Morley, leader of London society, then who the devil was she?

And who would give Abigail the future she deserved?

Alexandra turned her head toward the window, to the bright patch of sky hanging above the valley and the lake in the trees below the terraced vineyard. She reached down for the envelopes on the table and sorted through them until her blurred and stinging eyes identified the name of Mr. Phineas Fitzwilliam Burke, R.S.

Horseless carriages. What did she know about damned horseless carriages?

Evidently, she would have to learn.

Taking up the letter in her hand, with the newspaper tucked beneath her arm, she slipped through the gap in the wall and headed down the hillside.

SIX

Finn couldn't make out the precise nature of Giacomo's complaints, what with his own head stuck beneath the automobile's rear axle, but he gathered it had something to do with the women. With Giacomo, it always did.

Cheese . . . something something . . . *smell* . . . something . . . *stables* . . . something something . . . *devil-woman* . . .

"I say, there," Finn called out, "could you perhaps tilt the lamp in this direction? I'd be much obliged."

A pause. "*Che cosa?*"

"Never mind," sighed Finn. "Carry on." He struggled out from beneath the machine and reached for the kerosene lamp on a nearby table. Hardly what he was used to, of course—his workshop in England was equipped with electricity and hot running water and central heat and a telephone—but he'd adjusted quickly. The Castel sant'Agata's distressing lack of modern conveniences was the least of his misery.

Giacomo's constant interruptions, for example, ranked considerably higher.

"Is impossible!" The man threw his hands in the air and looked heavenward, though his view to the Almighty was presently obstructed by a series of cobwebs and roof beams, and quite possibly a barn owl, though as the creature kept nocturnal habits Finn couldn't quite be sure. He'd meant to take a sample of the droppings back to the castle with him and consult an ornithological book in the library, but it kept slipping his mind.

For some damned reason.

"*What* is impossible?" Finn inquired, because it seemed the polite thing to do.

"The cheeses! In the stables!"

"What cheeses?"

"You no listening! Not a word! *Nome di Dio!*" Aloft went the arms again, and the imploring gaze followed them upward to the deity in question. "I begin again."

Finn gave the lampshade a last adjustment, frowned at it critically, and then set the device on the floor. "I'd rather you didn't, frankly."

"Is the women. All the day, they make the cheese, the *pecorino*, in the . . . what is the word?"

"The kitchen?" Finn hazarded.

"Yes! The kitchen! And in all the great big castle, they say they find no room, no room for the cheese to . . . what is the word? To put the cheese to become old."

"Ripen, I believe." Finn settled himself back on the floor and began to wriggle gratefully out of range.

"Wait, signore! You must listen! The duke, he does not care, and his brother . . ." Giacomo rolled his eyes and circled his finger about his ear.

"Mad as a hatter, at the moment. I quite agree. But you see, my good man . . ."

"Is that *woman*!" Giacomo spat earnestly. "The devil-woman, who keeps the house . . ."

"I haven't the least idea who you mean. The housekeeper? I can't tell them apart." Finn tried to shrug from his position on the floor, half submerged beneath the axle.

"Tell the ladies, the English! Tell them about the cheese! She will stop, if the English say to her, stop!"

"Look here, old chap. You really must endeavor to make yourself clearer."

"*Che cosa?*"

"I don't understand you. See? *No comprendo.*"

Giacomo's body slumped into a sigh. "The *cheeses*, signore. The so-great wheels of the cheese, the *pecorino*." His hands shaped the air before him into a circle of impressive dimensions.

"They put them—to ripe—in the *stables*!" He drew a large breath and hissed out the word again. "The *stables*, signore!"

Finn gave his lower lip a thoughtful chew. "And the horses object?"

"Not the *horses*, signore! *I* object! I, Giacomo!" Giacomo beat his chest with a gnarled rebellious fist against the tyranny of cheese-wielding housekeepers. "La Morini, she has all the attics of the *castel* for her *pecorino*, and she sends the cheeses to the stables! Is an insult! To me!"

"And the smell, of course," Finn said, not without sympathy.

"And the smell! *Si!* You see, you understand!" Giacomo's mouth bent out a smile. "Is good. You speak to the ladies. I am happy. I say to you, good day and good luck." He turned to go.

"Now look here! I *can't* speak to the women!"

Giacomo looked back over his shoulder. "What is this?"

"Can't speak to them." Finn picked up his discarded wrench and pointed it at the man's chest for emphasis. "It's an oath."

Giacomo's eyes rounded in respect. "An oath! Signore! An oath . . . against the ladies?"

"Of a sort." Finn cleared his throat. "Well, not precisely. But we've sworn to have nothing to do with them, a brother-to-brother sort of understanding, if you will. Except at meals, which necessitate . . . a sort of what the French call *détente . . .*" He swallowed. "Well, it's bloody awkward, that's all."

Giacomo's hands swept upward before him, palms out. "Is understand. Is understand perfectly. The ladies, no speak. Wise, very wise, signore. Is only trouble, you speak to the ladies."

"I couldn't agree more," Finn said, smiling with relief. "So you see, it's quite impossible . . ."

"A note," interrupted Giacomo, "a note, she is enough." He ducked his head in a little bow. "I go now."

"Look here!" protested Finn, but Giacomo had already crossed the floor with miraculous speed, had flung open the door and disappeared into the explosion of sunlight.

Finn blinked after him. "Bloody hell," he said aloud, fingering the cool metal of his wrench. Light now tumbled through the doorway, the full throb of the midmorning sun, shining directly on the rear half of his machine. He set down the wrench and reached out one long hand to the now-redundant lamp and put it out.

What on earth was wrong with these people? Couldn't Giacomo simply talk to the damned housekeeper himself? Finn
picked up his wrench again and swung himself under the axle.
Protocol, probably. Or separation of the sexes, or some other
obscure custom, hardly to be unexpected among a people living
in the same remote mountainous valley as their great-
grandfathers before them. He'd traveled extensively. He knew
what sort of taboos might grow up around isolated communi-
ties. He knew how necessary and how indestructible they
could be.

Which left Finn the task of informing the ladies of the Great
Cheese Insurrection.

He didn't have to speak to Lady Morley, he reminded himself. A word in the ear of Lady Somerton would do just as well,
or else the sister, what the devil was her name, nice enough girl.
He hadn't addressed a word to Lady Morley since that first
evening—an impressive feat, considering they'd sat down to
dinner opposite each other every night for the past three
weeks—because every time the most perfunctory of mealtime
greetings began to form in his brain, the image of Lady Morley's right breast appeared next to it, large and round and suc-
culent, nearly bursting from its corsetry like an overripe fig
might burst from . . .

He was doing it again.

Focus. Focus on the task at hand. He needed his wits just
now, clear and sharp and undistorted by lust. He had forsworn
the company of women for that very reason. He was already
behind in his rigorous schedule, with several unforeseen problems in the development of his electric engine and that damned
nuisance Delmonico down in Rome announcing success after
success, rot him. Lady Morley's breasts, however enticing, had
nothing to do with engines. Except, perhaps, in a metaphorical
sense, which . . .

Focus.

He slid with resolution back underneath the gleaming metal
of his prototype and concentrated his thought on the axle before
his eyes. The crankshaft still hadn't been connected properly,
and there was no point returning to the engine until . . .

"Mr. Burke? Is that you?"

Ignore it. Focus.

The voice broke in again, so very much like Lady Morley's it seemed almost as though it were real, rather than a hallucination: "Mr. Burke? Am I intruding?"

It's all in your head, Burke old man. Axle rods. Crankshaft.

Something touched his hair. "Mr. Burke? Are you quite all right?"

Bloody hell.

Finn jerked in shock, slamming his forehead against the axle with a metallic clang. "Damn it all!" he groaned.

"Mr. Burke! Are you hurt?"

Finn placed one hand on his brow and rubbed ferociously. "Not at all, Lady Morley. Not at all." He paused a moment, collecting his wits, and then edged out from beneath his machine, inch by resigned inch.

There she stood, framed by the sun, her features shadowed and the light casting an electric glow about the outline of her hair and the hourglass curve of her waist. "I'm so terribly sorry," she said. "That was a dreadful clang. Was it your head?"

He sat up. The downward flow of blood made his brow throb with a distinct and excruciating pain. "No. That was the axle. My head rather absorbed the sound, I believe, than originated it."

Her mouth, what he could see of it, made a little round O. "I'm so terribly sorry."

"A trifle, Lady Morley. Think nothing of it." Finn rose to his feet and brushed at his trousers. "I presume Giacomo sent you to me?"

She shook her head. "No, no. I . . . I came on my own initiative. I hope"—she offered a smile—"I hope it doesn't violate any oaths and wagers and so on. It's a purely businesslike errand."

Finn felt a twinge of something like disappointment. "Of course. May I . . ." He cleared his throat. "May I offer you a seat?"

"Oh, that's not necessary." She seemed to lose herself for an instant or two, staring curiously at his face, her fingers clutching at a small rectangular bundle she held next to her abdomen. She'd moved slightly, tilted her head, so that the sunlight struck her face at an angle, curving around the line of her cheekbone and illuminating her brown eyes into gold.

Finn crossed his arms. "Lady Morley, I should hate to be

impolite, but I'm rather engaged at the moment. If you'll come to the point?"

"I beg your pardon. I've not the slightest wish of intruding on your work. I only wished to deliver your post." She thrust the bundle forward.

"My post?" he repeated, staring at her hands.

"Your post. A letter and the *Times*. Which properly belongs to Wallingford, I believe, but I thought I'd bring it along and let you have the first go." She paused and smiled. "Aren't you going to take it?"

"Yes, of course." He took the papers from her, with care to avoid the brush of her fingers, and scanned them mechanically.

"There's an item on the front page that might interest you," she offered, after a second or two. "About a public automobile trial in Paris."

He looked back at her, feeling rather stupid. "Really? I shall have to take a look. Thank you."

She nodded at the paper. "A chap named De Dion. Have you heard of him?"

"Yes, yes. I daresay he'll be in Rome in July, with the others."

"His ideas seem most revolutionary. What do you think of them?"

He blinked in astonishment. "I beg your pardon?"

"With the boiler mounted on the front. I believe he was clocked at nearly sixty kilometers an hour. Does your vehicle have a steam engine?"

Finn felt his mouth drop open.

"I think steam power holds a great deal of promise, don't you? Though I should think it more useful for speed trials than for general use. So unreliable, and the danger of explosion, of course." Her voice went on, perfectly smooth and melodious, as if they were discussing the weather instead of the vanguard of automotive progress. She raised her hand to dismiss the danger of catastrophic boiler explosion with an elegant flick of her fingers.

"Yes, of course," Finn found himself mumbling. "I prefer an electric motor, myself."

"An electric motor!" A bright glow came to life in her eyes, which looked past him to rest longingly, almost lovingly, on his automobile. "How perfectly clever of you! I'm an advocate of electric engines, myself. Such a great deal cleaner and more quiet. The trouble's the power, of course. How fast is yours able to manage?"

"I haven't . . . quite . . . that is . . ." Finn took in a long steadying breath. "Lady Morley, this is all rather unexpected. I'd no idea you were a student of automotive engines."

"I suppose you think women incapable of mechanical inclination?"

"No," he said, having enough wits about him to know the proper answer to that question. "Not incapable at all. Only perhaps . . ."

"Perhaps?"

"Perhaps . . . less inclined to make a study of it."

She smiled widely. "Oh, I'm fascinated by motor-cars. The wave of the future, I'm sure." She took a bold step toward the machine and placed her hand upon the smooth metal of the carriage frame. "Tell me about yours."

"Lady Morley, I really haven't the time. I'm working on something rather particular, at the moment . . ."

She looked up, with a glance Finn might have called flirtatious. "Oh, be as brief as you like. As I said, I'm fascinated. Every little tidbit is of interest to me." Her body, supple and feminine, leaned toward the machine. She was wearing a simple pale blue frock, the sort of thing a lady might put on for a summer picnic, fitted tightly at the bodice only to fall in luxurious swags about the ripe curve of her hip. Finn closed his eyes, allowing himself to imagine for just an instant that his hand rested upon that hip, the warm flesh beneath those layers of clothing fitting his palm exactly.

"An electric motor," he said hoarsely, opening his eyes, "has a great many advantages over steam and internal combustion. I'm convinced I can overcome the problems of speed and reliability. I've rather a new take on the matter of the battery . . ."

"Really?" she pressed, when his voice trailed off. "What sort of take?"

"Look, I haven't the time to explain at the moment. Perhaps we can discuss it at dinner."

"Ah. But you never discuss anything at dinner, Mr. Burke. Your mouth remains resolutely closed." She rested her eyes on the mouth in question.

"I've a great deal on my mind at dinner." He made a concerted effort not to rest his eyes on the great deal in question; namely, Lady Morley's right breast, which was presently and disappointingly clothed with a respectable abundance of blue linen.

"I daresay. You probably don't think me worth talking to, do you? A mere frivolous aristocrat. Shallow and vain and all that. And you're quite right, of course." She turned to the motor-car and ran her hand along the frame. "It's beautiful, this machine of yours. You must be immensely proud of it. Of yourself." Her fingers idled in the seam of the doorframe, long, mobile fingers, the nails short and rounded. She continued, in a murmur: "I've always wondered what it must be like to have a brain like yours, so useful and serious. So . . . oh, I don't know. All encompassing, I suppose."

Finn's all-encompassing brain couldn't seem to produce anything to say to that. A part of him seemed to detach from himself, watching him watching her, a lanky oil-streaked giant transfixed by the play of sunlight in a lady's chestnut hair, by the way it caught the red brown tendrils that had come loose from her chignon to curl against the creamy skin of her neck. He regarded that lust-wracked man with pitying scorn. *Here's what comes of giving up women*, he told the poor speechless fellow, shaking his head. *You only end up panting with longing for the first one who crosses your path.*

"From whom is your letter?" she was asking, still facing the motor.

"What's that?"

"Your letter." She turned at last. "I couldn't help noticing the handwriting was distinctly feminine. An admirer of yours, I presume?"

He looked down at his hands, which held the newspaper and letter together in a crushing grip. He unwrapped his fingers from around them and straightened the envelope. "From my mother," he said, running his thumb along the delicate black ink.

"Oh! Your mother!" A laugh drifted up from her throat. She took a step forward, craning her neck at the letter. "Far less thrilling, then. Where does your mother live?"

"In Richmond."

"How lovely. Do you visit her often?"

"As often as I can." He tossed the letter and the envelope on the table and folded his arms, not sure what to do with himself, great awkward rutting beast that he was, and desperately afraid she could read his thoughts. She was that sort of woman: altogether too perceptive, altogether too keen.

She made that throaty laughing sound again. "Well! I can see I've stayed quite beyond my welcome."

"Not at all."

"Oh yes. I can read the signs. You're wishing most earnestly for me to take my frivolous self out of your workshop." She moved closer and placed her hand on his arm, looking up into his eyes with searching intensity, the faint scent of lilies drifting from her warm skin to fill his brain. Her voice lowered. "Though I should very much like to stay and watch, for I'm so awfully curious about . . . oh!"

She whirled to the door, just as Finn's stupefied ears picked up the same warning.

"Burke! Burke! Where are you? Burke, damn you for a reclusive damned . . ." An awestruck pause. "Good God!"

The Duke of Wallingford stood stock-still in the doorway, wearing a thunderous scowl and a fine coating of goose down.

SEVEN

Alexandra stared in wonder as the duke made a gasp like a scandalized matron. "Lady *Morley*!" he exclaimed, looking back and forth between her and Mr. Burke. Bits of goose down came loose from his hair to waft aimlessly across the shaft of sunlight from the doorway.

"Dear me." Alexandra concentrated on the progress of one particularly drunken white feather, in an effort to gather her wits. "Did the goose win?"

Wallingford stabbed his right index finger in the direction of Mr. Burke's broad, oil-spotted chest. "You! I might have expected Penhallow, but *you*!"

"Calm yourself, Wallingford," said Mr. Burke, his voice reassuringly deep and firm, vibrating the air around them. "Lady Morley was only delivering the post. A letter from my mother." He extended one long arm to the lamp table and produced the envelope.

"Delivering the post, was she?" Wallingford's eyes, black and terrible, shifted back to Alexandra. "You always were a damned unprincipled schemer, Lady Morley. Seducing the poor sod in broad daylight!" He waved an illustrative arm to the broad daylight at his back.

"Of course not," Alexandra snapped, lifting her hand to cover the madly throbbing pulse at her neck. "You and your filthy mind, Wallingford. The maids are all busy with cheese and whatnot . . ."

"Yes, about that cheese . . ." Mr. Burke began.

". . . and so I took it upon myself to deliver the letter. I thought I was being neighborly." With effort, she schooled her voice into the proper mixture of confidence and affront. In truth, she was badly rattled. She'd planned out the encounter with Burke with great care, as she descended one by one through the vine-tangled terraces on the way to the cottage. She would be calm, and a bit flirtatious. She would open the door for future visits. Nothing to be gained dishonorably, of course. No trickery, no seduction; she would only take what he might be encouraged to offer.

And then he'd looked at her from his great height, with his arms crossed atop his oily mechanic's smock and his green eyes enveloping her with such terrible scrutiny, and her knees had gone so wobbly she'd had to lean against his machine to support herself. She'd felt stained, and venal, and yearning for some nameless and tantalizing thing that lay quite beyond her reach. The yearning stayed with her still, a sharp ache at the back of her throat.

Wallingford removed a feather from his tongue with great dignity. "Very well. You've delivered your damned post. Now off you go."

"Look here, Wallingford," Mr. Burke said sharply. "That's quite enough. Lady Morley's intentions were entirely honorable."

"And *yours*, man?" Wallingford looked as outraged as a man covered in goose down could possibly manage.

As Alexandra watched, a smile crept about the corners of Mr. Burke's mouth, lighting the whole of his face, and somehow the ache began to recede, and the first bubbles of laughter began to replace her bemusement.

"From the looks of it, old man, my intentions were far more honorable than yours," said Mr. Burke. "Poor old goose. I do hope you were gentle."

Wallingford's face turned a livid red beneath the down, a sight Alexandra viewed with the deepest pleasure. "Yes, Your Grace. Do tell us about the goose. Unless the tale is too sordid for mixed company, in which case I shall be happy to eavesdrop from the other side of the door."

"There was no goose involved, Lady Morley," Wallingford growled. He raked a hand through his hair to loosen the feathers, and then watched with shock at the volume of goose down erupting into the air. His eyes snapped back to Alexandra. "It's that damned sister of yours! Again!"

"What's that? You've debauched my *sister*?"

"And *again*, you say?" added Mr. Burke. "Really, Wallingford, this is most irregular."

The duke's mouth opened and closed. "To hell with the pair of you!" he shouted, and wheeled about to stalk out of the workshop.

"Wait!" Alexandra called, laughing, running after him. "Wait! I demand to know the details!"

"The details are none of your bloody business!"

"Such language, Wallingford!"

He stopped and spun about and stabbed his finger at her. "Your sister is nothing more than a common hoyden, a damned mischievous . . ." He groped for a word.

"Sprite? Imp?" Alexandra supplied.

"Pixie?" suggested Mr. Burke.

"Shrew!" The word exploded from the duke's chest with a fine shower of indignant goose down. His mouth worked furiously, attempting to form some additional epithet, but without success.

"Shall I ask poor Abigail about it, then?" said Alexandra kindly.

Wallingford's face seemed almost to collapse on itself. "Do that," he said, and turned around and stomped through the olive trees, away from the vineyards and the castle, toward the beckoning sparkle of the lake.

"I expect he's headed for a bath," Mr. Burke observed, his tall body close enough to brush Alexandra's elbow.

"I should hope so." She faced him. He was still smiling, and it was astonishing how that smile opened his face, illuminated his entire expression, illuminated the very air around them. If a genie were to descend upon them at that very moment and offer her a single wish, she thought wildly, she would wish to keep that smile on his lips forever.

But no genie descended, and a second or two later his face

turned to hers and the smile began to fade. "I suppose we'll hear all the details at dinner," he said.

"I'll have it all out of Abigail. I'm legendary at that."

"Yes, I expect you are." His arm moved, his hand lifted, and for a reckless instant she thought he might cup her face and kiss her. But he only brushed a stray white feather from her shoulder with his blunt-tipped fingers, and then stepped back to a more formal distance. The sunlight, cutting through the trees, turned his hair a fiery red gold.

"Mr. Burke," she said, "I was quite serious, back in your workshop. I have an immense curiosity for machines such as yours. I hope . . . I don't mean to intrude . . . I thought perhaps I might stop by, from time to time, and help you in your work."

His brow descended. "Help me?"

"Surely you've need of an assistant, on occasion?" She swallowed heavily, awaiting his reply.

"I've always Giacomo to call on, I suppose. You needn't bother."

"It's no bother, really. Or perhaps"—she raised a challenging eyebrow—"perhaps you're concerned about our wager, and all that. I promise you I won't consider it a breach. I'm quite honorable about such things. You can think of me as a fellow scholar. As a kind of female eunuch."

He smiled, though not the same smile as before—a stiff smile, almost acerbic. "Oh, quite. A female eunuch. I don't foresee any difficulties at all."

"You needn't be sarcastic. I was only offering to help."

"It doesn't matter if you call yourself a fellow scholar or a female eunuch. Our friends will be convinced otherwise, and I'll be forced to pay the forfeit. Rather humiliating, you see, as I was the one who suggested it." His smile seemed to grow a little more rueful, and Alexandra found herself beginning to smile back.

"I'll be discreet," she told him. "And if anyone discovers me, I'll tell them it was my fault. That I was drawn irresistibly to you, and you were too much a gentleman to refuse me."

He watched her with his rueful smile, and the birds began to speak into the silence, chattering through the small silver-green leaves of the olive trees. Alexandra felt her skin grow warm;

whether it was from the noontime sun or the thoroughness of his
expression, she did not know. When he spoke at last, his voice
was cool and distant, and he was already turning to walk back
to the cottage. "They'll never believe that, of course," he threw
over his shoulder.

"Does that mean you'll let me help you?" she called after him.

"I don't suppose I can bloody well stop you," he called back.

She found Abigail in the kitchen, sitting next to Signorina
Morini and an enormous pile of small, pale beans.

"What the devil have you been doing to poor Wallingford?"
she demanded, dropping into the empty chair across from them.

"Have you come to help us with the beans? That's awfully
sporting. You can put the discards in this pile." Abigail pointed
to a small hill of unpromising specimens, tiny and spotted and
miserable next to their plump white cousins.

Alexandra folded her arms. "Abigail, darling. I've *seen* the
fellow, and while I don't particularly care *how* you managed to
cover him in goose down, I do most passionately care about the
retaliation he's sure to bring down about our heads."

Signorina Morini, her hands moving in a practiced blur
amongst the beans, looked upward with a wise eye. "Tell me,
signora, where it is you see the duke, with all his fine feathers?"

"He stopped by the . . ." Alexandra narrowed her eyes at the
housekeeper and plucked a bean from the mountain before her.
"At Mr. Burke's workshop, whilst I delivered the post."

Abigail clapped a hand over her mouth. "You were with Mr.
Burke?"

"Only delivering the post." Alexandra rolled the bean up and
down the hard dark wood with her finger.

Abigail's face turned back down to the beans, but not before
Alexandra glimpsed a smug smile creasing her mouth. "And
when exactly did you become Mr. Burke's postman?"

"Only today." Alexandra flicked the bean back into the pile.
"You know I'm curious about his work. I wanted to have a
look."

"Oh, his work. Of course."

"Look here," Alexandra snapped, "I can't conceive why
everybody thinks a man and a woman can't work sensibly

together without the question of sexual interest. It's . . . it's barbarian. We are civilized people, quite able to deal with one another on a purely intellectual level . . ."

Signorina Morini began to hum to herself, a little smile playing about her lips.

"In any case," Alexandra said, "we were talking about Wallingford and his goose down. At least I assume it's goose down."

"Oh, it's goose down, right enough." Abigail turned to Signorina Morini and addressed her in Italian, something that sounded like a question. The housekeeper shrugged her shoulders and replied, in rapid-fire syllables Alexandra could hardly distinguish.

"Stop that at once," she said crossly. "What on earth are you talking about?"

Abigail turned to her sister, those delicately wrought features arranged into something like amusement. "Nothing at all. Only goose down. Look here, I'd love to tell you about my adventures this morning, but it's a much more tedious tale than you think."

"Humor me."

Abigail sighed. "There was a misunderstanding as I was helping the maids turn out the rooms. An altercation. I suppose it all started with the cheese . . ."

"The cheese!"

"As I said," Abigail hurried on, rising to her feet, "all very tedious. And now if you'll excuse me, the two of you, I've a great deal to do this afternoon. Quite . . . quite essential sorts of things." She bolted for the door.

"Wait a moment! Abigail!" But her sister's pale skirts had already disappeared around the corner of the doorway. She watched the empty space for a moment or two, the plain whitewashed plaster walls of the hall, not a shadow to be seen. "What on earth was that?" she asked.

Signorina Morini made another shrug of her sturdy shoulders, going on with her bean-sorting as though nothing at all had happened. "Is a mystery. The young girls, they are full of mystery."

"She isn't so very young," Alexandra said darkly. "Twenty-three. A spinster, almost. She ought to know better. I suppose it's because Mama died before she came out, you know. I arranged things for her, of course, but it isn't at all the same. I had my own life to look after, my husband and household." She looked up at Signorina Morini, who sat calmly with her beans, nodding in sympathy. "I tried," she insisted. "I really did. But I'm not her mother—I'm not really motherly at all, particularly not to my own sister."

Signorina Morini nodded again. "Perhaps you will help me a little with the beans?"

Alexandra reached for the great pile of beans and began sifting through, setting aside the flawed ones on their hill of shame.

"Of course you try," the housekeeper said. She addressed her words to the beans before her, with the bright red pattern of her headscarf standing out in relief against the white walls of the kitchen. "Is a very hard thing, you teach a young girl to be a woman. Is more hard when you are also young."

"I ought to have been more responsible, when I had the chance. The resources." Alexandra watched the beans blur before her. It was quick work, she discovered. The mountain of unsorted beans began to diminish appreciably, and the piles of good and bad beans built up into respectable mounds. How reassuring it was, to watch the steady progress being made atop the smoothly worn wood of the kitchen table, beans being put in their proper places. Alexandra began to feel an odd sense of accomplishment, the way she used to feel when the pile of unwritten thank-you notes on her London desktop gradually transferred itself to the pile of neat sealed envelopes, ready for franking and delivery.

Except that bean-sorting actually served a useful purpose.

"I ought to have paid more attention," she went on. "But Abigail's always been such an independent little thing, studying and exploring and all that. She didn't seem to want a husband. And so I . . . I didn't bother as I ought. And now look."

"The lady Abigail is a beautiful girl," said Signorina Morini. "A good girl, a clever girl. Of this girl, you are much proud."

"Oh, she's marvelous, of course. Far prettier than I am, if anyone bothers to notice. But she isn't a girl anymore, is she? That's the trouble. She can't go on like this."

She heard her own words with bewilderment. What was she saying? Revealing all this to a domestic servant, as if she were a trusted relative! But there was something so warm, so com-

panionable about sitting at this table with the rounded figure of
Signorina Morini, and her dark hair curling from her red headscarf, and all the lovely kitchen smells surrounding them: bread
baking and broth simmering and, somewhere, the faint scent of
ripening cheese.

Besides, the woman probably couldn't understand a word in
three.

"Why she cannot?" asked Signorina Morini. She gestured
with her hand to the window, which overlooked the kitchen garden and, beyond it, the hillside covered in the pale green of
early spring. "She is happy, no? There is much to do here. If she
wants love, she will find it."

"Love is hardly the point," Alexandra said. "She hasn't any
fortune. She'll need a husband, and before she loses any more
of her youth. I ought not to have brought her here. Another year
wasted."

Another shrug. "If she is wanting a husband, she marry the
duke."

Alexandra laughed. "Marry the duke! I do hate to disillusion
you, signorina, but it's quite out of the question. For one thing,
he's not the marrying sort. For another, she's just opened a thun-
dercloud of goose down over his head."

The signorina smiled her wise smile. "Is perfect. The so-high
duke, he never has a woman give him the feathers before."

"No," Alexandra said, giggling, which was something she
never did. "I'm quite sure he hasn't."

"He fall in love with her," Signorina Morini predicted, with
a confident tilt of her head. "I am sure of it."

Alexandra, not nearly so sure, didn't reply. Her nimble fingers
slid the last few beans in their proper places. "There. All done."

"*Grazie, signora*," said Signorina Morini, rising from the
table. "You have give me much help. The beans, they will be all
ready for the dinner."

"Dinner," Alexandra repeated.

She found, to her surprise, that she was looking forward to it.

EIGHT

Wallingford's fist came down on the dining room table, giving the plates a satisfying rattle. "Look here, Burke. Haven't you heard a word of this?"

Finn looked down and adjusted his plate. "I'm afraid I haven't. I've a problem with the battery to sort out, and all this ranting of yours isn't a bit of help. Penhallow, my good man, may I trouble you for the olives?"

"Eh what?" Lord Roland's blank face turned in his direction. "Olives, you said?"

"Olives, sir. To your left. Yes, that's the one. Good chap."

Wallingford's fist rattled the table again. "Burke, you insufferable sod . . ."

"Really, Your Grace!" exclaimed Lady Somerton.

". . . I beg your pardon, Lady Somerton, but the man deserves it. It's his own miserable hide I'm attempting to protect." Wallingford reached for his wineglass and tossed down an impressive slug of raw Chianti, though not without shooting Finn a glare that threatened to start his hair on fire.

"My hide is in no danger whatsoever, I assure you," Finn said.

"His Grace," said Lady Morley, setting her knife and fork atop her empty plate, "thinks I mean to seduce you, in order to win this silly wager of yours."

Abigail's voice broke in from the other end of the table. "But that's absurd. If you seduced Mr. Burke, successfully I mean, the wager would technically be a draw, wouldn't it?"

All heads swiveled in Miss Harewood's direction. She bore the scrutiny with admirable composure, looking from face to face as if searching for a perfectly reasonable answer to her perfectly reasonable question.

"Yes," said Finn at last, in a grave voice. "Yes, I believe it would."

Miss Harewood turned to the duke. "You see? You may put your mind entirely at ease on the subject of seduction, Your Grace. No reasonable person would contemplate such a scheme. Two advertisements in the *Times*! It wouldn't do."

Wallingford's face took on an unholy shade of crimson.

"Dear me, Wallingford," said Lady Morley. "You really must endeavor to calm your nerves. I fear you will bring on an apoplexy. Have you any medical training, Mr. Burke?"

"Only a few rudiments, I regret to say," Finn answered, popping an olive into his mouth. "Hardly enough to loosen his cravat."

"I am happy," Wallingford said, in icy tones, "to be the source of such endless amusement. But you"—he turned to Finn, and pointed one broad finger at his chest—"and you"—another finger, this time at Lord Roland—"have no idea at all what these women have in contemplation. From the moment of our arrival last month, they've been scheming and harassing us, in order to make our lives here so hellish as to drive us away entirely, and leave them the castle to themselves. Do not, Lady Morley, be so insulting as to deny it."

Lady Morley shrugged her elegant shoulders. "I should be very happy to see the last of you, Wallingford. I make no attempt to hide the fact."

Only Wallingford. Finn popped another olive into his mouth. The tart saltiness spread pleasurably over his tongue. Either she was trying to make the duke jealous, for reasons of her own, or else . . . But his mind sheared away from that speculation. If Lady Morley meant to attach any man in the room, it would undoubtedly be the Duke of Wallingford. Anything less would be a comedown from her current social position, and Alexandra, Lady Morley never came down.

Wallingford's eyes narrowed. "Very well, then, Lady Morley. I should like to propose an amendment to our wager. To increase the stakes, as it were."

"Oh, good God," said Finn. "Haven't you a better use of your time, Wallingford? Reading some of that vast collection in the library, perhaps? It *is* what we're here for, after all."

"He's welcome to join our literary discussion in the salon," said Lady Morley. "We should be pleased to hear an additional perspective, although I would suggest bringing an umbrella, in case of inclement weather."

"No, damn it all! I beg your pardon, Lady Somerton."

"Not at all, Your Grace."

Wallingford leaned forward and pressed his right forefinger into the yellowed linen tablecloth. "My proposal is this: that the forfeit, in addition to Burke's excellent suggestion of an advertisement in the *Times*, should include an immediate removal of the offending party from the castle." He sat back again, with a look of immense satisfaction.

Lord Roland gave a low whistle. "Hard terms, old man. Are you quite sure? What if it's *us* that's given the old heave-ho?"

"You are, I admit, the weakest link in the chain," the duke said dryly, "but I believe I may rely upon Lady Somerton's honor, if nothing else."

"Really, Your Grace," whispered Lady Somerton. Her face had lost its color, looking pale and drawn even in the warm glow from the dozen or so candles in their polished brass holders.

Lady Morley replied briskly. "This is beyond absurd, Wallingford, all this talk of conspiracies and whatnot. I assure you, I haven't the slightest intention of seducing poor Burke, and I daresay he has even less desire to be seduced. This is all about this business of the feathers this morning, isn't it? You're trying to have your revenge on us . . ."

"If I'm wrong, Lady Morley, you should have no reason at all to object to the increased stakes." Wallingford reached for the bottle of Chianti and refilled his glass with great care. "Isn't that so?"

Lady Morley cast a glance at her cousin, eyebrows furrowed. An expression of inquiry, or was it apology? Finn frowned, idling his thumb around the stem of his wineglass, looking back and forth between the two of them.

"Of course I shouldn't object," Lady Morley said at last. "Other than a sense of . . . of the absurdity of it all."

Finn drew his eyes away from the terrified expression on Lady Somerton's face and cleared his throat. "Really, Wallingford. It's hardly necessary. I don't see any reason why we can't continue to muddle on as we are. A tuft of goose down, here and there, doesn't much signify. And I'm fairly confident I can resist Lady Morley's charms, however determined her attempts on my virtue." He managed, with enormous self-control, to avoid looking at her reaction.

Wallingford leaned back in his chair and surveyed the table, composure restored, the picture of a self-satisfied English duke. "None of you, then, not one of you has the fortitude to meet my offer? Lady Morley? Your competitive spirit can't be tempted?"

She shook her head. "You always were an ass, Wallingford," she said, very softly. She held her full lips in a ghost of a smile, but her eyes were hard and calculating, and Finn had the uncanny impression that she was stalling for time, that she was thinking over a great many things in her mind.

"Why not?"

Finn started and turned in Miss Harewood's direction. She sat there as ingenuous as ever, her plate clear, her knife and fork crossed correctly atop the white porcelain. She really was a pretty girl, after all. Those delicate bones might be overshadowed by her sister's striking features, but they held a certain grace, a certain well-balanced symmetry, a certain whimsical charm. Especially now, with her hair drawn back from her face, and the candlelight dancing against her cheekbones: She was like the fairy version of her beautiful sister. "Why not?" She looked Wallingford directly in the eye. "I can't speak for your side, Your Grace, but we three are simply going about our business, studying and learning just as we intended. If it amuses you to turn this into a game, to raise the stakes, consider the wager accepted." She shrugged and looked at her sister. "It means nothing to us, after all. Does it, Alex?"

"No. No, of course not," Lady Morley said. "Very well. We accept your stakes, Wallingford. Though it hardly matters, as your suspicions are entirely wrongheaded. In fact, your head *itself* seemed to be wrongheaded at the moment, and I suggest you turn away from your wild speculations and put it firmly to work as you intended in the first place. We're on Aristophanes ourselves, just now, and my dear Abigail has already reviewed it twice in the original Greek. I'm certain she would have some useful insights for you. Perhaps she can assist you with your alphas and omegas."

By God, she's a thoroughbred, Finn thought, admiring the elegant angle of her jaw, the long, sinuous column of her neck, the look of defiance in her rich brown eyes. Her hair, like her sister's, was drawn back from her face, the shining chestnut kept in check by a dozen or more hairpins at the back of her neck. He imagined himself pulling out those hairpins, one by one, until the thick mass tumbled about her shoulders and down her neck. He imagined plunging his hands into those curls, burying his face in them.

His fingers clenched around the wineglass.

"My alphas and omegas are quite in order, I assure you, Lady Morley." Wallingford sounded deeply pleased with himself. "And now, ladies, if you'll pardon the unpardonable." With an elegant flourish, he dabbed his face with his napkin and folded it next to his plate, before rising and tilting his body in a polite bow. "I must excuse myself, and leave you to the far more appealing company of my fellow scholars."

He left the room in long strides, shutting the door behind him with a decisive sound that echoed about the table.

"Now why do I have the distinct feeling," Lady Morley murmured, "he's just played us all for fools?"

Lady Morley arrived at his workshop at precisely ten o'clock the next morning, just as Finn had stepped outside to relieve himself against an olive tree.

Her voice wafted through the open back door of the cottage. "Mr. Burke! Are you there?" A crash and a clattering noise, and then: "Dear me."

Hell and damnation. Finn stuffed himself back in his trousers and fumbled with the buttons. "Don't move!" he shouted, a whole host of possibilities racing through his brain, nearly overwhelming the mixture of dread and anticipation that had preoccupied him all morning at the possibility of her presence.

"I shan't," she replied faintly, and an instant later he ducked through the doorway to see her standing motionless next to the automobile on its blocks, wearing the same blue frock as yesterday, only with a dainty white apron tied improbably about her waist. An assortment of wrenches scattered across the floor before her.

He heaved a relieved sigh. She had only turned over a toolbox.

"It's nothing, Lady Morley. Only a few tools." He bent down and began picking them up, one by one.

"I'm so terribly sorry," she said, bending down next to him. "I seem to have a dreadful effect on you. If I weren't so impossibly selfish, I'd turn around this instant and leave you in peace." She tossed a wrench back in the toolbox and reached for another just as Finn grasped the handle himself. Her fingers closed around his for an instant, lean and firm, sending a jolt of sensation down his arm. "Oh! I . . . your pardon . . ." She snatched her hand back, nearly oversetting herself.

"Not at all." His knuckles burned. He dropped the last wrench back in the box and straightened next to her. "So you've come," he said, unnecessarily.

"Yes, I've come." Her eyes dropped downward for an instant to the fastening of his trousers.

He felt his face begin to flush. No doubt he'd left a button undone, or a corner of his shirt sticking through some gap in the placket.

Or worse.

He turned hastily to his worktable, where his mechanic's smock lay slung across the sand-smoothed wood surface, and thrust himself into it, not daring to look downward at whatever it was that had captured Lady Morley's attention. Phineas Burke, he reminded himself, did not care for such trivialities. Phineas Burke had far weightier, far more substantial, far more *consequential* things to think about than the correctness, or lack thereof, of his clothing. He tied the strings of his smock with slow deliberation, savoring the sturdy workmanlike strength of the material under his fingers, and gathered to his mind the phrases he had worked out in his mind the night before. Just in case, he'd told himself, she had the temerity to present herself the following day.

"I do hope you understand, Lady Morley, that you're not in

one of your damned salons." He turned around, smock fastened securely to form a shield of grime against her encroaching femininity. "This is a workshop."

She cast her eyes modestly to the ground. "I quite understand."

"Moreover, it's *my* workshop. I've a great deal of work to do, and I can't be bothered with appeasing feminine sensibilities."

"Of course not."

"My language will be indelicate, from time to time."

She waved her hand. "Profane at will, I assure you, Mr. Burke."

"I shall give orders and expect them to be obeyed."

"Obedience itself."

"There will be considerable dirt and oil."

"I've brought an apron." She indicated the lace-trimmed confection at her waist.

Finn crossed his arms. "No indoor plumbing, I'm afraid."

"Used to it." She looked back up at him with steady eyes, dark and unwavering in the liquid morning light. Every line of her face was set with fierce determination.

Finn took a single step closer and met her gaze with equal force. "One last thing. You've come here as a scholar, nothing more. I shall not tolerate any tricks, Lady Morley."

She lifted one eyebrow. She had beautiful eyebrows, neat and high and not too fine, perfectly matched, each rising at a slight angle that bent pertly near the tip. When she lifted one, as she did now, with exquisite control, she sent an unmistakable challenge. "I'm not at all sure I understand you, Mr. Burke. Did you have something else in mind?"

"Assuredly not. But forgive me if I don't quite trust your motives."

She smiled. "Really, Mr. Burke. You're not nearly as irresistible as you think."

She said it lightly, but her words slipped between the joints of his armor. "My dear Lady Morley, I would never accuse you of harboring a tender feeling in that calculating heart of yours," he replied, in something near a growl. "But I can perfectly imagine you spending an hour or so in my company and then skipping off to find my friend Wallingford and to demand the forfeit you so cheerfully arranged. Which will end, of course, in our being removed from the estate."

She did not reply. He could almost hear the echo of his words, hard and cold, in the silence between them, until the jabbering of some small animal outside the door interrupted the frozen air. Two of them, in fact, from the sound of it; squirrels quarreling over a newly unearthed nut, or else working up the courage to enter the cottage and trace the tantalizing smell of his ham sandwich, wrapped in paper in the pocket of his duster coat.

"I see," she said at last. Her voice was soft, small, quite unlike her; her features remained in place, betraying no emotion of any kind. "There it is, of course. I'm venal and petty and vain, and altogether spoilt by a life of idleness and uselessness. Yes, very true. None of my friends would deny you there."

"I beg your pardon," Finn said. "I spoke quite without . . ."

She held up her hand and spoke with greater strength. "But for all my sins, Mr. Burke, I do have my own peculiar brand of honor. I do have this: I'm loyal to my friends. It may not weigh much in the balance, I suppose, but as it's my only virtue, I tend it with the most devoted care."

Finn allowed her words to hover between them, taking on weight as the seconds ticked by, transforming into a kind of pledge. Her eyes seemed to bore through his, to will him to believe her.

"Very well, then." He reached for the toolbox and handed her a spanner. "Close the door before we begin. That should at least give us a moment's warning, should we have an unexpected visitor."

At some point well before noon, as an unreasonably strong sun beamed through the old glass window, and her fingers trembled with the strain of holding a pair of wires in place for— she peered at Mr. Burke's pocket watch, laid out on the work-table next to him—thirty-eight consecutive minutes, Alexandra began to think she had made a dreadful mistake.

"Tell me," she said, and was surprised to hear her voice come out in a husky, bedroom-y sort of growl. She cleared her throat, swallowed carefully, and tried again. "Tell me, Mr. Burke. What exactly does this contraption do? And what exactly are we doing to it?"

"Shht-shht," came his response, shot between his teeth like a pair of bullets. His head bent down toward a rectangle of polished metal, a magnifying monocle strapped to his eye; his fingers worked with delicate precision at the mass of fine wires crisscrossing the metal plate.

Alexandra, who had never received a "shht-shht" in her life, restrained herself with great effort from sticking the ends of her wires directly into Mr. Burke's two ears.

A good thing, because they were lovely ears. Too lovely for a man, really. Such a neat, perfect question mark of an ear, such a glorious peach-blush seashell of an ear, should have been bestowed on a woman, who had much greater need of ornamentation than sturdy Phineas Burke. Somewhere, she thought, lived some poor lady with monstrous wide ears that stuck out from her head like a pair of deformed potatoes, while Mr. Burke sat there with his wires and his monocle and his pincers, entirely indifferent to the beauty of his ears. Alexandra's eyes followed the curve of cartilage downward to the tender nubbin of his earlobe, where it merged into his neck. Rather a nice neck, too, solid and strong, with clean pale-gold skin that seemed to beckon . . .

"Lady Morley!"

She started. "What's that?"

"You may remove your hands. I've finished up the wiring."

"Oh, thank God." She drew back her hands and rubbed the joints furiously. "Whatever were you doing?"

"The wiring," he repeated, frowning downward at his handiwork. With one hand he unbuckled the monocle and drew it away from his right eye.

"Yes, of *course* the wiring. I mean the wiring for what?"

He looked up at last, and she caught her breath at the expression in his eyes, the intensity of his concentration.

Lucky wires, she thought.

"For the *battery*." His tone conveyed a certain sense of bewilderment at her ignorance.

"Well, if you'd *told* me." She straightened in her chair and forgot all about his ears and his neck and his eyes. "It's only *do this, Lady Morley*, and *do that*, and perhaps *if you please, Lady Morley*, if I'm quite fortunate."

He had the effrontery to smile. "I did warn you, if you'll recall."

"I thought you must be exaggerating. No one could possibly be that beastly."

His smile grew into a laugh. "Oh, I'm a right old beast in my workshop. I'm the last to deny it. Look here, would you like a cup of tea? I'm parched."

"Tea? You've got tea?"

"Oh yes. Couldn't do without it." He rose from the worktable and stretched his lean body to an unimaginable length, his hands reaching almost into the rafters, his muscles flexing powerfully beneath the dense cotton of his mechanic's smock. "Ah, that's better. One begins to cramp most abominably, after an hour or two."

"Yes, quite," she said, under her breath, and watched him saunter across the room to an enormous wooden cabinet along the wall.

"What's that?" He opened the cabinet door and extracted a large tin canister and a pair of chipped earthenware cups.

"Nothing. Can I help you at all?" she said, more loudly, rising from her chair.

"No, no. Quite capable. Besides, it's all a bit rough-and-ready for a lady." He set down the cups and the tin and turned to a high narrow table against the wall, next to the cabinet, on which rested a jumble of implements, both scientific and practical. He muttered something, searching through the objects, until he found a large glass beaker.

Alexandra sank slowly back into her chair, keeping a wary eye on the proceedings.

"Nervous, are you?" He chuckled and reached for the pitcher, pouring water into the beaker until it was nearly full. "Don't worry, Lady Morley. I've made myself thousands of cups of tea over the years, and at all hours. I fancy myself a bit of an expert, in fact." He set the beaker atop a gas ring and lit a match beneath, releasing a neat circle of blue flame.

"Have you really got a gas line here?" Alexandra asked in amazement.

"No, no. I've brought my own," he said, tapping a cylinder

underneath the table with the toe of his shoe. He went back to the cabinet and took out a teapot.

"Good God."

He half turned to grin at her. "Rough-and-ready, as I said. Do you like ceylon?"

"Yes, very much."

"Excellent. I've a particular blend I favor. A bit strong, but I imagine you like it that way, don't you?"

She faltered. "Yes . . . yes. How did you know that?"

He removed the lid from the teapot and began spooning in leaves from the tin canister. "I'll admit I'm no expert on women, but I do know what sort of lady prefers a weak blend of tea, and which likes it strong."

She began to laugh, carried away by this new mood of his, easy and familiar and equal. "I daresay you know a great deal more about women than you let on."

A blush crept up from his collar to spread through his neck and into his cheeks. "Then I daresay you'd be surprised," he said. The water in the beaker had already begun to bubble, spurred on by the intense efficiency of Mr. Burke's scientific gas ring, and he picked it off the flame with a pair of metal tongs and poured off the water into the teapot.

"How terribly intriguing," Alexandra said. "I wonder what you mean."

He replaced the lid on the teapot. "I haven't any cream to hand, I'm afraid, nor sugar. I like to use a bit of honey, myself." The blood remained high under his skin.

"Honey? How rustic."

He turned to face her, propping his long body against the table as the tea steeped behind him. "I picked it up from a fellow in India. Eats a spoonful or two of honey a day, and claims never to develop a cough. The stuff has a remarkable effect on germs."

"You're a traveler, then?" She drew her finger along the grain of the wooden table, up and down, watching the blush begin to fade from his cheekbones, leaving only a pink glow beneath the scattering of freckles.

"From time to time. Curiosity, you see." He turned back to the teapot and went through the mass of objects on the table until he produced a square of fine wire mesh, which he placed on top of the first cup to strain out the tea leaves.

"Which countries have you visited?" She watched the tea as it fell in a smooth amber stream from the pot into the cup. The mesh worried her. What was it doing with his scientific equipment? Was it used for experiments with highly volatile chemicals?

Had he washed it since?

"Oh, India, as I said. Siberia. The Caucasus, Mesopotamia. Much of the Continent, of course, though not yet Athens, sadly. I was on the point of making the crossing from Brindisi last year, when the most violent storm kicked up. Dreadful nuisance. Here you are, then." He picked up the cups and brought them to the worktable then went back to the cabinet. "Did you want the honey after all?"

"Yes, please," she said. His long legs dwarfed the journey from table to cabinet to table again, covering the distance in an easy stride or two. In his broad hand, the pot of honey looked like it belonged to a doll's set. "I should have loved to travel like that," she went on, stirring the honey into her tea, "but Lord Morley's gout made that sort of thing quite impossible."

"You never thought to go without him?" Mr. Burke settled into the chair next to her and dipped his spoon into the honey pot.

The chairs were still set close together from the wiring operation. Alexandra could feel the heat from his body shimmer against her skin, could sense the air hum with his vitality. "No," she said. She bent over her teacup and let the steam drift into her nostrils, warm and spicy and faintly sweet from the honey. "As I said, Mr. Burke, I'm loyal to my friends. And my husband was one of them."

Perhaps he felt the alarming closeness of their bodies, too, for his chair scraped briefly against the wooden floor, and his voice reached her ear from a greater distance. "And you never felt burdened by this? Confined?"

No one had ever asked her such a thing before, not her closest friends. No one had ever supposed how she might feel about remaining in England, season after luxurious, monotonous season, with her aging, gout-afflicted husband. "Of course not. I had a perfectly agreeable life. I . . ."

A brisk knock sounded on the door.

"Burke! Burke, I say!" The doorknob rattled furiously. "Burke, you ass!"

Alexandra froze in place. Mr. Burke's eyes locked with hers, round and stricken.

"Wallingford!" she hissed.

NINE

But it wasn't Wallingford at all.

"What the devil sort of hovel is this?" demanded Lord Roland Penhallow, entering the workshop in brisk strides. Or at least they sounded like brisk strides, from Alexandra's limited vantage beneath the chassis of Mr. Burke's automobile. "And why have you got it all locked up?"

"Security," Mr. Burke replied. "A competitive lot, we motor enthusiasts."

"Ha-ha. And rather useful for keeping seductive marchionesses at bay, eh what?" Lord Roland's footsteps halted at the center of the room. Alexandra could just see the high polish of his shoes at the edge of her vision.

"That, too, of course," Mr. Burke replied, rather too readily.

"What do you think Wallingford was on about last night? I hardly recognized the man. All that business about goose down."

"I suspect, old boy, that your brother's got troubles of his own in that quarter," Mr. Burke said.

Lord Roland gave a low whistle. "You don't say! Wallingford and Lady Morley! I suppose it's a natural match, both of them high-tempered schemers and whatnot. And it explains last night's doings, all those accusations about her seducing you. Jealousy, from my brother! Ha-ha. Very good."

"I don't mean Lady Morley," Mr. Burke said tersely.

"What's that? But who—good God, you can't mean Lilib . . . you can't mean Lady Somerton! Damn you for a slandering . . ."

"Pax, old man!" Burke chuckled. "Not her ladyship. Good God, no."

"What, then? Not Miss Harewood!" Lord Roland sounded thunderstruck. "You can't be serious."

"Mere speculation."

Alexandra craned her neck, straining to see more. Or, failing that, at least to breathe. The chassis sat low to the ground, with the rear axle mere inches from her nose and gleaming with grease, hiding her effectively if rather terrifyingly. She tried not to imagine the whole works crashing down upon her, and instead concentrated on the four male feet nearby. Lord Roland faced away from her, the heels of his shoes planted squarely before her eyes; Mr. Burke appeared to be leaning against the worktable, at ease, one foot crossed over the other. Distracting Penhallow from the motor-car, no doubt.

A warm feeling gathered inside her. He was only doing it to keep himself from being found out, of course, but it was pleasant (*pleasant*, she told herself firmly, nothing more) to imagine that he was protecting her. That he leaned against the worktable to save *her* disgrace.

"Hmm. Miss Harewood. Any port in a storm, I suppose," said Lord Roland. "But what has goose down to do with it all?"

Burke replied impatiently. "Haven't the slightest. Look, have you got a genuine purpose to your visit, or have you only come to harass me? I've got rather a lot of work to do."

Alexandra's ear began to ache, pressed against the hard wooden floor, while the smell of oil and dust and metal flooded her brain. Her shoulder blades felt as if they were pressing through her skin. How the devil did Mr. Burke stand it, hour after hour?

"Yes, yes. Of course." Lord Roland paused and shifted his feet, turning to the right. "So. This is it. The workshop of a genius, where mere mortals fear to tread. All sorts of . . . of doings . . . and . . . I say, what's *that*?"

Alexandra started, bumping her nose against the axle.

"A few spare parts. Look here, Penhallow . . ."

Lord Roland turned again to point his feet in her direction. She cringed away, trying to melt herself into the floorboards.

"And this! The machine itself!" He took a few steps away, apparently surveying it. "Absolutely marvelous! Really, old chap. I'm floored. Er . . . is that the engine?"

"Yes, I'm almost certain."

"Ha-ha. The old sense of humor, eh? What a card you are." He paused and sniffed, audibly. "Do I smell lilies?"

"Penhallow, for God's sake. Leave me in peace. Save it all for the dinner table."

"Burke, you ass. I've come for a friendly visit, to buck up your spirits . . ."

At that instant, entirely without warning, a mote of dust found its way into the back of Alexandra's throat.

Mr. Burke spoke firmly. "My spirits don't need bucking. Out."

Lord Roland paused, his indecision almost palpable in the air. And then, like a dam under flood, he broke. "Damn it all, Burke. It's the most confounded coil. Last night . . . all that non-sense about raising the stakes . . . oh, you must know I'm most frightfully in love with her."

"Oh, for God's sake," Mr. Burke muttered.

The dust mote, with unerring precision, burrowed itself into the most sensitive spot of Alexandra's throat, just below the epi-glottis.

"I know you can't possibly understand, you with your cold scientific heart and all that, but . . . well, damn it all, I had to confess to someone! And you're such a brick, Burke. You'd never tell my brother, or the ladies. My secret is perfectly safe with you."

"Perfectly. Now if you wouldn't mind . . ."

Very delicately, taking care not to make the slightest out-ward noise, Alexandra shifted her throat.

"That damned beast of a husband of hers. We all know he's treated her badly, of course, that's why they're all here to begin with. But the dear soul's so loyal and honorable . . ."

"Penhallow, another time perhaps. I'm really quite busy."

"But now that Wallingford's taken this notion into his head, anything I say or do might cause her to be tossed out entirely. And that shrew . . ."

Tears began to stream from Alexandra's eyes, rolling down the two sides of her cheeks and into her ears.

". . . that shrew Lady Morley, taking Wallingford up on his

wager! I should have rebuked her. I meant to, but Lilibet . . . but Lady Somerton gave me *such* a look."

"Lady Morley is not a shrew," Mr. Burke said sharply.

"Well, that's charitable of you, old fellow, considering how she's done her best to lure you in, ha-ha. A handsome woman, of course, but one can't imagine sitting across from her at the breakfast table." Lord Roland chuckled.

"Penhallow," Mr. Burke said, speaking apparently through his teeth, "I'm deeply sorry for your troubles, but you really must see me another time. The battery . . ."

Alexandra's throat gave way at last, with a muffled choking gasp of a cough.

"What's that?" asked Lord Roland, wheeling about.

"Nothing. Hydraulics. As I was saying . . ."

Alexandra managed to suppress the next cough, but the third caught her by surprise.

"There it is again! What the devil sort of hydraulics have you got in there? It don't sound at all healthy."

Mr. Burke cleared his throat. "A mere . . . simply to do with . . . the braking system. A new design I'm trying out. Quite trying, involving the most immense concentration, and rather dangerous at that. I shall really have to ask you to leave." His footsteps moved toward the door.

"But see here, Burke. That's exactly what I came to speak with you about. I was thinking . . ." Lord Roland paused. "I was thinking that perhaps you might take me on as your assistant. To keep me busy, to keep me out of her way, you see. It's the most honorable course."

"My assistant?"

"Yes. Don't you need another pair of hands to . . . well, to help sort out . . . all this . . . this whatnot you've got here?"

Mr. Burke sighed, so loudly Alexandra could hear the rush of air. "Penhallow, old man. Do you have the *slightest* idea how an electric battery works?"

"Well, no. That is, I have some notion that . . . the sparks rather . . . well . . . no. No, I haven't," Lord Roland said humbly.

"Can you even distinguish one end of my motor-car from another?"

Alexandra saw his lordship's highly polished shoes turn in her direction. She shrank into the recesses of the chassis.

"I daresay . . . one would think that . . . well, if I should hazard a guess . . ."

"Precisely," said Mr. Burke. "Now if you'll be so good as to return to the library and resume your quest for knowledge. Perhaps compose a verse or two, cataloging the anguish of doomed love. And if the delights of that endeavor should pall, you might consult with Giacomo regarding the cheeses in the stables, as a more practical matter."

"The cheeses?"

"He'll tell you all about them. But for God's sake, Penhallow, whatever you do, *leave . . . me . . . alone!*" The door opened with a forceful scraping of wood against doorjamb.

"I say, Burke, that's hardly sporting."

"Really? How ungentlemanly of me."

"In any case, old Giacomo sent me down here to begin with. Said you needed help. It's what gave me the idea."

"Did he, the old bugger?" Mr. Burke sounded dark, almost menacing. "Now *that's* hardly sporting."

"Very well. I take your point," Lord Roland said. His feet marched toward the door and beyond Alexandra's vision. "But just remember, Burke . . . Oh, hullo there, Wallingford! Out for a stroll?"

No. Not Wallingford. No merciful God would allow it.

Alexandra held back a groan and shifted her bones against the agonizing hardness of the floor. She couldn't hear the duke's reply; he was still on the other side of the door.

"Well, that's the devil of a coincidence!" Lord Roland said. "He told me the same thing, about Burke wanting help in his workshop, and I thought to myself, Penhallow, old man, that's just the ticket . . ."

"Giacomo was entirely mistaken," Mr. Burke said, in hard tones. "I'm in no need of assistance. Quite the opposite."

"Yes, yes. You've made yourself quite clear on the subject. I'm taking myself off directly, and I'd advise my dear brother to do the same." Lord Roland's voice drifted away, out the door and into unintelligibility.

"And you, Wallingford?" asked Mr. Burke. "Aren't you taking Penhallow's excellent advice?"

"No," said Wallingford, quite clearly.

Alexandra, staring in despair at the dark metallic gleam

of the axle before her nose, felt her heart sink into the floor-boards.

Wallingford's booted footsteps rapped against the wood, rattling her head. "It occurred to me, in fact, that our friend Giacomo's suggestion might just solve our problems at a single stroke."

"Which problems?" Mr. Burke sighed.

"For one thing, the problem of keeping Lady Morley away from your vulnerable heart," Wallingford said, "and for the other, the problem of avoiding that Harewood witch."

Alexandra's mouth tightened indignantly.

"Those are *your* problems, Wallingford, not mine," Mr. Burke said.

Alexandra turned her head to watch their feet and saw that Mr. Burke had resumed his pose against the worktable, leaning against it with insouciant ease.

Wallingford turned to face him. "The problem of Lady Morley is entirely yours."

"No, Wallingford. The problem of Lady Morley is entirely in your imagination," replied Mr. Burke, not moving an inch. "A scientist of no particular charm, an untitled Irish bastard of no social standing. I daresay the impeccable Lady Morley would sooner cut off her right arm than share my bed."

He spoke with firm assurance, with deliberation, each word cutting through the air between them to pierce her exact center. *Social standing. The impeccable Lady Morley. Share my bed.*

Bastard. She hadn't known that.

"You sell yourself far too short, old man," Wallingford said quietly, and then, with greater strength, "You're a bastard of high breeding indeed, after all. And in any case, the inducement is high. She'd give anything to have us out of the castle."

Mr. Burke uncrossed his long legs and straightened, making some motion with his arm that Alexandra couldn't see. "For God's sake, man. Do you see her here?"

"I've no doubt she's assembling her plan of attack this very instant. Which is why I've come to help. No, don't thank me." Wallingford squared his booted feet on the floor, five unbearably short feet from Alexandra's nose. "It's my duty, you see, to protect you from designing females. You haven't any idea what they're capable of. Lady Morley would make mincemeat of you."

"I daresay," drawled Mr. Burke, "but at the moment I'm entirely absorbed in the improvement to my battery. I shouldn't notice if Lady Morley herself were right here, holding the wires for me."

"Holding wires?"

"For hours on end, I'm afraid. Very tiring work. I'd be so terribly grateful if you'd take it on. I believe I've got an extra smock somewhere, though it's perhaps a bit oily. And then there's the acid . . ."

Wallingford took a step backward. "Acid?"

"Yes, of course. How do you think a battery produces its charge? Sulfuric acid, non-dilute. Strong stuff, of course. Liable to blind you if you're not careful. I've got patent protective goggles, myself." Mr. Burke's legs moved briskly over to the table against the wall, where he'd made the tea. "Look, here's the stuff. Take a look?"

Wallingford took another hasty step backward, bumping into the automobile. It shifted slightly, with a faint groan of protest, the axle just grazing the tip of Alexandra's nose.

Mr. Burke's feet dashed to the machine. His voice exploded in the air. "Good God! Careful, man! Step away from that!"

Alexandra's breath froze in her throat. She squeezed her eyes shut and crossed her arms above her face, because by God she'd be damned if her corpse weren't viewable, like poor Lady Banbury who fell through the skylight last June, during an ill-advised equestrian-themed bacchanal on her lover's rooftop.

But the machine held. She cracked her eyes open and fastened them on the curving metal, the individual bolts and fastenings, confirming their immobility. Somewhere through the machinery, she sensed Mr. Burke's strong, capable hands steadying the shifting mass, returning it to equilibrium.

"Well, then! What a lucky thing you weren't underneath just now. Assisting me, that is," Mr. Burke said, between hard breaths of air.

"Look," Wallingford said, "perhaps I could come back another time. When you're working on . . . the steering mechanism. Or the wheels."

"Don't you think, Wallingford, you've done quite enough already?"

"Christ, man. It's for your own good."

"Why," Mr. Burke said, sounding cross, "does everybody think me incapable of self-restraint, despite a lifetime of evidence to the contrary?"

Wallingford laughed, in his short, bitter way. "Good God, old fellow. Haven't you seen the look on your face when she's about?"

"As I am not, in fact, equipped with a mirror, I should expect not. Now if you'll excuse me, I've had enough assistance from the Penhallow family this morning to set me back a week or more."

Share my bed.

The words echoed back unexpectedly in Alexandra's brain.

Share my bed. His bed, Mr. Burke's bed, Phineas Burke's bed, warmed by his body, smelling beautifully of oil and leather and male skin; full of his sturdy limbs, his red gold hair, his lawn green eyes, his rare, luminous smile. She closed her eyes. Lying there, with perhaps half a ton of poorly supported automobile hovering above her, she felt an ache in her chest build and grow. Felt herself revel in the unfamiliar burn of want.

". . . for your good intentions," he was saying. "You'd be useless as my assistant, as you very well know."

Wallingford grunted. "Very well, then. I'll leave. But do be on your guard, old man. She may have a viper's tongue, but by God she can kiss like a Parisian opera dancer."

A tiny pause. "I shall take that under consideration, thank you."

The duke's booted feet began moving, at last, to the door, creaking the floorboards in the most beautiful music Alexandra had ever heard. "Right-ho, then. I'm off," he said. "Shall I see you at . . ."

Wallingford's sentence arrested in midair, dangling there in the preternatural stillness like a boom about to fall.

"What's that?" Mr. Burke said.

The duke spoke with dangerous calm.

"Tell me, Burke. Why, exactly, are there *two* teacups on the table behind you?"

TEN

Phineas Burke had first learned the value of composure in crisis at the tender age of six, when he'd released a jar of toads down the hallway of his godfather's London mansion just as several white-bearded Cabinet ministers were emerging from a meeting in the study. Instead of breaking down under interrogation, he'd explained the situation in rational terms: "Your Grace, in order to properly determine the relative speed of the toads"—Finn was that sort of nauseatingly precocious youngster who hadn't said a word until shortly after his fourth birthday, at which time he'd opened his mouth and begun speaking in complete and grammatically correct sentences—"I required a long stretch of uninterrupted territory, and the sudden entrance of your friends into the racecourse was a variable that I could not reasonably be expected to predict." By the end of this speech, his godfather was working too hard to suppress his laughter to inflict any sort of meaningful corporal punishment on him.

But faced with the thundering accusation in the voice of the Duke of Wallingford, Finn's ordinarily nimble mind stumbled and fell. "*Two* teacups? How extraordinary. I suppose . . . well, I wanted another cup."

Wallingford inspected the cups. "Half-full, both of them." He turned back to Finn, eyes glittering. "You didn't think simply to refill the first?"

"Oh, for God's sake, old chap. You're like a detective from one of those dashed sensational novels." Finn drew breath, folded his arms against his chest, and stood firm. "I suppose I forgot about the first cup. One tends to get a bit distracted, fiddling with machines all morning."

Wallingford began walking to the cabinet.

"Look here!" Finn exclaimed, but Wallingford had already thrown open the door with an enthusiastic *Aha!*

"You see?" Finn said triumphantly. "Nothing there."

"Oh, she's here, all right. I know it. I can feel her, sneering at us." Wallingford stalked about the room, peering behind the piles of chests, the spare parts, the stack of new state-of-the-art pneumatic tires. He looked up into the rafters, as if expecting to see her ladyship swinging by her marsupial tail.

"Wallingford," Finn said, as dryly as he could manage, "you're boring me. Can you not learn to control this . . . this clinical paranoia of yours? Find some other baseless obsession. Resume your goose feather flirtation with young what's-her-name. Oh, *really*. I assure you, she's not in the damned *sink!*"

Wallingford spun about, nostrils flaring. His gaze fell upon the automobile on its blocks. "Yes," he whispered. "Of course."

"You're mad."

Wallingford didn't reply. In two long strides he swallowed the distance to the automobile. She sat there innocently in the center of the room, wheels removed, seats unbolted, a bare hollow shell of molded metal. Finn had had her made to his own design a few months ago, had shipped her with almost maternal care on her own special railway car, across the Belgian plains and Swiss mountain passes, covered with flannel-lined tarpaulins against the cold and the damp. Even now, raw and unfinished, her beauty still took his breath away, long and lean and unlike anything else yet designed. Finn could almost see the air slipping along her top and sides, could almost hear the rush of speed against his ears. Breathtaking speed, unheard-of speed.

He adored her.

Wallingford's large hands gripped the edge of the doorframe, exactly where Lady Morley had run her fingers not twenty-four hours before, and peered inside. The tips of his shoes protruded slightly under the chassis, no more than a foot away, Finn judged, from her ladyship's elegant ear. Outside the open doorway, the squirrels were chattering again, oblivious to the knife-edge silence within the cottage.

Wallingford made a growling sound from the bottom of his throat. "Empty." He turned around to face Finn. His eyes had narrowed into slits. "Where is she, then?"

Finn spread his hands before him, trying desperately not to smile. "Haven't the slightest. Back in the castle, perhaps?"

The duke's eyes slid to the old carriage doors at the back, closed and innocuous. "She slipped out, didn't she? When Penhallow arrived." He stomped toward the portal and flung it open on one side, allowing a bright beam of noontime sunshine to burst into the room, illuminating the high shine of the automobile's metal frame. "The question is," he continued, turning his head one way and then the other, "whether she's gone back to the castle or lingered about, waiting for us to leave."

Finn shrugged. "Search away."

"My guess is that she's still about. She's a persistent woman, after all. Tenacious." He glanced back at Finn. "Come along. I'd like to keep an eye on you."

Finn sighed. "You bloody dukes. You don't understand the first thing about actual work. How, for example, it requires hours of uninterrupted concentration . . ."

"Humor me."

Finn threw his hands in the air. "Bloody hell, Wallingford." He stomped after the duke into the warm spring air, mild and silken against his cheek, laden with the rich scent of apple blossoms from the orchard above. Next to the olive tree he stopped and crossed his arms. "I'll wait here," he said.

The duke walked the perimeter with excruciating care, as if he were stalking a particularly canny stag through the autumnal mists of his Scottish estate. At each tree, he looked up and searched the branches, rotating his head this way and that, all but sniffing the air.

No, check that, Finn observed in amazement: He *was* sniffing the air, damn him. Trying to detect that telltale hint of lilies, perhaps? Finn's fists curled into balls against his ribs. It offended him, somehow, that Wallingford knew her scent.

"There, you see?" he called across the grass. "She's not here. Now would you mind taking yourself off?"

The duke kept walking, until he'd arrived back at the door.

He swiveled his head in Finn's direction. "Well done, Burke. Admirably played. But next time, I assure you, I'll be ready."

"Whose blasted side are you on?"

"Yours, though you may not believe it." He put his hand on the latch.

Horror flooded through Finn's veins. What if she'd thought the alarm was over and broken cover? "Look here, man. You've already searched the damned cottage!"

"Only retrieving my hat, for God's sake," Wallingford said, disappearing into the doorway.

Finn ran up behind him. "I'll retrieve your hat!"

But it was too late; they were already inside. Finn glanced around the room and closed the door discreetly behind him. No sign of her, thank God. She'd kept her composure, remained in hiding until he came back to sound the all clear.

"For God's sake," Wallingford began impatiently, and then he turned around and took in Finn's expression.

"Aha," he said, quite soft. "She's still here, isn't she?"

"She was never here. You and your damned imagination."

Wallingford ignored him. He rotated slowly about, eyes sliding along the rough stone walls. "Now," he said conversationally, "if I were a lady, caught in flagrante . . ."

"In flagrante, my arse."

". . . where would I scurry to hide my shame? A slender lady, mind you. And one with plenty of nerve. None of your missish airs about Lady Morley, I'll say that."

His gaze landed once more on the automobile, and then slid to the ground. "By God," he said. "You damned clever thing."

"Wallingford, you're mad."

"Do you know, Burke," said the duke, walking with slow deliberation to the automobile, as if savoring the moment, "I almost admire this Lady Morley of yours. It takes a certain amount of fortitude, not to say cheek, to lie beneath an automobile for such a considerable period of time. I do wonder whether she's sincerely in love with you after all." He stopped a few feet away and spoke in a soft voice. "Are you, Lady Morley? Are you in love with my friend Burke?"

Finn stood frozen, willing himself to remain calm, to give nothing away until the final instant, when he would . . . what?

Leap to her defense? Spirit her away? What, really, was the proper etiquette?

The duke eased downward. "Although," he continued, bracing one hand on the floor, "I daresay she wouldn't recognize the emotion if it slapped her on her pert little . . ." He stopped. "Bloody hell," he hissed, and struck the floor with his fist. "She's gone!"

With every atom of his self-control, Finn resisted the urge to bend down and see for himself. "Let me repeat: She was never there."

Wallingford straightened at last and turned to Finn. His face, hard with suspicion, gradually softened into something like sheepishness.

Finn allowed a smile to curl the corner of his mouth. "Can't a man make himself a second cup of tea without having his workshop ransacked, after all?"

"I suppose not." Wallingford returned the smile, albeit grudgingly. "All right, then, old man. My apologies. I'll just take my hat and be on my way." He turned and picked up his peaked cap from the worktable, next to the white porcelain cups with their fatal tea still rippling inside. With a lithe motion he settled the cap on his head. "But do remember what I said, eh?"

"I shall."

"And if you find yourself in dire straits, well, there are solutions *to hand*, as you yourself pointed out. Been driven to it myself more than once lately, ha-ha!"

"Delighted to hear it," mumbled Finn, wondering just how far away Lady Morley had hidden herself.

"Daresay you're a regular expert, with all your monkish notions about a quick . . ."

"Wallingford. *Go*."

"Until dinner, then!" Wallingford slipped through the front door at last and closed it with a decisive slam.

Finn closed his eyes and began counting off seconds, quite slowly. When he reached twenty, he called out, in a low voice, eyes still closed, "Lady Morley?"

From his left came the sound of a door opening. He turned and opened his eyes to see her, face smudged, dress disheveled, emerging from the cabinet.

"Is the coast clear?" She wore the barest hint of a rueful smile.

"Yes. Are you all right?"

"Yes." She stood there, hesitating, smoothing her dress with both hands in long, mechanical strokes, then moving on to pat her hair, which straggled from her chignon in untidy waves.

Finn realized he was trembling. "Can I . . . I suppose your tea is cold . . ."

"Oh, the damned tea . . ." She brushed a strand of hair from her cheek.

"Do sit down," he said, more decisively. "You must be done in. I'll make more tea."

"Why?" she said, shaking her head. "Why did you do that?"

"Do what?"

"Hide me like that. And it would be so much easier if Penhallow or Wallingford assisted you, instead of me. Why did you chase them off?" Her eyes were bright, gleaming, watching him with peculiar intensity.

"It was the honorable thing to do." He wanted to shrug, to demonstrate a certain amount of nonchalance, but his shoulders wouldn't obey him. "I let you stay, after all. You were under my protection. You had a right to expect it."

Her eyes fell away at last, down to study the tips of his toes. "Thank you."

Silence gathered between them, thick and full and expectant. The sun had shifted and was now pouring through the south window, warming the air, striking the back of Finn's neck in a hot beam and turning the skin of Lady Morley's face into gold. He turned and strode to the long table against the wall, where he'd made the tea less than an hour ago, a lifetime ago. His hands began to fiddle with the objects there, arranging them, gathering up the tea things to put back in the cabinet, forgetting entirely that he'd promised her another cup.

She cleared her throat behind him. "Rather fascinating, hearing you gentlemen talk with one another. You're all quite frank, I see."

"Just the usual sort of rubbish."

"I couldn't help wondering, of course, just what you meant by it all."

Wallingford, may God damn you and your descendants to the darkest pit of Hell.

"Oh. Yes. That. Hands and . . . and whatnot. Haven't a clue, in fact. Your guess as good as mine."

"No, not that. I mean before. What was rubbish, as you say, and what was sincere." Her voice was clear and plain, not at all like her usual voice, as if all the layers of artifice had been stripped away.

"Oh, I daresay . . . that is, I don't remember much of it." He looked down at his fingers, which were shaking. He pressed them hard against the tabletop.

"Wallingford said . . ." She hesitated, and went on. "I suppose you were wondering what Wallingford meant, about . . ."

"About?"

"About . . . kissing."

Finn squeezed his eyes shut. The sound of her voice, floating behind him in the warm, still air, was almost unbearable. "Yes. That. I seem to recall he'd mentioned it before."

"I want you to know . . . I want you to know that it only happened once. A very long time ago." Her voice slid downward, soft and low. "I was so young, you see. I'd just come out. I thought"—a little choke—"I had all these romantic notions, as girls do. I thought I had only to fall in love with the highest in the land, and he would love me, and it would be all rainbows and sunshine and . . . Well, anyway, he kissed me, there on the terrace at Lady Pembroke's ball, and it was lovely, sunshine and rainbows, just as I'd hoped. So *ardent*. You can't imagine . . . a girl of nineteen . . . I was so silly. I thought it meant he loved me. The way he looked at me . . ." She stopped.

He wanted to go to her, to take her in his arms, to tell her . . . what? He'd no name, no birth, no standing, nothing at all that Lady Morley sought. His mother was a fallen woman, living in Richmond in a house bought for her by a man who was not her husband.

"Very silly indeed," she said, more brusquely. "For you see, I went off to find him afterward, and at last came upon him in the library . . ."

Finn drew in a sharp hiss of air.

"Ah yes! I see you've heard the tale. So there I stood—oh, all very tragic and pathetic, his kiss still burning on my lips and all that—and there *he* stood, heaving away, his trousers about his ankles, a woman bent over the desk before him. Rather a clean break with one's girlhood illusions, I daresay. I accepted Lord Morley's offer a week or so later and have laughed at the notion of *love* ever since."

"I'm very sorry," Finn said quietly.

She didn't reply. He felt her presence behind him, could sense the steady rhythm of her breath into the stillness.

"Yes," she said. "I expect you are."

His fingers idled about the bottom of the gas ring. "Don't lose hope, Lady Morley. You're young and beautiful. There are a few good fellows left in the world, I assure you."

"Beautiful. But I'm not beautiful, not really. I give a good impression of it, I suppose, but it's not the same thing."

"Rubbish. You're quite beautiful."

She hesitated. "Well, that's very kind of you. I wish . . ."

"You wish?" His hand clenched against the metal ring.

"I wish . . ." Her shoe moved against the floor, a single hesitant step. "I wish . . . I want to tell you . . . how very beautiful *you* are."

His heartbeat thundered against his ears. "That's absurd."

"No, it isn't." Her words came in a rush. "Your brilliant mind, and your face, and your eyes. And your hands—how I love your hands, large and clever, cracking walnuts and soldering wires . . ."

He turned at last and saw her, standing in the middle of his workshop, gilt with sunshine, her face open and vulnerable and more beautiful than anything he'd ever imagined. Something shattered within him, a sharp, almost audible crack, and in two strides he'd crossed the distance between them. Her pink lips parted, releasing a gasp of surprise or perhaps anticipation, and he took her face in his hands and bent his head and kissed her.

When Alexandra was eight years old, she had come upon the cook in the pantry in late autumn, filling glass bottles from a large iron-hooped oak barrel, one by one, and sealing them tightly with cork and wax. She'd asked the cook what she was doing, and the cook had answered that she was bottling last year's yield of apple brandy—the Harewood estate was a respectable one, but hardly extravagant—for the master and mistress to drink through the winter. Alexandra, who loved apples, thought this sounded like an excellent plan, and the next afternoon, feeling thirsty, she'd tripped down the stairs to the pantry and opened a bottle of apple brandy and drank herself legless.

Kissing Phineas Burke was rather like that.

For all the suddenness of his approach, for all the passion with which his hands clasped the sides of her face, his lips moved gently on hers, slowly, as if he were savoring her, and the tottering remains of her composure collapsed at last. He tasted of tea and honey and himself, sweet and exotic and so perfectly delicious that her lips opened up beneath his, wanting more, wanting to absorb his flavor through every channel of her body. "Lady Morley," he murmured, "Alexandra," and she had never heard anything so deep and harmonious as the sound of her name in his throat, against her lips.

"Phineas," she breathed back—what luxury, to speak his name—and his hands moved deeper, speared into her hair, dislodged the rest of her pins as he caressed the back of her head in long strokes. "Phineas," she said again, dreamily.

He stopped and drew back, his breath warm on her skin. "Finn," he said.

His eyes looked into hers so deeply, so sternly, it took a moment for the word to make its way to her brain.

"Finn?" she repeated breathlessly.

"It's Finn, not Phineas. My mother calls me Phineas."

She felt a smile spread across her face. "Finn," she said, testing the word, and stretched her arms upward to circle his sturdy neck. The hair at his nape felt soft as down under her fingers. "Finn. Darling, marvelous Finn. Say my name again. Say it."

"Alexandra." He settled her against him and kissed her again, boldly now. His silken tongue grazed hers, his hands slid downward to span the hollow of her back, and she strained hard against him, wanting to feel every inch of his body, to be surrounded and engulfed by him, until she no longer had to think and plan and act and pretend: She had only to exist.

Had only to be herself at last.

She hadn't intended to entice him, not exactly. Almost until the end, she'd kept herself under exquisite control, reminding herself that the Dowager Marchioness of Morley maintained an irreproachable dignity at all times, even when wedged underneath the greasy reaches of an experimental motor-car with a feral dust speck gnawing at her throat. She'd listened to the patter of conversation, heard the way Finn defended her, heard the way the Penhallow brothers abused her—rather humbling, that—with admirable fortitude. Even the seductive effect of Finn's forthright *share my bed* had been shrugged off in the end, in the surge of relief at the duke's initial departure.

No, she'd held out beautifully, and had even constructed an opening line to dismiss the experience as beneath her notice (*What shocking dust beneath that motor of yours, Mr. Burke! Another minute and I should have been as dirty as you are . . .*) when Wallingford's words invaded her ears.

Are you, Lady Morley? Are you in love with my friend Burke?

And the answer her brain had returned, reflexively, before she'd had a chance to consider the question, made her legs give way underneath her. Only the thick wooden walls of the cabinet had kept her upright.

Now, of course, that particular task was being performed by Burke himself, to glorious effect. His mouth traveled away from hers, down the line of her jaw to the hollow beneath, some sensitive spot she'd never dreamed existed, now nibbled delicately by his warm lips. The breath left her body. She sagged into his enclosing arms. She could have sworn that the sunlight dimmed for just an instant, beaten back by the mighty flame of their passion.

Finn stiffened.

"What is it?" she gasped out, clinging shamelessly to his neck. It could not end yet. It could not. She hadn't had nearly enough of him.

"Damn it all." He took her hand and hauled her back to the cabinet and pressed a hard kiss against her lips before shoving her inside.

A brisk knock sounded on the front door.

"No." She braced her arm against the cabinet door and eyed him fiercely. "Not this time. I shan't hide any longer. I'll call off the wager, do whatever . . ."

The door began to open. Alexandra slipped under Finn's arm and smoothed at her dress in desperate strokes. Not that any improvement to her disordered clothes would make any difference, she realized, given that her hair tumbled freely around her shoulders and down her back in wild, slatternly chestnut waves.

Perhaps this wasn't the cleverest idea, after all.

But it was too late. A figure was entering the room, a male figure of medium height, backlit somewhat by the sunshine and not quite distinguishable to Alexandra. It was not, she grasped at once, with a gust of relief, either of the Penhallow brothers.

"Why, Delmonico." Finn stepped forward. "What a great pleasure. I . . . I hadn't expected to see you here."

"Signore Burke! There you are." The newcomer doffed his hat and held out his hand for a vigorous shake. "How pleased I am to have found you at last." His English was nearly flawless, enunciated with great care and attention, as if he'd spent considerable time among Englishmen.

"You received my last letter, I take it?" said Finn.

"Yes, I did, though your location was nonetheless difficult to find. What has brought you to this—ah—remote idyll?" Delmonico took in his surroundings with a sharp black eye, which settled with polite brevity on Alexandra before looking away.

Finn laughed. "Privacy, of course. But I beg your pardon, signore; I've been remiss. Will you allow me to introduce to you my assistant, Alexandra, Lady Morley?" He turned to her with the greatest respect, as if presenting a valuable treasure for Delmonico's inspection. "Lady Morley, this is Signore Bartolomeo Delmonico, under whose hospitality we gather in Rome in July, for the automobile exposition."

Delmonico lifted his eyebrows. The sun struck his olive skin at an angle now, allowing Alexandra a better view of his face, with its regular dark features and friendly expression, cast in relief by a collar of startling height and whiteness. He wore brown English-style tweeds and a round bowler hat, which he removed with one hand while extending the other to grasp the tips of her outstretched fingers with unctuous correctness. "A pleasure, Lady Morley," he said, and looked back at Finn. "A fortunate fellow you are, to have acquired such an amiable assistant."

"Lady Morley is remarkably able."

Alexandra found her voice. "Oh, very able," she said, acutely conscious that she looked more like a five-shilling strumpet than the assistant of a legendary scientist and inventor. She indicated her grease-streaked dress. "Indeed, I've spent most of the morning under the chassis, as you see."

Delmonico ran his eye up and down her figure. "Indeed. Really, my dear Burke, your gallantry is wanting. Ought you not to have allowed the lady to wear your smock? It is a great shame, I believe, that a dress of such loveliness should be exposed to such filth."

"You're quite right, of course," Finn said, looking guilty. "Remiss of me."

"I have an apron," Alexandra protested.

But Delmonico wasn't listening. His attention had already turned to the automobile in the center of the room, still on its blocks. "So this is it, Mr. Burke? Your great project?" He took a step forward, and a distinct *crunch* rose up from his shoe. "Dear me. Are these perhaps your hairpins, Lady Morley?"

Alexandra's face grew hot. "Why, yes, Mr. . . . Signore, that is, Delmonico. I believe they are." She and Finn lurched forward at the same time, but Delmonico beat them to it, leaning downward in a graceful gesture and brushing the dozen or so pins into his left hand, which he held out to her with a knowing smile.

"Thank you." She twisted her hair back into its knot, shoving the pins ruthlessly into place as the cottage teemed with awkward silence.

"They came loose, you see, while Lady Morley was removing her eye protectors," Finn burst out.

"Yes, I see," Delmonico said.

Alexandra tried to remember whether Tuscany was susceptible to earthquakes, and if so whether one (of the mild variety, of course) might be persuaded by fervent prayer to strike at that precise moment. Which was, of course, ridiculous. She was a marchioness. The opinions of a lowly foreign mechanic ought not to carry any weight with her whatsoever.

Nonetheless, the time seemed right for a strategic retreat.

"If you'll forgive me, Signore Delmonico," she said, in her loftiest voice, "I believe I shall retire for luncheon. No doubt you and Mr. Burke have a great deal to discuss." She did not miss

the relieved look that flickered across Finn's rather thunderstruck features.

Delmonico removed his hat and tucked it under his arm.
"Lady Morley, I should be desolated to cause you to leave."

"Nevertheless, leave I must. Good day, signore. Mr. Burke,
shall I see you at dinner?"

"Yes, of course." His green eyes burned into hers.

"Splendid." She turned and walked with ladylike dignity out
the door and into the verdant Italian noontime, acknowledging
the murmured masculine farewells behind her with a little wave
of her hand. When she had cleared the cottage entirely she
began to gather speed, and by the time she had reached the first
terraced vineyard she was running, her skirts and petticoats all
tangling about her legs, her face and lungs burning, her eyes
aching with a half decade's worth of tears.

There you are!" exclaimed Abigail, as Alexandra thrust
through the door from the kitchen garden. "You're just in
time! He's just arrived! Good heavens, you're a dreadful mess.
What on earth have you done to your hair?"

"Who's just arrived? Rosseti?" Alexandra asked hopefully.
Perhaps the landlord could straighten everything out. Perhaps
Signore Rosseti could issue edicts that would return her life,
somehow, to the quiet order she had envisioned last winter,
without any ginger-haired Irish scientists to disturb her equilibrium, to distract her from her practical goals.

"No, not Rosseti. For goodness' sake, don't you remember
the priest is coming today?" Abigail slung her arm through
Alexandra's and led her down the narrow hallway to the back
staircase. The sun shot directly through the narrow windows,
but the stone walls still held the nighttime chill, cooling Alexandra's flushed body as she brushed past.

"The priest? Good heavens, Abigail. You've not gone *papist*,
have you?"

"No, goose. But it's the most charming tradition. You must
join in; it will be ever so unsporting if you don't." She tugged
Alexandra up the stairs with eager energy. "It's why the maids
have been tidying like mad, as I told you yesterday. Sort of a
ritual cleansing, I suppose. In any case, the priest has just arrived

to do the Easter blessing, sprinkling holy water hither and yon, and then . . ."

Alexandra stopped short, three steps from the top. She put her hands to her head. "Good God! But you must hide me at once! I'm . . . I'm quite *unclean*."

"He's only downstairs yet, with his assistant. An adorable young man, the assistant I mean. Such a thumping great pity about that vow of chastity. Come along, I'll help you scrub off all that grime and change your dress. What on earth have you been doing? Rolling behind the plows?" Abigail pulled her up the rest of the stairs and urged her into a run, down the flagstone hallway to her bedroom.

Ten minutes later, a bit dazed, but clean and modestly clothed in a high-necked gray dress and neat headscarf, Alexandra found herself being presented to Don Pietro, the parish priest, in Abigail's fluent Italian. Not quite sure of the etiquette, and hardly wishing to incur eternal damnation, she eyed his enormous ring of office and decided against kissing it. She made, instead, a polite little curtsy. "Welcome, Don Pietro," she said, feeling as though Phineas Burke's decidedly unchaste kisses were written in scarlet ink on her swollen lips. "We are, er, pleased to offer you hospitality."

He looked at her quizzically with his elderly eyes, and turned to the young man next to him. Abigail was right, Alexandra thought, casting her eyes to the ground. A fetching chap indeed, all pale skin and golden hair and large poetic eyes, bearing the vessel of holy water with grave care.

The two exchanged a few words, and then the young man stepped forward and spoke in halting English. "We have make the blessing of the downstairs. Now is time for blessing of the upstairs."

"Oh, right-ho." Alexandra gestured to the doorway and the great hall beyond. "Sprinkle away. I've no objection whatsoever."

Abigail whispered in her ear. "I think he means us to accompany him."

"For heaven's sake, Abigail, does he not realize we're Protestants?"

"It seems the polite thing," Abigail insisted, and Alexandra, heaving a great sigh, tucked her headscarf more closely behind her ears and turned to follow the priest and his server in stately procession through the great hall and up the main staircase. A small rank of maids and gardeners fell in behind them, giving Alexandra the uncomfortable sensation that she was performing in a play for which she had no script.

Or even, come to think of it, any basic notion of the plot.

"Are you quite certain this is all right?" she hissed at Abigail.

"What do you mean?"

"Can't we be excommunicated for this sort of thing? Condemned to eternal purgatory and whatnot?"

"Oh, rot," said Abigail. "In any case, who's to know?"

"Well, the Almighty, for one. I daresay we can't disguise it all from him." Alexandra tucked again at her headscarf and rounded the corner of the staircase, nearly bumping her nose into the dark vestments of the handsome young server. "I shall either be damned as a Protestant for encouraging a papist ceremony, or else damned as a heathen for pretending to be Catholic."

"I think it's a beautiful tradition, whichever side one's on. The renewal of life each spring is an ancient rite, dating well before Christianity or even classical pantheistic religion. It's . . ."

Don Pietro had stopped and turned to the server, who held out the vessel of holy water with deep reverence. Dipping his fingers into the water, the priest began to murmur in Latin, and went to the first room on the right. Lady Somerton's room.

Alexandra turned to Abigail. "Where's Lilibet?"

Abigail shrugged. "She and Philip went off this morning with a picnic. I expect they're not back yet."

The priest emerged from the bedroom and moved on down the hall, followed by the server. Alexandra bowed her head in feigned supplication and glanced out the narrow window to the gardens and fields and vineyards beyond. A glorious view, really, all the way down to the valley and the village nestled at its bottom, surrounded by olive groves and terraces, by fruit blossoms and the newly plowed earth. Nature reawakening, sending out shoots of hopeful green into an uncertain world.

Somewhere in that mass of expectant life lay Finn's little cottage, and his automobile, and Finn himself.

With mechanical steps she followed Don Pietro down the hall-ways, past the bedrooms, and then on into the other wing, where the men's bedrooms were located. Alexandra hadn't been down this particular corridor in weeks, not since that first afternoon at the castle, making up the beds in the cold, musty March air and doing rather a poor job of it. She watched each door as Don Pietro opened it and stepped inside, letting her eyes rest on the interior of the sunlit room beyond as the priest performed his offices.

She didn't mean to look, exactly. The Dowager Marchioness of Morley did not snoop. But if, in the course of one's ordinary and perfectly legitimate activities, one chanced to notice a detail or two, quite inadvertently—well, that was hardly snooping, was it?

Such details, for example, as a newly washed mechanic's smock, folded neatly on the shelf by the window, clean and white, with a shaft of sunlight casting a diagonal shadow across the top.

That particular shelf belonged to the last room in the corridor, set off by itself near the corner, where a back staircase stretched down to the scullery.

Not that any of those details were of the slightest interest or usefulness to the Dowager Marchioness of Morley.

They arrived downstairs again half an hour later. "And now the eggs," Abigail said gleefully, as they passed through the doorway back into the dining room.

"The eggs?" Alexandra inquired.

Abigail nudged her elbow. "On the table."

Sure enough, a small bowl of eggs sat in the center of the large wooden table, covered by a neat white linen cloth. ("Freshly laid, just this morning," whispered Abigail with pride. "I gathered them myself.") The entire household filed into the room to stand respectfully by the walls; Alexandra saw Signorina Morini's neat, round figure between the two servant girls, Maria and Francesca, watching the priest with adoration.

Don Pietro advanced to the table and drew the bowl toward him, his crooked old fingers shaking alarmingly, setting the eggshells to rattle against one another in a dangerous fashion.

The entire room seemed to hold its breath.

How pagan, Alexandra thought, wanting to dismiss it all, but there was something about the reverent way in which Don Pietro's hands moved above the eggs, stilling them, it seemed, with his gesture. She could almost have sworn that the eggs tilted toward those fingers, listened to the murmured Latin words, and sighed with ecstasy as the droplets of holy water trickled down their delicate shells.

Which was rubbish, of course.

Don Pietro stepped away from the eggs, and the staff exhaled in unison, smiling broadly at the priest and at Alexandra, as if she were somehow to be congratulated. As if she had laid the silly eggs herself.

"Er, thanks ever so much," she said, feeling something should be said to mark the occasion, whatever it was.

Don Pietro wiped his hands on the linen cloth held out by his assistant and turned to bestow a polite nod on Alexandra, before addressing Abigail. "What did he say?" Alexandra whispered, when the priest turned away to greet the servants, all of whom seemed on deeply familiar terms with him.

"Oh, he's just invited himself to lunch, of course!" Abigail patted the knot of hair at the back of her head, beneath her modest scarf, and sighed. "I do hope his assistant stays, too. Do you expect I shall burn in hell for it?"

"Yes, a very particular circle of hell, reserved for young Protestant girls who lure innocent Catholic priestly chaps away from their callings. Really, Abigail. I don't think I understood a bit of that. Do you mean to say they do it every year?" She backed up to the wall, as the maids began scurrying about, setting the table for luncheon. The eggs were covered with a cloth and whisked away, like a chest of gold doubloons.

"Well, one can't be too careful, after all, with a cursed castle," Abigail said.

She said it so calmly, Alexandra thought for a moment she'd misheard.

"A *what*? What did you say?"

Abigail turned to her. "The castle's cursed, of course. Isn't it delicious? Morini told me all about it the other day."

"Oh, for heaven's sake, Abigail. What nonsense." She folded her arms.

"It isn't nonsense! It's a historical fact. Something to do with an Englishman who visited the place a few centuries ago and got the signore's daughter with child. Hideously careless of him, of course, but that's a man for you. In any case, the signore caught them in the very act of eloping, and of course the Englishman was too honorable to duel the father, but somehow pistols got involved anyway—honestly, *men*—and the signore was delivered a mortal wound. And before he died, he laid down a curse upon the Englishman, and his daughter, and the occupants of the castle, and I suppose his own childhood nurse for good measure. As was proper, under the circumstances; you can't expect a wronged Italian father not to go flinging curses about, willy-nilly, while he bleeds to death on the flagstones. I'd be disappointed if he hadn't, frankly."

Alexandra began to laugh. "Abigail, this is all superstitious rubbish. The castle's not cursed. Look around you. Everyone's absolutely shimmering with health."

"Oh, but it is. Ask Morini. Frightful history. And until it's lifted, ill fortune will dog the footsteps of those who . . ."

"Abigail!"

"Which I suppose explains why we got such a good price on the lease . . ."

"Abigail!"

"What?"

"For goodness' sake, my dear. Remember yourself. You've good, sensible British blood running through your veins—in theory, at least—and I expect a little more phlegm from you." She brushed at her sleeve and watched the progress of the roasted lamb as it entered the room on a broad platter and came to rest at the head of the table. From her belly arose a growl of appreciation, which her folded arms hardly muffled at all. "Curses, forsooth."

"Well, all right." Abigail's voice turned sulky. She moved forward and placed her hands on the back of her chair, her eyes following the food as it appeared on the table. "But don't blame me if disaster strikes."

Alexandra joined her. "I won't," she muttered. "It appears I'm perfectly capable of creating disaster on my own."

ELEVEN

"I must thank you for the excellent tea," said Delmonico, rising at last and taking his hat. "I cannot help but feel that I was very much what I believe the French call *de trop*."

"Not at all." Finn rose as well and gathered the cups from the table. "Lady Morley was on the point of leaving." His fingers tingled, remembering the way the small horn buttons nestled along the long, supple length of her back, the ease with which he might have slipped them free.

"I am sure of it." Delmonico hesitated, swinging his hat between his elegant fingers. "You have progressed a great deal in recent months. You are to be congratulated."

"Not nearly so much as you, from what I hear." *Her soft lips moving against his. The delicate brush of her tongue.* He carried the cups to the sink and set them inside, before turning around to regard the Italian. "The papers speak of nothing else."

Delmonico shrugged. "Ah, Rome. My friends at the newspapers, they have difficulty containing their enthusiasm. You are wise, my friend, very wise, to hide yourself here in the hills." He made a sweeping gesture with his hand.

"Not so very well hidden." Finn leaned back against the long table and crossed his arms. *Her hands at the back of his neck, her thumbs stroking his skin. Her low, throaty voice, saying his name.* "You found me readily enough."

Delmonico spread out his hands. "We have friends in common. I was on my way to Florence and thought, I shall stop and see my good friend Burke."

"Hardly in your way at all, really. Quite out of it, in fact. I'm deeply flattered." *The erotic press of her breasts against his ribs, round and lush and promising. Far too copious, in his expert judgment, for one hand: he should have to use both, and his mouth . . .*

"Your company is worth any trouble." Delmonico glanced at the automobile and nodded. "A fine machine. Perhaps you may change my mind about electric motors. I look forward to seeing her in July."

"As I look forward to seeing yours." Finn straightened and uncrossed his arms. "Do you know your way back to the road?"

"Ah yes! Do not trouble yourself." Delmonico tapped his finger against his forehead and smiled broadly. "I have a good head for direction. Your groundskeeper was most helpful in pointing the way down."

"Giacomo! Of course, Giacomo. What a chap. I must have a word with him, to thank him for all his trouble this morning. He's sent a veritable legion of followers my way."

Had she felt the stiffening of his flesh against hers? Thank God for the mechanic's smock, for all her layers of apron and dress and petticoat and . . .

Delmonico's mouth twitched. "Perhaps he felt you were lonely."

"No doubt at all."

Oh God, had she been wearing the same corset he'd glimpsed in March, with the delicate white lace lying against her flushed skin . . . ?

"But I can see your mind is elsewhere," said Delmonico, settling his hat upon his head. "Struggling, I do not doubt, with the technical challenge of your electric battery. I wish you much luck and success with it."

Finn smiled. "But not too much, of course."

"Ha-ha. Of course, not too much."

Finn. Darling, marvelous Finn.

Had she meant it?

He walked Delmonico to the door, shook his hand, said the usual farewells. When the Italian had reached a decent distance, his brown-suited figure ascending to the vineyard terrace above, he shut the door and turned the lock.

For a moment he stood there, leaning against the doorjamb, listening to the expectant rustle of the leaves against the roof, letting the deep tranquility of the Italian afternoon steal over him.

Alone at last, and yet alone no longer. His gaze, traveling around the room, saw her everywhere. Her image had stained itself indelibly: under the automobile, in the cabinet, at the worktable, standing there in the middle of the floor and looking at him as though he held some essential key to the universe.

In his arms, kissing him like a Parisian opera dancer.

He had never met anyone like her. His acquaintance with women had always been limited. A lonely youth, with a strong dislike for clichés, he had resisted the ritual deflowering by the dairymaid in his youth and remained chaste until the middle of his first year at Cambridge. There he had met a sort of bohemian intellectual, a Girton woman, who smoked cigarettes and made a point of ignoring sexual morality, and who for a very short time had appeared to him as the very zenith of desirable womanhood. A month or two of her company had put him off both cigarettes and bohemian intellectuals for life.

There had been a few others: a willing widow whose husband had been a professor at the university; the nymphomaniac landlady of his local Cambridge pub, who put him off nymphomaniacs for life, though luckily not pubs. After university, the occasional discreet liaison, at home and abroad. In none of these affairs, except perhaps for a small degree in the first, had his heart been particularly committed.

But though he was no monk, he was no libertine, either. Until a short while ago, he had always been able to exercise a cast-iron control over his sexual impulses. Even at the eruptive age of fifteen, when confronted unexpectedly by the dairymaid's enormous naked breasts, he had managed (after heroic effort) to walk away and silence the *rut-rut-rut* in his brain. He had never been overtaken by ill-thought passion, never woken up the next day to self-recrimination. He could look back over the entirety of his experience and feel nothing but satisfaction.

Well, that had all gone to hell.

His eyes traveled across the room to the long table against the wall and came to rest on the thick, expensive weight of the envelope propped behind the stack of reference books at the end. He'd read it yesterday evening, just before heading into the castle for dinner, when dusk had fallen and the lamp cast a golden pool against the grainy surface of his worktable, scattered with bits of wire and tools and his battery in the middle.

Getting news from his mother was rather like receiving dispatches from the front of war: brilliant victories, stunning reverses; plans and strategies without number; conflicting accounts of battlefield action; and, of course, the endless logistics of the supply train, keeping the whole enterprise in motion. Even now, even after he'd settled a fortune on her, she remained essentially herself, charming and beautiful, with the God-given ability to drive men mad.

Darling Phineas, the letter read, *I do desperately hope you are well, for I heard the most shocking things about Italian winters from the Colonel last night, who tells me that the annual mountain thaw . . .*

Last night. His mother liked to convey her little facts that way, in clauses and conditions, so as not to embarrass her son with anything so vulgar as an outright admission. It seemed the Colonel was ascendant, at the moment, which was hardly surprising, considering the elegance of the diamond earbobs he'd bestowed on her at Christmas.

He went on, scanning most of it, not really wanting to parse the words for further meaning. As a boy, he'd paid as little attention as possible to the gentlemen progressing, one by one, each in his own pattern of ascent and plateau and inevitable descent, through his mother's parlor and, presumably, beyond. He hadn't understood until much later—embarrassingly later, really, for who wanted to think such things about his own mother?—that the parlor itself, and everything in it, and the kitchens and servants and food and clothing and school fees, were all paid for by this succession of gentlemen.

He might, indeed, have continued in this state of studied ignorance, had the unvarnished truth not been presented to his face, as might be expected, by another boy at Eton.

The young heir, as it happened, to the dukedom of Wallingford.

He'd split the boy's lip, of course, and blackened his eye, and then gone on to become fast friends with him. And Wallingford had never again mentioned the shameful facts of Finn's case. The two of them were, in the laws of schoolboys, square.

... and you know that I love you above everything, my dearest boy, and am so deeply and passionately proud of you. Do take the most scrupulous care of yourself, darling, and return home whole and victorious to your loving mama ...

Return home. How long had it been since he'd presented himself at his mother's door? He'd missed his annual Christmas visit this year, his train having been thankfully snowbound in the Alps for a week, and he'd felt so guilty at his relief at the sight of the enormous white drifts covering the tracks ahead that he'd cabled her a particularly affectionate Christmas message: AT SPITTAL FROM 20TH STOP TRAIN BURIED IN SNOW STOP FURTHER STORM EXPECTED TONIGHT MAKING CHRISTMAS ARRIVAL IMPOSSIBLE STOP EXPECT PRESENCE SHALL NOT BE MISSED AMONG YOUR MANY ADMIRERS STOP ALL BEST LOVE AND WISHES FOR HAPPY CHRISTMAS

He'd made arrangements for a mink-lined dressing robe to be wrapped and delivered to her house in Richmond (his first and more practical idea—a patented dry-earth closet for the disposal of bodily waste, far more sanitary than the modern water closet—had been discarded after mature consideration) and it had proven a splendid success. Gifts of discreet luxury were always welcome to Marianne Burke.

They'd met for tea at Fortnum's in London a few weeks later, which had proceeded exactly as it always did. Marianne had appeared in an elegant rose silk tea dress, with a modest bustle and an equally modest necklace lying atop her unpowdered bosom. Her hair was gathered on her nape in a fiery ginger knot. She had held her teacup in one gloved hand and a cucumber sandwich in another, the last finger of each hand extended in a gentle curl, and had gone on at length about herself and her admirers and their gifts to her, Finn making noises of approval and dismay at the appropriate intervals. A final question about his doings just as he was helping her into her fox-trimmed coat, which he'd answered in the most general terms possible, and then Finn had kissed her moist cheek and gone away with the relieved satisfaction of having discharged his duty.

What would Lady Morley think of Marianne Burke?

Finn straightened from the doorjamb, as if stung by the

disloyal thought, by the possibility it suggested. What did it matter? What did it matter what Lady Morley thought about anything? She'd kissed him without thought, after the high drama of the Penhallow menace, out of relief and gratefulness and perhaps a touch of loneliness. But it wouldn't happen again. She was unlikely to repeat such an unguarded action, unlikely even to visit the cottage again.

When the sun slipped down behind the rounded tips of the mountain to the west, he would return to the castle for dinner. Lady Morley would sit primly in her chair, avoiding his gaze, and he would avoid hers with equal perseverance. They would eat roasted lamb and small white beans and stewed artichokes, served by a pair of stern-faced young maids, and Lady Morley's sister would discuss the merits of sheep and Socrates, and Wallingford would thunder on about the unsuitability of classical languages for the female mind, and that would be that.

He ran both hands through his hair, until the short, fine strands stood up in shock like an animal's pelt. With renewed determination he walked back to his worktable and sat down on the chair, the wood hard and unforgiving beneath his legs, and finished reassembling his new battery design.

B ut when Finn presented himself at the dining room at the usual hour, neatly scrubbed, having gone to the extraordinary trouble of both combing his hair *and* changing his shirt, he found it deserted.

"Hullo!" he called out, straightening his collar.

No answer.

Alarm filled Finn's belly, an easy thing for alarm to do, because the belly in question was otherwise quite empty. He'd had nothing but tea and honey since breakfast. The prospect of now losing dinner quite eclipsed all other concerns, from the reassembly of his automobile to his dread of begging Lady Morley to pass the sex when he really meant to ask for the salt.

He started off immediately in the direction of the kitchens.

After a false start down a dark corridor smelling ominously of ripening cheese, Finn glimpsed an open hearth through a doorway and plunged through, though not before smacking his forehead on the wooden frame.

"Bloody hell," he grunted, rubbing his skull.

"Signore!" A woman straightened up from the hearth, wiping her hands on her apron.

"No, no. As you were." He glanced at his fingers. No blood, at least. The last thing his forehead needed was another scar from a height-related accident.

She looked at him quizzically. Her hands still worked away at her apron. "*Che cosa*, signore?"

He switched to Italian. "Your pardon, signorina. The dining room is empty. Am I late for dinner?"

Her pretty young hands went to her cheeks. "Oh, signore! We had the luncheon today, for the priest, for the Easter blessing. It is all finished now. You did not come for the luncheon?"

"No." His brain swirled with the dull stench of disappointment. That, or he had just concussed himself. "Nobody told me, I fear. Is anything left over?"

"Yes, certainly, signore. We have lamb and bread and other things . . ." She turned to the larder and drew open the door and began pulling objects out from the shelves. "You are very hungry, no?"

"Very hungry." He dropped himself into an empty chair at the large wooden table in the center of the room.

"Oh, be careful!" she exclaimed, and then checked herself.

"Be careful?"

"The chair, signore." She set a plate down on the table before him. "It has . . . it has a weak leg."

He tested it, rocking back and forth. "It seems strong," he said, "if a little small."

"The chair is not small, signore." She flashed him a dimple. "It is you who are so tall, Signore . . . ?" The word trailed expectantly.

"Burke," he supplied.

"Signore Burke." She took a knife and began to slice a half loaf of crusty bread. Finn's eyes followed the movement, watching the tiny flakes of crust fly away from the blade, the soft white bread fall like a pillow to the tabletop. The scent wafted toward him, rich and yeasty. He swallowed.

The knife stopped slicing.

He looked up in agonized bewilderment. She was frowning, as if concentrating her mind on some important matter, her head cocked slightly to one side. "Signore Burke," she repeated.

"Signorina?" He reached one hand across the table and snatched a slice of bread.

"Oh, but . . ." she began, and then sighed. "Signore Burke, I remember I have a message for you, from Signora Morley."

His hand, conveying a large ripped hunk of bread to his mouth, froze on his lips. "From Lady Morley?" he repeated.

"Yes, Signore Burke. She asks . . . will you meet her . . . tonight at ten o'clock . . ." Her lips pursed disapprovingly.

"Go on," Finn whispered.

"Tonight at ten o'clock in the peach orchard." She threw up her hands and turned back to the larder. "That is all, do you hear me? All!"

"No, no," Finn said, still whispering. "That is sufficient. *Grazie.*" He put the bread back to his mouth and chewed in mechanical movements, watching her bring out the remains of a leg of lamb and fling it onto the table with a distinct air of censure. He swallowed his mouthful of bread and cleared his throat. "It is likely something to do with the automobile," he said. "Lady Morley is my assistant."

She looked upward at him through her eyelashes.

Finn cleared his throat and summoned his fragile command of Italian. "Tomorrow we go to perform a delicate operation, to put the engine back together again with her new battery. I think Lady Morley has a few final questions. Ah, is that your lamb? It looks excellent."

"It is excellent lamb. Tender and new and innocent as Our Lady." She turned away and marched to the hearth, where two large cauldrons shot steam into the air in a mighty boil. With one sturdy arm she lifted each pot from the fire and attached it to a wooden yoke, which she hoisted onto her shoulders as if it were nothing.

Finn half rose from his chair, astonished. "Can I help you, signorina?"

The look she tossed him was of purest scorn. "Is milady's bath," she said, and apparently no further explanation was necessary, because she marched from the room without another word, leaving Finn to his bread and his innocent lamb and his nighttime assignations.

TWELVE

The approaching footsteps startled Finn out of a tantalizing reverie involving Lady Morley's lace-edged corset.

He'd been trying to focus his mind on his automobile, as he sat there on the damp grass, propped up against the slim trunk of a peach tree laden with blossoms. After all, he had a complicated operation to perform the next morning, reattaching the improved battery to the motor and installing it back in the chassis. If he did it well, he might even be able to fit in a trial before sundown. That, indeed, was something to look forward to. That, indeed, was exciting. A triumph.

His brain, however, was uninterested. His brain kept turning to Alexandra, to her mouth and hair and breasts, to the silken skin of her neck under his lips. To her underclothing, and how he would remove each piece, slowly, revealing first the slope of her bosom, and then the curves of her breasts, and then her . . .

Snap, snap went the footsteps on the fallen twigs, and Finn jumped up, searching through the trees for the sight of a pale dress bobbing against the darkness.

Awfully heavy tread for a woman, he reflected, placing one hand on the rough bark of the trunk.

Then he dove behind it.

"Still, still, still," said a masculine voice. "Pill? Kill? Oh, God, no. Mill? Hang it all. Shall have to try something else."

Finn pressed his forehead into the tree trunk, hard, until the ridges bit sharply into his skin.

Lord Roland's voice came louder, drifting between the trees. "*. . . the memory is with me still . . .* no, *the memory is with me* yet. *The memory is with me yet*, there's the ticket. *The memory is with me yet, and something something . . . shall forget?* Or *regret? And never shall my love regret?* Oh yes. Very good."

Very good? Was he mad?

Finn peered cautiously around the tree. Though the moon was nearly full, the profusion of leaves and peach blossoms swallowed its light, and he could only just make out the dark-coated figure of Lord Roland Penhallow as he settled himself against a tree trunk ten or twelve yards away, paper in hand, face turned dreamily into the blossoms above.

"*The memory is with me yet, and never shall my love regret*," murmured his lordship.

Finn had never gone in much for poetry as a youth. Still less as an adult, come to think of it. But he recalled hearing, at some point, amid the ale-soaked midnight conversations of his Cambridge years, that young Penhallow was reckoned a dab hand at a verse. Colossal promise, it was said. Perhaps another Byron, or that mad chap with the sister.

This was not Byron. This was some of the most appalling rot Phineas Burke had ever encountered.

Would Lady Morley hear him? Would it stop her in time? Finn slid his pocket watch free and squinted at the face, tilted it this way and that, trying to catch the meager light. Five minutes past ten, it looked like. Where was she? Perhaps he could sneak away and warn her, without alerting Penhallow. A risky move, though.

Lord Roland glanced back down at his paper and straightened. "Excellent. From the beginning, then."

Finn turned his forehead back into the tree and began to pound, softly, in time with the meter of the poem. Was it a sonnet? Only fourteen lines in a sonnet. Five little iambs per line, five strikes of the old forehead against the tree. No, no. Wait. Something was quite wrong. Penhallow had only four iambs per line, which meant . . .

Snap, snap.

Finn bolted to attention. So did Lord Roland. He stuffed the paper inside his coat and scrambled behind the nearest tree.

The footsteps drew closer, slow and deliberate, striking firm earth and crisp twigs. A nightjar called out a warning through the darkness, low and trilling.

Hell and damnation. What was he to do? Reveal himself and expose their meeting to Lord Roland? Or allow her to walk away, thinking he'd played her false?

The footsteps stopped. Heavy footsteps again, Finn realized in shock. Which could only mean . . .

"I know you're there," growled the deep, impressive voice of the Duke of Wallingford, carrying through the orchard with enough force to make the tender young blossoms vibrate in fear. "You may as well come out."

Not on your bloody life, Wallingford, Finn thought grimly. Not a chance in the world he'd confirm Wallingford's suspicions, not until the last second, not until it was too late and Lady Morley had actually walked into full view and confessed. He concentrated every nerve on the effort to remain still, to let not one movement of his body catch the duke's attention.

"I have your message," Wallingford went on, his tone turning pleasant. "There's no need to hide. No need for any more tricks."

Finn's mind raced. Message? What message? Had Lady Morley left him a note?

Or was it Penhallow's note? Had Penhallow actually managed to defeat the inflexible virtue of Lady Somerton and arrange a tryst in the orchard?

He didn't dare risk looking across at Lord Roland, hidden behind his own tree. He could only stand there, frozen, and pray that Lady Morley had been unavoidably detained by her sister's account of the goat milking that evening.

"Now look here." The duke's voice gentled further, until it seemed almost coaxing. "You asked me to meet you tonight. Don't be afraid, my brave girl."

Brave girl.

Finn's breath caught in his throat.

Unless, of course, the maid had made a mistake. Unless Lady Morley hadn't intended to meet Phineas Burke in the orchard at ten o'clock at all.

Unless she'd set her sights on a duchy instead.
Snap, snap.

Alexandra stared, stupefied, at the Duke of Wallingford. The words *what the devil?* rose in her throat, but her vocal cords seemed unable to activate them.

"Lady Morley." The duke ran his eyes down her pale figure and back up again to her face. He lingered on the headscarf, which still clung modestly to her hair. "This is charming indeed."

She didn't panic long. She never had, after all. A few seconds' indulgence was all she ever allowed herself before practicality took over. Options flitted through her brain, one by one, and in the end—that is, after a split second's consideration—she decided to brazen it out. "Your Grace," she said. "You're looking well. Courting the moonlit shades for your studies, perhaps? Or a dalliance with a village girl?"

His face was deeply shadowed, the eyes mere black pits above the dark blur of his nose and mouth. "I might ask the same of you, Lady Morley," he said, in a silky voice.

"Village girls are not in my preferred style."

"Ah, more's the pity." The duke exhaled with regret. "You're a lover of nature, then?"

She took a deep breath, filling her senses with the heady scent of peach blossom. "I walk here every evening," she said. "The cool air braces one wonderfully before bed. Dare I hope you're picking up the same habit? You'll find it puts you to sleep directly."

"Now why do I have trouble believing this charming tale?"

"Because you've a fiendish mind, I suppose," she replied, tilting her chin. "You're a devious fellow, and you can't imagine that everyone else isn't scheming just as you are. I expect you think I'm meeting Mr. Burke here tonight, don't you?"

"Since you asked, yes. I do."

"Then tell *me*, Wallingford, whom *you're* meeting here tonight."

He lifted one hand and examined his fingernails. "Perhaps I came to catch you out."

She made herself laugh. "That won't do at all. Even if I were meeting Mr. Burke tonight, I shouldn't be so careless as to let anybody else know of it. No, the shoe is quite on the other foot. I've caught *you* out. The question, of course, is whom."

"There is no question. I've no meeting at all."

"Your Grace," she said, smiling into the darkness, "I should never be so indelicate as to call into question a man's command of the truth . . ."

"I should very much hope not." His tone was deadly.

"Though of course, in affairs of the heart, one's allowed a bit of rope. After all, it would be far more shabby to expose one's sweetheart to disgrace than to insist on an exact adherence to the facts. Wouldn't it?"

"We have strayed, Lady Morley," said the duke, his words striking her ear in precise notes, "rather far from the point at hand. Are you meeting Burke here tonight?"

"I'm not under any sort of obligation to answer your question. Why don't you ask him?"

"He's not here, at present."

"Isn't he?" She cast about in confusion. "But I thought you said I was meeting him! Dear me. What a dreadful muddle. Perhaps I got my times mixed up. Or perhaps it was the seventh tree, twelfth row instead of the twelfth tree, seventh row. I burnt his note, you see, in the fireplace."

Wallingford folded his arms and regarded her steadily. "Well played, madam. I commend you. My friend Burke, I must concede, is an exceptionally lucky man."

"Mr. Burke is twenty times the man you'll ever be." She folded her own arms. "Your Grace."

"So I perceive," he said softly. His fingers tapped against the dark wool of his jacket. "What now, then, Lady Morley? We seem to be at an impasse. Do we await his arrival together?"

"Do as you like, Wallingford. I shall continue with my walk." She started forward, in a direct line from the way she had come, brushing past him with only a foot to spare.

His hand reached out and snared her arm. Up close, his features emerged from shadow, familiar and severely handsome, fixed on hers. "A shame, Lady Morley," he said, his voice still soft, "to waste this lovely evening."

She shrugged off his hand. "I don't intend to, Your Grace. Good evening." She walked on a pace or two, and then stopped and turned back to him. "Tell me, Wallingford. Why does it mean so damned much to you? Can you not simply let people do as they please? Can you not simply look to your own affairs for happiness?"

He stared at her for a long moment. "No. It appears I cannot."

The flagstones beat cool and hard underneath Alexandra's slippers when, an hour or so later, she slipped down the rear hallway to the little staircase in the back of the library wing.

The castle was quiet. She'd waited until the last sound had died away, until the door to the gardens had ceased opening and closing, until the muffled noises of booted heels on stone had ceased to echo through the hallways. And then she'd waited another half an hour, just to be certain.

Even in her fury, she showed patience.

It might, of course, have been an accident that Wallingford had appeared in the orchard instead of Mr. Burke. Perhaps the housekeeper had muddled the messages, or perhaps Wallingford's presence had been coincidental. The peach orchard, after all, was rather an obvious place to arrange an assignation; she was probably fortunate that she hadn't tripped over any number of trysting couples as she made her way through the trees.

On the other hand, Mr. Burke might have been sending her a very clear message.

Regardless of what had actually happened, she refused to rest tonight until she'd reached the bottom of it. Her reasons, of course, were entirely practical. Mr. Burke must be brought to understand that he couldn't treat the Marchioness of Morley in such a cavalier fashion, and that dodging appointments with ladies smacked of cowardice. More importantly, their earlier kiss must be explained away in rational terms, and firm rules established to ensure it wouldn't happen again.

No, her eagerness to meet him had nothing at all to do with the happiness that sang through her veins at the sight of him. That was entirely beside the point, and best ignored.

She ignored, too, the delicious thrill that snaked through her body as she crept up the staircase. A clandestine activity naturally produced an excited physical response, in order to heighten her senses against discovery. Nothing at all to do with the anticipation of seeing Mr. Burke in his bedroom, perhaps half-clothed, perhaps even in the bed itself, perhaps with his hair charmingly tousled and his eyes half-lidded and his chest . . .

You are angry, she reminded herself. You have grievances. He *failed to keep an appointment.*

She reached the top of the stairs and peered around the corner into the darkened hallway, lit only by the glow of the full moon outside. It stood empty, doors closed, shadows settled comfortably into the corners, holy and blessed just this day by Don Pietro and his beautiful young server. Rather sinful of her, presumably, to desecrate the hallway's state of grace so quickly, but it couldn't be helped.

The door to Mr. Burke's room stood almost at the top of the staircase, just a few feet away. She stepped over to stand in front of it and raised her hand for the fateful knock. For an instant she hesitated, as a terrible thought occurred to her: What if she'd been mistaken? What if—God forbid!—it hadn't been a mechanic's smock on the shelf? What if it had been one of Wallingford's white shirts?

Rubbish. She knew a smock from a shirt. Besides, Wallingford's shirts were always rigidly starched, and the garment on the shelf had carried a distinct droop.

She tapped the door. Solid wood, of course, and quite heavy. Unlikely Mr. Burke could hear such a fainthearted sound, particularly if he were already half-asleep.

She tapped more smartly and listened, ear to the door. Through the wood she could hear, just barely, the sound of the castle as it groaned and shifted its old stones through the night. Comfortable, inanimate noises, and nothing at all like the rustle of a man rising from his bed to answer a midnight knock.

Well, then. There was nothing for it. Alexandra reached one hand toward the old brass handle and pushed.

The door swung open, unlocked, carrying Alexandra with it. She staggered into the room, nearly falling to her knees on the worn braided rug covering the stone floor.

"I beg your pardon," she whispered, gathering herself, smoothing her dress. "It's only me. I tried knocking, but . . ."

Her words trailed off. The room—tidy and immaculate, its single trunk sitting at the end of the bed and its books stacked in perfectly leveled order on the shelf, altogether unlike the comfortable disorder of the workshop—was quite empty.

THIRTEEN

Lady Morley appeared in Finn's workshop doorway just after daybreak, sooner than he'd expected. "Good morning, darling," he said. "Tea? I've just started the water."

She stood stock-still and stared at him.

"Did you sleep well?" he continued. "I confess I'm a wreck. Spent the entire night here, fitting in the new battery and putting the motor back together." He ran a hand through his hair and felt the ends stand up stiffly beneath his fingers. "I expect I'm a less than salubrious sight. Do sit down; you're looking pale."

Her eyes widened farther. With one hand she clutched at a shawl of light green India cashmere about her shoulders, the first sign of movement since she'd stopped in the doorway. "Pale?" she repeated hoarsely. "Pale? *Darling?*"

"I tried to find you last night, once bloody old Wallingford took himself off, but you'd quite disappeared, and I was too electrified, so to speak, to go to bed." An understatement, of course, but how could he describe to her the sense of elation he'd felt at her words to Wallingford last night? How those simple words—*Mr. Burke is twenty times the man you'll ever be, Your Grace*—had revealed a shining magnificent truth, her true regard for him, as clearly as if they'd lifted a veil from before his eyes. How they'd charged him with confidence, with determination, with purpose.

He could no more have gone quietly back to his room and slept than he could have gnawed off his own right ear.

Though, just now, she looked at him as if he were doing exactly that. He stepped toward her and took her hand and led her to the chair. "Sit, darling. You're alarming me."

"Alarming you? *Alarming* you?" Her voice rose in pitch, directly up the scale to land in some impressive octave well beyond its usual range. "I went to your room, last night, did you know that? You weren't there. *Darling?* I sent word for you to meet me in the orchard, to talk about this . . . this *madness* . . . and instead . . . *Wallingford!*" She poured all her meaning into that one word, spitting it out with unbridled loathing.

"I was there, darling. I heard it all." He looked down at her tenderly, at her beautiful face, the faint lines of fatigue just visible around her eyes and mouth. Her scent crept into the air around them, soap and lilies and morning air. "It took all I had not to march out from behind that tree and wrest you away, but I thought . . ."

"You *thought*?"

"I thought you might perhaps not want me to do it." He reached out with his thumb to brush her cheekbone. "I thought the decision should be left to you. Whether Wallingford should know."

Her face, already pale, seemed to lose its color altogether, though her eyes glowed brown and enormous. "Should know what?" she breathed.

"About this." He bent his head to place a gentle kiss on her mouth.

He felt her surprise, felt the slight tentative movement of her lips under his, the pressure of her fingers as her hand slid up his chest to his shoulder, coming to rest on his neck, her thumb just grazing the lobe of his ear.

"This," she said, breathlessly. She pulled back. "*This* isn't right, Mr. Burke."

"Finn."

"Mr. Burke. We'll be found out, and everything will be ruined . . ."

"No, it won't. Wallingford and his damned silly wagers and tyranny." He put up his other hand and cupped her face between his palms. "I won't be bullied away from here, and neither will you."

"Please. I can't take any sort of chance. Neither can you, for that matter. You've your automobile, and your race." Her voice faltered. "We can't . . . how can it go on, if we're . . . if we . . ."

"Sweetheart. Alexandra." He stroked his thumbs against her skin and pressed another kiss on her lips. "I put together an entire automobile last night. Have you noticed?" Another kiss. "There she sits, ready for trial." Against the tip of her chin, the line of her jaw. "*This* in no way prevents me from working effectively. Quite the opposite." He drew back and smiled into her blurred eyes. "You *inspire* me."

"This isn't fair. I came here to tell you what a cad you are."

"A dreadful cad," he said, kissing her again. "Though twenty times better than Wallingford."

"A hundred, but it's not the point."

"What is the point?" He lifted the shawl from her neck and placed a kiss along the delicate skin of her collarbone.

"That there's too much to be lost if we're discovered . . ."

"Nonsense. Wallingford can go to the devil. Send him there myself, if I have to."

"   and too little to be gained otherwise." Her hands tightened at his neck, and she spoke into his ear with an intense whisper. "I'd be dreadful for you. You're so marvelously good, so pure and straightforward, and I'm weak and vain and mercenary . . ."

"You're not," he murmured, against her neck. "You pretend to be, but you're not. If you were really mercenary, you'd have seduced Wallingford by now."

She laughed. "You've got bags more money than Wallingford."

"But he's got position, grand houses, a title. You'd want that, if you were really ambitious, and not just pretending. Besides, you've a fortune of your own."

She began to speak, but he lifted his finger and held it gently against her mouth. Her eyes squeezed shut, blocking him out.

He spoke in a low voice. "When I saw you approaching last night, I thought at first you were meeting *him*, that the maid had confused her messages. And then I heard you speak to him, I heard you *reject* him—*him*, the Duke of Wallingford—" He swallowed. "And I realized what an idiot I'd been, that I'd read you all wrong, that I'd allowed myself to believe what everybody else does, because it was the easiest thing. The most convenient thing."

"They're right," she said, eyes still closed. "You're wrong, and they're right. You've no idea . . ."

Tenderness filled him. He leaned forward and pressed his lips against her brow. "I'm an idiot with women, generally. Most awkward fellow in the room. I don't understand the first thing about this business of wooing . . ."

"Oh, God, Finn . . ." Her forehead dropped into the hollow of his throat. She nestled there, like a bird, the quick drumbeat of her heart striking madly into his ribs.

"But I shall do my best, darling. Proud, stubborn girl. I'll wear you down, bit by bit. Seduce you with tea and oily smocks and engines and trips to Rome for motor races. With everything I have." He bent his words into her ear. "Because you're worth it."

She stilled against him. Her hair felt soft and feathery under his jaw, making him want to pull out all her hairpins and toss them back on the floor and spread the gleaming strands about her shoulders. He brought his arms down to her waist and held her, absorbing the warm, compact feel of her, the way her body fit neatly into his.

She cleared her throat at last. "I begin to find all this talk of Phineas Burke's genius rather hard to credit," she said, in a voice that was remarkably clear, considering she spoke into his shirt collar. She leaned back and eyed him. "Because I doubt I've heard anything so perfectly idiotic in all my life."

He leaned back his head and burst out laughing. "Oh, you splendid thing," he said. He slid his arms away from her waist and down her arms to her hands, and kissed each one. "Lady Morley. Tell me, have you ever driven an automobile?"

WHAT if somebody sees us?" Alexandra hissed. She clutched the cold metal of the steering tiller as if it were a life buoy and stared ahead, her eyes unblinking and her back ramrod straight.

"Nobody will see us. Far too early," came Finn's voice, calm and steady behind her, and only slightly breathless from the effort of pushing the automobile through the tender spring grass toward the cart track leading to the village.

"But what if someone's up already?"

"You're assisting me in a motor trial. We're hardly locked in an embrace, you perceive. Could you kindly remove your foot from the brake lever, my dear?"

She glanced downward. "Is that the brake? I beg your pardon." She shifted her foot, and the automobile lurched forward at renewed speed.

The abrupt movement shook loose the question she'd pushed to the back of her brain all morning long: What the devil was she doing, really?

What was she doing, driving an automobile through the meadow grass with Phineas Burke?

She'd told herself, at the beginning, that she'd sought him out to discover information about horseless carriages. Not outright espionage, perhaps, nothing so brutal, but something like it. Some idea, some invention that might save the Manchester Machine Works, might save her future and Abigail's, without doing Finn any real harm. Might regain for her the life she'd lost, the person she'd been.

But here she was, her lips still tingling from his kisses, her senses tracing every movement of his body with aching precision, without so much as a stolen nut bolt to show for it. And why? Hartley's automobiles were steam powered, if she remembered correctly, while Finn's was electric: She could learn nothing useful, nothing but theory.

And she had a feeling, a dreadful, sick feeling, that she'd known this all along. That her vague schemes had been a mere excuse, a useful fiction to disguise the real attraction of the little workshop in the olive trees: Finn himself.

If only she had the will to resist him. If only she could look at his tall, loose-limbed body, hear his deep, expressive voice telling her God only knew what thrilling things, without melting into a puddle at his feet. Puddles were weak. Puddles were transparent, with all their secrets and imperfections clearly visible to observers standing above them.

Puddles could be stepped on and splashed through and ruined.

But he's not like that, she told herself. Phineas Burke was not a puddle-stomper, not by any stretch. Might she not, just for a short while, just to satisfy her curiosity . . . ?

No. She must not. She would not. She must return to her original purpose, to find a way to make that damned Manchester Machine Works profitable, if she were ever to return to London and her old life, if she were ever to give Abigail a chance at the future that was her birthright. If Phineas Burke's workshop held no useful information for her, if she hadn't the stomach or the knowledge for the task, then she must stop all this dalliance at once, before she committed the unforgivable act of falling in love.

Unless her reflexes had spoken true yesterday, in Finn's wooden cabinet. Unless—oh God!—she had fallen in love already.

It must end now. Not another kiss. Not another . . .

"Darling, the tree!"

Her eyes flew open. "Christ!" she exclaimed, turning the tiller just in time to avoid the slender trunk of a young olive tree.

The automobile rolled to a stop. She didn't dare turn around.

"Weren't you looking?" he asked.

"I had . . . there was . . . a bit of dust. In my eye. Sorry. All clear now. Carry on."

A surge of breeze struck the back of her neck, or perhaps it was his exasperated sigh. "You do realize how long it takes to repair an automobile in this wilderness, don't you? No spare parts for miles. No skilled mechanics."

"I don't mean to criticize, but perhaps you ought to have considered that before you took out a year's lease on a remote castle."

"I considered it," he said evenly, "but I decided that the advantage of privacy outweighed the risks. I planned every detail, with parts and supplies and a dynamo—a *dynamo*, Alexandra, carried by steamship and its own damned railway car— for electric power to charge the battery. I failed, however, to anticipate the introduction of an unpredictable new variable."

"Unpredictable variable?"

"*You*." He said it with rather excessive terseness.

"Oh, of course." She fingered the tiller and examined her gloves. "Well, you did invite me to drive, after all."

He sighed again. "So I did. In the very madness of my passion." He went silent a moment, apparently considering the matter, and then said, "Very well. Keep your eyes open, then, if you please."

"Right-ho. Eyes open."

"Foot off the brake lever."

Alexandra looked down and adjusted her right foot. "Quite off."

The automobile began to move forward again, bumping through the grass toward the yellow gray line of the cart track up ahead. "Why can't we simply drive it to the track?" Alexandra called, over her shoulder.

"Because, dear girl, I want to save the engine. In case I haven't fixed it properly."

"What do you mean, haven't fixed it properly? Don't you know if it's working?" She glanced back in alarm. His hands rested on the rear of the motor-car and his tweed cap bent downward toward the grass between the large round balls of his shoulders. Beneath his chest, his legs moved like piston rods, steady and powerful.

He looked up at her. "That's why it's called a trial, after all," he said patiently. "Again, darling, I'd be most abjectly grateful if you'd keep your eyes facing forward."

"Oh . . . yes." She turned back. The track was only yards away. "But you're reasonably sure it will work, of course."

"Yes, reasonably. I shouldn't go to the trouble of pushing it out if I weren't. Here we are, then." The machine rolled more smoothly now, its front wheels easing into the dirt of the track. "Turn us westward, that's it. The track's flatter that way, and the glare won't bother us. Now press the brake lever, if you please. Excellent."

The automobile stopped, and Finn came around and reached inside, across her lap, to pull another lever with his hand. Heat radiated from his body, through his clothes and smock, and into the skin of her legs.

He straightened, his eyes just level with hers. "Now then, if you don't mind sliding over a bit."

"Sliding over?" she whispered. His face seemed far too close, those lawn green eyes far too alive with energy and anticipation.

He smiled. "I'm quite happy to teach you to drive her, at some point, but I'd rather do the trial run myself."

"Oh yes. Of course." She slid to the left and straightened her skirts, absurdly conscious of the easy, athletic swing with which he tucked himself under the steering tiller. His body loomed large and vibrant next to hers; his left arm just grazed her right.

"Now then," he said. "If we were driving one of those internal combustion engines, like those chaps in Germany are raving about and Delmonico's busy perfecting, we'd have a complicated business on our hands. You've got to set the choke, and turn the crank, and spark the ignition. Bloody awkward business, to say nothing of the danger of breaking your arm on the crankshaft. But the first lovely thing about an electric motor is this." He reached forward and turned a switch. A low hum vibrated the air. "Easy as can be. And splendidly quiet, as well. That damned motor of Delmonico's roars like a lion."

"How clever," Alexandra managed. A hint of queasiness began to curl in her belly. She hadn't quite thought through the actual business of driving an automobile. Finn sat next to her, relaxed and easy, his voice purring with confidence, but her own body was beginning to feel rather like a pudding, and a wobbly one at that. "How . . ." Her voice squeaked. She cleared her throat and began again. "How fast will it go, do you think?"

"Fifteen or twenty, I hope."

"Yards?"

He laughed. "Miles per hour, Alexandra. Eventually I'd like to achieve something more like forty, but today's just a trial. And of course I'd never take such a risk with you." He said it carelessly, as a fact almost too obvious to be said aloud.

"Yes, of course. I wouldn't stand for it anyway."

She must have sounded shakier than she intended, because he turned his head to look at her. "Nervous?" he asked kindly.

"No, not at all."

"You don't have to come, if you'd rather not. I nearly lost my breakfast, the first time I rode in one."

She straightened her back. "How picturesque. But I've a much stronger stomach than *that*, Mr. Burke."

"Excellent. Have you secured your hat?"

She touched the crown. "Three pins."

"Off we go, then." He released the brake lever, and the automobile rolled forward.

Alexandra clutched at her hat with her right hand and at the doorframe with her left. Her breath seized in her throat. The quiet whine of the motor built in pitch, higher and more intense, and the yellow gray dirt ahead disappeared under the automobile's front with increasing speed, building and building, and the seat beneath her bumped and jolted at the rocks and pits in the road. "Oh!" she gasped out, her knuckles aching with the force of her grip on the doorframe.

"Seven miles an hour!" Finn exclaimed, exultant.

"Splendid!" she croaked. The brim of her hat flapped with excitement.

"In a combustion motor, we'd be shifting gears by now. Ten! Bloody hard work, disengaging the engine each time, moving the new gear in place. Complete nuisance. There we are! Fifteen!"

Her hat brim was waving madly now. The wind pushed against her face, cool and vigorous, sending stray tendrils of her hair tangling across her face. She let go of the doorframe for an instant and pushed the strands aside with her hand. "Fifteen miles an hour! Marvelous!" Her voice strengthened. "Like riding a horse, without all the rocking about."

"Do you ride much?"

"Oh, constantly. I adore it. But this is splendid!" She raised her hand to catch the draft and felt it stream around her fingers, warmed by the morning sun. The green shawl slipped down her back, exposing the thin line of skin between her hat brim and her dress.

"In one of Delmonico's machines, we wouldn't be able to hold this conversation," Finn was saying. "Incessant racket. Eighteen!"

Both of his hands rested on the steering tiller, gloved in leather, broad and strong. What would he do if she took the one nearest and slipped off its glove and wrapped her hand around it? If she closed her eyes, she could feel its warmth, its firmness, the way his fingers would enclose hers, the way his thumb would brush against her palm. She wanted that hand so much. She hurt with it.

She felt something move against her leg and glanced downward to realize it was his own. It pressed against her from hip to knee in shocking intimacy, the curve of his thigh muscle quite clearly outlined by his woolen trousers.

He was speaking again, talking about his motor, something about horsepower and voltage and cells, which she knew she ought to be memorizing. "So we really should turn about now, you see," he said, "because I don't fancy pushing the whole works all the way back, should the battery pack up earlier than expected."

"Oh, naturally." Disappointment tinged her. The machine began to slow, the splendid breeze quieting across her ears and her skin, the brim of her hat subduing its exuberant flutter. His leg moved against hers, pressing on the brake lever, bringing them to a stop in the middle of the dirt track, where the warm sun settled onto her shoulders and the nape of her neck and trapped itself in the wool of her shawl.

"There we are! A solid mile, I believe, and without a hitch. By damn, I'm relieved. I beg your pardon."

"Oh, not at all." She injected a note of cheerfulness into her voice. "You warned me in the beginning about your language, remember?"

"Yes, but that was before . . ." His words trailed off. He dropped his left hand from the steering tiller and rested it on his leg.

"In any case," she went on, "that was splendid. Perfectly splendid. An entire mile! I'm quite amazed. It was all just a . . . a collection of parts, only yesterday." She wanted to move her leg, but quarters were too tight; they were both pressed against their respective doorframes. Another few inches and she would be in his lap.

This was beginning to prove a bad idea indeed.

She spoke up with determined cheer. "Could we have gone forty, do you think?"

"Not yet. I plan to expand the battery, add a couple of cells, which should increase my horsepower considerably. This was just to test the efficiency of the new design."

"And it worked?"

"Exactly as I'd hoped. Absolutely revolutionary." His voice sounded curiously flat, as if he'd lost all interest in automotive revolutions.

She took a deep breath. "Tell me all about it. I want to know every detail."

He laughed. "Good God. Not just now, in the middle of the road. I'll sketch it out for you, if you like, when we get back."

"That would be perfect." She looked back down at their legs, pressed together.

"In the meantime," he said, straightening, "I suppose we should turn around." His feet shifted against the floor, against the pedals springing up from the boards below, and the automobile curved forward to the right, and then went backward, and then pushed forward again, until the full force of the midmorning sun hit their faces. Alexandra tipped her hat brim down to shade her eyes.

"Well, go on," she said.

His fingers tapped against the tiller. "Tell me. Would you like to drive her?"

"Me?" she gasped. She turned toward him and found his face looking down on her with a curious expression, his left eyebrow raised in question.

"Yes, of course. There's nothing to it, really, not like your combustion engines. Simply press the forward pedal when you want to go, and the brake lever to stop. The steering, you'll find, is almost automatic."

"Automatic?"

"I mean it's a sort of reflex. You don't need to think about it." He smiled, warm and encouraging. "Come along, then. Try it. I'll be right here next to you. Jump in and take over at a second's notice."

"I don't know . . . I . . ."

"Come now." His smile broadened, and his head tilted challengingly. "Surely the indomitable Lady Morley isn't afraid of a mere machine?"

"Of course not," she snapped. "Remove yourself, if you please, Mr. Burke."

He laughed and ducked out under the steering column and into the road. Around the edge of his tweed cap, his hair glinted fire from the morning sun, and the little dusting of freckles across the bridge of his nose seemed almost to dance.

She slid across the seat and positioned herself once again in front of the steering tiller. He'd made it to fit himself, of course, and since he outmeasured her by a good ten inches, her feet had to stretch to reach the pedals.

He leaned over the doorframe. "That's it. You'll have to sit forward a bit, with those short legs of yours."

"My legs are not short," she said indignantly.

"Like a crocodile's."

She rapped his gloved knuckles.

"Like a gazelle's," he amended, "only rather a short gazelle. A lovely, graceful, proportionately long legged, but rather short gazelle."

"I'm not short at all. I've got sixty-six and a half inches, which is more than sufficient. It's only because you're a damned monstrous giraffe, yourself, so everybody else seems like a pygmy. Now where are these pedals of yours?"

He chuckled. "Right there. That's your forward pedal, and that's the reverse. Not that you'll need it, of course. And the brake lever. Most important."

"Yes, I know the brake lever." She gripped the steering tiller tightly, hoping it would keep her hands from shaking.

"Right-ho, then." He swung around the front of the car to settle his long limbs in the seat next to her. His leg, she could have sworn, pressed against hers with even greater insistence than before.

"You're trembling," he said.

"How absurd. I'm not trembling."

"Alexandra, the seat is positively shaking."

She tightened her fingers even further around the steering tiller. "It's only your dodgy motor. Are you ready?"

"You don't have to drive if you'd rather not . . ."

In answer, she released the brake lever and pressed down firmly on the forward pedal. Or at least she thought it was the forward pedal.

The automobile jerked backward and bumped down the track.

"The brake!" exclaimed Finn.

Flustered, she pressed the forward pedal instead of the brake. A horrible confused whirr rose up from the engine. The automobile ground to a stop, and then, mercifully, began to edge forward.

"I daresay she's all right," Finn said, after a moment.

"It sounds so," said Alexandra humbly. She tested the pedal, very gently. The automobile eased its way down the road, into the sunshine.

Finn made a coughing noise. "Perhaps you might venture a little more speed?"

"I have already."

"Then, if you don't mind, I believe I'll just slip out and walk alongside. For the exercise, you see."

"How droll you are." She pressed down firmly on the pedal. The car leapt ahead, like a greyhound from its traces, shocking her for an instant before the familiar breeze caught in her hat and swirled past her face, sweet and invigorating.

"There you are! Ten miles an hour!" came Finn's jubilant voice, next to her. "Just keep her on the road. She steers beautifully."

It did steer beautifully. Finn was right: She hardly needed to think about steering at all; the machine simply went where she wanted it, down the long, straight track and into the sun. A laugh rose in her throat at the sheer magic of it, the speed building beneath her, the power flooding through her from the motor. The great, shimmering strength of the man sitting next to her, his leg pressed into hers.

"Fifteen! Excellent! You're doing splendidly. A natural." His arm lay along the back of the seat, nearly touching her shoulders. Its warmth reached into her skin.

"Thank you," she said. She was beginning to feel a little giddy. Or perhaps dizzy. It was rather hard to sort through all the sensations at the moment.

He tilted his head to speak into her ear. "Dashing Lady Morley. Do you know, you look particularly beautiful driving an automobile. It brings a lovely flush to your complexion. Perhaps I should build you one of your own."

"This one is quite sufficient, thank you. In any case, I should much prefer a new hunter."

He laughed. "Are you quite sure? I find the automobile's seating accommodation far more convenient."

She shouldn't ask. She knew she shouldn't. She knew exactly what his answer would be.

But she couldn't help herself.

"Convenient for what?" she asked, as innocently as possible.

He laughed again, as if he'd read her thoughts and knew what she was after. "Convenient for this." With one hand he lifted the brim of her hat and kissed the tender skin at the nape of her neck.

"Stop that," she said, angling her head to give him better access.

"Can't." His warm lips trailed around her throat; she could feel his nose brush against her hair. "You're so delicious . . ."

The road bent a few degrees, bringing the sun directly into her face. Her eyelids sagged, unable to withstand the drugging warmth of the sunlight and the narcotic sensation of Finn, this new and amorous Finn, teasing her neglected flesh with such hunger. What had happened to the old Finn? The cold and scientific Finn, the ambitious genius with no regard for frivolous women, who had cracked walnuts between his fingers and examined her with such arctic reserve?

He hadn't been aloof at all, had he? He had only been . . . shy. *Shy.*

His lips moved upward to caress the curve of her ear, not shy at all now. Quite in command, in fact, and drawing her inexorably under his spell, into the palm of his hand, while her heart thundered against her ribs in fear and joy and anticipation.

Her half-lidded eyes caught the flash of color at the last second.

"Oh damn! A cart!" she exclaimed, and jerked the tiller to the right. Finn's automobile flew obediently off the road and into the grass.

FOURTEEN

"It was entirely your fault." Alexandra flashed her eyes at him in her haughtiest Lady Morley expression.

He straightened from his examination of the automobile's right front tire and looked down contritely at her face. "Entirely my fault. I accept full responsibility."

Her expression softened. "Good, then."

"I've learned my lesson, never fear."

"Excellent. I quite agree. No more of this rubbish about kissing . . ."

". . . until the automobile has come to a full stop," he finished. He glanced back down at his patented pneumatic tire, which settled into the tough meadow grass in a long, flat line.

"That isn't at all what I meant."

"I'm afraid the tire's quite flat, however. I ought to have thought to bring my mending kit." He glanced back at her and winked. "I suppose I was carried away."

"You're impossible." She lifted her hand to shade her eyes and looked down the track. The cart's astonished driver had been dispatched at last, after a badly executed Italian explanation, and now continued on his way, already a small, distant figure against the dun-colored dirt.

Shy men make the best lovers. Where had she heard that? Lady Pembroke, probably. Her ladyship spoke with authority on such matters, having an extensive frame of reference. *Your inexperienced young matron always falls in love with the arrogant ones,* she'd told Alexandra once, over tea in the conservatory, her starched white sleeves buttoned to the wrists and her starched white collar buttoned to the neck. *All very well if you'd like to be sorted out and on your way in twenty minutes. But the shy, quiet fellow takes his time, Alexandra. Remember that. He has imagination. And underneath his trousers, he's invariably a tiger.* A sip of tea, a gleam in her eye. *Give me the shy fellow, every time.*

Alexandra had sipped her own tea and smiled knowingly and gone home to dear Lord Morley and his gout and his monthly heave-ho over her nightgown-clad body. She hadn't minded. Lord Morley smelled pleasantly of sherry and wool, kissed her breasts with touching enthusiasm, and plainly adored her. He didn't take long, and never removed his nightshirt, and complimented her afterward on her beauty and vigor. There were times, early on, before gout had made him too irascible, when the sound of his brisk knock on her bedroom door had even excited her. Perhaps it had been the thrill of having such power over a powerful man—Lord Morley had had the ear of the Queen, for a time—or perhaps it was just the notion of the act itself, the intimate friction, the sense of some glittering prize lying just out of reach.

Shy men make the best lovers. She'd never had a lover. She'd never wanted one. Why risk everything, one's reputation and one's independence and one's peace of mind, for a few moments of physical pleasure?

Finn—Mr. Burke—knelt in the grass again, considering his tire. He'd left his smock back in the workshop, and a brown tweed jacket now stretched across the breadth of his shoulders. On the side of his face visible to her, brightened by the sun, she could see his narrowed eye and his furrowed brow. He reached out his right hand and ran it along the side of the tire, blunt-tipped fingers smudged with oil.

What sort of lover was he?

She knew the answer. Hadn't he kissed her already, caressed her already? He was the clever, patient sort, who took his time and had imagination. In bed, he would be a tiger. He would stalk her, subdue her, deliver her that glittering prize and drop it into her lap. He would gather her in his arms and keep her safe.

"Mr. Burke"—what was she saying, what was she doing?— "Finn."

He looked up at her and smiled.

Her blood thudded drunkenly in her veins. She couldn't speak.

"I know it's a nuisance," he said. "I'll just dash back to the workshop for my mending kit. It won't take a minute. You can sit here in the sunshine and listen to the bees."

"I'm afraid of bees," she lied. "I believe I'll come with you instead."

Imagine that," he said, to fill the awkward silence as he fumbled the key into the workshop door. The significance of opening a locked door into a private room, with Lady Morley by his side, had just crashed down about his ears. "Eighteen miles an hour on the first go! By God, I'm thrilled."

"Why on earth do you keep your workshop locked?" she asked. Her voice held an odd note. Quiet, almost subdued.

He turned the knob and slipped the key back into his jacket pocket. "We motor enthusiasts are a competitive lot, after all," he said, motioning her through the door before him. "There's a great deal at stake. It's one of the reasons I picked this spot."

"And the other?" She didn't turn toward him, only drew the pins from her large straw hat, one by one, and set them on the table.

"Fewer distractions." He thought she would laugh at that, her ironic, musical laugh, but she didn't. She only pulled her hat away from her head and set it down on the table, next to the pins.

"I suppose I should feel lucky you allowed me in here at all," she said, still turned away. The morning sun hadn't quite reached the window yet, and in the diffuse light the skin of her cheek seemed to glow from within. "You must trust me a great deal."

"Of course I do." He watched her as she stood, motionless, her hair loosened slightly by the hat's removal. One hand rested on the table, next to her hat and pins, and the other hung next to her side. "Are you all right?"

"Yes, quite," she whispered.

"Have I offended you? It was rather a long night, and with all the excitement . . . succeeding at last . . ."

"No. No, you haven't offended me at all." Her voice came more firmly now. She turned to him at last, her hands gripping the edge of the table behind her. "Not at all," she said, meeting his gaze with large, round eyes, looking rather like a prisoner left at the scaffolding to perform her own execution.

His mouth opened and closed. What the devil had come over her? "I'll just . . . I'll just gather my mending kit, then, shall I? We'll head back down to the road and . . ."

"No!" The word burst from her.

"I beg your pardon?"

"No. Let's . . . let's stay here a moment." She swallowed heavily. "Please. Please, Finn."

He watched her a second or two longer before understanding dawned. "I see," he said. His head was still heavy from the sleepless night, and his muscles drained from the effort of moving and installing the immense battery and pushing the automobile to the road. Altogether it was much the same as the poleaxed feeling of having drunk the better part of a Scots distillery the night before.

"Please," she said again, in a whisper, and the heavy feeling in his head dropped into his groin, and his muscles, much like his battery the night before, flooded with new energy.

He stepped toward her, watching her eyes widen and gleam as he came close. He removed his peaked cap and his gloves and tossed them into the chair, next to her skirt-covered legs.

The scent of her seemed to reach out and wrap around them. He leaned his head down next to her ear and breathed it in. "Tell me. Is it your soap or your perfume?"

"What?" she asked breathlessly.

"Lilies. You smell like lilies."

"My soap, I think," she said, with a little gurgle of a laugh.

"Bloody reckless of you." He liked that he could drop words like that around her, that she wouldn't mind, wouldn't even notice. He lifted one hand around the back of her head and began to pull out her hairpins, letting the heavy swags tumble about her shoulders. "Have you any idea what your lilies do to a man?"

"No, I don't." She tilted her head, exposing the long column of her throat.

He removed the last pin and set it down on the table, next to her hat and hatpins. Her eyes were closed, the lids pressed down tightly, as if she were afraid of opening them. He brought his hands into her hair and spread it about her shoulders, long and thick and shining in the floating late-morning light, smelling of fresh air and sunshine. "They give him ideas, Alexandra. Improper ideas. May I confess something?"

"I hope you will. I adore confessions. The more shocking, the better."

"I've been consumed with improper thoughts for you from almost the first moment of our meeting." He lifted her hair with one hand and kissed the side of her neck.

"*Almost* the first?" Her voice wavered.

"You *were* rather ungracious."

"I'm so terribly sorry. I'll make it up to you."

"Yes, you will." He straightened and gazed down at her face, at her closed eyes and her wide, ripe mouth. "Look at me, darling."

"Don't, please. I can't." Her arms came up, wrapping around his neck, pulling his head into hers. "Just kiss me."

The words sent fire racing across his exhausted brain. He sank his lips into hers and felt her instant response, her gasp of shock, her fingers digging into his neck. God! Her mouth was so sweet, so eager. Her velvet tongue met his, tentative and then ardent, returning each stroke, drawing him deeper, as if she couldn't get enough of him. He could hardly think from the lust billowing up inside him, months and months of control and frustration, and now came this passionate woman into his arms, this astonishing and beautiful Alexandra, her mouth open and hungry under his, as desperate as he was.

His hand slid downward, along the curve of her back, anchoring finally at her waist, his thumb rubbing between two long whalebone stays, searching for the flesh underneath. "Please," she said, into his kiss, "oh please." Her hand slipped down from his neck to the buttons of his jacket, fumbled between their locked bodies, slipped out the top button and the next, and then she slid her fingers underneath the thick woolen tweed to burn through the cotton weave of his shirt and into his chest, finding the buttons.

His breath drew sharply into his lungs. With one hand he trapped her fingers against him, stilling her movement. Her face tilted upward, eyes open now, searching his own with a pleading gleam. "What is it? Don't you . . ."

"Yes." He exhaled. "God, yes. But darling, you're . . . Are you quite sure?" His brain spun dizzily. Every nerve seemed to have gathered underneath the sensation of her fingers against his chest. *Stop*, said a distant voice, through the maze in his head. *Stop. Wait. It's too soon. Not yet.* "Are you quite sure?" he repeated, both to her and to himself.

Her other hand, her free hand, came up to rest against his cheek. "Finn, it's all right. I want this. I want it . . . oh, you can't imagine how much. Don't draw away. Please. I'm a disaster for you, I really am, but I'm selfish and lonely and I . . . oh!" Her head dropped into his chest. "Oh, you damned noble brute. I shouldn't. You deserve better. You deserve some sweet young thing, some noble girl . . ." She shook against him, clutched her hands around his waist.

"Shh." He laid his chin gently atop her hair, feeling the silken strands tickle his jaw. Her hands dropped back to circle his waist. "Alexandra, listen. You've got it all wrong. My mother . . . you ought to know this . . . before you . . . before we . . ."

She went still against him, the gentle rise and fall of her breath steady beneath his hands.

"She's . . . you may have heard of her . . . her name is Marianne. Marianne Burke." The name sounded strange and foreign on his lips.

"Marianne Burke? What . . ." Her breath caught. "Oh!"

"Yes," he said. "Exactly."

"Oh. I see." She turned her head against his shirt and stared at the window, absorbing it all. She would have heard of his mother, of course. Everyone had. No one became the acknowledged mistress of the Prince of Wales at the tender age of seventeen without acquiring the patina of legend. "Richmond, of course. The little cottage. My God! And you're her son!" She drew back and searched his face with wide, astonished eyes.

"The hair, of course. And her eyes, though mine are a shade lighter, I'm told."

She nodded, eyes still round. "I've heard she's quite striking. As one would expect, I suppose. Was she . . . is she very tall?"

"Not particularly. I've that from my father."

"Your fa . . ." She checked herself, covering her tactless curiosity with a nervous laugh. "I never imagined . . . It's a common name, Burke, I suppose . . ."

"Yes. So you see, as far as my being noble, it's quite the opposite. It's I who belong to a world beneath yours." He took her gently by the arms, set her away, and looked down in her face. "I thought you should know, that you had a right to know, before you decide. Before you say anything, before we do anything, that might . . ."

"Finn," she whispered, "I've already decided. It doesn't matter about your mother. Who will know, after all?"

"Everyone. Your friends. They'll find out eventually."

"No, they won't. We'll be discreet. Not even Wallingford . . ."

"I mean eventually. When we're back in England."

She stared at him a moment, without speaking. Her lips parted, and then closed again.

A leaden weight settled down around his heart. "Ah," he said. "I see. You'd rather keep things unofficial." A lock of hair swung down across her face. He reached out with one hand and brushed it away, tucking it behind her ear.

"Don't," she said brokenly. "Don't. Don't spoil it."

"Spoil what, my dear?"

Her hands grasped the lapels of his jacket. "You see? This is what I meant. Vain and frivolous. *This* is what I am, Finn." She spoke defiantly, eyes blazing. "If you want me, you'll have to take me as I am. You'll have to *accept* what I am."

She stood just apart from him, her dress grazing his jacket, the corners of her eyes tilted upward in that catlike way of hers. Watching her, he was reminded of a fox he'd once seen caught in a trap long ago, on one of his many solitary childhood rambles through the woods near his mother's cottage, before he'd been sent off to boarding school at the age of eight. The fox had looked up at him with that same expression, brazen and fearful both at once, daring him to get close enough to free her.

He placed his hands atop hers, where they gripped his lapels. "I've known any number of selfish women in my life, Alexandra, and you're not anything like them." He slid his hands upward along her arms, rounding about her elbows, drawing her body against his, and spoke in a low voice. "Let me show you, darling. Let me show you what sort of woman you really are."

He felt the moment she gave in, when the taut resistance in her muscles eased away and her body melted into his. He moved his hands to her waist, and in a single easy movement he lifted her onto the worktable.

"Oh." Her eyes widened.

He set each hand on either side of her hips and kissed her forehead. "Now then, Alexandra. Marchioness of Morley, leader of London society."

"How did you know that?"

He reached deep inside himself for his calm, scientific detachment. "I'm not a complete recluse. I emerge from my workshop from time to time. I hear things. How the drawing room of the dashing Lady Morley is the only place to be seen on Thursday evenings." He kissed her right temple, a light silken kiss. "How her sixty-eight-year-old husband died of an apoplexy two summers ago, and she has been seen only in deep mourning ever since. As is perfectly proper." He kissed her left temple. "How puzzling it is that, though she never lacks for admirers, she has no known lovers, past or present. Much to the disappointment, I'm told, of the admirers in question."

"Perhaps I've been discreet." Her voice brushed against his cheek, hardly more than a whisper.

"I considered that possibility." He kissed the tip of her nose. "And I dismissed it. You yourself said you were a loyal wife."

"You've given the matter some thought, I see."

"Endless thought. You've no idea. But to return to the point, his lordship found his eternal reward nearly two years ago." He reached behind her neck for the top button of her bodice. "Which leaves us a long period of time to consider. Why, I asked myself, would a lady of legendary charm and beauty, still in the flush of youth . . ."

"Hardly that." Her eyes were closed now, the dark curl of her lashes lying against her creamy skin.

He undid the second button. "You're younger than I am, after all. Why wouldn't such a woman take herself a lover?" The third button gave way, exposing the edge of her chemise under the tips of his fingers, beneath the parting plackets of the bodice.

"Perhaps I have."

"No, you haven't." The fourth button. "You're shivering, darling. Your eyes are closed. Hardly the actions of a woman experienced in clandestine liaisons." The fifth button, stiff in its buttonhole, slipped free at last. Her chemise was fine and thin and delicate, alive with the warmth of her skin beneath.

She gave a shallow laugh. "You scientists. Altogether too observant. I ought to have chosen Penhallow for my first lover."

"But you wouldn't, would you?" The buttons were coming more easily now, aided by the slackness of the bodice; a good thing, as his fingers seemed to be growing increasingly clumsy. Owing, he supposed, to the unprecedented concentration of blood in his fully aroused loins. "Because your cousin is in love with him. And because"—the last button gave way now, and her bodice sagged away from her breasts—"you haven't any interest in a chap like Penhallow, have you?"

"He's frightfully handsome."

Finn drew the bodice forward, extracting her arms from the sleeves with the greatest care, spreading his fingers along her skin. "Conventionally so. But you're impatient with the things everybody else likes. You're yearning for something different, though you don't know quite what it is."

"How do you know that?"

"Because you're here with me. And I'm hardly the sort of conventionally handsome, conventionally employed sort of lordling that hangs about your Thursday evening salons, am I?" He let her empty bodice pool about her waist and placed his mouth just below the hollow of her throat.

"No," she gasped, "you're not."

His lips moved against her skin. "And now you're wondering to yourself just how much I've discovered in my scientific studies. Whether, for example, I've made any sort of research into matters of human biology."

Her head angled backward, exposing the long white reach of her throat. "H-Have you?"

"We scientists are curious animals, Alexandra. And curiosity doesn't stop at the boundaries of one's chosen field of study." His mouth traveled downward, to where her breasts swelled abundantly above the boning of her corset. "Ah, darling. You're so beautifully made. So full, here." He set his open mouth atop her left breast and ran his tongue along the pink sliver of areola that escaped from the top of its confinement.

Her body jolted in his arms.

"There are those," he went on, kissing the valley between her breasts, "who insist that the human female feels no particular pleasure in the sexual act. Those are not, my dear, the sort of scientists you should invite into your bed."

"No," she whispered, "never."

His tongue traveled along the edge of her corset to find her right breast, and this time she was ready, this time she arched her back and moaned when he found the sensitive ridge, when he drew down the corset so her breast sprang free, when he covered the peak with his mouth and suckled her through the muslin of her chemise. Her hands clutched at the back of his head, taking fistfuls of his hair.

His brain was ringing, throbbing. She tasted so delicious, so pure and womanly, her nipple hard in his mouth, her breasts large and full against his face, her heartbeat so rapid and eager he could feel it pound beneath his lips. "Ah, God, darling," he muttered, and with his right hand he swept down the endless length of her skirts and found her ankle.

Such a beautiful ankle, trim and flexible beneath his fingers, covered with stockings of fine strong silk. He lingered over it, running his thumb around the little hollow beneath her ankle-bone, and then he drew his hand slowly up the inside of her leg, rucking up her skirts as he went: the curve of her calf, the round ball of her knee, the narrow silk ribbon of her garter. He was elbow deep in her skirts and petticoats now, and she had frozen, had stilled her breath in her chest, her only movement the involuntary quiver of her flesh.

He lifted his head back to hers and kissed her throat. "Shh. Don't be frightened. Did your husband never touch you like this?"

"Yes—no," she stammered. "Not like this. Not . . . I can't think . . ."

"Did *you* never touch yourself like this?"

"No! I—no, not like this, not—I don't know how—I thought . . ."

He thought, for just an instant, of the Cambridge landlady with her forthright use of anatomical terms, with her years of experience and experimentation. He'd parted from her, relieved and eviscerated, after two exhausting weeks, but the knowledge gained had been priceless.

"Darling, trust me. I'm going to show you something rather lovely, but only if you let me. Will you let me?" In his lust, in his raging need for her, he struggled to calm his voice, to sound patient and coaxing.

"Yes." But her body remained as tight as a bowstring.

He moved his lips across her face and captured her mouth again, measured and lingering. Bit by maddening bit, he deepened the kiss, following the pattern of her yielding; he stroked her lips and her tongue, let her sweet, intricate flavor fill his mouth and nose and memory. With his thumb he circled the delicate skin of her inner thigh, just above the knee, in infinitely slow circles, as if he had all eternity to make love to her.

Her mouth began to move with his, to find the rhythm of the dance. He felt the slow unwinding of her muscles as she gave herself up to it, accepted his touch, accepted his intrusion beneath her clothing. "Trust me," he said again, moving his lips back along her jaw, securing her against him with one hand, meandering his way up her thigh with the other, feeling utterly confident and powerful now, every nerve in his body trained on the vital task at hand.

Her skin felt indescribable beneath his fingertips; no silk had ever formed a weave this fine, this delicate, this warm and living. He found the edge of her drawers and slipped his fingers beneath them, schooling himself to patience, drawing out each moment, hardly daring to reach his objective.

Her head dropped into his shoulder. "Finn, *please*."

"Hush." His finger found the slit at the bottom of her drawers, slippery already, tiny curls springing against his touch. "You beauty," he whispered into her hair. "You lovely thing." His cock strained toward her, but he marshaled his ferocious concentration into the movement of his finger instead, the sensation of her slick, intimate skin, each precious detail of her composition imprinting itself on his brain.

She was gasping, sobbing into his shoulder; her fingers dug deeply into his back; her body rocked against his. With his thumb he found her tiny bud, that perfect cluster of nerve endings tucked under its protective hood, and began to circle it with slow deliberation. He imagined the way the sensation would burst along the pathways to her brain, setting off chemical reactions, leading to an ultimate eruption of pleasure; all the glorious science and mystery of her body, taking place by his own hand. "Let yourself go," he crooned. "Let me show you. It's all right. Don't fight it, darling, ah, precious love, that's it. Let it all go." He sensed her building response, the crescendo of sensation coming to a peak inside her, and moved a bit faster, a bit harder, murmuring all the while into her ear.

She cried his name, almost anguished, her body poised and shuddering in his arms. He slipped one finger inside her and absorbed the fluttering contractions of her orgasm. Shut his eyes against the wonder of her.

His. She was his, now. He would make her his, show her how perfectly they fit together. Would make her see, would make her believe her own beauty.

She gave a last tremor and went limp upon him, her face buried in his neck.

He held her for the longest time, savoring the way her breath heaved, the way her pulse knocked against his. The sunlight had found its way through the window at some point during the last tumultuous half hour, and the air itself seemed luminous, touched with gold. He watched the dust drift drunkenly in the light and felt, through the agony of his own withheld release, a most profound contentment settle inside him.

Hers. He was hers, body and soul.

She stirred at last, curling her fingers into his jacket.

"All right?" he asked.

"Thank you," she said, raising her head and avoiding his gaze. "That was lovely."

He let his right hand slide back down her leg, leaving a trail of moisture along her skin. "That, my love, was only the beginning." He straightened her petticoats and her skirt, slid her bodice back up her arms and into place, buttoned her up. He reached behind her for her hairpins on the table. With one large hand he gathered her hair, twisted it into a knot, and held it there while he stuck the pins, one by one, into place. The rich scent of her arousal drifted into the air between them.

"Thank you," she said again, in a whisper.

He bent forward and brushed a kiss along her lips.

"Very good, then, darling," he said. "I'm off to mend that tire."

He picked up his cap and gloves and found his mending kit, and then he ducked through the doorway and across the meadow, ballocks aching to end the world.

FIFTEEN

Only the beginning.
    What on earth did he mean by that?

She stared at the door in stunned disbelief. Had it all really happened? Had he just lit her body into a Roman bloody candle and then *left*? To mend his *tire*?

The beginning of *what*?

She slid off the table. Her legs nearly buckled beneath her, as if Phineas Burke had somehow managed to remove her bones as well as her capacity for rational thought.

She wouldn't put it past him.

Only the beginning.

She cast her eyes about the room, now flooded in sunlight. It must be nearly noon. How much time had passed? A fog seemed to have seeped through her brain, hampering its normal course of activity, so that the images striking her eyes took some time to work their way through her faculties. Said faculties, at the moment, focused instead on the raw, delicious throb still radiating from between her legs, on the feeling of his fingers there: a phantom sensation, the way amputees were supposed to feel a missing limb for months and years after its removal.

Two thoughts arose, disembodied and simultaneous. First, she wanted those fingers back, as soon as possible, and the man to which they were attached.

Second, she was alone in Phineas Burke's private workshop, with at least half an hour to herself before he could be expected back.

She wanted very much to concentrate on the first thought. It was pleasant and simple and perfectly understandable, this longing for his presence, especially after the monumental pleasure he'd just worked on her body. She was a woman of child-bearing age, after all; nothing more natural than physical desire, nothing more delightful than contemplating its execution.

But the second thought kept poking through, dark and insidious.

What if there *were* something here that might help the Manchester Machine Works?

No. It was horrible, disloyal even to think it, after what they'd just shared.

But wasn't this why she'd come here in the first place? Passion was all very well, but men soon recovered from passion, even noble-minded men like Phineas Burke. In a month, in a year, where would she be? Still destitute, her sister still unmarried, her life an unrecognizable ruin of its former self. No means of supporting herself, no means of finding her way.

She looked around her in despair. It was impossible. What use could Finn's workshop provide to a manufacturer of steam automobiles?

Still, he'd made a breakthrough with his battery, and an important one. Perhaps she could convince William Hartley to do the same, to turn to electrics if he hadn't already. If the advantages of electric power were obvious to her, a mere layman, they must be sound enough.

She only needed the company shares to rise in value. Only needed to sell them at a decent price and have her money back, so she could return with Abigail to London and her salons, to the life that had always defined her. To the luxury of footmen and decent French wine and fine dresses, to the duty of settling her sister in life, to the feeling of being rich and important amongst the richest and most important people on earth.

To the feeling that she mattered.

To the feeling that she was safe and whole and invulnerable once more.

She wouldn't steal anything, wouldn't pass on information

directly. That would be wrong. She would only . . . study. Learn. Come to her own conclusions, and then write to Mr. Hartley with her advice. Nothing at all that would harm Mr. Burke.

And then . . . and then perhaps she could have both. She could have her comfortable place in London society, and Finn as her lover, coming to her bed in the evening, after everyone else had left. They could take a discreet cottage in the country, perhaps, and meet there together on little holidays. It would be idyllic. She'd make it all up to him, lavish him with love and care, cover his beautiful body with kisses. She'd make the best mistress a man had ever had, and never cost him a penny. She might even help him with his work. For as long as he wanted her, for as long as he desired her, he could have everything she had to give him.

Her hands were gripping the edge of the worktable in an iron hold. She released them with conscious effort and looked around the room. He must have notes, papers of some kind. Where would he keep them?

She drifted to the cabinet and the long table next to it, against the wall. Cylinders, bottles, boxes illegibly labeled, the gas ring over which he'd made her tea. No papers of any kind, perhaps because of the fire hazard.

She turned around. The worktable, of course, was clear of everything except her hat and her virtue.

The lamp table held only the kerosene lamp.

The pile of spare tires, the empty blocks where the automobile had sat, the chests stacked neatly upon one another, across the room . . .

Something caught her eye atop the chests. They sat apart, in a shaded corner where the sunlight couldn't quite reach. Good, solid English oak, the kind once used to make English ships, to withstand cannon fire and hurricanes.

She walked toward them, briskly and with purpose. A stack of papers sat upon the nearest, topped by the envelope she'd handed him a few days ago. The letter from his mother, from the infamous Marianne Burke. She brushed her hand over the tidy copperplate handwriting and set it aside.

Beneath the personal letter lay papers, covered in the same unreadable scrawl she'd seen on the box labels. Finn's handwriting, she supposed. She hesitated for an instant, her hand hovering atop the stack.

She closed her eyes.

Her body still seethed, still vibrated from the force Finn's fingers had unleashed, that engulfing wave of physical pleasure that had lapped into every tip and corner of her. Her knees still wobbled, her breath still felt new and quick in her lungs. Behind her eyelids, she could still see him, his hair lit into golden flame from the sun, his green eyes looking up at her with tender warmth.

With trust.

Let me show you, darling. Let me show you what sort of woman you really are.

She opened her eyes and looked down at the topmost page. Notes, mostly, with drawings and diagrams scattered throughout. None of it made much sense to her. His handwriting was too difficult. Small, hasty letters, as if his hand had trouble keeping up with his brain. She could just make out the title: *Lead-Acid Battery (improv 4 Mar 1890).* Or perhaps the 9th of March; the number had an odd curve to it that might have gone either way.

I've known any number of selfish women in my life, Alexandra, and you're not anything like them.

She closed her eyes again.

When she opened them, she looked not at the stack of Finn's notes. Instead, she reached for the letter, the letter from his mother, and put it back in its place, obscuring all the arrows and drawings and the quick black handwriting. Finn's handwriting. She smoothed the creamy envelope with her fingertips and wondered what she was like, this woman who had given birth to beautiful Finn, who had raised and loved him in a cottage in Richmond.

Another way. There had to be another way. She was clever, resourceful. She would think of something that had nothing to do with Finn and his workshop and his illegible notes. Perhaps if she wrote to her nephew and told him to stop his nonsense and give up steam engines, or perhaps if she actually attended a board meeting for once and used her vote as a shareholder . . .

The back door rattled.

For a few seconds, the sound didn't quite register, so deep in concentration she'd become. It only jangled at the back of her mind, an annoyance.

"Hullo there," said Finn. "What are you up to?"

She jumped from the chair and hid the papers behind her dress. "Oh! You're back!"

"Yes, I'm just opening up the carriage doors. I won't be a moment." He frowned. "What have you got there?"

"Nothing. Nothing at all. I mean," she added, realizing that she was making things worse, "just a few papers. Your notes, I think. I was curious. About the battery."

A smile spread across his face. "Were you, now?"

"Well, I did help you fix it, after all."

"So you did." He turned to the carriage doors at the back and unbolted the center. "Were you able to read my notes at all? My assistant back in England finds them impossible."

"Not very well." She watched the easy movement of his shoulders, his arms, as he spread the doors wide, letting in a gust of fresh air, already warm from the morning sun and heavy with the fragrance of blossoms from the apple trees nearby. The automobile sat just outside, paint gleaming in giant pools of reflected light.

"Then take them back to the house with you, if you like." He turned his head in her direction and tapped his temple with one finger. "All in my head now anyway. I'd be happy to explain things, if you find yourself stuck. Or can't decipher my scribbling, which is more likely." He said the last words over his shoulder, as he went back out through the carriage doors and braced himself against the right-hand side of the machine, next to the steering tiller. With one hand on the tiller, he pushed the motor-car inside, rolling past the doors and into the space before the blocks. "There we are. All in."

He reached inside, presumably to set the brake, his long, beautiful body stretched out before her in its sturdy English tweeds. Her breath stopped in her throat.

Are you, Lady Morley? Are you in love with my friend Burke?

He turned to face her. "Are you all right, Alexandra?"

She gathered herself. "I'm quite all right. I'm splendid, as

you very well know. It's you who . . . You must be tired.
Exhausted. You should go back to your room and rest."

He extended one arm to her, and she couldn't resist, couldn't
resist going to him and laying herself against that warm, broad
chest and feeling his arms enclose her. "I'm sorry, darling.
You're quite right; I'm completely done in. Would you mind
terribly if I left you to yourself?"

"Not at all." His woolen jacket felt comfortably scratchy
beneath her cheek. She closed her eyes and absorbed the sensation. Memorized it, just in case.

His hand stroked along the back of her head. "Will I see you
later tonight?"

"At dinner, of course." Her belly fluttered.

He spoke softly. "And after?"

"It's dangerous. Everyone will be about, Wallingford and my
sister and the rest of them . . ."

He shrugged beneath her. "If you'd rather not . . ."

"No! I do . . . I want . . ." She swallowed. She wanted everything. She wanted him, all of him, every last ounce to fill the
great emptiness inside her. "May I . . . if you're not too tired . . .
I might perhaps stop by your room . . ."

His arms tightened around her. "No. If anyone's going to be
lurking about, it should be me. If you're caught . . ."

"I won't be caught. Your room's right by the back staircase.
No one will see me."

His breath warmed her hair. She could feel the beat of his
heart through all the layers of shirt and tweed between them.

"If you're certain," he said at last. "If you're quite sure."

She pulled back from his arms and met his gaze steadily.
"I've never been so sure of anything, Mr. Burke."

His thumb brushed along the line of her lips. "Then, Lady
Morley, I'll be waiting for you."

A voice burst through the warm stillness. "Signora Morley!
At last!"

Alexandra looked up in dazed bewilderment. Her eyes ached
with concentration and her head swam with Aristotle. Several
seconds passed before she remembered that she was in Italy, in

the room she had begun, euphemistically, to call *the conservatory*; and that the woman addressing her was Signorina Morini.

An agitated Morini, headscarf askew and hands wringing the air. "Signora! The eggs!"

Alexandra blinked. "The eggs?"

"The eggs, the blessed eggs! They are gone!"

"The *blessed* eggs?" She frowned. "Do you mean the eggs from yesterday, the ones the priest . . . did that sort of . . ." She made a motion with her hand.

"Yes! The blessed eggs! They have been stolen!"

"Stolen! Oh, come now, signorina. Surely not. Why would anyone steal such . . . such saintly eggs? It would be blasphemous, wouldn't it?"

Morini's eyes narrowed. "Is that Giacomo. *He* is not being afraid of blasphemous."

"Ah yes. The infamous Giacomo. He does seem a troublesome sort of fellow." Alexandra set her book on the table next to her and steepled her fingers. "But why on earth would he steal your eggs?"

Signorina Morini flicked her hand. "He did not steal the eggs himself, oh no. He had the men of the stable do it. Because of the cheeses."

"The cheeses?"

"Is necessary to put the *pecorino* to ripe in the stables. Is the tradition. Now, this year, the men of the stable say it is too much trouble. *I* say, is Giacomo." Morini wagged her right index finger in emphasis.

"*Giacomo* is too much trouble?"

"No, no, the *cheeses* are being too much trouble," Morini said impatiently. "To the men of the stable. Is the smell, they say. Giacomo, he stirs the pot. He tells the men, go to the castle, take the eggs. Tell the women we are keeping the eggs until the cheese is take away."

Alexandra leaned forward and set her elbows on her knees, the better to rub her temples. "Does he know the eggs are sacred?"

"He knows," Morini said, in a bitter tone. "He is not caring."

"Oh, an atheist! Splendid. One needs a bit of variety. I do hope he doesn't break the eggs on purpose. Imagine!"

Morini looked at her in horror. "Break the eggs!"

"I do beg your pardon. Only thinking out loud." Alexandra tossed her a reassuring smile. "Of course, I see it's a great problem indeed. But I'm afraid I don't fully understand these matters. Why would your Giacomo begin all this trouble?"

The woman heaved a great sigh and crossed her arms. "He is disappointing."

"Oh, dreadfully so. I quite agree with you. All because of cheeses, really! I've never been so disappointed in a man. Not in some time, anyway."

"No, I mean *he* is disappoint. He . . . he has disappointment."

"Ah." Alexandra paused respectfully. "Crossed in love, I expect?"

Signorina Morini ducked her head. "Yes."

"Oh! With *you*?"

The housekeeper looked up again with fierce black eyes. "Is long ago. Is finish! But Giacomo, he . . ." Her hands flailed helplessly.

"He isn't over it?" Alexandra guessed. "He's made a vow to harass the kitchen staff for all his days?"

"Yes, yes! All those things. Is terrible, milady. The things I am suffering. And you!" She leaned forward and spoke in a loud confidential whisper. "Is Giacomo who sends the people to Signore Burke, when you are being there. Is Giacomo who sends the great duke to the orchard last night."

Alexandra took in an outraged gasp. "He didn't! He wouldn't!"

"Yes!" Morini nodded briskly. "He hates the lovers. He hates the women. He tries to make you and your friends to leave."

"Well, I won't have it!" Alexandra sprang from her chair. "The nerve of the fellow! I shall tell him straightaway exactly . . ."

Morini stepped backward. "No, no! Is not . . . is not possible."

"And why isn't it possible, I should like to know?" Alexandra's veins flooded with anger. Not only had the man abducted the eggs, over which Alexandra felt a certain maternal protectiveness, but he'd set Wallingford on her! On purpose! The act demanded vengeance of the most medieval kind.

"Is not possible." The housekeeper was emphatic.

"I protest it *is* possible. *I* am the mistress here, after all. I won't be plotted against by my own servant!" She began to pace across the room. "Have we a dungeon here? Is it sanitary?"

Morini made a nervous adjustment of her headscarf. "Perhaps . . . perhaps it is better if I am speaking to Signorina Abigail."

"Abigail? Miss Harewood? What on earth?" Alexandra stopped her pacing and turned to face the housekeeper. "She has no sense of authority *whatsoever.*"

"I speak to her. She is . . . she is knowing the men of the stable. She can tell them, we take the cheeses back to the attics. They give the eggs to us. Is all happy again." Morini turned to the door.

"Now wait just a moment, signorina," Alexandra said, in her most commanding tone. "You just described this to me as the greatest crime in history, and all of a sudden you're standing down. That's not at all cricket."

Morini's head swiveled. "Cricket, milady? Like the insect?"

"Fair, I mean. It's not fair. Because cricket is a sport, an English sport, that requires a sort of strict adherence . . . oh, never mind. The point is, you've changed your mind, and I should like to know why." Alexandra planted her feet firmly on the wooden floor and regarded the housekeeper with unswerving authority.

The woman sighed deeply and sank into the opposite chair. Her face seemed to wilt, to take on a faded translucence, blurred at the edges. "You must understand, signora, we are living here many years. We are fighting; we are loving. The men of the stable and the field, the women of the house and the garden. The English, the visitors, is making things different. Is . . . is . . ." She looked at her palms, spread open in her lap.

"Is upsetting the order?" Alexandra asked.

"Yes! The cheeses, I am maybe a little wrong, putting the cheeses in the stable. The maids, they do not like the climb to the attic, and I am feeling . . . is so good, to have the women in the castle again, just as . . ."

"Just as?"

"Just as in the old days, the long-ago days."

Alexandra cleared her throat. "Was there a Signora Rosseti, then?"

Morini looked at her sharply. "Yes. But is a very long time

ago. I am forgetting . . . I am hoping . . . But is too much, the cheeses. I send Signorina Abigail, she speaks to the men, it is done. We have the eggs again."

"I am quite capable of undertaking negotiations," Alexandra began.

"No!" The housekeeper stood up abruptly from her chair. "No, signora. Is better sending Signorina Abigail. The men, they are liking her. She is milking the goats, watching the *pul-cini*, the little chickens."

"Yes, quite. Perhaps you're right." Alexandra glanced down at the papers on the table. "I'm rather occupied, at present, in any case. But this Giacomo. I really can't allow . . ."

"No, signora!" Morini shook her head vigorously. "I am taking care of Giacomo. I know Giacomo. I am speaking without thinking, telling you these things. Is the anger that speaks. Now is nearly dinner. You go to dinner, you see your so-handsome Signore Burke, you go to his room when the moon is rising . . ."

"What! What do you know of that?" Alexandra stared at the woman in full astonishment. Had she been eavesdropping? Had Finn said something to her, asked for her help?

Signorina Morini raised one finger to her lips and smiled beneath it. "I know everything, signora. I am giving you a little of wine, a little of bread, a *torta* of almond. I am making sure the hall is empty. You are never worrying. You are only . . . loving."

Alexandra bit her lip. "Look here, Morini. That's not at all necessary. Really, I've no idea at all what you mean." But the confidence of authority was missing from her voice.

Signorina Morini tucked her headscarf securely and winked. "You are never worrying. In this castle, signora, I am the mistress." She turned to leave.

"Wait, signorina! One more thing."

The housekeeper turned her head, one hand on the door.

"Abigail said something to me yesterday about a curse. A curse on the castle."

Morini's expression turned to stone. "The curse, signora?"

"Yes. Dastardly Englishman and so on. The thing is, Abigail's quite young and impressionable, and I'd appreciate it . . ." She cleared her throat. "Well, it might be best if you didn't tell her such stories, in the future."

One of Morini's hands smoothed her apron. "No, signora. Of course not."

"It *is* all a story, isn't it, Morini?"

The housekeeper regarded her for a second or two, and lowered her eyes. "A story, signora. Nothing more."

She turned once more and left the room.

SIXTEEN

The basket had appeared inside her door, as if by magic, while Alexandra was bathing after dinner, and it weighed down her arm as she stole her way down the narrow back hallway. It was covered with a blue-checked cloth and filled with all the bounty of Signorina Morini's larder. Including the almond cake, which Alexandra knew to be ravishing.

Moonlight spilled through the ancient windows, illuminating the worn stone staircase at the end of the hall. In the pale glow, it might have been centuries ago, and she some ruthless Medici princess, off to meet her lover on the stroke of midnight. Such a convenient little staircase. How many other women had traveled this same route, for this same purpose? Had slipped up these stairs in stocking feet, hearts pounding, veins pulsing with decadent anticipation?

Perhaps even the young lady Abigail had been talking about yesterday. The one who'd been cursed.

Not that she believed in curses.

In a moment, in an instant, she would be in Finn's arms. His kiss would cover her lips. She would see him at last, know him at last, every contour of his body.

Dinner had been torture. She'd walked into the dining room to find Finn, and only Finn, standing there with a glass of grappa in one hand and a letter in the other.

They'd stared at each other in horror.

Hello there, she'd said, and *Good evening, Lady Morley*, he'd replied, with a slight bow, and then the kitchen maids had arrived with platters of roast lamb and Wallingford had stormed in with lurid tales of the cheese wars (Abigail had apparently employed infamous methods to secure a sweeping victory for the women of the household staff against the men of the stable) and they were able to sink into their seats without being noticed.

She'd done her best to keep up appearances (*I daresay, Your Grace, if you should take a turn with Miss Harewood's goats, you might find them equally as agreeable as the geese*) but Finn had sat there in absent silence, not a word escaping his mouth except to trouble Lord Roland for the pepper, which only made her want him more. Made her envy the wineglass as his lips parted to drink from it. Made her want to leap across the table and into his lap, from where she would feed him bits of airy *panettone* with her own hand and lick the crumbs from his skin.

When the final dish had been cleared, he'd risen at once from the table and bid them all a good evening with such arctic formality he'd nearly frozen the potent dessert coffee in its cups. Only the split-second lingering of his eyes on her own had stopped her from impaling him on a sugar spoon.

The memory made her hand clench around the handle of the basket.

A few steps from the top, she paused, listening. Signorina Morini had promised her an empty hallway, but she was hardly about to stake her all on the ability of an Italian housekeeper to keep the Duke of Wallingford from crashing around the corner just as she raised her hand to knock on Phineas Burke's bedroom door.

Silence met her, so profound she could hear the pulse of blood in her own ears. From some distant corner came a muffled scraping; the maids, probably, putting the kitchen to bed. Alexandra drew in a fortifying breath and climbed the final steps.

She nearly faltered as she raised her hand to tap the old impassive wood of his bedroom door. The act reminded her of last night's disappointment. What if he'd changed his mind, decided she wasn't worth the risk? What if he were back down in his workshop, fiddling with his beloved machine?

The door moved beneath her fingers, and a large, blunt-tipped hand emerged to draw her inside the room.

"This is madness," Finn said. "You shouldn't have come." His hand remained in hers, warm and firm. She'd forgotten his height; he seemed to tower above her, the leaf green color of his eyes softened by the candlelight and his ginger hair sticking in odd directions, as if he'd been thrusting his fingers through it. He was in his shirtsleeves, the cuffs rolled halfway up his forearms, the white cotton emphasizing the sturdy breadth of his shoulders.

She let the basket slip from her fingers and placed her hands on his chest. All around them flickered the golden light of Signorina Morini's best candles, thick white beeswax tapers, a dozen of them at least. "Were you hoping I wouldn't?" she asked. Her voice prickled in her chest.

With one hand he touched her hair then cupped the side of her face. "No. I was praying you would, God help me. You've no idea how much."

"Really? You seemed so indifferent at dinner."

"Alexandra." His voice was low, intimate, reproachful. "You must know better than that, by now. You must know what it means when I'm quiet."

She gazed up at him and met the penetrating intensity of his eyes, this time without flinching. "Yes, of course I do. You're no more indifferent than I am." His chest glowed with heat beneath her fingers. She wanted to sink herself into it, to surround herself with him.

He didn't reply, only lifted his other hand to capture her face and brought his mouth down to hers. An eager kiss, an impatient kiss. The rhythm of his lips went straight through her body in long licks of flame, melting her core, melting her wits, until all she had left was sensation: the taste of sweet wine in his mouth, the hard shock of his body against hers, the scent of his soap and the faint lingering traces of leather and oil. She heard a dark, satisfied growl and realized it came from her own throat.

Her hands reached higher to grip his shoulders, his neck, anything to secure herself to him, and all at once she was swinging upward in his arms, his mouth still plundering hers, and he was carrying her across the room to lay her on the bed.

She had no chance to regain her wits, no chance even to take in her surroundings. He followed her, planting his knees on either side of her calves and his hands on either side of her head, like a beast of prey, and kissed her again, on and on, as if he meant to spend the rest of his life like this, his lips and his tongue mingling with hers.

She ran her fingers up his neck and around the firm line of his jaw and up to his cheeks. His skin felt smooth, sleek, newly shaved. "You're so beautiful," she whispered, "so marvelous. Let me see you, Finn. I want to see you. I want to know you."

He smiled a little and drew back, allowing her to prop her head up against the pillows. His long arms still bracketed her, and though his features, backlit by the candles, were shadowed and inscrutable, she felt she had never seen him so clearly. "Yes, beautiful," she said softly, and moved one hand to his collar to unbutton his shirt.

His eyes rolled. "Blinded by passion, I see," he said, and kissed the tip of her nose.

She didn't answer. She was concentrating on the buttons, on the skin of his chest appearing before her, inch by inch. She'd never really seen a living man's chest; Lord Morley had always worn his decorous nightshirt, and her only glimpses of true masculine architecture had been through pictures and statues. Of course, these were idealized models, works of art. She didn't really expect Phineas Burke's chest to look as if it belonged to a Greek god. She didn't need it to. She was already mad for him.

But still. A lady could hope.

His skin was pale beneath the shirt, beneath the spreading V, and nearly hairless. Her fingers brushed against the light scattering of red gold along his breastbone, pulled impatiently at the fine white cotton of his shirt, and freed it from his trousers. She worked quickly now, with both her hands, nearly ripping the last button free, and with a sigh of relief she drew the shirt over his shoulders.

He was perfectly made, in lean, precise proportion, his muscles flat and hard and spare and his skin pale gold in the candlelight. Her hands traveled in wonder across the width of his chest, around the curve of his shoulders, up the angled cords of his neck. He dipped his head to press a kiss against her palm, his eyes never leaving hers, and she felt weightless, boneless, floating atop the soft cushion of the mattress in some dizzy haze of bemusement. Was she really here? Was she, Alexandra Morley, really lying on this bed, running her bold hands across Phineas Burke's bare skin?

What on earth had she done to deserve him?

He bent his head and kissed her again, gently this time, and she felt his hand moving across her chest, cupping her breast through the material of her dress. She'd worn a loose gown, free of all the tight lacing and decoration of her formal evening attire, and his lips hardened as he realized how little lay between his hand and her flesh. "You're a seductress, aren't you, darling," he murmured, and his hand slipped around her back to her buttons, fumbling impatiently against the bedclothes.

Giddy laughter bubbled up inside her. "Stop. You'll never get them like that." She struggled upward against the pillows and turned around. Her hair had come loose from its pins, and she lifted the heavy mass from her shoulders as his fingers grasped at the fastenings of her dress.

"Why on earth couldn't you have worn a dressing gown?" he muttered. His hands were heavy and impatient, almost tearing the buttons from their holes. All signs of scientific detachment had fled him.

"Because if I'd been caught in the hallway in my dressing gown, I'd have had a devil of a time trying to explain it." The bodice loosened and brushed against her sensitized skin, sending shivers down her body.

"You're shaking again," he said, more softly, and his hands slowed. She closed her eyes and felt his breath stir her hair, his fingers graze her spine.

"I can't help it," she whispered, and it was true. Desire and fear and anticipation coiled together in her belly, indistinguishable from one another. She'd never been so nervous, not even on her wedding night. That had been formal and sanctioned and proper, no more strange than the experience of standing before the altar, and Lord Morley had been nothing like the man in bed with her now. She'd been clothed, and he'd been clothed, and it had all been quite safe. A ritual.

This was something else. This was unknown and thrilling and illicit; this man was young and brilliant and handsome. He wanted to give her pleasure, *would* give her pleasure, by some mysterious means she hardly knew how to imagine. She would be naked, bare, exposed; so would he. They would lie together as man and wife, except that they weren't; he would clasp her afterward in his arms and hold her while she slept. All these things would happen in the next few hours. By daybreak she would know them all.

He seemed to sense her mood. He worked carefully now, his fingers trailing down her spine as he went, and when at last the final button parted and the bodice sagged away from her, he drew his large hands around her waist and upward to cup her breasts, reverently, as if holding a nest of baby birds. "Ah, God, darling," he said in her ear, his voice catching. "You're beautiful, so full and round and perfect." His thumbs brushed against her hardened nipples, and a shudder went through her. She reached her arms upward, behind her, to enclose his head, to spear her fingers through his thick hair.

"I want you, Alexandra," he murmured. "I want to know every inch of you, to sink myself inside you."

She turned then, and pressed her naked chest against his, thrilling in the sensation of his skin on hers. "I want you, too. I want . . ." *I want to be part of you. I want your body inside mine. Your strength, your life, everything. I want you.* She stroked her hands down his body. "Now. *Now.* I don't want to wait any longer." He brushed her fingers away as they tangled in the fastening of his trousers, removing them himself, in rough, impatient jerks, taking off his drawers at the same time, until he returned to her fully naked, his shaft jutting proudly from his body, his long, heavy limbs pressing her backward into the bed. She felt his hand at her hip, struggling with her dress, and she arched her back and closed her eyes as he removed the last of her clothing, laying her body bare before him.

He went still.

"What is it? What's wrong?"

"Nothing." His voice was hoarse. He lowered his head to her breast and drew his tongue over the nipple. Pleasure coursed through her, down to the tips of her fingers and toes, pooling hot and liquid between her legs. "You're beautiful," he said. "This, and this"—his mouth went to her other nipple and sucked, hard, so her entire body lifted from the bed and her gasp filled the room—"and the curve of your waist . . ." His lips trailed down her belly, and his hand, so large it seemed to cover her, settled

along her hip, his thumb brushing at her curls, parting her flesh
with such exquisite gentleness she couldn't breathe. His breath
fanned hot across her skin.

She was shaking, burning. She clutched his head between
her hands and drew him up to her mouth. "Now. Please. *Please*,
Finn. I need you. I can't . . . I can't bear it . . ."

His cock pressed against her, heavy and urgent. She reached
down with unthinking freedom to clasp him in her hand, to
discover this last frontier of his body: forbidden and masculine
and mysterious, and yet so essentially Finn. He let out a low
groan when her fingers found him, when she circled his broad
length, relishing the contrast between silken skin and cast-iron
flesh beneath. He seemed enormous, but then what did she have
to compare him to? She'd never touched her husband's organ
like this. She couldn't say for certain she'd even seen it properly.

Finn's eyelids dropped. His body stilled above her, except for
a faint tremor across his shoulders. In the candlelight, his skin
seemed lit from within, glowing with controlled power as she
learned his shape and texture. He waited in patience for her,
offering himself up to her. She brushed the tip of him against
her inner lips, testing the sensation, the luxurious feel of his
strength against her slickness.

For an instant he dipped his head, as if gathering himself,
and then he looked up again, found her gaze with fierce eyes,
and thrust forward.

She nearly shrieked, so great was the shock of pleasure, of
force perfectly rendered, of fullness after famine. He rocked
against her for a moment, finding equilibrium, working himself
deeper, looking into her eyes with such intensity she thought she
might break apart.

"Sweet Christ," he groaned. "You're tight as a winch."

"A . . . a *what*?" She couldn't think beyond the irresistible
push of his body taking hers. "Is that all right?"

"God, yes." He kissed her and moved his hips against her.
"God, yes, darling. If I can bear it without disgracing myself."

He was so large; he filled her so completely. The deepness
thrilled her. She felt her body stretch and clutch at his length,
felt an indescribable pressure against some madly throbbing
core; she wanted more of it, more of that feeling, more and more
and forever more of him.

She wrapped her legs around him, urged him on with her hands and her lips, and he understood, he responded, he thrust again and again, watched her keenly, adjusted his angle, thrust again, hitting her on the mark with a precision that tossed her head back in shock. She'd never dreamed of pleasure like this. She'd never dreamed, in all the nights she'd lain with her husband, that a man's possession could feel like this. She felt Finn's penetration all the way to her belly, felt him reach far inside her, felt their sinews strain together for more depth, more union, more sensation. Her body wound upward, coiling higher and higher, impossibly high, teetering toward an unknown brink she couldn't quite reach.

"Let go, my love," he said hoarsely in her ear, "marvelous, marvelous girl, you're nearly there, just let yourself go," and at last she soared off the edge, she shimmered; flawless waves of energy rippling through her body, her cry mingling with his. Dimly she felt him pull out of her, shuddering, supporting himself with one arm while his seed pulsed harmlessly onto her belly.

She reached up, still shimmering, and drew him against her, savoring for long, still moments the softness of his hair against her cheek, the heavy weight of his body, the wetness of his essence on her skin.

He came to himself by slow degrees, hardly recognizing his own befuddled brain. Alexandra's arms were wrapped around him, one hand stroking through his hair, her breasts crushed beneath his chest. "I'm sorry," he muttered, lifting himself away. "I meant to have a handkerchief ready . . ."

"Hush. It's all right. It's marvelous; you're marvelous."

He propped himself on his elbow, reached for his shirt, and wiped the smooth white skin of her belly. He wanted to say something, but the sight of her beauty, the idyllic contours of her body, stole his breath.

"It doesn't matter anyway," she said, in a low voice. "I mean you needn't have bothered. I'm barren."

He returned his gaze to her face. She was watching him solemnly, her catlike eyes turned to gold in the candlelight. "What makes you say that?"

She shrugged. "I was married for five years, with never a sign."

"Darling, you were married to an older man. Whose previous two marriages were also childless, if I recall correctly. I daresay you're as fertile as the next woman." He leaned over to kiss her magnificent right breast, as lush and perfect as he'd dreamed, and forgave it unreservedly for the torment of the past several weeks.

"What, Lord *Morley*? How is that possible? Men . . . I mean, it seems . . . well, as I understand it . . ."

"Oh, it's likely enough. All sorts of things can go wrong. Have you never seen a sample of ejaculate under a microscope?" He moved on to the left breast, which was looking lonely and neglected.

It took her a second or two to reply. "Shockingly enough, I haven't."

"It's extraordinary. Some subjects teeming, others quite deserted." He drew back and laid his hand around her breast, admiring the way it overflowed his long fingers. "You certainly *look* quite capable of conceiving. When were your last menses?"

"*What?*" Her eyes flew open.

"Your monthly courses."

She stammered. "I don't . . . how did you . . . a week, I suppose . . . oh, for God's sake, Finn . . ." Her skin remained flushed from arousal, but a fine pink still managed to intensify the blush in her cheeks.

He moved his hand to her belly. "Then I suppose we're safe enough. Once we're in Rome I'll track down proper prophylactics. Withdrawal by itself isn't foolproof, after all; there is some secretion before climax, which . . ."

She rolled over and planted her face in his pillow. "Oh, God. *Scientists.*"

He didn't reply, being rather enjoyably distracted by the sight of her firm, round buttocks curving into the air. An ardent walker, no doubt. Perhaps tennis as well. Who knew that her skirts disguised such a decadent derriere? It was a crime, really.

"Finn?" Her voice emerged from the pillow.

"Yes, darling?"

"You're sounding very matter-of-fact."

"I'm generally a matter-of-fact sort of fellow, my dear, as I daresay you've noticed before." His gaze still lingered lovingly on the arc of her arse.

She turned her head. "What *are* you doing?"

"Admiring you."

She scrambled upward. "Look here, Mr. Phineas Burke. We've just . . . well, we've done the most intimate things together, lovely things, *passionate* things, and I'd really . . . I'd rather appreciate it if . . . well, if you'd *say* something about it. Take me in your arms and tell me how wonderful it all was. How all the other women . . ."

"Not so many."

"Well, how you've never felt anything like it. Even if you have to make it all up."

She looked adorable, all pink and tousled and utterly his. "Oh, is *that* what's the matter?" he said. He reached out, enclosed her with his arms, and brought her down into the pillows with him. "It was wonderful, darling. I've never felt anything like it."

"Thanks frightfully much."

He chuckled. "Glorious. Shattering." He trailed his hand along her arm. "In fact, I'd very much like to have another go, when you're feeling up to it. Are you cold?"

"A little."

"I expect the air feels chill, now that your body's cooling off." He felt for the edge of the sheet and blankets and worked them out from beneath their entangled bodies. "There," he said, spreading them over her. "Better?"

"Much." She tucked her head beneath his chin.

He lay there a moment, working his fingers through her hair, trying to summon the right words. "I realize I'm not particularly glib with women," he began.

She snorted.

"Yes, all right. Thank you. Look, what I mean to say is this: I'm no libertine. I don't take women to my bed on a mere whim, and what happened just now . . . the beauty of it, darling, the beauty of *you* . . . was very special indeed. Unique in my experience." He took a deep breath. "And you should know . . . It's important you know this, you *must* know this . . . My intentions, as I intimated before, in the workshop, are . . . are entirely honorable. Are entirely permanent."

She said nothing, but he could feel the tension hum like a current through her body.

He picked up her hand and brought it to his lips. "Was that sufficient?"

"Yes." She spoke hoarsely. "I . . . you're a darling, Finn. I adore you; I've told you so. But let's not . . ." Her voice broke, cracking through the middle. She pulled her hand away from his mouth and placed her arm across his midsection. "Let's not think so far ahead, shall we? We've months and months left here. Anything might happen."

"You think my sentiments will change?"

"Anything might happen."

He moved quickly, slipping free from her arms and turning over, so he hovered above her, his mouth inches from hers. "Listen to me, Alexandra. Listen closely. I'm not your bloody Wallingford. I'm a constant man. I'm not after swiving women in libraries and that sort of rubbish." He captured her mouth in a tender kiss. "I've found you, darling. Found you alone, only you, and I don't intend to let you go."

"You don't know me," she whispered. "If you knew me, you wouldn't say that. You don't know what I'm capable of. I'm not the right woman for you, Finn."

"Yes, you are. You're clever and brave, full of wit and life and strength."

"And vanity and selfishness."

"No more than the rest of us mortals. Really, Alexandra, what do you think? That I should find myself a weaker woman? One who parrots my words and hides in my shadow and flatters my vanity? Do you think so little of me?" He spoke fiercely, intensely, willing his words to penetrate her.

"That's not what I meant. I'm a creature of society, Finn," she said, looking up at him with bitter eyes. "Conventional to the core. You need someone adventurous, willing to sacrifice for you."

He heard himself laugh. "Look at yourself, darling. Listen to yourself. What other creature of society would take up a remote and inconvenient castle in Italy for a year's academic study? How much more unconventional a woman could I find? One more willing to make sacrifices?"

She struggled upward and took his face in her hands. "That's not why I came to Italy. Not at all."

"But you said . . ."

"Do you want the truth? I'll tell you."

At the word *truth*, a thin layer of frost seemed to crystallize in his chest, stilling his blood. "Tell me what?"

She took in a long breath. "I'm destitute, Finn. Do you hear me? I've scarcely a penny to my name."

He stared at her a moment, at the hard set of her features and the ferocity in her eyes, belying the softness of her voice. Her fingers held his cheeks with painful firmness. "Are you—are you serious?"

"It's true! I gave up my house in London because I had to, because the lease was far beyond my means. I haggled with that fellow Rosseti . . ."

"But that's impossible!" He covered her hands with his and gripped them tightly. "Surely . . . haven't you a jointure of some kind? My God, that villain Morley, did he really leave you . . ."

"It wasn't his fault." Her hands fell away and twisted in her lap, and her eyes followed them. "His nephew invested the money in . . . invested it badly. I can't get it out. I've scarcely fifty pounds a year on what's left."

"Fifty pounds!" The frost in his chest had melted, and now his blood whirred back into motion to feed his reeling brain. There was something important about this information, something that tantalized him with possibility.

"So you see, I'm not adventurous at all. I'm only rusticating, hoping things will improve, so I can return to London and my old life. The life I love, Finn. The life I'm used to, the life I'm good at." She paused and ended flatly: "The life I want."

His jaws worked, trying to take it all in, trying to find the vital hole in her logic. "But Lady Somerton . . ."

"That was only part of the reason."

"Surely not. I've heard tales about that husband of hers . . ."

Her eyes shot back to his. "For a recluse, you're awfully current on London gossip."

"Darling, darling." He took her unresisting hands in his and kissed each one. "I'm sorry for your troubles, dreadfully sorry. I daresay it's been a jolly awful sort of year for you. But don't you see? There's an obvious solution, a quite satisfactory solution."

Her head was shaking, slow and steady, like a pendulum, anticipating him.

He leaned forward and spoke in her ear. "Marry me, darling. God knows I've money enough. Buy a house in town; buy ten of them. Do exactly as you like. You'd be perfectly free from any worry of that kind."

"Stop, stop." She was trembling. A teardrop fell from her face into their entwined fingers. "Don't be ridiculous. I can't marry you. I *won't* marry my way out of this. Not this time, not with you."

His blood fired. "Why *not* me?" he demanded, squeezing her hands. "For God's sake, Alexandra! What does *that* mean? Some other man, perhaps, but not *me*?"

"No! *Not* you!" She looked up at last. Her eyes were red and heavy; tears leaked from the corners. She dashed them away with her hand. "I won't let this be about money! Everything else, but not this. This *one thing*, Finn. I want to keep it precious and sacred and unspoiled . . ."

He gathered up her shaking body against his. "Hush, darling. Hush."

"Not marriage. Not a bargain, a contract."

"Never that."

"I shouldn't have told you. I never meant to tell you."

"Hush, darling. I'm glad you told me. I want everything open between us. No secrets."

She gave a hysterical little laugh.

"Alexandra. Sweetheart. I'll be damned if I let you marry *any* man for money." He set her away, tucked her hair behind her ear, and spoke firmly. "Including me."

Her eyes traveled across his face and stopped at his mouth. "Very sensible," she whispered. "Very wise."

He looked at her tenderly. He saw the way her skin glowed pink from the pleasure he'd given her, the way her eyes cast down, unable to meet his. The way her hair tumbled madly about her shoulders and curled atop her breasts; the way the high curve of her cheekbone gleamed in the candlelight.

He pressed his lips against her forehead.

"You're going to marry me for love," he whispered.

SEVENTEEN

He was serious. He had that look on his face, the same look he wore when he was working on his battery, filled with passion and conviction. She ought to be flattered, she supposed. To be ranked as high as a lead-acid battery was an honor few women, if any, could claim.

He was guiding her downward now, taking advantage of her momentary stupefaction to settle her on her back in the bed. "I realize, of course," he went on, clasping her lips in gentle little kisses, "it's a thoroughly bad bargain for you. Stubborn, taciturn chap that I am, liable to spending days on end in musty workshops and factories. Or, God forbid, laboratories."

Her body stirred, responding to his touch. She couldn't resist him. She put her arms about his neck and closed her eyes.

"Questionable colleagues littering the drawing room at all hours, leaving oil on the upholstery and drinking all your best brandy." He drew his lips along her jaw and blew at her ear.

She giggled. "Surely not."

"No title. No birth. My mother's a scandalous Irish courtesan, no better than she should be, and my father . . . well." He shrugged that off and kissed his way down her neck to her breasts, taking her nipple in his mouth with hungry enthusiasm.

"Your father!" she said, trying to pursue the thought past the delicious rushes of sensation smothering her brain. "Oh, tell me. Who is he?"

He ignored her. "And then there's the physical package. Unpromising, of course. Too long, too lean, head overlarge. Damned gawky youth, I was. A pumpkin on sticks."

"You're beautiful. Magnificent. Oh!"

His tongue flicked into her navel with a lightning jolt to her senses.

"Finally, of course, there's the ginger hair. Unlucky business. Nothing at all to be done about that."

"I adore your hair." She wrapped her fingers around it with a little purr of satisfaction.

"So I quite understand your reluctance to marry me. Most sensible. Levelheaded, even. Though, on the other hand, there *is* this." He kissed his way down her belly and settled himself between her legs.

"What?" she gasped.

"This."

At which point the thinking portion of her brain exploded into a cloud of useless particles, leaving only sensation: the hot slide of his tongue in her intimate flesh, exploring each fold in patient detail. She clutched at his hair, clutched at his shoulders, clutched at a pillow; tried to secure herself to something in the throes of this unbearable pleasure. His tongue circled her slowly, too slowly, driving her beyond madness; his mouth touched her everywhere but *there*, that raw, magical core, the part of her that cried out for him. "Oh please, oh please," she heard herself say, and something glided inside her—his finger, two fingers—and then at last, *at last* his tongue found that locus of sensation and stroked it, expertly and lovingly. Her body jerked and spasmed beneath his mouth, outside all control, but he kept on licking her, steady and constant, the immutable center around which her world spun.

Climax bore down on her like a juggernaut, unstoppable, and when it came she threw her head back and flung the pillow over her face just in time to cover her howl.

He knew what to do: damn him, bless him. At the first throb he stilled his tongue against her, stilled his fingers inside her, let her body ricochet off the gentle pressure to even greater heights.

The waves rolled on and on, gradually diminishing, leaving the most delicious floating languor in their wake. She was only vaguely aware of Finn's body sliding upward, warm and solid; of his mouth covering hers with her own scent and taste. "Mmm," she said, twining her arms about him.

He made a growling noise and went on kissing her, delicately at first, patient, letting her drift to earth by easy degrees. Then his tongue stole deep, hungry, and with gentle hands he turned her over onto the pillow.

"What . . ." She drew in a gasp at the insistent brush of his cock, hard and massive between her thighs.

His breath curled around her neck, her ear. "Trust me, darling. Let me. Let me show you. Let me love you."

He eased himself between her swollen lips, millimeter by exquisite millimeter. She could feel the slickness of his penetration, her own arousal lubricating his passage, and her hips rose upward to take more of him, all of him, until her buttocks nestled intimately into his groin and the skin of his chest brushed along her shoulders. A deep groan came from her throat at the marrow-deep satisfaction of his cock buried so solidly, so snugly inside her, exerting wholly new pressures on her tender flesh. She was surrounded by him, immersed in him, her existence encompassed in the space of their two bodies rocking together as a single united whole.

Impossibly, beautifully, it was rising up again, the excitement and the friction, that now-familiar sensation of her building peak. He seemed to sense the escalating tension inside her. He rose up on his hands and began to thrust, slow, deep strokes in perfect rhythm, tilting himself just so. It was too much; it couldn't be borne, pleasure so intense it was almost painful. She needed to escape, to climax, but he wouldn't let her: He kept on thrusting at that same relentless pace, trapping her on the brink, just short of release.

On and on he went, holding her hostage, while her hands fisted into the bedclothes and the moans spilled from her throat. It might have been minutes; it might have been hours: She lost all sense of time and place, all sense of anything but the slow, infinite beat of his body, the weight of pleasure bearing forever down on her.

Finn. She heard her own impassioned groan as if from a stranger.

Just when she thought she couldn't take it any longer, when she thought she might actually expire from the eternally building crescendo, he quickened his thrusts, slipped his hand beneath their bodies, and pressed his broad palm against her, just above his own sliding flesh.

Release came hard and sudden and gorgeous, sweet relief and mindless exhilaration all at once. Her cry ripped into the pillow. She felt his swift withdrawal, felt him take up his shirt again in an agile gesture, felt him sink gently against her, bracing himself on an elbow and nuzzling at her neck as the spasms receded.

She couldn't move, couldn't think. Every last particle of energy had drained from her body. Her limbs were like lead.

He settled himself behind her in the bedclothes and gathered her up against his body, his hot, damp chest cradling her back, his legs following the bend of hers. "Now, my love," he whispered, his breath rough in her ear, "*now* will you marry me?"

She hadn't planned to sleep, hadn't planned to waste a moment of the few precious hours allowed them, but she found herself emerging from a velvet unconsciousness to a darkened room, all the candles out except one, and Finn's body curled solid and protective around hers, one hand cupped beneath her breast.

"What time is it?" she gasped, fighting upward.

"Shh. Not two o'clock, I should think." His voice was low and soothing. His arms urged her back down in the warm cocoon of blankets and drowsy flesh and the mingled scents of lovemaking.

"You let me sleep," she said accusingly.

"You were exhausted."

"And you've been awake all this time?"

"Darling, I slept until five o'clock this afternoon. I'm as sharp as a dagger point."

She turned in his arms to face him. "I'm sorry. You must have been frightfully bored, lying there."

"Not at all." He kissed the tip of her nose.

"Are you hungry? I've brought a basket from the kitchens. Cheese and bread and wine and the most divine almond cake. It might help to make you sleep."

"I don't want to sleep."

She put her hand to his cheek. "You're an idiot. Go fetch that basket."

He laughed and turned his head to kiss her palm. "As my lady commands."

They ate in his bed, feeding each other, crumbs dropping indulgently into the blankets, and then they made love again with marvelous slowness: shifting positions, tasting and exploring, drawing out the pleasure until at last, when she dissolved into climax, it was hardly more than an intensification of an ages-long simmering of incomparable sensation; when he withdrew and spent himself, it was as if he'd ripped away a part of her own body. *Stay inside me*, she wanted to say, *don't leave*, but that was tantamount to an acceptance of his proposal. Taking his seed inside her meant absorbing the possibility of his child, of a future with him, of marriage.

She must have drifted off to sleep again, because the next thing she knew, she was in his arms, her gown hanging loosely about her body, being carried down the darkened hallway to her room.

"No, don't," she whispered, muzzy headed. "Someone will catch us."

His kiss touched her hair. "I almost hope someone will."

He found her door without direction and tucked her into bed just as the fine gray light of dawn outlined the ragged hills to the east. She remembered his lips on her forehead and the faint scrape of the closing door, and nothing else.

EIGHTEEN

Midsummer's Eve —

Finn couldn't see Giacomo's disapproving gaze, but he could feel it infuse the warm air of the workshop with pious contempt.

After all, he'd grown quite familiar with the sensation over the past two months.

"Come to berate me again for my folly, Giacomo?" he asked, not looking up. He was reinstalling the battery yet again, after still more improvements, and he dared not remove his gaze for an instant.

"Is only trouble, the women," Giacomo muttered.

"Yes, and so you've observed to me on perhaps dozens of occasions now, yet I remain most steadfastly in love with her. So bugger off, if you'll pardon the expression."

"Bugger? What is this?"

Finn made a last clamp of the cable and propped himself up on the edge of the engine block. "A crude term, I'm afraid, referring to a peculiarly British preoccupation with carnal vice. What can I do for you, my good man?"

"Is the letters." Giacomo slapped a few envelopes on the worktable with unnecessary vigor. "Is also a question."

"Oh, Lord, Giacomo. Not another one of your questions. Can't it wait?"

"Is she telling the ladies, the other ladies?"

Finn paused. "No."

"Is she saying to marry you?"

"Not yet."

"Is she saying she love . . ."

Finn pointed the remaining battery cable at him. "Look here, Giacomo. That's quite enough. I'm not in the habit of telling a lady's secrets, and certainly not to a woman-hating fellow like you. I don't know how you've discovered these things, or think you have . . ."

Giacomo sighed. "Is not hard, Signore Burke. I see your face in the morning. I see the light in the window in the night, when the others are dark."

"I often study late."

Giacomo rolled his eyes. "*Study*. Ha. Is that what the English are calling it?"

"We are not calling it anything at all."

"Is only trouble, this *studying*. You will see. One day you will see I say the truth. The women, there is no trusting them."

Finn straightened. Tomorrow was the first day of summer, and though the carriage doors were wide open to the breeze coming down the hillside, the air in the workshop now grew warm and dense by noontime, particularly when the dynamo ran at full pitch, recharging the battery for the usual afternoon trial. He felt a trickle of sweat roll down under his collar and into his shirt. "Lady Morley is a woman of honor," he said. "I'd trust her with my life." He reached with his free arm for the glass of water perched rather precariously on a nearby axle rod.

Giacomo shrugged. "Ah, the lovers, the young lovers. They think they discover everything. They think they discover the great thing no person ever discover before. But I tell you, Signore Burke"—his fist dug into the worktable—"is not possible for woman to be true. Always, she is fuckle."

Water sprayed from Finn's mouth in an elegant triangle. "Fuckle?"

Giacomo gestured in the air. "She is fuckle, *mobile*, like the wind in the springtime."

"Like the . . . ? Oh. Yes." Finn set the glass down and dabbed at his chin with his sleeve. "I believe you mean *fickle*, old chap. *Fickle*."

"Think of the song, Signore Burke." Giacomo's voice slid into a surprisingly lyric tenor. "*La donna è mobile* . . . Is true."

"Yes, but as it turned out, she wasn't fickle at all. That's the point of the aria, after all. The duke was the fickle one. Irony, my good man."

Giacomo frowned. "I am confuse."

"The opera, Giacomo. *Rigoletto.* Your aria's from *Rigoletto.*"

The man pulled himself up with dignity. "I am not seeing the opera. I am only hearing the song from the men."

"Well, it's a charming tale, I assure you. Delightful sort of yarn, except perhaps for that sobering bit at the end, when she dies for the cad. In any case, it quite disproves your point about women. Noble to the core." Finn bestowed a smug smile upon the groundskeeper.

Giacomo's eyes narrowed. "So you think, Signore Burke. So she says to you." He picked up the small stack of envelopes from the table and brandished them menacingly. "But perhaps you read the letters. Perhaps you see what I am meaning."

"Oh, for God's sake, Giacomo. How can you possibly know what's in my letters? And what on earth have they to do with Lady Morley?"

Giacomo returned him the same smug smile he'd just bestowed. "When you are not busy, signore. When you are having the time."

Finn opened his mouth to reply just as Alexandra swept through the open carriage doors, blue skirts gusting about her legs in the sun-scented wind. "Good morning, Finn. How's your battery coming along?"

Giacomo's smile melted into a scowl of glowering proportions. "I leave now. Good day, Signore Burke. Signora Morley."

She only raised her eyebrows as he brushed past, ignoring him in her stately way. She and Giacomo had never been on what might be called speaking terms. "Everything all right?" she asked Finn, placing her hands on her hips.

"Yes. Yes, of course. Battery's nearly in. I'd greet you properly, darling, only I'm rather attached to the cable at the moment."

She laughed. "Then I suppose I'll have to do all the greeting," she said, and crossed the room to plant a kiss on his lips over the engine block. "Mmm. You smell divine. All oily and sweaty. I adore you this way. You're in your element."

"*You're* my element, but I'm flattered nonetheless. Could you perhaps toss me the clamp on the bench over there?"

"With pleasure." She found the clamp and slipped it into his waiting hand. "I meant to bring the post, but it's already disappeared. Wallingford, no doubt, rifling through your correspondence in desperation. I'm certain he suspects."

"He's always suspected, darling. It's just that he's given up caring anymore. Troubles of his own, I gather. In any case, Giacomo's brought the post already. There." He stepped back from the engine, wiped his hands on a reasonably clean rag, and captured his lover around her waist. "And *now*, my dear, I'll greet you properly."

She responded ardently, as she always did, with her gurgle of laughter and her soft figure curving into his and her face reaching upward for his kiss. As springtime had advanced, as the sun had mounted high in the hot blue sky and the grapevines had unfurled their leaves in long, undulating rows down the sides of the hills, she'd shed most of her petticoats and loosened her corset, like the rest of the women in the village. Now her body glowed warm and vibrant beneath his hands, a thing of summer; the luxurious swell of her hips teased him with memories of the night before, and all the nights before that. He caught her familiar scent curling around them both, and his body, recognizing all the signs, hardened like the well-conditioned beast it was.

She must have felt him stirring. A little groan escaped her throat and her lips slid across his face to whisper in his ear. "Do you remember what you told me about swiving women in libraries, those months ago?"

"That I'd never even begin to contemplate it, I believe," he said, doing exactly that. He pictured Alexandra bent over a gargantuan lion-footed desk, positioned perfectly under the lamp's soft glow, her round, firm arse beckoning him inward. Or else sprawled naked on a leather-upholstered chesterfield, her hair spilling over her abundant breasts, one leg propped atop the sofa's low back.

Well, he was only a man, after all.

"Mmm." Her hands slid down his body to cup his buttocks,

urging his arousal into her belly. "I don't know about libraries, but I daresay workshops would be perfectly suitable."

"Strumpet. Coming into my sanctum with your lilies and your lascivious ideas, expressly to distract me."

She laughed and pulled back. "You began it. And if you hadn't insisted on denying yourself last night, I daresay you'd have no trouble at all resisting me now."

He took her hands and brought them around front, where he could keep a watchful eye on them. "You're in the exact middle of your month at the moment, darling. I daren't go near you. Or that salient part of me, in any case."

She groaned and pulled her hands from his, covering her face with them. "How on earth do you calculate these things? It's mortifying."

"It's my business to calculate these things, my dear." He kept his words quiet, gentle. "I know enough about a bastard's lot to make quite certain I don't cause another to be brought into the world."

Her shoulders sagged. She parted her hands and peered at him, her face flushed and resigned between the fingers. "And yet, my dear, I'm eternally grateful your own father wasn't so careful."

He extended his long arms and drew her unresisting body back against him. "Only marry me, darling. That's all. It's quite simple."

"You know I can't." Her voice was low and implacable.

"You needn't take a penny of my money. I'll give it all away if you like. Only be *mine*, for God's sake."

"I *am* yours."

She had burrowed her face into his chest, her breath warming the sturdy cotton of his smock until he could feel it against his skin, could still taste it in his mouth: sweet with tea and jammy toast and her own particular essence. His arms tightened around her. "In any case," he went on, more lightly, knowing better than to push her, "what difference is it to you? I made jolly fine work of consoling you last night, after all."

Her back vibrated with a chuckle. "You were splendid. I woke up this morning and instantly thought of a dozen ways I might have reciprocated, had I any remaining faculties after you were done with me."

"Ah. I should very much like to hear them all."

She drew back and touched her finger against his lips. "Not now, I'm afraid. I only came to tell you that I won't be able to assist at the trial this afternoon. This wretched Midsummer's Eve feast tonight. Abigail has the household in an absolute tizzy over it."

He opened his lips and sucked her fingertip into his mouth.

"Mmm. I've been drafted to help with the preparations—oh, that's very nice." She withdrew her finger and traced around his chin and down his neck, leaving a damp track behind. "I shall be in a frenzy of decoration and whatnot all afternoon. Abigail-ish sorts of things, quite impossible to explain."

He frowned. "Exactly what is this feast of yours? Is it for the village?"

"It's Abigail's idea. Signorina Morini says it's an old tradition on the solstice, quite deliciously pagan, though of course the Church now sanctions it and the village priest will be there and all that." She circled her finger around the hollow of his throat, the action absorbing all of her concentration. The innocent touch went straight to his groin and tingled there, almost painfully. "We're going to have masks and torches and music and dancing. All very decadent. You must come, of course."

He thought wildly. "I haven't a mask."

"We're making the masks ourselves, this afternoon. Oh, do come." She looked up and smiled at him with her charming, catlike smile, glimmering eyes tilted upward at the corners. "It will be most dreadfully dull if you don't. Who the devil would I flirt with?"

The thought of a masked Alexandra, dancing in the torchlit midsummer twilight outside the castle, made his heart thud in his chest. "You're to flirt with no one else but me, of course," he said firmly.

"Then you'll be there?"

"I suppose I must. Though my dancing may put you off forever."

"I'll have dragged you into the orchard long before that." She went up on tiptoe to kiss him. "I'm already late. Abigail will be wondering where I am. Do mind the time. You're to be downstairs by eight o'clock, washed and shaved and presentable."

He opened his mouth to ask for more information, like

whether the Penhallows were attending as well, but she had already slipped out of his arms and hurried to the doors. "Good-bye, then! Don't be late!"

Bloody women, he thought. He closed his eyes and concentrated on bringing his raging flesh back under control. Not an easy thing to do, either, considering he'd brought her twice to orgasm last night without so much as a palliative pat to his own organ, which had remained decorously clothed throughout to prevent any fatal indiscretions. Twice, he'd watched her in the throes of pleasure, her head tilted back, her ripe flesh contracting around his fingers, his lips. He could still taste her salty tang, could still smell the erotic musk of her arousal. With a single stroke, he could have taken her, spilled himself inside her, created a life between them, perhaps. Bound her to him for evermore.

But he hadn't. He'd shut his eyes and thought about alternating circuits while her body cooled and the heavy thud of her pulse had returned to normal, and then he'd gathered her into his arms and watched her eyelids drift downward into sleep while he calculated the number of days until he could once more bury his eager cock inside her without much fear that some stray swimmer might find its mark. Calculated the speed at which he could track down the necessary equipment in Rome, and no longer have to deny himself during the peak of her cycle or tear himself away from her at the critical moment.

Actions he found more arduous with every passing week.

No, the stakes were too high for carelessness. He wouldn't trap her into marriage, wouldn't take the chance that she might not allow herself to be trapped. A woman like Alexandra must be won with great care. She must come to him willingly, pledge herself willingly. And it would be worth it, because once she was won, once she had laid her hand in his, she would never let it go. Beneath all her charming, complex, contradictory layers beat the heart of a lioness.

His lioness. Fierce and graceful and seductive . . .

Hell.

Finn's gaze, searching for distraction, fell upon the letters on the worktable, white and glaring in the light from the window. Business correspondence, from the look of it. The reports tended to arrive in clusters toward the second half of the month:

fat summaries of his affairs, responses to his queries, statements of account, contracts needing signature; all gathered together by his man of business with annotations and suggestions. The envelopes had arrived with increasing heft and frequency of late, now that his long-contemplated purchase of the Manchester Machine Works was nearing its final stage.

He'd had his eye on the company for some time. Though he'd focused his own energies on electrically powered vehicles, he thought the Manchester outfit's steam prototype held promise, once the boiler-control issues had been sorted out. More than that, though, he lusted after the works themselves. A few years ago, a fresh capital infusion had allowed the company to build a state-of-the-art factory that was miles ahead of others—miles, indeed, beyond its own current needs—in size and capability and efficiency. Location and transport links were excellent.

And the stock was trading at a fraction of its worth. Ignorant City investors, no doubt, had been scared away by the lack of immediate success without any thought to the value of the physical plant and the whole burgeoning future of automotive transport. Finn's business manager had been completing his due diligence, discreetly, of course, and he was almost ready to begin buying shares.

Finn sat down heavily on the chair and picked up the envelopes. One from Delmonico, rather thin, probably with last-minute instructions for the exposition. A fat packet from his solicitor, marked URGENT, which meant it contained the latest patent applications for his signature. Bankers, of course: no mistaking the indulgent thickness of *that* envelope. Finn opened it and learned that he was still in possession of his fortune, that the sale of British consols with which he had recently instructed them had been effected, and that his pile of immediate cash was more than sufficient to buy the Manchester Machine Works—lock, stock, and barrel—at whatever price its shareholders demanded.

On that note, he lifted the flap of the last envelope in the pile. *My dear Burke*, it began, in Malcolm Gordon's plain and precise black writing, *I have completed my assessment of the shareholder composition as you requested, and have listed on the enclosed sheet the fifteen largest owners of the Company. Most, as you see, purchased their shares some years ago at much higher prices than the current quote, and may well be amenable to private offers of a reasonable nature, which I suggest should be no more than ten shillings, representing a premium of greater than 200 percent on the current price per share . . .*

Finn ignored the rest and turned with interest to the other sheet of paper.

Lord Albert Lindsay, 32,500 shares
Mr. William Hartley, 30,200 shares
Sir Philip Macdonald, 28,350 shares
Dowager Marchioness of Morley, 22,800 shares . . .

The letters seemed to blur together. Finn set the paper down on the table, squared it precisely with the worn wooden edge, and smoothed the creases in the middle.

He rose from the chair and paced to the carriage doors, and then back again. The heat pressed with suffocating strength against his skin; he drew off his heavy smock, folded it, and placed it on the table, next to the paper.

Then he thought better of it and went to hang it in the cabinet.

When he returned, the paper still lay immaculate on the worktable, edges squared, creases smoothed. He sat down before it, thrust his fingers through his hair, and read again.

Her name looked unnatural, written in black ink in his business manager's somber Scots handwriting. It was not her. It was the other Lady Morley, the London lady, salon hostess and society leader. The Lady Morley one read about in the newspaper columns, a stranger.

His nephew invested the money in . . . invested it badly. I've scarcely fifty pounds a year on what's left.

Lord Morley's nephew. Maternal or paternal? What was the family name? Finn scanned the list again.

William Hartley. Of course. He'd forgotten that Hartley's mother was an aristocrat, daughter of the sixth marquis and sister of the seventh; that she'd married a rich City banker back in the days when marrying rich Cits was still something of a scandal. Her son Hartley had put his own fortune into starting Manchester Motor Works, along with those of his partner and motor-enthusiast Lindsay and that brilliant engineer Macdonald. Alexandra's jointure, no doubt, had provided the equity capital required to finance the gleaming new building that Finn coveted with such lust.

Finn leaned back in his chair and stared at the flat ceiling high above him, at the long, meandering cracks in the plaster between the beams. He felt curiously numb, as if the enormity of this information were too much to encompass, too much to understand. He ought to feel some gash down his middle, its ragged edges screaming with pain, but he did not. Only . . . numb. And something else, something large and crushing about his head and shoulders, some black weight.

It might be a coincidence. She might not even know the name of the company in which her fortune had been invested to such spectacular failure. Perhaps she was simply interested in automobiles.

Or perhaps he was the greatest fool alive.

The women, there is no trusting them.

A breeze gusted in from the open carriage doors, carrying the fragrance of the terraced fields: corn ripening in the sun; vines sprouting out thousands of bunches of tiny Sangiovese grapes for the sultry air to enlarge and sweeten; olives still small and hard and green at the ends of their branches.

Finn rose from his chair and went back to the cabinet for his smock. A great deal of work remained before his automobile would be ready for its final trial this afternoon.

NINETEEN

Alexandra held up a mask for a last critical inspection. "I say, it's a shame we didn't save Wallingford's feathers. Think how many of these we might have done."

"Really, Alex, if you'd visit the barnyard occasionally, instead of that musty old workshop of Mr. Burke's, you'd know we've no lack of feathers." Abigail stuffed the glue brush back in its bottle with unnecessary force. "There. That's the last one."

"Mr. Burke's automobile is much more interesting than any of your livestock," Alexandra replied. She ran her fingers across the fine, sleek softness of the feathers edging her mask, imagining how they would tease her skin. How they would tickle Finn's nose when he kissed her beneath the peach trees.

"To say nothing of Mr. Burke himself. Here, Lilibet. This one will do very well for you. Lily-white."

"Oh, for goodness' sake," snapped Lilibet.

Everybody turned to stare at her: Alexandra and Abigail; Signorina Morini, from her seat at the kitchen table, stuffing the last of the olives; Francesca at the hearth, turning the beef on its spit. Lilibet's cheeks had flushed in two large patches of color, and her blue eyes flashed in a most un-Lilibet-like manner.

"My dear cousin," Alexandra said in awe. "Are you well?"

Lilibet thrust herself up from her chair. "I am quite well," she said, and burst into tears and fled from the room.

Alexandra rose to follow her, but Signorina Morini laid a restraining hand on her arm. "Is well. She is wishing to be alone."

"Alone? Where? Why? And where's Philip, come to think of it?" Alexandra demanded, looking about. She hadn't seen the boy in ages.

"Out with Penhallow, of course." Abigail shrugged one shoulder.

"*Of course?* What do you mean by that? Do they go out together often?"

"Really, Alexandra. Where on earth have you been the last few weeks?"

Alexandra sank downward into her chair, looking at the faces around her with penetrating inquiry. Each pair of eyes slid away at the contact. "I see." She picked up her mask. "It seems our wager has become irrelevant."

"Oh, I wouldn't say that," Abigail said cheerfully. "Wallingford's stuck to his guns admirably. No complaints at all from the village girls."

"Well, they wouldn't, would they?"

Signorina Morini cleared her throat. "The olives, they are finish. Signora, signorina. Is time to make ready."

Alexandra tied her mask around her face. "There! Quite ready." She snatched an olive from the housekeeper's platter, earning herself a slap on her knuckles. But the result was worth it. No one stuffed olives like Signorina Morini, with bits of savory herbed sausage meat, or else cheese, or that lovely artichoke paste. Really, she would have to wrangle all the recipes out of the woman before she returned to London.

Better yet, she could bring the Italian with her and install her in the kitchen.

"No, you're not ready," said Abigail. "You've got to put on your costume, too."

Alexandra chewed and swallowed. "Excellent, Abigail. Ha-ha. But really, I must be seeing about that bath." She rose and called out to Francesca. "Has the water been taken up yet?"

"No, really. It's all part of the tradition." Abigail picked up her own mask and tied the long ribbons around the back of her head. "We're to dress like the women from the village and help to serve the food. Everyone will be masked so nobody will know us. Such fun!"

Alexandra clapped her hands. "Marvelous! Splendid lark. Awfully jolly. That is, if I were ten years old again, which I decidedly am not."

"I see. I expect you're afraid Mr. Burke won't be able to pick you out amongst the crowd."

"I've no idea what you mean by that."

"Or that perhaps he might find one of the young village maidens more to his liking . . ."

"That's absurd!" She checked herself. "Yes. I *mean*, of course, absurd that I should care. He may have all the village maidens he likes, as long as he's prepared to pay the forfeit for the wager."

Abigail leaned back in her chair and nibbled at an olive. "Mmm. These are lovely, signorina. Really, I can't wait to see what else you've devised for tonight's festivities."

Alexandra turned her gaze to the housekeeper, who sat smiling beatifically in her chair, arranging olives. She began, belatedly, to sense a current in the air, a current of understanding that seemed to link her sister and the Italian woman.

She planted her hands on her hips. "See here. I really hope you haven't gone out of your way, signorina. I should be deeply sorry to find you've been troubling yourself over matters that *don't concern you*."

Signorina Morini smiled her wise smile and rose from her chair to take Alexandra by the arms. She pressed a kiss on each cheek. "*Bella donna. Bellissima* Signora Morley. Tonight, she is a beautiful night, a beautiful feast. The girls of the village, they say the night of the midsummer has a little of the magic." She leaned closer, so that Alexandra could smell the comfortable scent of baking bread rising from her skin. "You are young, you are beautiful, you are in love. Is magic. Is . . . is *il destino*, destiny. You let the destiny come wherever it is wishing. The destiny, it is knowing what to do."

The clock in the hallway chimed distantly, seven faint rings of its ancient bell.

"How perfectly ridiculous," Alexandra said. "I shan't wear

your silly costume, Abigail. It isn't dignified. Don't think for a moment you can convince me."

This is so undignified." Alexandra straightened her apron and picked up a tray from the kitchen table.

Abigail picked up another tray and began to walk to the door. "Nonsense. You look marvelous."

"Marvelously undignified. At least Lilibet's neckline isn't cut down to her navel. I feel as though I'm presenting my bosom on this platter." She looked downward critically.

"Your necklines are exactly equal. It's your magnificent chest that makes all the difference. Now do come along. Lilibet's out there by herself. And don't eat all the olives on the way."

"I shan't." Alexandra sighed. "They're the only things protecting my modesty at the moment."

She followed her sister out the kitchen and down the hallway to the door.

Outside, in the fading light, the terrace had been filled with long trestle tables and chairs and strings of lights and torches, and at least sixty or seventy laughing people from the village milled about the old gray flagstones in the masks they'd made that afternoon. From some unseen corner, a band of musicians sent lyric music into the warm twilight, briskly rendered, violins and woodwinds and the distinct *oom-pah* of a grandfatherly tuba.

"Just set the platters on the nearest table," Abigail called to her, over the din. "They'll sit down when the first course is in."

Alexandra didn't have time to look for Finn in the throng, didn't have time to do anything but run back and forth with Abigail and Lilibet and Francesca and Maria, setting out food and jugs of wine until the tables were full and the guests, by some unseen signal, piled into their chairs.

"Do we welcome them at all?" she whispered to Abigail, when everyone was seated. She'd just spotted Finn, whose ginger head spiked far above his neighbors, down at the opposite end of one of the tables. He wore a simple black mask and looked rather dashing. He was engaged, she saw, in animated conversation with the woman next to him, whose crimson mask was bedecked with feathers and sequins far exceeding their own efforts this afternoon.

Alexandra narrowed her eyes.

"Of course not. That would give the game away. Don't worry. Signorina Morini and I have it all planned perfectly."

"That's exactly why I'm worried. May I eat now? Or is fasting part of your grand scheme as well?"

"Oh, eat, by all means. Lilibet's saved a seat for you, over there in the corner."

Alexandra looked and saw Lilibet's slender white arm raised in greeting. Philip sat next to her, eyes round and dancing in the torchlight, and a plate full of food lay before the empty seat on her other side.

All very inviting, except that it was all the way across the terrace from Phineas Burke and his charming crimson-masked companion.

"I say, Cousin Alexandra," said Philip, as soon as she sat down, "that's a bully mask. Don't you think I've got a bully mask?"

She examined him. "Without question, the bulliest mask in the history of the world. Is that an eagle feather?"

"Yes, it is. Uncle Roland found it for me. I think Uncle Roland's top-notch, don't you? A damned trump."

Lilibet gasped. "Philip! Where on earth . . ."

"You've hit the nail quite on the head, my dear boy," Alexandra said. "Your Uncle Roland *is* a damned trump. There's no other word for it. Don't you think so, Lilibet?"

"Uncle Roland shouldn't be teaching you such words."

"Uncle Roland took me fishing on the lake this morning. Have you ever been fishing on the lake, Cousin Alexandra?"

"Well, no," she said. "Not for fish, anyway."

A firm kick crossed her shin.

"You should. It's rotten fun. I caught heaps of fish, but Uncle Roland made me put most of them back, the damned scoundrel."

"Philip!"

"But I thought he was a damned trump," Alexandra said.

"Well, he is generally, but . . ."

"Look here, Philip," Lilibet said, "why don't you finish your dinner like a good boy? Then Mama will take you inside and put you to bed."

"Not bloody likely," Philip said. "Not with all the fun out here."

Lilibet bent and whispered in his ear.

"Oh, all right. But sometimes it just slips out, Mama. I'm only five, after all." Philip picked up his fork and stuck it squarely into a stuffed olive. "These are rotten good."

"I'm partial to them myself," Alexandra began, when a shadow cast across her plate. She looked up hopefully.

"Hullo, all," said Lord Roland, unmistakably Lord Roland, his dark gold hair ruffled about his navy blue mask and his smile spreading wide below it.

"You're not supposed to be able to recognize us," Alexandra said. "I was told the costumes would quite confound you."

It was difficult to tell the direction of Lord Roland's gaze beneath the mask, but Alexandra had the impression it dove straight down the front of Lilibet's dress. "I'm gobsmacked, I assure you."

"I've just heard the most horrifying language from Philip's mouth," Lilibet said sternly. "It can't have been yours, can it?"

Lord Roland looked as stricken as was possible in a masked man. "I'm shocked you should accuse me of such a thing. I pay the most scrupulous heed to my words around the boy."

"Nevertheless," said Lilibet.

"Look here," Alexandra said. "I've just had the most cracking idea. Penhallow, why don't you take Philip up to bed, so that Lilibet and I can resume feeding our esteemed guests? I'm sure you have any number of properly edifying bedtime stories for a boy his age."

Philip bounced in his seat. "Yes, yes, Uncle Roland! You can read me the one about Persia! The one with the pirates and the harem girls."

Lilibet's wineglass hit the table with a crash.

A red flush crept downward from the bottom of Lord Roland's mask and spread across his jowls.

"Oh yes," Alexandra said. "That's perfect. I should like to know myself how that one turns out."

So. *Uncle Roland*, is it? How charming."

Lilibet nodded across the terrace to where Phineas Burke's ginger head bobbed obligingly next to his companion. "Tell me, do you mean to marry him?"

"What's that?" Alexandra brought her glass to her lips and drank deeply. They had just set down the desserts at last, sweet cakes and almond macaroons and fruits, and the crowd was growing restless and jolly with all the wine.

"Will you marry him? And don't for God's sake begin all this nonsense about not knowing what I mean."

Alexandra opened her mouth and found she hadn't a word to say.

Lilibet plucked a macaroon from the platter in front of them and placed it on Alexandra's plate. "I think you should. I think he's marvelous for you. Look at you. You're blooming."

"I can't," Alexandra said. She stared at that distant shock of ginger hair, fiery red gold in the torchlight, and her voice, when it emerged, choked painfully at the base of her throat. "I won't. Marriage is a bargain, a contract. You know that as well as I do. I won't take something so beautiful as this and turn it into something sordid. I won't ruin it."

"Is it because of his money?"

Alexandra picked up the macaroon and placed it in her mouth, where it melted sweetly on her tongue, coating her mouth with the rich taste of almond. "It spoils everything, money."

"Do you love him?"

Alexandra's throat closed.

"Because if you do, the money won't matter."

"But it will," Alexandra whispered. "Money always does. What if . . . what if it *is* the money? And if I marry him, I'll never know. I'll be comfortable and luxurious, and never know if it was just the money, after all. If I wasn't just deceiving myself about the rest of it." Oh God, what was she saying? The wine, the stupid wine, making the thoughts tumble unchecked from her mouth.

"Rubbish. I've never heard anything so absurd. Listen to me, Alexandra, you little fool," Lilibet hissed. "If you love him, hold him. Don't even think about anything else. Don't condemn yourself to misery, for God's sake."

"As you did."

Lilibet hesitated. "As I did."

The musicians struck up suddenly behind them, lilting and jovial. A ripple of laughter cast through the throng. People began rising, clasping hands, hurrying to the open center of the terrace.

"Find him," Lilibet said, next to her ear. "Don't let him go."

Alexandra rose without speaking. Men and women thronged about her, feathered masks sailed past her face, reds and golds and purples, mouths beneath open with laughter. She had to push against the tide, to sidle her way around them all. A table corner bumped bruisingly against her thigh, though she hardly noticed the pain. Step-by-step, she made her way to the corner where Finn had sat, deep in conversation with an Italian woman in a crimson mask, eating his dinner.

When she arrived at last, he was gone.

TWENTY

The dancing went on and on. Alexandra held back at first, watching the kaleidoscope of dancers shift beneath the flickering golden light of the torches. She'd always thought of the Tuscans as rather a somber lot, given to serious works like cheese making and vineyard-pruning and bean-sorting, or perhaps a bit of egg thievery in their wilder moments. But now, under the influence of wine and masks, all that had changed. They threw back their heads in laughter, turned this way and that with the merry dance of the violins, swished their homespun skirts, and stomped their feet. She recognized Maria's dark curling hair, Francesca's rosebud mouth.

It was Abigail who took her hand and drew her into the throng. She moved reluctantly, her limbs weighed down with longing for Finn, but Abigail had no respect at all for the bittersweet torment of a mad passion, and she forced her to move about, to join in the lines of dancers. She didn't know the steps, of course, and she'd never heard the music before. But somehow she made it down the line, guided by strange hands, by the inexorable *oom-pah* of the grandfatherly tuba.

Eventually she lost sight of Abigail, lost sight of anything else but the immediate present, dance and music and fire and the wine now singing in her blood.

She stepped out at last, breathless and laughing. "Here," said someone at her elbow, "drink this, *mia donna.*"

It was Signorina Morini, holding a tiny glass filled with clear liquid. Her eyes danced gold in the torchlight.

"What is it?"

"It is a little drink I am making. It is a little of the limoncello, a little of other things. Is traditional, on the feast of the midsummer."

"How delightful." Alexandra took the glass and tossed down the contents. It burned a pleasant lemony track down the length of her throat, filling her brain with its fumes. She handed the glass back in wonder. "Oh, that's very nice. May I have another?"

The housekeeper leaned closer. "He is at the lake, near the boathouse. He will be wanting one of the drink."

Something cool slipped into Alexandra's hand. She looked down and saw another glass, exactly the same. "Thanks ever so much," she said, and started it to her lips.

Signorina Morini caught hold of her wrist. "No, signora. This one, it is for Signore Burke. You must be giving it to him now."

"Why, yes," Alexandra said. "So I must."

As she turned to leave, she caught the corner of Signorina Morini's smile, wide with approval as she stepped from the flagstones, outside the circle of torchlight. She made her way down the terraced fields, each one burgeoning with the endless ripening bounty of summer.

The gibbous moon loomed large and heavy between the stars, tracking her progress between the rows of vines and the cornstalks and the fruit trees. Her feet knew the way, of course. She could have skipped down the terraces blindfolded by now. Still, she kept her steps measured, careful. There was something odd in the air, something watchful and vibrant just outside the periphery of her senses. Which were not terribly acute at the moment, she had to admit. Not so long ago, in her London days, a few glasses of wine meant nothing to her.

Now, she was stumbling on every root.

Near the last terrace, with Finn's workshop a black mass off to her right, her foot caught a fallen branch.

She staggered forward, grasping Signorina Morini's glass

with both hands, as if it were a Fabergé egg. One step, another, the ground rushing up to meet her, and then her third step caught her hurtling body. A few drops of the limoncello splashed onto her skin, cool and tingling.

A man's figure hurried across the shadowed path before her.

"Who's there?" she snapped.

He stopped and stared at her, startled. For an instant, the moonlight caught his face: dark hair, thick mustache, skin so pale he seemed like a ghost. She couldn't quite distinguish his features, but as the seconds stretched between them, she saw his eyes narrow from astonishment to something like malevolence. He clutched at his jacket pocket. One of the villagers, probably, returning from the castle.

"Hello there!" she called. "Can I help you?"

He turned and bolted onward. She stared after him, but it was as if the night had swallowed him up. Even the breeze was still. The trees poised motionless in the hot air, leaves and branches disappearing into the shadows.

"I'm not afraid," she said aloud. The drink still glowed warm in her belly, radiating outward into her heart and limbs and brain. She began to walk again, a bit more swiftly, peering ahead for the silver flash of the lake between the olive trees.

Just before she emerged at the shore, she caught its scent: cool and clear and fresh as it cut through the drugging fruit-laden warmth of the vineyards and orchards. Moonlight trailed across the glassy water, gilded the planes and angles of the boathouse nearby and the tall figure of a man standing next to it, leaning his broad shoulder into the wall.

"Hello there," she called softly.

He turned to her deliberately, as if he'd already sensed her presence. He was still wearing his mask, and she could only just see the flicker of his eyes through the holes. They enveloped her, all of her, taking in every inch, every nick, every flaw. "Lady Morley," he said.

At the sight of him, at the feel of his eyes upon her skin, the lemony burn of Signorina Morini's drink seemed to pulse throughout her body, reaching the outermost point of every tingling nerve, making her heart sing out and her brain dance.

I love you.

"*Lady Morley*, is it? You must be cross with me." She walked toward him, as if he'd hooked her with a string and pulled her in. "I've brought you a glass of limoncello. You must drink it. I'm told it's traditional." She came to a stop mere inches from his chest and held the glass to his lips.

He lifted his hand and took the glass from her and drank.

"Delicious, isn't it? Signorina Morini gave it to me."

"Signorina Morini?" His voice was thick.

"The housekeeper."

He was looking at her intensely, examining her, his face cleansed of all color by the pale moonlight. She could feel her heart pounding in her chest, hard and rapid, making the blood spin past her ears. "You left before the dancing started. I was looking for you."

He shook his head dazedly. "I thought I'd take another look in the workshop before I leave for Rome."

"But you're not leaving until next week!" The words burst from her throat. Something about his tone, his face, sent a thread of fear unspooling around all the fuzzy warmth in her middle.

He pressed the empty glass into her hand and folded her fingers around it. "I changed my mind. I thought perhaps it might be better to leave sooner, rather than later. To familiarize myself with the grounds, find local help."

"It sounds as if I'm not going."

"You didn't want to go to Rome," he said. "You insisted you wouldn't, that we shouldn't be seen together."

He stood so close to her, his breath caressing her face. In the whiteness of the moon he loomed even larger than she remembered: taller, broader, longer. She searched his face, trying to read his expression beneath the black mask. "Perhaps I've changed my mind," she whispered. She raised her hand to his cheek and rasped her thumb against the sandpaper ends of his beard.

"Have you?"

"Finn. Darling, what's wrong? Have I done something?"

"No," he said, voice cracking, "it's just . . . I thought it would be simple, leaving tomorrow, and I find . . . I have only to look at you and . . . God, I can't help it . . . I'm caught, aren't I?" His hands came up to cradle her face. "I'm yours. I . . ." He shook his head and bent down to kiss her with hard, unforgiving lips.

The empty glass dropped from her fingers.

She opened her mouth and took him in, met him stroke for stroke, kissed and nibbled and caressed him. With shocking force, lust flooded her veins: lust for him, for his body and his spirit, for every last beautiful particle of him. She wanted to absorb him through her skin, to somehow fuse herself into him. She wanted the beat of his heart, the dazzling impulses of his brain, everything that was and would be Finn.

He kissed her urgently, as if struck by the same compulsion racing through her own body. His tongue roamed deep, tasting of lemons and wine, hot and silken against hers; she felt his hands at the back of her head, tugging at her mask.

She drew back and grasped his wrists. "No," she said, smiling. "No."

"No?"

She kissed each hand with her open mouth. "You do so much for me, darling. You laugh with me, love me, pleasure me until I'm blind and helpless. I give you nothing."

His eyes closed. "You give me everything. You give me life."

"Let me give you something, Finn." She leaned into his chest and pulled aside his collar and kissed the salty hollow of his throat, licking little circles around it. Her hands slipped down under his thin wool jacket to his waist, to the fastening of his trousers, already tented with arousal. "I want to taste you, darling," she whispered, into his warm skin. "I want to drink you in, to fill myself up with you."

His breath sang out in a sigh. She heard it as agreement.

Somehow she fumbled his buttons free and knelt into the pebbles of the lakeshore, pressing kisses through his shirt as she went, down his lean chest and his flat, corded belly, urging him back against the side of the boathouse. Her hands slid around his thighs to cup his buttocks, to hold him in place as she nuzzled his straining shaft through the thin cotton of his drawers, taking in the richness of his scent, the silken hardness of his flesh. She felt his fingers creep into her hair, clutching rhythmically, and she smiled.

Oh, how she wanted this. She wanted the taste of him, the essence of him. She'd have all of him at last.

She slid his drawers downward and his cock sprang free into her mouth, swollen and eager and beautiful. She circled it with her tongue, exploring the hard, thick circumference, the smooth head emerging from within its velvety fold of skin, the bead of liquid welling at the tip. She lapped it up eagerly, tasted the electric tanginess of him. She'd never imagined such temptation.

"Is that all right?" she breathed.

"Yes . . . good God . . . no . . . more . . ."

He groaned as she took him inside her mouth, as far as she could, encompassing his great length to the back of her throat. She didn't know what to do; it was probably all wrong, but she didn't care: She wanted to draw him into her, to devour him, to torment him the way he did to her, to give him exactly the same shattering consummation he gave to her.

She slid one hand underneath to caress his ballocks, round and tight and snug against his body, and her own flesh seemed to vibrate with desire. She pictured how she must look to him, with her white feather-edged mask covering her eyes and forehead, and his cock sliding in and out of her pink mouth as she sucked and pulled and stroked. His pleasure was her own; his building tension seemed to melt through her body and pool between her legs; his groans sank like music into her ears.

His hands gripped her hair in fistfuls. Through her lips and fingers she sensed his muscles coil, approaching the peak, and in that instant he jerked away with a guttural cry. "No," she said, and took him back in, absorbed the final thrust of his hips, heard her name tear hoarsely from his throat. She took the hot pulse of him inside her, stroked release from behind his sac with featherlight fingers.

Gradually the throbs of his body subsided, and his muscles relaxed into a blissful quiescence against the side of the boathouse. She pressed her forehead into his belly, gathering her wits, savoring the taste of him where it lingered in her mouth. His hands traveled through her hair, gentle now. From somewhere quite distant, quite outside the small circle of their intimacy, came the sound of water slapping restlessly against the rocky lakeshore.

She staggered upward, knees aching, and wrapped her arms around his waist. "Thank you," she whispered.

His chest vibrated beneath her ear. "Christ Almighty, Alexandra," he gasped. "You're thanking *me*?"

"It was beautiful."

"Oh, God. Oh, God." His arms swept around her, tightening like a vise, holding her against the shaking laughter in his chest. "Alexandra, you mad creature. Oh, God. Forgive me." His hand went back to her hair and stroked it relentlessly.

"Forgive you for what?"

"Nothing. Just . . . oh, God."

His body steadied at last, and she laid herself into his embrace, luxuriating in the feel of his arms around her, his hand in her hair, the rise and fall of his breath under her cheek. His hand plucked at the strings of her mask, untied it, let it fall to the pebbles below.

"You'll let me go to Rome with you, then?"

He didn't reply at first, only gathered her face between his palms and looked into her eyes, the muscles of his cheeks stiff behind the feathered edges of his mask. "Alexandra, tell me. Why did you visit my workshop, that first time? Why did you begin helping me with the automobile?"

His eyes seemed to sink right through the skin of her face and into her soul. "I don't know. I think . . . I wanted to find a way to know you, and so I took the first excuse that came to me."

His thumbs moved against her cheekbones. "Really, Alexandra? No other reason?"

"Don't be ridiculous." She tucked her hands under his jacket, at his waist. What the devil did he mean by this? He couldn't know about the Manchester Machine Works. She'd hardly even thought about the damned company for weeks; such unpleasant memories had a way of puncturing the sweet haze of love in which she'd been drifting since April, since that first night in his bed. The Lady Morley of London society and automobile shares seemed like another woman. She could hardly even remember her own intentions. "In any case, what does it matter anymore?"

"It might. Hmm, Alexandra?"

She clutched his shirt between her fingers. "My motives may not have been pure in the beginning," she said fiercely, "but they are now, Finn. I'm yours, now."

"How am I to know that, Alexandra?" His hands dropped to idle at the base of her throat. "You've drawn me in until I'm your creature, your devoted fool. Have I, perhaps, been deceiving myself, all this time? Am I an idiot to think that the Marchioness of Morley would really fall in love with an Irish bastard, so obviously beneath her? That she would give up her title, her precedence, her place in London society?"

"You know that means nothing to me anymore. Finn, what is it? What have I done?" Tears began to well in her eyes, as she experienced a sense of something precious slipping away.

He said nothing, only went on examining her, thumbs stroking gently against her collarbone. As if he were waiting for her.

She opened her mouth to say something, anything, to break the unbearable silence between them, but in that instant his hands froze on her skin.

"Finn?" Then she heard it, too: the swift snap of shoes against rock, the rattle of pebbles, a male voice raised in anger.

Finn took a step forward. Glass crunched beneath his foot.

"The limoncello! Are you all right?"

"Hush." He dragged her flat against the side of the boat-house.

A masked woman flew by, dress fluttering in the moonlight, and disappeared into the trees nearby.

"Damn it, Abigail!" roared the male voice.

Stones scraped. From around the corner of the boathouse, a large figure loomed in pursuit against the silvery waters of the lake, scrambling barefoot over the rocks.

Stark and utterly naked.

"Wallingford!" Alexandra gasped.

He stopped and turned to them, male equipment swinging with the force of his movement. His trousers dangled from one hand. "Where did she go?" he roared.

Finn pointed. "Into the trees, old man. Right over there."

Alexandra buried her face into his chest.

"And Wallingford?" Finn continued.

A clash of pebbles. "What the devil?" growled the duke, from somewhere behind her.

"Good luck, old chap."

"Oh, bugger *off*, you goddamned Irish bastard."

They collapsed together against the side of the boathouse, helpless with laughter, tension dissolved for the moment. "Let me," Alexandra said, and she fastened the buttons of his trousers, tucking him inside with a final pat. Then she reached up around his head, drew off his mask, and kissed him tenderly, his eyes and cheeks and nose and chin and lips.

"Alexandra," he said at last, running his hand along the side of her arm, sending tingles running throughout her body, "you must tell me the truth."

"About what?"

"About all of this. About you, and me, and . . . and everything. You must trust me. Trust that I care for you, that I believe in you. That I'll forgive you anything, because of that." He was no longer stiff, no longer angry: only tender and anxious.

She swallowed. What could she say? *Oh, I started out spying on you, you see! Trying to see if I could glean some information to turn to my own profit! Rather rum of me, I admit, but I do have a sister to support, and a position to maintain, and all that.* Yes, he'd understand perfectly. "I've told you, Finn. I . . . I couldn't admit to myself that I wanted you, that I wanted to know you better. I needed an excuse. But I've changed, Finn. *You've* changed me, and Italy, and being away from London. I've realized that all those silly trappings I've prized all my life are nothing, nothing at all, compared to this." She reached up bravely to kiss him again, cradling his face against her palm. "This is what matters, Finn. This is all I care about. You, and my sister and cousin, and . . . if you'll allow me, if you'll let me prove myself to you . . ."

She felt his arm harden into steel around her. He scrambled upright, dragging her with him, and peered through the trees.

"What is it?" she asked.

"Oh, hell," he said. He released her and sprang into a run. "Oh, goddamned *fucking HELL!*"

TWENTY-ONE

She pumped until her arms ached, filling bucket after bucket for Finn or Wallingford or Abigail to toss on the fire. No time to check its progress, no thought to anything but the cold stream of water into the next bucket, the wet slide of the pump handle under her fingers.

"That's it," someone said, a male voice, but she kept on pumping like an automaton, like Finn's electric dynamo, because that *couldn't* be it, she *wouldn't* give up.

A hand gripped her arm. "Alexandra," said Wallingford huskily, "it's out. You can stop now."

She looked at his hand and then at his face, grim and wet with sweat and water. His chest gleamed bare and white in the moonlight above the dark line of his hastily donned trousers. "It's out," he repeated.

She turned to the building, to the carriage house, Finn's workshop, where she'd spent countless precious hours of toil and laughter and companionship. It still stood, of course, but its dun-colored stones had blackened with soot, and the window next to the long, narrow table had blown out. A great hole gaped through the roof tiles above.

"Where is he?" Her voice was raspy with effort and smoke.

"Inside." His hand gave her arm a little squeeze. "I'm awfully sorry, Alexandra. We did the best we could."

Gentle words. She couldn't remember the last time she'd heard them from him. "Thank you," she said, and covered his hand with hers.

Inside the building, the light was nearly gone, and the air was hot and damp and reeking of smoke. She could just make out Finn's lanky figure near the cabinet, which still stood, though burned nearly to charcoal.

"Are you all right?"

He didn't turn. "A bit singed here and there. The machine's all right, thank God. I got it out before the fire reached it."

She looked across the room to the carriage doors, which stood open to reveal the faint gleam of moonlight on metal, some twenty yards away.

With great care she stepped across the puddled floor to where he stood, sifting through the remains of the cabinet. "Oh, darling. Let me see you. Are you burned?"

"Quite all right, as I said. It's the devil of a nuisance, though. The spare battery's a complete write-off, I'm afraid, and all my equipment . . ." His voice trailed off.

"Do you know what started it?"

"The gas ring, I think. I must have left it on, though I can't imagine how. The explosion's what I saw through the trees, though again it's not clear what set it off. The dynamo's too far away for any stray spark to reach, and . . ."

She placed her arms around his waist. "Hush. You're all right. That's all that matters."

"And the machine."

Laughter choked her throat. "Yes, that, too, of course. It could have been much worse. We might have lost everything."

He didn't reply. His body was stiff and hot against hers, his jacket gone, his collar unbuttoned. Her eyes, accustomed to the darkness, began to pick out details: the black pit where the table used to be; piles of shattered glass and sooty shards of wood and metal; the gas canister poking through the rubbish, catching the faint gleam of moonlight through the blown-out window.

"The canister!" she exclaimed. "Thank God! It might have blown up everything!"

He shrugged. "There wasn't much gas left, actually. No, it's cursed bad luck, but you're right. It might have been worse."

"Darling. At least you weren't inside when it happened."

"If I'd been inside, it wouldn't have happened." His voice was flat, emotionless.

She drew back. "Don't you dare blame yourself! It was an accident! It's nearly midnight; you wouldn't have been here anyway. You'd have been where you belong, in bed with me."

He laughed. "Yes, you're rather bad for my discipline, aren't you?"

"Tell me what I can do to help. We've two weeks before the race. Surely we can build another battery."

His body softened at last. His palm touched her cheek, warm and callused. "I'll have to start by cleaning up. I won't be able to properly assess the damage before daybreak, and then I'll need to make a list of what's needed and head into Florence."

"I'll help you clean up. We'll get it all done tonight."

His thumb stroked her cheekbone. "Go to bed, Alexandra. I'll manage."

"Not bloody likely."

Footsteps sounded through the door. "I've stashed the buckets and swept up the glass outside," said Abigail. "How are things in here?"

"Absolutely buggered," Alexandra said cheerfully, stepping away from Finn, "but we'll manage. The automobile's all right."

Wallingford spoke up. "Burke, old chap. What a damned nuisance. Are you all right? Anything I can do?"

"You've done more than enough, my friend." Finn stepped through the puddles and grasped the duke's hand. "I can't begin to thank you."

"You know damned well there's no such thing as thanks between us."

Something seemed to pass between the two of them, some bone-deep understanding. Alexandra watched in bemusement as Finn nodded, once, and dropped Wallingford's hand. "I'll just tidy up a bit. You head on back to the house and let the stable lads know. I shall require carts to haul off the rubble, that sort of thing."

"Done." Wallingford hesitated and turned to her. "Lady Morley?"

"I'll stay and help," she said, her voice clear and final. "But I'd be much obliged if you'd see my sister safely back to the house."

"I should think I'd be much safer without his help," muttered Abigail.

"Oh, for God's sake," muttered Wallingford.

When they left, she put her hands on her hips and looked at Finn with her most efficient expression. "Now, then. Is it safe to light the lamp?"

They worked through the night. Together they sifted through the remains for anything salvageable and swept the rubble into piles outside the door, to be picked up in the morning.

Finn was exhausted. It showed plainly in his shadowed eyes, his bent shoulders. Near dawn, when the last whole object had been placed in the pile on the worktable, and the last shard of glass had been swept from the floor, she guided him to a chair. "Sit. I'll bring you some water."

"I'm all right," he said. He placed his arms on the table and laid his head upon them, his hair tufted about his pale face.

She went outside to clean and fill a soot-streaked cup from the pump, and when she returned he had drifted to sleep. She sank into the chair next to him and watched him for a moment, in the light of the lamp. Watched his purple eyelids twitch with the force of his dreams, watched his incongruously long eyelashes shadow the skin of his cheekbones. Last night, in his room, he'd stretched his long body on the bed and talked with her about Hannibal—the women were working through Livy just now—and the route he'd taken through the Alps with his army and his elephants. "It must have been a good deal warmer back then," he'd been saying, "for I've been through that pass in the summertime and I'll be damned if I can see an African elephant making the journey." She'd been lying on her stomach, watching him exactly as she did now, and she'd noticed at that precise moment, for the first time, the luxurious reddish curl of his eyelashes. *Do you know, you've got splendid eyelashes*, she'd said, and he'd turned to her with a rakish gleam in his eyes. *And have you only just noticed, darling?*

Alexandra rose from the chair and went to the chest on the opposite wall, the undamaged wall. He kept blankets in there, mostly for protecting his automobile against the dust at night. She took out the blankets and arranged them on the floor.

"Come." She laid her arm about his shoulder and urged him out of the chair. "Come and rest."

He stumbled out of the chair and crashed atop the little nest onto his belly, his arms spread out on either side. A long, satisfied snore emerged from his nose. She smiled and slipped another blanket on top of him, and then she sat by his side and watched him sleep, her happiness like a giddy lemon-scented narcotic running through her blood.

F inn woke as the first ghostly hint of dawn filtered through the open carriage doors and across his face. His brain spun heavily, groggily. Where the hell was he? What was going on?

Smoke. The smell of smoke.

Alexandra.

His eyes dropped down to the blanket next to him, where she curled in slumber, still dressed. In sleep her features took on a curious innocence, softened perhaps by the diffuse early light. He resisted the urge to trace his finger along the soot-smudged arch of her cheekbone, along the graceful line of her jaw. She needed to sleep. She'd labored at his side like a heroine last night.

Slowly, without really wanting to do it, he raised his head and cast his gaze about the workshop. It wasn't as bad as he feared. Last night, the shadows had magnified the blackness and damage; now, with all the rubbish cleared away, the burns seemed superficial, the scorched furniture replaceable. His automobile, at least, was undamaged. The second battery might even be worth salvaging, on closer inspection. No, the damage wasn't catastrophic. It could have been far worse.

He glanced back down at Alexandra and felt again that crashing wave of love, as strong as it had been last night, when she'd looked up at him beneath her feathered mask, her eyes returning the gleam of the moonlight. *You left before the dancing started*, she'd said, her voice lonely and hurt, and his every resolution had crumbled. In that instant, everything else had disappeared, and there was only Alexandra: brave, stubborn, resourceful, beloved Alexandra. And he would do anything for her. Would forgive her anything.

But could he trust her? She hadn't admitted her involvement

with Manchester Machine Works, though he'd given her every opportunity at the lakeshore. Why? Because she didn't believe he'd understand? Or because her allegiance still lay with his rival?

No. She couldn't be working for William Hartley. No one, man or woman, would have done what she had just now, putting out that fire, risking herself, if she were playing a part. No one could have loved him the way she had these past months, with her eager body and passionate kisses, if she were really false.

But he needed his every wit about him in Rome, and until he knew the truth, until she'd trusted him with her reasons, he couldn't allow himself the distraction of her presence. It would be better that way. Cleaner, easier.

When he returned from Rome, they'd sort it all out. And in the meantime, he'd show her she could trust him with the truth. He'd show her just how much he'd do for her, just how much he loved her.

With great care he tucked the blanket around her and lifted her into his arms. So exhausted, so soundly asleep she was, she hardly stirred, only turned her face into his chest with a contented noise.

He carried her up the mist-shrouded terraces to the castle, where the trestle tables still sat on the flagstones outside. The door stood ajar; he pushed it open with his foot and made his way to the stairs. She opened her eyes, blinking sleepily. "The elephants are so lumpy," she told him, and closed her eyes again.

The window in her room stood open, letting the cool dampness of dawn drift through the air. He tucked her in bed and closed the window. At the door he paused, letting his gaze travel around the room a final time.

She'd been profligate with the library. Books stacked about the room, Latin and English and Italian, with bits of notepaper sticking haphazardly between the bindings. On the dressing table sat a silver brush and comb, a hand mirror, a pitcher and basin, hairpins, an ivory box. She'd left the wardrobe door ajar, and he could just glimpse the clothes within, dark wools and brighter silks and something that might have been the blue frock she'd worn to his workshop that first morning.

He imprinted it all on his memory: the room, the objects

within; Alexandra herself, lying on the bed, her face turned at an angle and her chestnut hair spread in dark waves across the whiteness of her pillow.

At last he turned to leave, and walked straight into the naked chest and wild-eyed face of Lord Roland Penhallow.

"Good God! Penhallow! What is it?"

Lord Roland clutched him by the shoulders. "Have you seen her?"

"Seen whom?"

"Lilibet! Lady Somerton!"

"No, I haven't. Not since last night. What's the matter?"

Lord Roland shook his head and ran the length of the hall to disappear down the main staircase, his bare feet slapping against the old stones like a rifle tattoo.

The whole damned castle had gone mad.

F inn worked fast, packing up his trunks and preparing the automobile for the journey to Rome. Around seven o'clock that morning, Giacomo appeared at the carriage doors with carts and men, and Finn helped them load and secure the machine and its accessory parts while the sun rose hot above the trees and burned the mist from every corner of the terraces.

"I shall take the train from Florence," he told Giacomo, "so your men should return by tomorrow if all goes well. Keep a sharp eye on things while I'm gone. Other than the roof repairs, no one's allowed in the workshop."

Giacomo's eyebrows lifted. "But Lady Morley?"

Finn hesitated for only an instant. "Lady Morley's allowed, of course."

"You are not perhaps thinking she made the fire?"

"Rubbish. Of course not. You're to give her this letter, when she emerges this morning. I daresay she'll be a bit cross that I've left, but I've tried to explain . . ." He thrust the envelope at Giacomo's unwilling chest. "Well, take it, in any case."

Giacomo plucked it gingerly from Finn's hand, as he might extract a snake from its basket.

"Don't fail me, Giacomo. You must promise me scrupulously you'll give it to her. None of your tricks."

Giacomo sighed. "I make the promise. I give the letter."

Finn swung aboard the cart, next to the driver. "Right-ho. I'll return in three weeks. Do endeavor to make yourself more charming in the meantime."

The cart rolled away, just as the clock in the village tolled nine o'clock, and the men tying back the vines in the fields paused for a drink of water.

TWENTY-TWO

For a brief moment, on waking, Alexandra was surprised not to find herself engaged in vigorous sexual congress with Phineas Burke atop an African elephant.

She lay against her pillows for a long moment, recovering from the disappointment. The dream was so real, so vivid. She could still sense the sway of the elephant, feel Finn's steely arms encircling her, smell the earthy mingling of oil and smoke and sweat on his shirt . . .

Smoke.

She bolted upright. What time was it? Why the devil was she sleeping in her own bed?

Where was Finn?

She flew to the window. Late morning, from the height of the sun. The hills rolled away from her, exactly as they had the day before, every detail in its place. In the vineyards the men tended to the grapes, shirts billowing white against the greens and browns of the earth. No sign of anything out of place. No sign of Finn.

In swift movements she shed her smoke-laden clothes and cleaned her face and hands and neck with cool water from the pitcher on her dresser. Dressed anew, she hurried down the silent corridors to Finn's room and found it bare and lifeless in the brightness of day.

In the kitchen, she encountered signs of life at last. Signorina

Morini stood at the kitchen table straining the jugs of milk from the goats.

"Has Mr. Burke been downstairs?" Alexandra asked breathlessly.

Signorina Morini looked up. Her face looked rather pale. "No, signora."

"There was an accident in his workshop yesterday. A fire."

"Yes, I have heard this." She hesitated and picked up another jug to pour through the strainer. "But there is nobody hurt?"

"No, nobody. I stayed to help Mr. Burke clean up, and then . . . then I suppose he must have brought me back here, though I don't remember it. Did you see anything?"

The housekeeper shook her head, not looking up. "Nothing, signora. You are perhaps a little hungry? A little thirsty?"

"Yes, rather. Only I'd like to run down to the workshop first, to see if he's there."

"Eat first. Drink first." Signorina Morini wiped her hands on her apron and turned to the cupboard. "The feast, it is a long time ago."

"No, really. I'll only be a moment. Where is everybody?"

"Signorina Abigail was milking the goats." She set out bread and cheese on the table and went to fill the kettle with water. "There is a letter for you."

"What, a letter? So early? From whom?"

The housekeeper nodded. "On the table."

Alexandra saw the folded sheet and picked it up.

My dear Alexandra, I have been obliged to depart unexpectedly early this morning. I shall return as soon as possible. You must not follow me.

It was not signed, but the copperplate handwriting, though hasty, was unmistakably that of her cousin Lilibet.

"How odd." Alexandra fingered the edge of the paper. "Did you see her leave this here? Did you speak to her?"

Signorina Morini hung the kettle above the fire. "No, signora. I did not. A little of the bread?"

"But surely you heard something? Horses, a messenger?"

The housekeeper went back to the cupboard for the tea. "Signore Penhallow, he is not here this morning."

Alexandra dropped into a nearby chair. "Penhallow! She's run off with Penhallow?"

"Perhaps." The housekeeper cleared her throat. "Or perhaps there is something else . . ."

But Alexandra wasn't listening. She clapped a hand to her mouth. "Oh, good God! Good God! Why didn't you say anything? And the boy?"

"He is gone, too."

"Oh, how marvelous! She's done it! Oh, the darling girl!"

Signorina Morini managed a strained smile and turned back to the kettle on the fire.

"Perhaps you don't approve, with her husband and all that, but I assure you Lord Somerton has quite forfeited any claim on her." Alexandra took up the bread. "It's marvelous. I'm delighted."

"You are wanting a little of lemon with your tea, signora?"

"No." Alexandra rose. "I'll drink it later. I'm off to the workshop. I can't wait to tell F—. . . to tell Mr. Burke."

"Wait, signora! Your breakfast!"

But Alexandra had already fled out the door, bread clutched in her hand.

It was just the news to raise Finn's spirits.

A t first, as she pivoted about in the smoke-scented center of the workshop, she thought he must be testing out the automobile on the road.

Of course he would want to make sure the machine hadn't been damaged in the fire. He'd probably woken early, unable to rest until she'd achieved her forty miles an hour to his satisfaction.

Odd, though. The spare battery was missing as well.

Perhaps he'd had it tossed out with the rest of the rubbish. It seemed a tremendous waste, but if he thought nothing could be salvaged from it, well, that was that.

The blankets had been picked up from the floor, she noticed. A tidy gesture. But where had the chests gone? The spare parts? The tires?

The hydraulic lift for the battery?

Her heart thudded in her ear. Nothing to be concerned about. Any number of likely explanations.

If only she could think of one.

I changed my mind. I thought perhaps it might be better to leave sooner, rather than later.

With leaden steps she walked back outside and around the building, past the carriage doors, tightly shut, to the protective shed that housed the dynamo. Massive black steel machine, custom-made to his specifications, too large and loud to be housed inside the workshop. He'd shown her how it worked, how it converted the mechanical energy from the nearby stream into the electrical energy that charged the battery.

Her hands trembled as she opened the wide door to the shed. It swung easily, as if the hinges had been recently oiled, and revealed nothing but a great dark void where the dynamo had been.

Empty.

She shut the door at once and turned and leaned against it, staring upward at the pure, depthless blue of the sky, at the small silver green leaves of the nearby olive trees. Under her feet, she knew, there would be marks: scuffed dirt and wheel tracks and footprints. Signs of Finn's leaving.

All at once, she pushed herself upright. He wouldn't have left without a word. A note of some kind must exist somewhere.

She strode back purposefully through the clipped green grass to the workshop and flung open the front door. Where would he leave it? She scanned the worktable, the long counter. She opened the scorched wooden door of the cabinet. The window-sills, the walls—he occasionally pinned notes and diagrams into the wood, where he wouldn't miss them.

The chests? Mostly gone, but a pair remained, near the lamp table. She drew near and saw a stack of envelopes, today's post perhaps. She picked them up and flipped through them, curled and browned at the edges, but thankfully far enough from the blaze to have escaped destruction.

A sheet fluttered to the ground.

She bent to pick it up and caught, from the corner of her eye, her own name written there in tidy handwriting.

Precise, even, legible handwriting. A lawyer's handwriting, a businessman's.

Nothing like Finn's.

Dowager Marchioness of Morley, 22,800 shares

She folded the paper before she could read more, running her fingers along the creases to sharpen them, but it made no difference. The letters still burned in her brain, black and stark and impartial, stating the undeniable fact of the case.

A world, a lifetime of guilt, packed into those few brief words and numbers.

Alexandra, you must tell me the truth. You must trust me.

So he'd found out. Had questioned her, and found her wanting. Now he'd made his decision: to leave for Rome without her.

She could follow him. Could beg him to forgive her, to understand. But how could she face the look in his eyes, the distance, the pity? The power it would give him, having forgiven her? The chance, possibly, that he might not understand, that he might not forgive her?

And how could she forgive herself, for deceiving him in the first place?

She couldn't do that, couldn't come to him as a pauper *and* as a supplicant. Everything she had would depend on him: on his money, on his mercy.

She replaced the papers on top of the chest and walked out of the workshop, into the sultry midsummer air, where the birds chattered impatiently in the trees and the men in the fields had gone in to lunch.

TWENTY-THREE

Two weeks later

The goat eyed her balefully, ears flattened with suspicion.

"Don't be ridiculous," Alexandra said. "You're supposed to look grateful. That udder of yours looks as if it's about to burst."

Abigail sighed at her from two goats over. "Alex, there's no point trying to win over goats with irony. They don't appreciate it."

"I should think a goat would adore irony." Alexandra reached for the bucket and placed it with due care underneath the pertinent udder. "I think it suits them."

"Now there's where you're wrong. It shows you have no real understanding of goats at all, not after two full weeks of instruction." Abigail gave her goat a final squeeze and rose with her bucket. "I'm ashamed of you."

"They may hate me all they like, but they can't argue with my technique."

"You're a natural, I admit." Abigail poured the milk into one of the tall jugs lining the wall and moved on to the next goat. "One look at you, and the poor thing lets its milk down in a torrent. Probably out of sheer fear."

"I expect they know I have nothing left to lose." She took hold of the teats and squeezed with vigor, enjoying the sight of the swift white lines shooting into the pail, enjoying the visible proof of her own usefulness. Or perhaps *enjoying* was too strong a word for this rather subdued sense of satisfaction she felt just now. The most, really, she was capable of feeling.

Still, it was something. It gave her a reason to rise out of bed in the morning. To dress, to eat, to speak, to carry on.

Tomorrow she and Abigail would be returning home. Their trunks were already packed. She had no desire to be near when Finn returned from his exposition in Rome. No, they'd leave the men in peace. They'd do what they ought to have done long before, and let Wallingford and Finn pursue their studies without further hindrance.

Back to London, then, to a rented house in Fulham or perhaps Putney. She would sell her shares in Manchester Machine Works and invest the meager proceeds in sound British consols. Together with her remaining capital and Abigail's small inheritance, they would have perhaps two hundred pounds a year. Enough to live in genteel dignity, with a servant or two. An occasional dinner party, if she were economical. Books from the lending library, as many as she liked. Visits from Lilibet and Penhallow, perhaps, whenever that pair turned up again: They'd had no word at all in two weeks.

Somehow, the prospect didn't seem as bleak, as desperate as it had a few months ago. The physical details of her life no longer mattered much.

"What did you say?" asked Abigail.

"Nothing."

She went on milking alongside her sister, in the warm, companionable silence of the goat shed, the final milking before tomorrow's dawn departure. When the last animal's udder had been emptied, she picked up two of the tall metal jugs and carried them across the stableyard to the door to the kitchens.

"Hullo," said Abigail, "what's that?"

Alexandra turned her head and stopped. A trail of fine yellow dust rose up in the air from the long main driveway. "I've no idea. Penhallow and Lilibet, perhaps?"

"It can't be. They'd have written; there's been no word at all. Perhaps a guest?"

Alexandra frowned. "I can't think who. Unless . . ." A shiver of trepidation crawled up her spine.

"You don't think it's Lord Somerton?"

"Of course not." She stared at the cloud of dust, at its hard brown center that might possibly be a carriage of some kind. "Come along. Let's get this milk in the kitchen. If we're to entertain guests, we ought at least to clean the goat droppings from our shoes."

And indeed, no one would have mistaken the polished, well-dressed lady who descended the main staircase, twenty minutes later, for the homespun woman bringing in the milk jugs from the goat shed. Not that she cared, particularly. Good grooming was a matter of habit, ingrained in her by her mother and a succession of nursemaids and governesses from the time she could walk.

One brushed one's hair and pinned it neatly in place even when one's heart was breaking. One extended one's thoroughly washed hand in greeting to visitors, even when one wished all the people of the world to the devil.

"Good morning," she said now to the young man in the great hall, whose tweed-covered back was turned as he contemplated the medieval vastness of his surroundings. "I know, it's a great deal of empty space, and most inhospitable, but . . . Good God! Mr. Hartley!"

Her nephew-in-law whirled around and dropped his hat from under his arm. "Lady Morley!"

"What on earth are you doing here?"

His thin mouth opened and closed. "I : . . I . . . I should ask the same! I thought . . . Isn't this . . . Isn't Mr. Burke staying here?"

"Oh! Mr. Burke! Of course."

William Hartley bent over and picked up his hat. "I beg your pardon. I'd . . . it's the devil of shock. I knew you were away on the Continent somewhere, but . . ." He checked himself, hands chewing at the edges of his hat, the wheels of his brain visibly whirling. "Did you . . . you and Mr. Burke . . . I say, I . . . I didn't know you were acquainted." His voice struggled audibly for tact.

"Oh, we weren't. It was all a great misunderstanding. A muddle with the estate agent." She smiled and took his arm. "Come with me to the library. It's the only habitable reception space, other than the dining room."

By the time they'd settled into the moldering sofa in the library, and Francesca had arrived with tea, Mr. Hartley seemed to have recovered himself. "Lady Morley! Gad! Here of all places. Charming surprise."

"Charming." She reached for the teapot and poured.

"I say, you're looking splendid. Roses in your cheeks and all that."

"Why, thank you. I find life in Italy agrees with me tremendously. Would you like cream and sugar?"

"Oh yes. Both, if you please."

"I'm afraid you've missed Mr. Burke, however. He's already gone down to Rome for his automobile exposition." She dropped in the sugar and stirred it, the muscles of her fingers remembering the ritual even though her brain found it oddly foreign.

"Yes, of course. Headed down there myself." He took the cup and saucer from her and beamed. "It's just as well I found you, in fact. The most tremendous news. We've had our breakthrough at last!"

"Breakthrough?"

"Splendid, splendid business! Finally sorted out the steam transmission, ridiculously complicated affair, had my engineers confounded for ages." He leaned forward. "It's highly privileged information, of course. You're not to tell a soul. I shouldn't tell you, if you weren't a shareholder and all that."

"Why, no. I mean, yes, I'm a shareholder, and no, I shan't tell a single soul." She set her own tea on the lamp table. Her fingers were shaking too hard to keep the cup from clattering.

"We've entered the automobile in the exposition. The race, you see." He set down his own cup and knit his fingers together. "We fully expect to win it, and then—well, once the news is out, I daresay you'll finally be able to sell those shares of yours at a handsome profit. Yes, a very handsome profit, ha-ha!"

She blinked. "Win it?"

"Oh yes. I've clocked her at forty-five miles an hour, Lady Morley. Forty-five! Well, I daresay that means little to you, but I assure you it's tremendous." He picked up his tea again and took a dainty sip. "Tremendous."

"Yes. I'm . . . I'm quite thrilled."

He replaced the teacup in the saucer and coughed into his hand. "Always felt a bit rotten about that, you know. Investing your jointure, and having things work out . . . well, rather poorly. Never expected old Morley to kick off so soon, you see. Oh, egad! I beg your pardon."

"No, not at all," she said dazedly. "But I'm afraid I don't

quite understand. Why were you coming to see Mr. Burke, if it's all meant to be a great secret until after the race?"

"Oh, that. Well, it was a bit of an impulse, really. I was on my way down and realized I was no more than a few hours' drive away, so I thought I'd come to refuse his offer in person, ha-ha. Just to see the look on his face." Mr. Hartley grinned.

Her throat went dry. "His offer?"

"Why, he's been sniffing after the company himself! A week or so ago, we received a formal offer from his business manager to the tune of fifty shillings per share. Fifty shillings, ha-ha!"

She dropped her teacup into its saucer with a sharp crack. "Fifty shillings a share!"

"Fifty! Can you credit it? When the stock's trading at under five shillings at the moment." He drank his tea and shook his head in the same gesture. "The man must be mad, unless he's had some wind of our success."

"Quite mad."

"Of course I shall jolly well refuse him now. If we win this race as I expect, Manchester Machine Works will be worth a great deal more than that, ha-ha. And I've no doubt that we will. No doubt at all."

"Fifty shillings per share." Her mind went over the calculations again, and returned the same extraordinary number.

"Charming figure," Mr. Hartley agreed. He reached for one of Signorina Morini's fine almond macaroons. "These are jolly splendid. Have you a good cook here?"

"Marvelous. It's . . . it's been altogether the most delightful time of my life."

"What, tucked away here in the middle of nowhere? Lady Alexandra Morley?" He laughed and took another macaroon from the plate.

"Extraordinary, isn't it? But I find that the longer one spends away from London, the less one tends to miss it."

"No doubt, no doubt! I like a nip of the old country air myself, from time to time." He brushed the crumbs from his lap and consulted his watch. "But I must be off. I've a train from Florence tomorrow morning, and all sorts of arrangements to manage. The machine's coming in by steamship to Civitavecchia."

She stood up and held out her hand. "A pleasure, Mr. Hartley. A charming coincidence. I wish you much luck at the exposition. Do . . . do stop by when you're next in London, and tell me all about it."

"I shall, Lady Morley." He took her hand and shook it vigorously. "I shall."

She saw him out to his waiting carriage and walked in a daze back inside to the kitchen, where she collapsed in a chair at the table and stared at the swirling grain of the wood.

What had Finn meant by it?

A week or so ago, Hartley said. Finn had known she was a shareholder by then. He knew her fortune depended on the company. It couldn't be coincidence.

But he'd left. Without a note, without a kiss. Without a word.

So was this, then, his good-bye? The most generous, most selfless of gifts: her independence. The restoration of everything she valued most. A tender, dignified farewell.

Or simply payment for services rendered. A slap in the face.

She put her head into her arms. The sobs overtook her in a gust, wracking her body, relentless and unfamiliar. She hadn't cried, really cried, in years. Not since before her marriage, not since that night at Lady Pembroke's ball.

She couldn't explain why. She had what she wanted, after all. She had her money back, or nearly so. In a few weeks, assuming Hartley won his race, she could go back to London and resume her old life, as if nothing had changed, as if she'd never been away. No more Fulham or Putney. No lending libraries. No shabby dinner parties, the remains of the roast carefully husbanded to last the household for the rest of the week.

She should be laughing, not crying.

She should feel full, complete. Not empty.

Not hopeless.

Something touched her shoulder, warm and steady. She caught the faint scent of baking bread just before she heard Signorina Morini's voice.

"Signora, what is wrong? Why the crying?"

"Nothing. Oh, nothing!" A fresh burst of tears overwhelmed her.

"Signora, signora." The housekeeper settled into the chair next to her. "You are missing Signore Burke."

"Of course not. I'm . . . I only cracked my elbow on the . . . the corner . . . and . . ."

"Hush, signora." Her plump arm lay across Alexandra's back

with gentle pressure. A comforting warmth seemed to radiate from the contact. "Hush."

". . . and it hurts so . . . hurts like the *devil* . . ."

"Of course it is hurting you. Of course. Hush, hush, *mia cara*." She stroked Alexandra's hair. "I have the post from the village."

Alexandra let out a shuddering sigh. "Just put it on the table. I'll have a look."

"There are letters for Signore Burke, for the duke. There is also the newspaper."

"How charming. I'll see that Wallingford gets it." She rolled her head sideways, away from Signorina Morini, facing the wall of cupboards. No point letting someone else see one's misery.

"Hmm, yes," said the housekeeper. She went on stroking Alexandra's hair with light fingers. "Of course, it is possible you see something in the newspaper, something to give the smile back into your face."

Alexandra managed a choking little laugh. "Oh, quite impossible. Nothing but death and scandal and mayhem in the newspapers. The best one can hope for is bad news for one's enemies."

"Ha. You are clever, signora. Is what I am loving best about you, this clever head. Is making me laugh. Is making Signore Burke laugh." She gave Alexandra a squeeze across the shoulders. "The laughing, it gives a long life. Signore Burke, he is wise to choose you."

Alexandra straightened and wiped the tears from her cheeks. "Well, he seems to think it a poor bargain indeed. He has, thankfully, come to his proper senses, so we can all resume our . . . our former lives without further ado."

"Hmm, yes." Morini rose from her chair with a last pat to Alexandra's shoulder. "Still, signora, there is the chance you see something you like. Something of the good news. Is rare, the good news, but perhaps that is the reason it make us happy."

She left as quickly as she came. Alexandra sat staring at the table, still feeling a warm tingle in her scalp from the housekeeper's stroking fingers. So soothing, so comforting. Morini would have made an excellent mother.

The post lay on the table where the housekeeper had been sitting. Alexandra glanced at the pile of envelopes and the newspaper underneath and tried to summon the barest scrap of interest in the doings back home. Which ministers were in favor and which were out. Which opposition members had given scintillating speeches against this or that law and which had fallen flat. Railway disasters, diphtheria outbreaks, mine cave-ins, food shortages. Lady X's party had featured servers dressed as centaurs; Lord Z was conspicuously absent from his wife's latest confinement.

Once, she had eaten it all up.

Footsteps pattered through the doorway. "Oh, there you are!" said Abigail. "Who was the visitor? So awfully sorry to have abandoned you like that, but you know I'm hopeless with strangers. Either can't say a word, or else ask some frightfully indecent question by mistake. Oh, is that the *Times*? Do let me see it. I put a fiver on a Derby horse before we left, and I'm desperate to see if I've won."

Alexandra waved her hand. "By all means."

Abigail picked up the paper and lifted herself onto the table, legs swinging. "I shall skip right over the first few pages, if you don't mind. Nothing but railway disasters and mine cave-ins. Oh, bugger it! I've lost. To a nag named Sainfoin, if you will. Such rotten luck. That chap down the pub positively *assured* me. Well, that's that. Perhaps next . . ." She stopped in midsentence.

Alexandra looked up. "What is it?"

"Alexandra," she said, in a strangled voice, "you haven't seen the newspaper yet, have you?"

"No. It only just arrived. Has somebody died?"

"No. Quite the opposite."

She folded one side behind the other and handed it to Alexandra.

MR PHINEAS FITZWILLIAM BURKE, R.S.

in respect of a Scientific Experiment, conducted to Rigorous Standards and to his Thoroughgoing Satisfaction, concedes the following to

A . M .

THAT the Female Sex enjoys Unrivaled Superiority
to the Male Sex with regards to steadiness of purpose
in pursuit of Academic Enlightenment;

THAT the Male Sex is by far the more easily
distracted from its Intellectual Labours
by Thoughts of Love;

THAT in Courage and Steadfastness
the Female Sex has no Superior;

THAT all of the above are Scientifically Proven to
hold true at speeds exceeding Forty Miles per Hour.

On the TRUTH of these FINDINGS,
Mr. Burke declares himself prepared to stake
both his LIFE and his HEART.

*WRITTEN and ATTESTED
this 22nd day of JUNE, 1890*

"Good God." Alexandra looked up and met Abigail's eyes.
"Good God."

"Quite. A full sheet, just as we agreed, back at that inn."
Abigail peered over the edge. "His name must be five inches
tall. Rather sporting of him, to use only your initials. Do you
think anyone will smoke you out?"

"I don't know. I don't bloody care." Alexandra rose from her
chair and folded the paper back again. Her nerves sang with the
return of her fighting spirit. He loved her. He must love her. And
she'd be damned if she let him walk away again. "Abigail, my
dear."

Abigail looked at her, eyebrows raised. "Yes, Alex?"

"How would you like to go to Rome with me?"

TWENTY-FOUR

Borghese Gardens
Rome

I say, Mr. Hartley," said Alexandra, "this is really most inconvenient. Did you not consider your propensity for motion sickness before taking up automobiles as your life's work?"

William Hartley lifted his pale head and cast her a mournful look. "Trains are all right. I thought the same would hold true for horseless carriages. It's why I . . . oh dear."

Alexandra sighed. "Take my handkerchief, sir. What a damnably sticky wicket. No, do keep it. I have several, I assure you." She cast her eyes across the exhibition grounds, which were still empty of people in the early dawn light. Across the field, the temporary sheds housing the machines rose like ghosts from the shadowed grass.

In one of those sheds sat Finn's automobile.

"I'm quite all right up to twenty miles an hour," Mr. Hartley said hopefully.

"That's no use at all. Mr. Burke's machine can do forty with ease. Really, I'm most put out. The race begins in little more than twenty-four hours, and you're all but eviscerated." She tapped her fingers against the edge of the seat. "We *must* show well in this race. We *must* have a resounding triumph, or we'll be forced to accept Mr. Burke's bid after all."

And I'll be damned if I take his money, however he tries.

"No, no. There's talk of an exposition in Paris next fall. Or perhaps the spring . . ."

She looked back at Mr. Hartley. "Can one of your mechanics drive?"

He dabbed at his face again with her handkerchief. "Possibly. But they've never tried it before, I'm afraid. Ought to have brought one of my engineers down, but the cost . . ."

She heaved a great sigh. "There's nothing else for it. I shall have to drive."

Mr. Hartley nearly toppled out the open door of the automobile. "You!"

"Me, of course. Do you plan to win the race by discharging effluent across the faces of those competitors in your backdraft? I should think not."

"Do you . . . do you know how to drive?" he asked feebly.

"Yes, I do. Quite well. I shall have to take a bit of instruction from your mechanics, of course"—she nodded in the direction of the three men nearby, who leaned against the white fence circumscribing the grounds, faces purpling with suppressed laughter—"but I daresay I shall get on very well."

"You . . . you *daresay*?" He clutched at the handkerchief.

She smiled at him and administered a pat to his shoulder. "There, there. You're in no condition to drive in any case. Weak as a lamb, poor thing."

"I say." He straightened manfully.

"Don't worry. I've studied the course. It's a shame we didn't arrive earlier, to familiarize ourselves with things, but you could hardly have foreseen the delay with the customs officials."

"Deuced bureaucrats," Mr. Hartley said, under his breath.

"Off you go, then! The general public will be herding on through in little more than an hour. Gentlemen?" She motioned to the mechanics.

They grinned at her as they came up: no tugging of forelocks, no ducking of heads, no *your ladyships*. An egalitarian lot, these motor-car enthusiasts. "Yes, ma'am?" one of them asked, folding his arms.

"As you've perhaps noticed, Mr. Hartley is unwell."

"Sick as a dog, ma'am, looks like."

"Dogs ain't in it," agreed another.

She cleared her throat. "Yes, well. As it happens, I have some experience with automobiles myself, and I shall be taking over the driving for the upcoming race."

A slight breeze rustled the brim of her hat, the only movement in the stunned silence among them. She allowed the news a moment to digest.

"*You*, ma'am?" asked the first man at last.

"Yes, that's right. I've driven an electric motor at forty miles an hour on roads far inferior to tomorrow's route. Of course, you'll have to give me some brief instruction on the operation of a steam-powered engine, but I imagine . . ."

"But ma'am," broke in the second man, "it ain't that easy! Begging your pardon."

"Of course it isn't easy. If it were easy, Mr. Hartley wouldn't have become unwell."

"And . . . well, it ain't exactly what a lady might call safe."

"I'm not *exactly* like other ladies."

The men looked at one another and shrugged.

"That's that, then," Alexandra said. "Mr. Hartley, if you would be so good as to hand me your goggles."

Phineas Burke's head was priced rather high this morning, which rendered Delmonico's company only just tolerable on the short walk up the hill from the hotel on the via Vittorio Venetto to the exhibition grounds in the Borghese gardens.

"She is a beautiful creature, you must admit," Delmonico was saying, "though she makes rather much noise when one uses her hard."

Was he talking about his automobile or his mistress? Finn rubbed his aching temple. "I daresay."

"Yours, of course, has the advantage of silence," Delmonico went on, "and of course she doesn't lack spirit. But again, she tires too quickly. You'd be better off with my sort. Not so clean, I admit, and smells like the devil. But she's cheap to feed. Just fill her tank when she's empty."

Surely he must mean his automobile.

"I'm convinced I can solve the problem of battery endurance," Finn said. "I've already made astonishing progress. My motor's cleaner, more efficient, far easier to drive." He struggled to marshal his thoughts. He wasn't a drinking man in ordinary circumstances, but the revelry at the hotel last night had gone on and on, led by that Belgian fellow, and the waiters had refilled his wineglass with great dedication. Filled with restlessness, filled with uneasiness that Alexandra hadn't yet replied to his parting note, he'd emptied each round in due course. He'd stumbled into bed at two o'clock and thanked God, for the first time in well over a fortnight, that Alexandra wasn't there to witness his disgrace. He was still half-drunk, even now, and the remnants of intoxication paired most foully with the pounding of his head.

They had reached the white fence encircling the grounds and stopped to lean against the thin wood. "Ah, there we are," said Delmonico, gesturing at the open field, with its row of tidy sheds along one side catching the light from the rising sun. "Fully fifteen exhibitioners, eleven of them racing tomorrow. Even that compatriot of yours with the steam engine has come at last."

"Steam engine?" Finn shook his head, felt the resulting rattle, and stopped at once. "Who's got a steam engine?"

"A Mr. Hartley, from the Manchester Works in England. Perhaps you know him?"

"Hartley, by God!"

"He sent me a cable two weeks ago. He says he has made a very great breakthrough and wishes to compete." Delmonico leaned his chin on his hands. "If I am not mistaken, that is him now."

Finn raised his hand to shelter his brow against the flashing sunrise and peered into the field. A dark object sat in the distance, at the beginning of the track, surrounded by men. "What, there?"

"I believe so. The machine has only just arrived." Delmonico leaned forward. "It seems they want to give her a trial."

"By God," Finn whispered, ravaged head forgotten. "So they are." With one hand he reached inside his coat pocket and pulled out his watch.

The mechanics backed away from the automobile, revealing its silhouette against the sunrise. Finn had seen it before, touring the works with William Hartley several months ago: a rather

awkward body, with the driver perched high and the boiler positioned behind, delivering steam to the front-mounted motor.
Still, a steamer was capable of high speeds and rapid acceleration. No gear shifting necessary, no need to crank the engine. A
neat, efficient machine.

Except, of course, for the risk of boiler explosion.

Finn craned forward, trying to pick out more detail in the
watery light. Good God, that was an extraordinarily odd hat
Hartley was wearing. Almost . . .

The automobile surged forward like a shot from a cannon,
building speed with shocking ferocity. Finn couldn't hear the
engine from his post, couldn't see much except the rising cloud
of dust as the vehicle raced down the dirt track, beaten out of
the meadow turf just a few days ago.

Delmonico gasped next to him. "Such speed!"

The track ran in a straight line down the length of the exposition grounds before curving around to complete its oval. Finn
held his breath as the steamer drew closer, its contours emerging rapidly from the glare of the sun, resolving into detail. The
tires churned into the dirt, the rhythmic hum of the turbine
reached his ears, the driver . . .

The driver.

Finn felt the blood drain from his head, from his hands,
dropping like a stone into the center of his gut.

"By heaven," cried Delmonico, "they have a woman driving
her! A woman!" He pounded the fence with his fist.

The motor was slowing now, nearing the turn of the track.
Finn sensed, dimly, that he had vaulted over the white fence,
that he was running across the damp grass, that William Hartley's steamer was making the turn to head back to the starting
point.

"No!" he heard himself yell. "For God's sake!"

But the automobile was accelerating again, exploding back
down the track. It rushed past him, a hundred yards away, trailing a billowing banner of dust.

Finn turned and ran after it, legs pumping and lungs bursting,
as the long, hot rays of the Roman sunrise pierced his throbbing
skull. All he could do was chase after Lady Alexandra Morley
in her steam-powered automobile, while her delighted laugh

mingled with the throb of the engine across the motionless air between them.

Alexandra set the brake and jumped with delight from the seat. "Bloody splendid!" she called out, tearing off her hat and her goggles. Hartley and the mechanics ran up to her from the fence with identical mad grins on their faces. "Magnificent! How fast was it?"

"Forty-two miles per hour, by my watch!" Hartley brandished the instrument in question. "A record."

"I can't describe it! The acceleration! It was like bolting on a horse, only perfectly smooth, perfectly . . ."

"Alexandra!"

The word burst through the air, sharp and desperate.

Alexandra whirled at the sound. A man raced toward her through the yellow dust, long legs battering the ground like pistons. "Finn! There you are! Isn't it marvelous? I . . ."

He stopped a few yards away. "You fool! You bloody fool! You might have been killed!" He whipped about to face Hartley, chest heaving. "You damned idiot! Why did you let her drive?"

Hartley's face, already white, blanched even further. He removed his hat and wiped his forehead with Alexandra's lace-edged handkerchief. "I . . . She insisted . . . She told me she could drive . . ."

Finn threw his hands up in the air and turned back to Alexandra. "For God's sake, what were you thinking? A steamer's nothing like an electric. The boiler alone . . ."

She planted her hands on her hips and glared at him. "Well! That's a fine greeting. I thought you'd be pleased to see me."

He aimed his gaze upward to the pale morning sky. "Not tearing down a dirt track in an untested steam engine!"

"How perfectly unreasonable. You know I'm a competent driver. You taught me yourself."

"In *my* automobile, under *my* supervision. And for that matter . . ."

"I don't *need* supervision . . ."

". . . why are you here at all? And with *Hartley's* team?" His eyes blazed at her.

She glanced at her nephew-in-law, who stood with the
mechanics, hanging on every word. "I'm an owner of the company. As you know."

The lines of his face hardened. "Yes, I know."

"Oh, don't look at me like that! I only came down to watch,
to see the new machine in action, and then Mr. Hartley . . .
proved unable to drive this morning. I thought I might help."

"Risking your neck."

"No more than you do," she said quietly, "every day."

He didn't reply, only looked at her with his grave, penetrating eyes. His hands clenched and relaxed by his side. "Perhaps
we should continue this discussion later," he said at last.

"Yes, of course." She gathered herself and turned to the
other men. Her heart pounded hard in her chest, shocked with
awareness of Finn's gaze, Finn's body once more crackling with
energy and emotion a short distance away. "I beg your pardon.
Mr. Burke is extraordinarily protective of his friends. Shall we
put the automobile back in the shed? I expect you'll need to get
her ready for the public viewing."

Mr. Hartley started forward. "Yes, yes. Of course. Shall
drive her back myself. You . . . eh . . . of course, Burke, you're
welcome to . . . eh . . ."

"I shall accompany Lady Morley," said Finn.

Mr. Hartley leaped into the automobile and grasped the tiller, while the mechanics started off on foot. Finn stood motionless, watching them go. Alexandra's heart gave another dizzying
thump.

He turned. "So. You're here." He wore that fixed inscrutable
look of his, the scientist's look, studying her.

She swallowed. The glowing self-confidence that had filled
her since the sight of the newspaper advertisement drained
away, under the weight of that impassive gaze. Perhaps she'd
misread. Perhaps he'd arranged for the advertisement earlier,
before he knew about her ownership of his competitor.

Perhaps she'd just made the greatest blunder of her life.

"Would you rather I hadn't?" she asked carefully.

He shook his head. "At the moment, I suppose, I'm only glad
you're alive and whole."

"I didn't mean to worry you. I didn't know you were there.

I . . ." She checked herself, and then asked, "Why did you leave like that, without me?"

His expression softened at last into a rueful smile. "For one thing, darling, you're the devil of a distraction. And as I explained in the note . . ."

"Note? What note?"

He started. "You didn't get my note?"

"No! I looked for one, I thought you'd left one, and then I found that list of shareholders, that stupid, stupid . . ."

He stepped forward and took her shoulders. "That damned Giacomo! You thought I'd left without a word? Oh, darling."

"But the list . . . the shareholders' list . . ." A tear leaked from her right eye. She brushed it away in an angry gesture. "I knew you'd think the worst, that I'd betrayed you, but I didn't, Finn, I swear it!"

"Of course not. I realized that, once I thought it through. Once I saw you fighting to save the workshop. Oh, Lord, darling, don't cry." He reached up one hand to touch her cheek.

"At first . . ." She shut her eyes to keep the tears in. "At first I wanted to find out about what you were doing, to see if there was something I might learn, something that might help. I was so desperate. But, really, it was *you*, Finn. I realize that now. It was all an excuse to see you. I knew in my heart the idea was all useless, because yours was electric and Hartley's was steam, but I told myself . . . I told myself . . ."

"Shh. I know." His hands caressed her shoulders.

She opened her eyes and looked at him steadily. "From the beginning, from that first dinner in the inn, when you looked at me with those eyes of yours, looking straight into my heart. It was *you*. You must know that."

He drew her against him and wrapped his long arms around her body. His heart beat against her ear, still rapid from his sprint across the field. "I know it now."

She closed her eyes and savored him, flush and living against her. She could almost feel the blood rushing through his veins, the vibrant strength of him enfolding her. How she'd missed him! Only now, in his arms, did she realize just how much. How dull, how empty life had been without him. "What did your note say?" she whispered.

His chuckle rumbled against her ear. "All sorts of lovesick rot. I'm rather glad you didn't read it, after all."

"I'd have come to Rome straightaway, if I had. I'd have taken the next train."

He shifted beneath her head. "Hmm. And why *did* you come?"

"Why, to help Hartley, of course. If he wins the race . . ."

He started backward. "If *he* wins the race? *Hartley?* You're on *his* side?" He took her by the arms and set her away, looking directly in her eyes.

"Well, yes. From a practical point of view. I'm a shareholder, after all." She caught his incredulous expression and patted his elbow. "Of course I want you to do well, Finn. It's just that he *needs* this. *I* need it. He's got to prove to the City that the automobile's a winner."

Finn's voice took on an ominous note. "And why is that, *exactly*, Alexandra? Why does he need to prove the automobile to the City?"

A rather uncomfortable feeling began to work its way through the Finn-induced bliss in Alexandra's brain. "Well, so that . . . so that the shares will go up. So that I can sell my stake and have my money back and . . ."

"I assume, of course, you're aware that the company's owners have already received an offer to tender their shares at a generous price?"

She cleared her throat. "Er. Yes."

"I assume you're aware of the identity of the individual making the offer?" he pressed, in a dark growl.

"Oh, Finn, really." She smiled up at him. "It's too kind of you—noble, really—but I simply can't allow you to throw your money away on another company, just to give me my jointure back. I have my pride."

He removed his hands from her arms and ran them through his hair. "Christ, Alexandra. You haven't convinced Hartley to *refuse* the offer, have you?"

"I didn't need to. He thinks we can do a great deal better than fifty shillings a share."

"He's mad!"

She crossed her arms. "Well, I won't let you do it! I won't

tender my shares to you, by God, even if you offered me a hundred!"

"Why not? Why the *bloody* hell not?" He stood before her, arms akimbo, bristling, looking two or three inches taller and a good foot broader. The rising sun had caught his hair aflame, radiant red gold against the pale hazy sky.

Anger filled her, hot and unreasoning, at the glorious sight of him, at the way he glowed with brilliance and power and infallibility. Even the sun couldn't resist him.

"Because I won't! I won't let you buy me! The way Morley did, the way every man does!" she blazed back. "I am not for *sale*, Phineas Burke! And neither is Manchester Machine Works!"

She whirled away and strode off in the direction of the automobile sheds. The grounds were scattered with people now: exhibitioners readying their automobiles, members of the public arriving early to peer at the machines, photographers setting up cameras.

"Wait, Alexandra!" he called from behind her.

She broke into a run, stumbling across the field in her cumbersome skirts and her awkward shoes, half hoping he would catch up with her.

But he didn't.

TWENTY-FIVE

W hy, I believe it is Lady Morley!"
Alexandra turned to see a man of medium height tilt his bowler hat courteously in her direction, his black eyes flashing. He must have sensed her confusion, for he supplied, quickly, "Bartolomeo Delmonico, your ladyship. We met in the spring at my friend Mr. Burke's workshop near Florence."

"Signore Delmonico! Of course." She held out her hand.

He took her gloved fingertips and bowed over them. "Am I mistaken, your ladyship, or was it you who drove Mr. Hartley's automobile on the track yesterday morning? A dazzling spectacle."

"Yes, it was. Thank you." She allowed her eyes an instant to dart past him, searching for Finn's ginger head above the crowd. All day yesterday, she'd watched him stalk about the exhibition grounds, half a head taller than anyone else, radiating confidence and command. This was his turf, his kingdom, and he roamed about the crowds like Jupiter down from Olympus. She'd lost count of the number of times someone had nudged her and said, *Look, there's Mr. Burke, all the way from England!* or *Have you seen Mr. Burke's machine? The man is a genius!*

Deeply annoying, and also deeply arousing.

She'd told herself she was too proud to approach him, or that they were all too busy. In truth, she found him too strange, too intimidating, here in this foreign place where aristocratic English titles were as flimsy as paper, and only genius and initiative had the power to impress anyone. At the exhibitioners' dinner last night, she'd been seated at the opposite end of the table, with Hartley's team, and had hardly spoken to Finn all night. *You're enjoying yourself?* he'd asked at one point, when the shifting crowd had brought them together, his voice as cold and reserved as the rainy March evening they'd first met. *Yes, very much,* she'd answered, chin tilted high, and then some half-drunk Belgian exhibitioner had claimed his attention, and that was that.

It had been an exceedingly restless night for her.

"Have you met my friend Herr Jellinek?" Delmonico was asking her, turning to a tall bearded man at his left. "My dear Jellinek, I have the honor to present Lady Morley, an English rose of the highest bloom."

Alexandra fixed a smile to her mouth. "Signore Delmonico is too flattering. A pleasure, Herr Jellinek."

"The pleasure is mine," said the man, in a thick German accent. He straightened from her outstretched hand.

"Have you brought an automobile to the exposition, Herr Jellinek?" she inquired.

He shook his head. "An enthusiast only, Lady Morley."

Delmonico laughed. "Herr Jellinek is in great demand among our exhibitioners, Lady Morley. He has a great passion for the automobile, and seeks one with particular promise in which to invest."

"How brave of you!" Alexandra said. "I'm surprised our dear Delmonico lets you out of his sight at all."

Jellinek smiled and glanced at the Italian. "His machine does impress me very much. He is far in advance of others with petrol engines, save perhaps for Herr Daimler."

"Oh, Herr Daimler!" Alexandra exclaimed. "I've heard of him! The fellow in Munich with the four-stroke engine. Is he exhibiting here this week?"

A scowl settled on Delmonico's face. "No."

"A great shame." Jellinek sighed. "I do not know why he has not come. It would be so much use to see the two machines side by side."

Alexandra glanced between the two men, at the black and restless expression on Delmonico's face. "A great shame," she echoed. She noticed a young woman by Jellinek's side, holding a large dark-haired baby against her hip and looking rather bored. She smiled kindly. "Have you brought your wife, Herr Jellinek?"

"Forgive me!" Herr Jellinek put his hand to his wife's back. "My wife, Frau Jellinek, Lady Morley. She has no English, I fear."

Alexandra took Frau Jellinek's free hand and squeezed it. "You have a lovely child, Frau Jellinek."

Jellinek murmured something in his wife's ear, and she smiled a great proud smile. "*Danke, mein Dame. Sie heisst Adrienne.*"

Jellinek turned to Alexandra. "She thanks you, Lady Morley. Our daughter is named Adrienne. Though we call her Mercédès, because she is our gift."

"Mercédès." Alexandra bent and placed her finger in the baby's grasping fist. "What a lovely name."

Though Finn located William Hartley readily enough—in the center of a phalanx of photographers, his steam motorcar hissing behind him—finding a quiet moment in which to intimidate him proved more difficult.

In the end, he resorted to brute strength.

"A word with you, sir," he said, grasping the man by the arm and pulling him away from the battery of camera lenses.

"Why, Mr. Burke!" Hartley straightened his cuffs and craned his neck to meet Finn's gaze. "What can I do for you?"

For most of his life, Finn had regarded his excessive height as a matter of personal grievance between himself and his Maker. There was nothing at all wrong with being a tall, sturdy chap like Wallingford or Penhallow, but all good things had their limits. Once he'd passed seventy-four inches, during the weedlike summer of his fifteenth year, Finn cursed each successive inch—there were four of them—more roundly than the last. He grew from gangly, awkward youth to broad, longshanked adult, always half a head taller than his companions, always bumping into doorframes and folding himself into train compartments and hanging his feet over the edges of beds. To have his six and a half feet crowned by a shock of ginger hair was only the final insult.

Now, staring down at the hat brim of the modestly proportioned William Hartley, who continued to straighten his cuffs as if his life depended on it, Finn recanted.

Height was good.

"You can do a great deal," Finn said, in a drawling voice. "You can begin by telling Lady Morley you'll brave the rigors of the race yourself."

Hartley removed his hat, ran his fingers through his hair, and replaced the bowler on his head. "Oh, Mr. Burke. I'm afraid . . . well, the plans are already in place . . ."

"Change them."

"Well, I . . . I . . ." Hartley swallowed, and then burst out, "I don't see that it's any business of yours! Sir."

Finn bent his head a little closer. "Oh, but it is. Lady Morley is very much my business. Do you understand me?"

"Yes, sir."

"I don't want the slightest whiff of danger to so much as drift in her direction. Is that clear?"

"Yes, sir. But Mr. Burke," Hartley said, taking a handkerchief from his pocket and patting his forehead with it, "I don't see how. The race begins in an hour. How am I to find a substitute driver?"

Finn shrugged his shoulders with deliberate slowness. "If you can't find a suitable driver, I expect you'll have to cancel your entry."

"Mr. Burke! But you know—surely you know—we need to prove ourselves." Hartley's voice took on a pleading note, perilously close to a whine. His round cheeks worked in agitation. "We can't simply cancel. Our investors would . . ." He stopped. "Oh, I see. I see."

Finn narrowed his eyes. "What do you see, Mr. Hartley?"

"You *want* us to lose, don't you?"

"Naturally, I do. I'm fielding another entry, after all. But my primary concern is for Lady Morley's safety."

Hartley stabbed a finger in the general direction of Finn's chest. "You want us to lose so we'll be forced to accept your flimsy offer for my company. Eh?"

Finn raised his overlarge hand and folded it around Hartley's stabbing finger. "Fifty shillings a share is not flimsy. It's a damned windfall, and you know it."

"If we win . . ."

"If you win, then what? Your company will be worth over half a million pounds overnight? When current law in England prohibits speeds in excess of four miles an hour? When legal operation of motorized road vehicles requires the employment of no less than three accompanying men?" He brought Hartley's offending finger down to his side and released it with a pat. "I think not."

Hartley's face began to flush. "We expect those laws to be repealed."

"Not for years, I think. Not with railway interests pushing so hard to keep them in place. Eventually, perhaps, but not yet."

The photographers, noticing the intensity of the conversation, began to draw near. Hartley glanced nervously toward them and then back to Finn. He licked his lips. "If that's what you think, Mr. Burke, then I wonder why you're so keen to buy my company."

Finn shrugged and folded his arms. "Because I'm playing the long game, Hartley. I can afford to; I've got two million pounds in hard-won capital, and I'm going to use it to muddle around and experiment and find the solution that sticks." He leaned down and spoke softly. "Cash is king, Hartley. Remember that."

"Damn it all, Burke."

Finn straightened. "Now, look, Hartley. As I said, I don't particularly care if your automobile runs today or not. My only concern is for Lady Morley's safety. If you can find another driver, I'll raise my offer to fifty-five shillings a share." He reached out his hand and brushed at a piece of lint on Hartley's wool shoulder. "Should Lady Morley so much as step inside that machine of yours, however, I'll withdraw my offer entirely."

Hartley's mouth opened and closed. He threw a desperate look at the photographers, setting up their cameras a few feet away.

"Mr. Hartley! Mr. Burke!" called out one. "A photograph, please!"

"Why, Hartley, old chap." Finn linked his arm with the other man and turned them both to face the cameras. "Do smile, there's a fellow. You're looking a bit panicked."

"But surely you understand. When Lady Morley's determined about something, she always manages to get her way."

"Hmm. Yes. I've noticed," Finn said affably. "So I suggest you find a way to manage *her*. And soon." He started to turn away.

"Hold still, please!" shouted a photographer.

"If it's as easy as that," Hartley said, "why the devil don't *you* tell her to sod off?"

"Well, well!" broke in a female voice. "How very charming! Our two competitors, linking arms and all that before the race. Whatever can they be talking about?"

Hell.

Finn looked across the heads of the photographers. There stood Alexandra in another impeccable white dress, hat spreading about her head, arms folded across her bountiful chest. The expression on her face could have melted stone.

"Gentlemen," he said to the cameras. "Thank you. That will be all."

He withdrew his arm from Hartley's, stepped over to Alexandra, and drew her aside. "Darling," he began.

"You're plotting against me, aren't you?" she said, in a harsh whisper. "You're trying to convince Hartley to keep me from driving."

He exhaled. "Yes, I am. It's dangerous, Alexandra. Not just the race, but the automobile itself. I haven't looked at the engine. I don't trust it. It's untested, untried. And steam's a damnably tricky thing."

"Finn, if I don't drive, we won't win. It's as simple as that. Hartley's a fool, and the mechanics don't know the course."

"For God's sake, Alexandra! Better the automobile loses the race than you lose your life!"

"Don't be ridiculous. No one's going to *die*, Finn. Or perhaps you don't like the idea of my racing against you? Beating you, perhaps?" Her eyebrows rose in challenge.

"Nonsense. I . . ." He frowned into her gaze. "All right. Perhaps a little."

"I knew it!"

Finn looked up at the cloudless sky, hoping God might perhaps help him understand her. "Look, I don't see why you're so determined on it. It's as if you want to pit yourself against me."

"That's not it at all. Not exactly. It's just . . . oh, Finn, don't you see? It isn't just the money; it isn't just being able to sell my shares to someone other than you. I admit that. I *want* to do it, to prove to myself that I *can* do it." She put her hand on his arm, her slender fingers biting into the thin summer-weight wool of his jacket. "Look at me, Finn. When will I ever have another chance to do something like this?"

"You can drive my motor whenever you like."

"Would you let me race it today?"

He hesitated. "No. The course . . ."

Silence settled between them. In the back of his mind, he sensed the shift of people around him, the curious glances directed their way, the smug attention of William Hartley in his wilting bowler hat a few yards away. But in his sight there was only Alexandra, her golden brown eyes looking up at him in supplication, her hand still tight and pleading on his arm.

Pleading not for his permission, he realized, because she was going to climb into Hartley's motor-car and drive it anyway.

Pleading for his understanding.

"You see?" she asked, in a small voice.

"Oh, Alexandra," he breathed out. "The danger . . ."

"Far less danger than having a baby, I think, and most women face that all right."

He slid his hand down her arm to grasp her fingers. With his other hand he grasped her chin, heedless of their gathering audience. "In other words, you're going to risk your life just to prove to me that you don't need my money?"

She tried to pull away. "That's not it. You're twisting my words."

"Because I don't understand. I don't. What are you saying, exactly? That if you don't win the race, you won't have me? That your damned independence, this need to have a fortune of your own, is worth more to you than a life with me?"

"No, I . . ." She pushed his hand away. "Why do you put it like that?"

"Because that's how it is. You're risking everything just to prove that you're not the mercenary woman you used to be, when I already know that perfectly well. When I've been trying

to convince you all along. I don't need your proof, Alexandra."
He forced his voice to soften. "I only need your love. Can I not
have that, at least?"

"Stop that, Finn. Don't turn this into a test."

"It *is* a test, by God!"

"Is it? Is it?" Her voice grew, not in volume, with nearly
every ear on the grounds trained on them, but in intensity. She
folded her arms and leaned forward. "Very well, Finn. If it's a
test you want, it's a test you'll get. I'll back out of the race."

He let out his breath in a gust. "Thank God. Thank you,
Alexandra, for understanding. I promise I'll . . ."

She held up her hand. "Wait. As I said, I'll back out. But only
if you will, too."

He stared at her. "What the devil?"

"What's good for the goose is good for the gander, isn't that
right? If I've got to pull out of the race to prove my devotion, so
must you. If it's too dangerous for me, it's too dangerous
for you."

"That's . . . that's rot! That's the most unreasonable . . .
ridiculous . . . female convoluted . . . reasoning!" He knew he
was sputtering, and he didn't care.

"I think it's quite logical indeed, and I'm sure that if you
consider the matter carefully, you'll see that I'm right. After all,
I have a great deal more to lose than you do." She took her sleek
kidskin gloves from one clenched fist and fitted them carefully
to her hands. "Now, while you're busy thinking it all over, I
believe I have an automobile to ready for a race."

TWENTY-SIX

Of the eleven competitors in the race, Alexandra decided, only two were any real threat to her: Bartolomeo Delmonico, with his rumbling petrol engine, and Phineas Burke.

Phineas Burke, who should have been making a last-minute inspection of his own motor-car just now, but who instead hovered over the boiler of William Hartley's automobile, firing questions at all three mechanics at once.

"Impossible man," she said, as she wound her white cotton voile scarf securely about her head, trapping the hot afternoon sun in her hair.

"I think it's touching," said Abigail. "Aren't you going to speak to him?"

"I think we've done enough speaking for one day. Goggles, please." A flashbulb went off at her left elbow, scraping against the raw edge of her nerves.

Not that she would admit *that* to anyone.

Abigail handed her the goggles and helped her slip them over her head, with the lenses atop her scarf, ready to be pulled down. "This is so thrilling," her sister said, tightening the buckle on the leather strap. "I want you to know, I've laid twenty lire on you with the chap running the book at the hotel café."

"Where the devil did you find twenty lire?" Alexandra asked her sister. "Really, Finn," she said, more loudly, "that's quite enough. These men are really most frightfully competent. You should see to your own machine."

He straightened and turned to her. His forehead was creased with worry. A light sheen of perspiration shone on his temples, beneath the line of his driving cap. "You're certain of the course?"

"Perfectly. Around the gardens, down to the Colosseum, back up to the gardens. I tracked it yesterday. And it's marked."

He stared at her a second or two longer, his eyes the color of new leaves in the bright Roman sunshine. "Be safe," he said.

For an instant, her heart swelled painfully against her ribs.

"And you," she whispered.

He turned and walked away, his long limbs flowing purposefully through the thick, hot air. Alexandra watched him circle his automobile, checking the tires, and then swing into the driver's seat in a competent motion. Why couldn't he understand? Could he simply not imagine her need to walk into his arms as her own woman, with her own fortune, free and unencumbered? Could he not comprehend her desire to shut the door on her past, on the idle and useless Lady Morley she'd once been, the one who married for money and position instead of love?

"Lady Morley."

She was so absorbed, she didn't hear the words at first. It was Abigail who whipped about and exclaimed, "Good God! Wallingford!"

Alexandra turned. "Wallingford! What on earth?"

He stood there glowering in a light gray suit and straw boater, his black eyes flashing not at her, but at her sister. "You might have told me where you were going, you silly fools," he said.

Alexandra recovered in an instant. "And why is that, exactly?"

His gaze slid to her. "Because I woke up four days ago to find myself the only damned resident in the castle, and the entire pile gone silent, without a word of news from anyone, and . . ."

"I'm so terribly sorry," Abigail said. "How were the goats?"

"I don't," he said, between clenched lips, "give a damn about the goats."

"Such language, Your Grace! In front of Miss Harewood! I'm shocked. Shocked and appalled. Moreover, I've a race that begins in"—Alexandra consulted her watch—"five minutes,

and I beg leave to point out that you're a most unwelcome ob-
struction."

"You're *driving*? In the *race*?" He looked thunderstruck. His
eyes shifted back and forth between her and her sister.

"Certainly I am."

"But you can't simply leave your sister alone in a crowd
of . . . of *Italians*!" Wallingford exclaimed.

"Of course not. Mr. Hartley will protect her from any insult."
She nodded to where Hartley stood a few yards away, hat in
hand, scratching his ear, mechanics lounging at his side. He
seemed to hear his name, for he looked over at them, replaced
his hat, and worked his jowls.

Wallingford stared a moment and turned back to Alexandra.
"You're not serious."

"Well, watch her yourself, then. Though I'd be more concerned for the poor Roman fellow who dared to accost her. Mr.
Hartley!"

He straightened. "Yes, your ladyship?"

"I believe it's time. Is the steam up?"

One of the mechanics spoke. "Yes, ma'am. Full steam. She's
ready to go."

At that instant, a loud noise like a pistol shot cracked through
the air.

"The poor fellow," Alexandra said.

They watched in respectful silence as the injured man
passed by the ten remaining automobiles in a stretcher, arm and
face bound up in white.

"Did you see the way his arm swung about? Jolly lurid,"
Abigail observed. "To say nothing of his jaw. I thought they'd
never get all that blood off the bonnet."

"Damned cranks on these petrol engines," said Alexandra.
Her fingers drummed along the steering tiller. A solid weight
had been forming in the pit of her belly for some time. She
ignored it. She looked instead down the row of competitors,
lined up at the starting point, automobiles of all shapes and
sizes and engines, each more improbable than the last. One fellow balanced on what looked to be a sort of motorized bicycle.

She saw Delmonico chuckling with Herr Jellinek, whose

wife and daughter were apparently avoiding the hurly-burly of the race itself. The Italian's automobile perched next to him, its metal frame polished to a blinding sheen.

In the automobile next to her, Finn stared straight ahead, as if memorizing every paving stone on the road before them. With one hand he drew his goggles down over his eyes. Wallingford came around and leaned on the edge of Finn's doorframe, exchanging a few words, face intent.

On Finn's other side, Delmonico's mechanic cranked his shiny beast's engine with expert heaves of his arm. A deep growl rumbled through the air, and then another from down the line, smothering the boiler's hiss behind her. Delmonico glanced down the row of motor-cars in her direction, and the look in his eyes surprised her, fierce and piratical beneath the huge disks of his goggles.

A flash of recognition exploded in her brain.

She'd seen that expression before, those dark, fierce eyes narrowed in malevolence. She'd seen it among the olive trees, near Finn's workshop, on her way down to the lake on Midsummer's Eve.

The night of the fire.

Good God. It was Delmonico. Delmonico, who wanted Jellinek to invest in his company. Delmonico, who'd spent a fortune, who'd nearly bankrupted himself setting up this exposition, to showcase his own automobile.

Delmonico, who would apparently do anything to win this race.

She turned to Finn and called his name, into the roar of engines and the shouting of the crowd. He didn't stir, didn't so much as flicker a muscle of his face.

"Finn!" she screamed again.

He started and turned to her.

"Finn! Watch Delmonico!" She stabbed her finger at the Italian.

Finn swiveled his head and looked at Delmonico. His face returned to hers with a quizzical shrug.

"Watch him!" she screamed again.

Finn shrugged again and pointed in front of them.

She turned to follow his finger, to where the starter stood fifty yards down the track with his pistol raised.

It was too late. The race was about to begin.

The sultry smell of petrol exhaust filled her nose and lungs. Her right hand clenched the steering tiller with an unshakable grip, and her left hand stuck to the throttle.

The starter looked up and down the line, consulted his watch, and scanned the line again. *Watch the pistol,* Finn had told her. *You'll see the puff of smoke before the sound reaches your ears.*

She watched the pistol. Her pulse pounded in her throat.

Around her, the crowd of spectators had gone utterly still. Not a sound, except for the roar of the engines; not a movement, except for the starter swiveling his head up and down the line of automobiles. She sensed the eager pressure of the steam in the boiler behind her, ready to burst.

Puff.

An eternity passed before the crack rattled her eardrums, an eternity in which Finn's motor surged next to her and her foot lifted from the brake and she opened the throttle.

Hartley's steamer erupted forward with an eager burst of speed. She matched Finn, passed him, her acceleration carrying her to the front of the field with nothing but empty paved road before her, lined with trees and spectators. The wind flowed over her scarf, fluttered the ends, cooled her head from the burn of the sun.

Elation sang through her body.

She had the fastest machine. She'd stick to the front, draw Delmonico's attention, keep him from bothering with Finn. Delmonico would follow the greatest threat. All she had to do was keep her lead.

From behind her came the whining grind of the petrol engines, shifting gears and building speed. Somewhere in that pack Delmonico's automobile strained toward her, trying to catch up.

The dust from her tires must be stinging his goggles.

Ha-bloody-ha.

F inn knew something was off the instant his automobile leaped from the starting line.

She was quick off the mark, almost as quick as Hartley's steam engine. But some subtle spark was missing, some additional fraction of energy.

He couldn't pause to consider the question. Dust and motor-cars swarmed around him, jockeying for position. The screaming growls of the petrol engines filled his ears, drowning out the roar of the crowd. A race among gentlemen it might be, an exhibition of infant motor development, but a race was still a race.

And Alexandra was winning it, by God. Her motor streaked away under the full pressure of its formidable boiler, raising a billowing fug of dust and steam behind it. He had to keep her in sight, at least.

The paving stones shook under his tires and the cheering crowd streamed past. Eighteen, perhaps twenty miles an hour, he judged, holding position between Delmonico on his right and the motorized bicycle on his left. Just ahead, on the other side of the motor-cycle, rolled another motor-car, a high-wheeled petrol model with the driver mounted atop a converted carriage frame.

The four of them tore down the road, passing through the entrance of the Borghese gardens and angling right onto the via di Porta Pinciana. The crowds still pressed against the sides of the road, cheering wildly, stucco-fronted buildings rising up behind them: a noisy tunnel down which they barreled after the fleeing shape of the Hartley steamer.

Up ahead lay the sharp left turn onto the via Sistina. The motors began to slow. Finn's brain had split into two: one part followed Alexandra's progress as she disappeared around the corner, while the other jostled about with the three automobiles around him. Delmonico roared along steadily, ahead and then behind, his goggles flashing in the sun. The motor-cycle kept pace. Finn didn't know the driver, another dark-haired man who glanced at Delmonico in a constant rhythm, speeding and slowing, taking his cues from the Italian.

As they neared the corner, Finn saw the other petrol motor wobble.

He backed off and edged farther away, almost pushing Delmonico to the right. The other motor recovered, and then wobbled again, and recovered.

Just as they reached the corner, the tiller came off in the driver's hands.

Shouts, roars. The motor-cycle veered smoothly right, forcing Finn back. The disabled motor kept going in a straight line, right for the crowd. The driver waved the useless tiller, screaming, and dove out of his seat in a graceless tumble.

"'*Ware! 'Ware!*'" Finn shouted.

Delmonico glanced backward at him and cut across his path, angling around the corner. Finn turned sharply, nearly grazing the back of Delmonico's machine. His own motor strained mightily, sliding against the paving stones in a screech of tire rubber.

Out of the corner of his eye, he saw the crowd part in the path of the tillerless automobile, until nothing remained but a fruit stand. The vendor turned his head just in time to dive away, before the machine plowed straight through the middle of his cart to bury itself under a load of astonished bananas.

Finn judged the turn to a hairbreadth. Inches from Delmonico on his right, from the motor-cycle on his left, he rounded the corner and shot down the straightaway, where Alexandra's motor appeared once more, leading by twenty or thirty yards at least. Delmonico flung back a look of deep annoyance and wiped his goggles.

The buildings here were taller, denser, red roof tiles burning in the sunshine. They rushed past the yawning gap of the Piazza Barberini and glimpsed the Triton Fountain through the crowd. Finn fought to keep up with Delmonico and the motor-cycle, fought to keep them from closing him off in a pincer. Behind him came the shouts and rattles of other motor-cars; ahead of him lay the acute right turn onto the wide via Nazionale.

His heart climbed into his throat. He strained to watch the black shape of Alexandra's motor, to spot her white scarf rising above the boiler. *Slow down, slow down*, he begged her. *Don't risk the turn*. He had no idea what sort of steering Hartley's engineers had put in their machine, what strength of rubber contained the air in her tires. A blowout at this speed . . . a shade too fast around the turn . . . the motor rolling over, Alexandra crushed beneath it, Alexandra flung free to break her neck on the paving stones . . .

He couldn't watch, couldn't look away. He didn't notice when the motor-cycle swerved, didn't notice until the last second. He hit the brakes hard to avoid the churning tire, and Delmonico roared on ahead of him in a burst of speed, spewing mottled smoke from the back of his engine.

Damn it all! Bested, caught out in a moment's distraction. Another motor-car caught up with him, a steamer, ranging up on his right side. He gritted his teeth. He couldn't see Alexandra's motor now. He'd have to trust that she made the turn, that he'd taught her well. He pictured her hands on the tiller, elegant, capable white fingers, steering safely around the corner and onto the via Nazionale.

The corner neared. No smashup, no smoking wreckage. He sighed out in relief and leaned forward, judging the angle and his own speed and the motor rattling along beside him in a hiss of eager steam.

They slowed in tandem, turned the sharp corner in tandem. He glanced at the other driver, a fair-haired young man with an intent expression. The wide avenue of the via Nazionale stretched before him, lined with people who turned and cheered at their approach. Not so many, now. A sparser crowd, easing the claustrophobic tension of the early stage. Finn glanced down at the instruments on his dash, made to his own specification, measuring speed from the tire rotation and voltage and remaining power from the battery.

Something was certainly wrong.

Not enough charge.

He should have more. He'd recharged the battery fully last night and installed it this morning into the engine.

Twenty yards ahead, Delmonico surged along, the motorcycle dropping back behind him. Finn drove in lockstep with the fair-haired man in the steamer, down the via Nazionale and around another corner to the via dei Serpenti, his brain working madly to solve the problem.

Leakage? Had he left it running at some point? The drive over from the shed: When had he turned the engine on? When had he turned it off? He'd been so bloody preoccupied with Alexandra. He couldn't say for certain.

Did he have enough charge to finish the race?

Uphill?

The pale stone arches of the Colosseum rose up out of the pavement ahead. He'd lost sight of Alexandra ahead, but he could sense her. She'd be exhilarated at her speed, exhilarated at leading the race. She'd be carried along by the power of her steam engine, beginning the curve around the ancient stadium, drunk on the cheering of the crowd and the wind in her scarf.

God, let her make it. No disasters. Just let her make it.

The arches began to flash by. He curved to the right, around the Colosseum piazza. The steamer edged in front by a few feet, helped by the fractionally shorter distance. A smooth, round curve, beautifully executed, arches streaming by under the pure blue sky, and then they sprang out into the open before angling left up the via dei Fori Imperiali.

Finn spared not a glance for the familiar shape of the ancient ruins, rising up from his left in a jumble of crumbling stone. He glanced down again at the battery dials, calculating, measuring.

Enough. Just enough. Enough that he'd still have power left at the end. He could keep up with the leaders, make sure Alexandra was all right. Perhaps even enough left for a burst of speed. Enough to beat that rascal Delmonico, at least.

Up they charged, toward the Piazza Venezia, past cafés and fruit stands and cheering crowds. The knot in Finn's belly began to relax. Elation began to sing through him: at the speed and the hot rush of wind in his face, at the unrestrained joy and wonder on the faces of the Romans he passed, at the rear tires of Delmonico's motor edging closer and closer.

Not until they'd passed through the famous piazza, not until they'd started up the via del Corso, did anything go wrong.

Not until they neared the corner of the via delle Muratte, leading to the Trevi Fountain, did he notice the tire rolling merrily past him. Only then did he look, astonished, to his right, where the steamer and its fair-haired driver veered left toward him, and then right, and then, as another tire popped off, straight into the paving stones.

Motor-cars, Alexandra thought confidently, were without a doubt the wave of the future.

Such glorious speed, such ease of movement! She must convince Finn to switch to steam. His electric was well enough, but it couldn't accelerate out of a corner like this. Couldn't sail along, far ahead of everyone else. Why, she hadn't seen her competitors in ages! The cheering of the crowd went right to her head as she soared along the broad length of the via del Corso.

Well, perhaps soared wasn't quite the word. Vibrated. Bumped, even. Hartley's engineers seemed not to have put, as Finn had, so much attention into such comforting details as suspension.

But these were minor considerations. She narrowed her eyes as she approached the turn into the via delle Muratte and regulated the throttle with care. From behind came the distant roar of a petrol engine, Delmonico's probably. Of Finn there was no sign. Good. The farther back he was, the better. As long as Delmonico wasn't after him, he'd be quite all right. Nothing to worry about with Finn, strong, capable Finn, clever as the devil. After the race, she'd explain, she'd tell him what she'd realized about Delmonico. She'd quite happily let Finn exact whatever revenge he wanted on the villain.

Everything would be fine, as long as she stayed ahead of Delmonico. As long as she won the race. The money, the company shares, the glory: It meant nothing now. All that mattered was that Finn was safe.

She could do it. She could save him.

People were waving at her now. She slowed just enough to swing around the corner, one hand on the tiller and one on the throttle. She couldn't wave back, so she smiled and nodded, racing up the street and acknowledging her admiring public.

Really, Romans were so lovely. Waving and shouting at her like that. Encouraging, was what it was.

Pop.

Hiss.

POP.

Wrong. Something was wrong. The popping grew louder, insistent. The automobile was slowing down, as if someone had hitched a rhinoceros to its rear. She pulled desperately at the throttle. The engine gasped valiantly and lurched forward.

A sound came up on her right, a rattletrap roar, and the motorcycle appeared at the side of her vision. It pressed against her, forcing her to the left, where the Trevi Fountain loomed upward in a tangle of streaming Gothic intricacy.

"Bastard!" she shouted. "Bastard!"

The driver's head swiveled in astonishment, and so did his motor-cycle. She swerved to avoid him, bounced up the steps to the fountain's edge, and slid over the bonnet of the motor to land with a splash under Neptune's disapproving gaze.

TWENTY-SEVEN

Finn saw the dripping figure up ahead. White muslin plastered its legs, white cotton voile plastered its skull, and ropy dark hair plastered its back. It shoved a long, elegant finger into the chest of the motor-cycle driver, and its language was both forthright and picturesque.

It could only be Alexandra.

He took in the scene at a glance. The motor-cycle turned sideways in the middle of the road. Delmonico outside his automobile, pushing the other vehicle out of the way, his own engine coughing itself to death.

A narrow passageway remained between Delmonico's motor and the stucco-fronted building along the side of the street. He threaded his motor through, set the brake, and jumped out.

Relief hit him like a mighty club. Thank God, thank God. He still had a future before him. She was safe, she was moving, she was unhurt.

She was just . . . wet.

"Come along," he said to Alexandra, and caught her up in his arms. Cool water soaked through his jacket.

"Finn!" she began, but he didn't let her finish. He hauled her to his motor and tossed her into the seat beside him and released the brake.

"Try not to drip over all the leather," he advised, as they launched up the street.

"Finn! You don't understand! It's Delmonico!" she exclaimed, unwinding her scarf. The water trickled heedlessly over the seat.

He grunted. "It could be. Damn the bastard. Something's off. Wrong. A fix-up. I think that cycle driver's his man. Hold on!"

He swerved around a darting pedestrian, charged on up to the via del Tritone, and turned right.

She pounded the seat with her hand and spoke with passion. "Of course it is! Of course it is! Finn, he's desperate! You've got to hurry!"

"What the devil! What do you mean, desperate?"

"Delmonico! He set the fire, Finn! His face—I saw his face, just before the race, and I realized . . ."

"What was that? Realized what? Blast it! Hold on!" They whipped around the sharp turn, back onto the via Sistina. Finn glanced down at the battery dial and bit his lip. The stop and restart had cost him. With the additional weight of Alexandra's body, the finish would be touch and go. How much lead did they have before Delmonico got his engine running again?

"What's the matter?"

"Charge is running out."

"But you recharged it last night!"

Finn heard the unmistakable rattle of the motor-cycle behind them, like an angry mechanical bee. "Bloody hell."

She turned again. "Oh, he's gaining! Can't you go faster?"

"No, I bloody can't! I'm running out of charge!" They were climbing the hill now, upward toward the park. He could see the flash of trees ahead, see a man in front of the crowd, signaling wildly to the left.

"Left! Turn left!" Alexandra exclaimed.

"No! Straight ahead!"

The motor-cycle came up, rattling at their rear tires.

She gestured ahead. "The man! He's pointing us left!"

"Dash it, Alexandra!" He pounded the tiller. "If we turn left, we'll be going down the Spanish bloody Steps!"

She looked at him, and then behind. She grabbed the tiller. "Don't, you fool! I know Rome!"

"Not us," she hissed. "*Him!*"

She jerked the tiller. The car swerved, the motor-cycle jigged left. The driver tried to recover, but it was too late.

Down he went, down the elegant curve of the Spanish Steps, bumping toward the piazza below.

Alexandra stood up on the floorboards, flinging droplets. "I say!" she cried. "He's awfully good! There he goes, down the right side . . . oh, look out . . . but no! No, he's still up, by God! . . . still up . . . still up . . . oh! Oh, I *say*! Jolly luck!"

She sat back down in a giant squish of frock. "Straight into the fountain," she said, with smug satisfaction.

They were going to win.
The finish line lay a quarter mile ahead, just inside the Borghese gardens, shaded by trees. It was thick with spectators, all screaming and waving with mad enthusiasm, handkerchiefs flying in the air.

"We're going to win!" she screamed, joy surging through her blood. "We're going to win! Come on! Faster!"

"I can't," he said grimly.

She turned in horror. The automobile was slowing measurably, dragged down by some mysterious weight. "What do you mean?"

"I mean we're almost out of power. The battery . . . damn it all . . . Delmonico, I'm sure of it!" He pounded the seat with his fist.

"Oh no! Oh, come on!" She strained forward with him, hoping the tension in her belly would somehow carry them over the finish line. Screaming, cheering people, so close! "Come on!"

"She can't!" Finn howled. "By God, I'll see him *rot . . . in . . . hell*!"

His words punctuated the last desperate surges of the motor as it rolled to a halt, thirty yards from the finish.

The crowd ahead of them began to still. Curious faces materialized out of the throng.

A growl of engine emerged from behind.

"I'll get out! We'll push!" said Alexandra, in agony. The sound grew louder. She didn't dare turn around. She knew who it was. "Hurry!"

Finn's shoulders slumped. "No, dash it. No use. It has to cross on its own power."

"You don't understand!" she screamed. "We've got to do something! He might have a gun, he might . . . oh, come on!" She pulled at his arm, frantic.

A figure separated from the crowd ahead, walking swiftly toward them. Wallingford, dragging Abigail behind. Hartley trailed them at an awkward trot, followed by his three mechanics.

The engine roared triumphantly behind them. A tiny gust of wind, and then Delmonico's motor-car blew past them, bouncing along the paving stones to cross the finish line.

First.

A wave of confused cheering scattered through the air. Delmonico's car came to a stop. He stood up, fists raised. "*Vittoria! Vittoria! Viva Italia!*"

"*Viva Italia! Viva Italia!*" The crowd began chanting, whistling. The handkerchiefs fluttered up again in a delirium of national enthusiasm.

"*Viva Italia! Viva Italia!*"

"Well, that's that," Alexandra said dully. She reached for Finn's hand on the seat next to her. It was hot and damp, and curled around hers with a gentle squeeze. "At least we're still alive."

"Alive?" He turned and stared at her, goggles crusted with road dust. "What the devil do you mean?"

"The fire. I told you, Delmonico set the fire to your workshop." She said it flatly. It hardly seemed to matter now. He'd won. They were safe, all right, but the bastard had won. Relief and disgust tumbled through her, all tangled together.

"How do you know that?"

"I saw him, on the way to the lake. I didn't realize it until I caught sight of him, just before the race, and the expression on his face . . ."

"Good God! Are you certain?" His arm whipped around her and crushed her into his chest. "Good God! But he might have . . . he might have killed you!"

Wallingford came up. "Hard luck, old man. Why did you stop?"

"Out of charge. And that villain Delmonico . . ." Finn's arm tightened around her in a smothering act of protection. "By God, I'll kill him!"

"Darling, I can't quite breathe . . ." she began.

"Where's my motor?" demanded Hartley, at a high pitch.

Wallingford's brow knitted. "What's that? Out of charge? But . . ."

"*Basta!*" An outraged voice tore through the air. "*Basta!*"

Alexandra looked up. A man was racing up the street toward Delmonico's motor, brandishing a long, thin object that looked remarkably like a steering tiller.

"By God," whispered Finn. He flung her aside and stood up on the floorboards. "By God!"

Alexandra stood up next to him. "Who's that?"

"The chap who lost his steering, near the beginning . . . you missed it all . . . by God! There he goes!" Finn's hands gripped the edge of the frame.

The man plunged into the crowd, waving his tiller and shouting.

"*Basta! Basta!*" Another voice joined in. Alexandra cast about and saw, from the other direction, a man running toward the finish line with an engine crank in his hand.

"By God!" said Finn again.

"*Basta! Basta!*" came another shout. A man with a tire.

And another.

Delmonico looked wildly around. He spotted the approaching men. He dove from the bonnet of his automobile, straight into the crowd.

Melee.

The tide turned so rapidly, so completely, Alexandra could only watch in astonishment. Delmonico's mechanics plunged into the crowd, swinging fists. Women began screaming. Men began punching. Tires and steering tillers launched through the air.

Wallingford locked eyes with Finn. Finn nodded, once, and looked at Alexandra. "Stay here," he said. "Don't bloody move."

He jumped from the motor-car and turned to Hartley's mechanics. "Not a hair on their heads," he warned, and he and

Wallingford disappeared into the crowd, ginger head and black head bobbing together.

Abigail climbed in next to Alexandra. "You missed a jolly lark. All the other racers came back hobbled, claiming someone had sabotaged their machines. Such fun!"

"They're going to get killed!" exclaimed Alexandra. The noise had reached a crescendo, a mad fury of swinging arms and tumbling bodies. She watched a man take up another and toss him artfully through a café window. She strained to see Finn's fiery head amongst the crowd, but everything blurred together. Panic began to seethe through her body, hot and light.

Abigail shrugged. "They'll look out for each other, of course."

"But you don't understand! Delmonico will . . . he'll . . ." She couldn't explain. She hadn't the strength. Alexandra's hands clenched on the metal, exactly where Finn's fingers had lain a moment ago. Hartley's mechanics pressed up tightly against the frame, facing outward in a protective phalanx. Hartley himself was nowhere to be found.

"He'll what? Oh, come, Alexandra. The little dark-haired man? Either Wallingford or Finn could smash him to bits. Although I suppose," she added, with a regretful sigh, "they'll merely turn him over to the authorities."

From the sea of crashing bodies emerged a tall darker-haired figure, flanked by an even taller ginger-haired figure, with the disheveled form of Bartolomeo Delmonico stumbling, defeated, between them.

"Thank God!" Alexandra's legs crumpled with relief.

The crowd seemed not to notice. The fighting continued unabated. The man who'd been tossed through the café window came wobbling out again, bleeding from his forehead, and plunged back into the fray.

"You see?" Abigail said with satisfaction. "Family sticks together, Alexandra."

"Yes. Yes, of course. Thank God. I . . ." She stopped. "What was that?"

"Family sticks together, of course. Those two may fight between themselves, but you needn't fear if . . ."

"Family?" Alexandra's mouth went dry. *"Family?"*

"Oh, for heaven's sake, Alex. Don't tell me you don't know."

Alexandra turned to her sister, slowly, as if in a dream. "What do you mean?"

"Well, look at them. Don't you see it?"

"See what?" Something flashed inside Alexandra's skull. "But their . . . their coloring . . ." She faltered.

Abigail shrugged. "Oh, coloring, of course. But if you look past that, look at their faces, their bones. The shape of the eyes."

Alexandra felt her face stretch, felt her mouth elongate into an oval O of astonishment. Her brain spun in a dazed circle, trying to fit the pieces together. "Oh no. It's impossible. Are you saying Wallingford's *father* sired him? They're *brothers*?"

"No, of course not," Abigail said impatiently. "Not Wallingford's *father*, you goose. His grandfather, his mother's father. The Duke of Olympia."

Alexandra's legs wobbled. She sat down with a wet thump, staring forward.

"His uncle." A giggle escaped Alexandra, and another. "Finn is Wallingford's uncle." She laid her arm across her stomach and began to laugh, great hearty, hysterical laughs, all the madness and tension of the past several hours tumbling out of her in a flood of uncontrolled mirth. One of the mechanics looked up at her in shocked disapproval. "Oh, Lord! Oh, Lord! His uncle!"

She wiped away tears and watched as the two of them dragged Delmonico toward a brace of policemen standing idly against a tree, watching the brawl. Waiting, presumably, for things to die down.

"Horrible, odious man. At least that Jellinek fellow will have to find another automobile for his investments," she murmured to herself, as her giggles died down at last.

"Right-ho," Abigail said briskly. "This has been going on long enough. Someone's bound to get hurt before long." She took an object out of her pocketbook, a short, plump revolver.

"Good God! Where did you get that?" Alexandra demanded.

"From the starter, of course." She checked the primer. "I traded my aquamarine bracelet for it."

With that, Abigail rose to her feet, pointed the pistol into the air, and fired.

TWENTY-EIGHT

A shadow crossed the doorway of the automobile shed, blocking the dark red glow of the fading sunset.

"I'm sorry," she said.

Finn straightened from the battery, which he'd just hooked up for recharging. "Alexandra," was all he could whisper.

After the tumult, after the confusion, he'd had to stay with the police for hours, giving statements. Wallingford had escorted the ladies back to the hotel. He'd caught a glimpse of her in the lobby, much later, on his way upstairs to change from his dirty clothes. She'd had a crowd around her, hanging on her every word, just as they had at the dinner last evening. He could see, now, why London loved her. The way she smiled, the way she tilted her head and listened to her companion, the way she laughed in her throaty way. The way she had irradiated the air around her. She was made for crowds, made for parties. She'd been in her element, as far removed from his world as the sun from the moon.

"May I come in?"

"Of course."

She closed the door and moved forward in a rustle of skirts, looking elegant in her sapphire evening gown and intricate headdress, her waist cinched once more into a neat circle. "Wallingford is looking after Abigail. They told me you were here. I wanted to speak with you."

He gestured with his hand. "Certainly. I haven't a seat, I'm afraid."

She smiled. "Yes, you have." With graceful steps she walked to the automobile and perched on the passenger seat, the seat she'd occupied so many times before. Her feet rested on the edge, small pointed toes peeping out from the edge of her dress. "So you've sorted everything out with police?"

"Yes. I almost felt sorry for the chap, until I remembered how he'd nearly killed you." He cleared his throat. "Of course, you've lost the race. I'm sorry about that."

"Oh, God, Finn. When he might have done something worse. When *you* might have been killed." She shook her head. "It doesn't matter, now. There will be other races. People have seen how fast the steamer can go. Maybe even Jellinek . . ."

"Damn all that, Alexandra!"

She closed her eyes. "I know. I'm sorry."

Finn took a deep breath. "Look, I . . ."

She held up her finger. "No. Let me. I've been horrible to you, ever since I came to Rome. You'd made a kind gesture, an extraordinarily generous gesture, and I threw it back in your face. I insisted on racing, accused you of awful things, when you were only worried about my safety. I understand that. But *you* must understand . . ."

He reached out and touched the hair at her temple. "*Buy you*, you said. Before the race. Do you really think that?"

"Not . . . no. Of course not."

"No man could ever buy you, Alexandra. I never even meant for you to find out, at least until later." He let his finger drift downward to outline the edge of her ear. "Impossible woman. Why won't you let me help you?"

"I won't let you do it, Finn." Her eyes were huge, the pupils fully dilated in the dimness. "I can't let a single penny pass between us."

"Christ, Alexandra." He tore his hand from her face and ran it through his hair. "Don't you see what you're doing? You say you want to be something other than what you were, but that's not true. You've always got to be the one in control. You've always got to be her almighty ladyship, always the immortal marchioness, as if money and titles are the only things that matter."

She flinched, opened her mouth, and struggled for words. "I . . . That's not true, Finn. I don't give a fig about London society anymore."

"Don't you? Really, Alexandra?"

She looked at him steadily. "Really. These last few months, grubbing about in your workshop, have been the happiest of my life. I want to live like that forever. And I appreciate that you want to give me the choice, to have the resources to . . . to live with you, or not. It's just . . . I simply can't . . . I can't have that money come from you. I'd be forever obliged, because you've made such a tremendous sacrifice . . ."

"Sacrifice?" He frowned. "It's no sacrifice, darling. I *want* to buy the company."

She tilted her head and began to remove her gloves, pulling at each fingertip with great care for the delicate satin. "It's a steam automobile, Finn. What use would that be to you? You must give it up. I can't let you do it for me."

"For God's sake, Alexandra. Do you really think this is all about *you*?"

"Isn't it?" She tossed the gloves on the seat beside her and scoured him with her eyes.

He looked at her a moment and then turned away with a wrenching movement. "I need that company, Alexandra," he said, staring across the little shed at the battery hulking next to the wall, feeding hungrily from the wires strung in from the electric generator in the main exhibition building. Tomorrow, it would all be taken down. Tomorrow, he and Alexandra would be on their way. Together, or apart? "I've been thinking of buying it for months. Didn't you know that?"

"I . . . No. Not until Hartley turned up, a few days ago," she said, in a small voice.

"Not because of you, Alexandra. Because of the building works. Have you ever been there?"

"No."

He shook his head. "Your fortune's invested in it, and you've never been there?"

"*I* didn't invest it there. It didn't seem to matter which company had ruined me."

"It's got a bloody marvelous workshop for research, and a testing ground, and the shell of a factory, ready for production.

To build such a thing myself would take ages, and the devil of an amount of effort in planning and attention and supervision, which I can't afford." He looked back at her. She was watching him with wary eyes, her face shadowed by the wide curve of an ostrich feather. "I wanted Manchester Machine Works long before I met you, Lady Morley."

"Oh. I see." She fidgeted with the lace around her sleeves. "But the building isn't worth fifty shillings a share, is it? You overbid."

"In order to assure myself that shareholders would tender, yes."

"But you could have bid twenty," she insisted. "Twenty would have been more than enough."

Something cracked inside him.

He took her by the shoulders, hard. "Yes! Yes, I could have! But I didn't. I offered fifty shillings, Alexandra, and do you know why?"

She shook her head, wordless.

He moved his hands to her face, covering her cheeks and her jaw with his long fingers, and spoke in a harsh voice. "Because I love you. I love you desperately, ruinously. I can't see you unhappy without wanting to help. To fix things for you, to make you whole again. So I offered fifty shillings a share for that damned company, and by God I'd bid a million if I had to. I'd borrow or beg or steal every penny I could lay my hands on. I'd pick the jewels from the Queen's own crown and hang for it gladly, because nothing else on this earth means anything to me if a single wretched tear stands in your eye. Do you understand me?"

Her eyes searched his, round and astonished. From the other side of the thin wooden door of the shed came the sound of male laughter, hearty and unrestrained, and someone else joining in. It grew louder, drawing an almost visible line from the front of the shed to the center, before fading away to the back.

"Well then," she whispered. "Well then."

"Understood?"

"Yes."

He leaned his forehead against hers and exhaled. "Good."

She kissed him. A gentle kiss, and then another, her sweet breath mingling with his. Her arms stole around his waist, tugged his shirt from his trousers. Her shoulders shook; he realized she was laughing.

"Oh, God, how I love you," she said. "I love you so." She kissed him harder, met his tongue with hers, ran her fingers under his shirt to clutch at the skin of his back. "I love you, I love you. I . . . *Finn!*"

The last word came on a gasp as he dug his hands under her buttocks and lifted her up from the seat and onto the bonnet. Her skirts frothed around his legs, dark and endless. He reached up inside them and found her knees and drew them apart, settling himself between her thighs. "Say it again," he said, pulling off her hat, letting hair and pins tumble free.

She looped her arms around his neck. "I love you."

He pressed his nose against her throat and inhaled her scent, letting it wash through his head and body to awaken every last memory: kisses, laughter, bare skin, the hot quiver of her flesh against his.

"Oh, God," she said.

He kissed her neck, her jaw, her chin; devoured her thoroughly, learning again the shape of her lips, the contours of her mouth and tongue. The golden taste of her shot through his blood. "Say it again," he demanded.

"I love you." Her hands went to his trousers, deft and eager, unfastening the buttons until his cock leaped fully erect into her palm.

He lost all thought, lost all sense of everything but pure animal lust. His hands went to her knees, traveled up her thighs, found the opening at the bottom of her drawers.

His breath drew in with a ragged gasp. "Good God."

"I've been like this since yesterday," she confessed. She turned her head into his shoulder as if ashamed. "Watching you as you stalked about, towering above everybody else. Wanting you. Imagining you dragging me behind some corner and tossing up my skirts and . . . *Oh!*"

He thrust inside her wet channel, burying himself to the root in a single stroke. Her head fell back with a cry; she braced herself on the smooth metal of the bonnet and wrapped her legs around him and met him, tilting her hips to take him deeper. Her dress fell away from her thighs in a cascade of lace and silk.

He pulled back in a long velvet glide. "Say it again."

"I love you." She was laughing, crying, singing the words.

He plunged forward and drew back. "Again."

"I love you."

He took hold of her round bottom and lifted her, impaled her on himself. He felt her snug embrace along his shaft, the grip of her legs around him, the dig of her heels into the tops of his legs, and he carried her back to the seat of the automobile and tumbled with her onto the dark beaten leather. "Again," he growled.

Her fingers dug into his back. "I love you. I love you, Finn. Every atom of you. Oh, God, *now*, please, I can't bear it."

Neither could he. His need for her had been building for weeks. He rose above her and drove into her, hard and fast, while her hips lifted eagerly and her hands clenched in his hair and her back slid against the leather. He struggled for control, struggled to hold himself back, to wait for her; he felt himself rise inexorably toward the peak and gritted his teeth and reached down with his broad thumb, circling her in perfect rhythm with his thrusts, over and over.

Her back arched; she cried his name; her orgasm rippled around his cock and his own release burst from him in a blinding wave of pleasure.

Finn collapsed against her breast, heaving for breath, an infinitely precious weight on her heart. "Sorry," he gasped, and made a motion as if to roll away.

"Stay." She tightened her legs around him. "Stay."

"I'm crushing you."

"Stay." The smell of leather rose up from the seat below her to thread through the sultry scent of union. Her fingers stroked through his hair; down his back, damp with perspiration; around the hard curve of his buttocks. His shaft still lodged deep inside her, linking them together. "Stay forever."

His chuckle rustled against her ear, mingling somehow with the distant echoes of climax lapping through her body. Her muscles seemed to have taken on the consistency of aspic.

She'd never been so happy.

They lay quietly a moment longer, listening to the sounds outside the shed: the distant rumble of someone's motor, the rise and fall of a deep male voice. It occurred to her that someone could walk in at any moment and see them tangled together on the seat of the automobile, flushed and sweating and disheveled.

She found, to her surprise, she didn't give a damn.

He rose up on his elbows and studied her with a worried expression. "Bloody hell. I've blundered it, haven't I?"

She stroked his cheek and smiled. "Not in the least. No, don't," she added quickly, but it was too late. He withdrew from her with a wince and pulled a handkerchief from his pocket.

"Lord, I'm sorry, darling. What an ass I am. Stupid, blundering ass. Here." He helped her upright and gave her the handkerchief.

"It's all right. I wanted it. I wanted you."

He cast her a rueful look. "Not a child, though, I expect."

She took him firmly by the ears. "If I should be so fortunate as to bear your child," she said, locking onto his gaze to make sure he understood, "I'd love it with all my heart. As I love its father."

He didn't say anything. The lines of his face, if anything, seemed to harden beneath her hands.

"Do you know what I mean?" she whispered.

He leaned his forehead against hers. "If you mean that you've finally come to your proper senses . . ."

"I think I have. I think . . ." Giddiness overtook her brain, at the feeling of his breath floating over her skin, quick and uneven. "I think, today, just now, I've finally discovered what I really want, Finn. Who I really am. And it isn't the all-powerful Marchioness of Morley. It isn't Lady Anybody."

He pulled away and dropped to one knee, trousers still unbuttoned, long legs folded awkwardly between the steering column and the leather seat. He snatched her hands. "Marry me, Alexandra. I'll give away every penny, if you like. Put it in a trust for our children. I'll live in a damned hovel for you, if only you'll share it with me."

"Oh, get up." She laughed and kissed his hands. "Of course I'll marry you, though I shall require a good deal more than a hovel. Get up, before you hurt yourself."

He buried his face in her lap. "Thank God. At last, you damned minx."

She laughed again and tugged at his hair. "Oh, do get up,

darling. Of course I'll marry you. Darling Finn. I'd rather drive your automobiles, anyway. Poor old Hartley."

He ducked under the steering tiller and straightened himself. "Poor old Hartley, indeed. He can drive his own damned machines."

"No, he can't."

"Of course he can, the coward." He buttoned his trousers with swift fingers. "Why shouldn't he?"

"Because driving makes him sick."

"Makes him sick?" Finn stopped tucking his shirt and stared at her, incredulous. "Makes him *sick*? Bloody Christ, Alexandra! You stood in for him because *driving* makes him *sick*?"

"Well, yes," she said. "Yes, I suppose I did."

He fell against the back of the seat, laughing and gasping. "Oh, Lord! The poor damned fool!" His chest shook.

He was so infectious that she began to laugh, too, thinking of Hartley's face, stricken and pasty, hanging out the side of the automobile as the steam hissed impatiently from the boiler. "Stop it," she said, between spasms. "It's not at all funny, the poor chap. He was . . . He was jolly miserable . . ."

"It's *damned* funny! It . . . Oh, Lord." He went on laughing, holding his hand to his chest, shirt half tucked, until she gave in helplessly next to him.

"There's one bright spot, though," he said, when their laughter had died down at last, and they sat companionably together on the leather seat, fingers entwined, her head resting blissfully on his shoulder.

"Oh, aside from our engagement?" She tucked her feet up beneath her and closed her eyes in contentment. A great warm blanket of certainty covered her, from head to toe. She sat, at last, exactly where she was always meant to be: curled up on the seat of a horseless carriage with Phineas Burke.

"Aside from that." He gave her breast a congratulatory squeeze. "Reflect a moment, darling. I do suspect we've earned our place in the annals of automobile history, just now."

EPILOGUE

Across the room, a rectangle of Roman sunshine burst past the curtains to illuminate, in intricate detail, the lace edging of a corset slung atop the back of a nearby chair.

Alexandra smiled sleepily. It must be noon at least.

An arm lay across her belly, long and heavy, the hand loosely cupping her breast. The owner's breath stirred the hair at the top of her head. She listened for a moment, to the slow, regular rush of air, the far edge of it just brushing her ear. If she closed her eyes, she could measure the beat of his heart at her back.

My husband, she thought in wonder.

She'd never woken up next to a husband before.

Slowly, so as not to disturb him, she rotated under his arm. Her aching muscles protested at the movement. She settled her face into the nook of his neck and breathed him in, his salty essence, all trace of oil and leather scrubbed away. She lay there a moment, unable to move any farther, and let his warmth simply enfold her. Let the languorous memories of the night stir through her mind, spread bliss through her body.

My husband. The word seemed so different now.

"Good morning, love." His low voice vibrated the air.

She craned her face upward. "I'm sorry. I didn't mean to wake you."

He kissed her. "I'm glad you did. It must be frightfully late."

"We were up late, as I recall." She curled her hand suggestively around his bottom.

He turned her onto her back and rose above her, the thin rays of sunshine gilding his hair, making it seem more gold than red. Another kiss, this time long and lingering. "Apparently I lost track of time. Did you sleep well?"

"Divinely. The deep sleep of an honest woman. At last."

He laughed. "I did my best to arrange things quickly. Three nights alone in my bed, with my dear love sleeping a single wall away, were almost more than I could bear."

His skin hovered over hers, making her nerves jangle with anticipation. She drew her fingers along the taut, smooth skin of his waist. "And am I your dear love?" she asked softly.

Not because she doubted it, but because she wanted to hear the answer again.

"Daft woman. Did I not stand yesterday before the only ordained Anglican in Rome, obtained at considerable negotiation and expense, and pledge my life to you? Have I not spent an entire night doing my manful best to prove my devotion?" He kissed his way to her ear and whispered the words, "You are my own dear love, and always will be."

"Finn," she said, kissing his hair, relishing the feel of his weight against her. "Phineas Burke. I do love you."

"I should bloody well hope so, Mrs. Burke." He gave her earlobe a little nip. "It's all been an immense amount of trouble. I daresay I've had enough of hasty wedding arrangements to last me a lifetime."

"Well, that's the idea, after all." *Mrs. Burke*. The sound of it, the simple, commonplace name, sent a delicious shiver down her spine. "I did think Abigail made a lovely bridesmaid, on such short notice. And your nephew . . ." She loved saying the word. She employed it at every opportunity. *I suppose I can allow my new nephew a congratulatory kiss*, she'd told Wallingford yesterday, after the wedding, as she offered her cheek with an innocent smile.

Finn rolled his eyes. "He kept his scowls to a minimum, at least." His thumb brushed the tip of her nipple. "Poor chap. She's leading him a merry dance."

"Abigail?" Alexandra allowed a wise smile to curve her lips. "She'll never marry Wallingford."

"Yes, she will."

Alexandra lifted her head against the pillow. "Of course she won't. She has much better sense."

"You're biased. He's a good fellow, really. He'll have her in the end." Finn nuzzled her neck. His voice was supremely confident.

"Rubbish. I'll wager you any odds. I'll wager my fifty shillings a share . . ."

"No more wagers," he groaned. "Please."

His breath tickled her ear. She drew her hands up his back, into his hair, and closed her eyes. His cock, she noticed, was now pressing firmly into her leg, full of husbandly ardor. "Fair enough. No more wagers."

"Besides, the bet's unfair. Wallingford will marry her."

"No, he won't."

"Yes, he will." Finn began to kiss along her collarbone, caressing little nibbles. "For one thing, he hasn't got Giacomo undermining him at every turn."

"Giacomo. That horrible man. I don't know what he holds against me." She sighed. "I've never even met him."

Finn's face stilled against the hollow of her throat. He looked up. "Yes, you have. You've seen him in the workshop, any number of times."

She examined him curiously. His face was drawn in serious lines. "No, I haven't. Not once. I've heard you speak of him, that's all."

He started back. "Oh, rubbish. You must remember. Wiry, dark-haired chap. Scowls all the time. Rather like Wallingford, only shorter and more tyrannical."

She shook her head. "No. No, you're mistaken. I've never seen him."

"Oh, really, Alexandra." He sat up, bare chest dusky in the muted light. "He was right there, that last morning. The morning of the midsummer feast. When you came in, he was just on the point of leaving."

"Finn, you're mad. There was no one else there."

"Alexandra, I was *talking* to him. You must have heard us!"

She looked at him closely. His eyes lit strangely, penetrating her with that serious gaze of his. "I heard you muttering. But you're always muttering to yourself."

He let out a great gust of air and ran a hand through his hair. "What the devil," he muttered. "What the devil. I swear it, Alexandra. He was *there*. In the room."

Her heart began to hammer in her chest. "I've heard of him, of course. All the time. He and Signorina Morini . . ."

"Morini." He latched onto the word. "Morini. The housekeeper. Which one is she?"

"Why, the older one. There's Francesca and Maria, the blond one who wears her hair with a ribbon. Signorina Morini's the older one with the headscarf, the one who gave you the message, when I wanted to meet you in the peach orchard."

"No, that was Francesca. Definitely younger. No headscarf. Deeply disapproving."

Alexandra's thoughts began to whirl. "Morini doesn't disapprove of you. Not at all. She encouraged everything. She and Giacomo kept . . ." She paused and watched Finn's intent expression. "You've never seen her, have you?"

"No." His voice was a mere whisper.

They stared at each other for a long moment in the quiet room. Alexandra felt a lock of her hair fall down over her shoulders, felt Finn's hand push it away in an absent gesture.

The castle's cursed, of course. Isn't it delicious? Morini told me all about it.

A knock sounded through the open door to the sitting room.

"I'll get it," Finn said hoarsely.

He rose from the bed, his beautiful rangy body like a shadow in the dim room. From the armchair he grabbed a dressing robe and threw it around himself in a giant swirl. He tied the sash in swift jerks and strode out of sight.

Alexandra found his pillow, still warm and scented with his skin, and sank her arms around the fine linen weave. She listened to his voice echo from the sitting room, low and resonant, and then heard the outer door close.

"What is it?" she called.

Silence.

She sat upright, still clutching the pillow. "Finn?" she called out, more loudly.

He appeared in the doorway, a bemused smile on his face. A paper dangled from his fingertips.

"What is it?"

"It's the devil of a good thing you didn't make that wager with me." He tossed the note in her direction.

She reached out and picked it up from the tangled sheets. It was folded in half, a few hasty lines scrawled in a hand she didn't recognize. "Why's that?"

"Because, my darling." He sank into the bed behind her and rested his chin on her shoulder. His voice hitched, whether with laughter or shock she couldn't quite tell.

"Because?" she prodded, opening the note with an odd frisson of foreboding.

"Because I'm afraid Wallingford and your sister have eloped."

A roaring sensation started up in her ears. She dropped her eyes to the paper before her.

My dear fellow, Miss Harewood and I have found ourselves obliged to depart Rome on a matter of great urgency. Shall advise further when I can. In the meantime, assure your wife that Miss Harewood will remain under my full and devoted protection.

She looked up. "Eloped, did you say?"

"Isn't that what it says?" His tone was innocent.

"No." She folded the note and turned to fix him with her patented death glare. "No, it does not. What it says, Finn, is that *your nephew* has run off with *my sister.*"

His jaw worked. "I'm sure his intentions are entirely honorable."

She planted her hands on her hips and said nothing, only went on staring without remission.

Many men had been broken by less.

"Hell," he said. "I'm going to have to go after them, aren't I?"

She lifted her eyebrows, to make sure her point was driven home.

"All right, then." He heaved a resigned sigh and reached for his shirt. "It's your honeymoon."

HISTORICAL NOTE

Today, we take the supremacy of the internal combustion automobile for granted, but at the turn of the last century only 22 percent of American cars were powered by gasoline engines, and the world land speed record of sixty-six miles per hour was held by the rocket-shaped *Jamais Contente*, an electric vehicle.

While Delmonico's automobile exposition is entirely a product of my imagination, the competition among steam, electric, and internal combustion engines formed a genuine and dramatic narrative for the development of the automobile in the 1890s and beyond. Each technology had its advantages and drawbacks, as Finn and Alexandra demonstrate, and it wasn't until the development of the electric starter in 1912 (eliminating the need for a hand crank) coincided with improved highway infrastructure (encouraging longer journeys) that the internal combustion engine finally roared ahead of its peers in popularity. By the start of the Roaring Twenties, electric and steam automobiles were all but unknown.

For dramatic purposes, I've anticipated some technological advancements. Forty miles per hour would have been within reach for a steam vehicle of 1890, but existing lead-acid batteries weren't capable of powering similar speeds for an electric one. I solved this problem as only a novelist can, by making my hero a genius who invents his own battery, as well as a more aerodynamic frame.

Finally, I couldn't resist stretching the facts to engineer a cameo appearance by Emil Jellinek, a wealthy entrepreneur and early automobile enthusiast, and his daughter Adrienne Manuela Ramona Jellinek, born in 1889 and known to her family as Mercédès. Herr Jellinek did indeed enter the motor-car business, eventually joining the board of Daimler-Motoren-Gesellschaft in 1900 with an investment of half a million marks and a mandate to build the car of the future.

That car rolled out of the factory in December 1900, and it was named for Jellinek's own daughter: Mercedes.

Turn the page to read an excerpt from
the next book in the trilogy

A Gentleman
Never Tells

Coming from Berkley Sensation
in November 2012!

PROLOGUE

*London
February 1890*

In six years of clandestine service to his Queen and country, Lord Roland Penhallow had never before been summoned to the private library of the Bureau chief himself.

It could mean only one thing: He had inadvertently killed somebody.

Roland couldn't imagine how. The last caper had tied up as neat as a bow, with hardly any noise and only a very little blood. *Even the most perfidious villain can be made to serve some purpose*, Sir Edward would intone, pressing one blunt forefinger into the polished mahogany of his Whitehall desk, *but a dead body is a nullity*. Roland had taken that advice to heart as a new recruit, and had lived by it ever since.

Standing now in Sir Edward's shabby Mayfair entrance hall, with the tips of his shoes squared against the chipped marble tiles and his eyes roaming across a series of dyspeptic family portraits, Roland felt the same mild dread he'd known at Eton, when called in by his housemaster to atone for some recent prank. He knit his cold fingers together behind his back and looked upward at the dusky ceiling. *Nothing to worry about*, he told himself. *You can talk your way past anything, Penhallow.* Was that a water stain spreading along the far corner? The old fellow really ought to have that looked at; rubbishy things, leaks . . .

"Your lordship."

Roland started. Sir Edward's butler stood before him like an avenging penguin. His slick dark hair glinted in the yellow glare of the incandescent lamp on the hall table, and his impenetrable shirtfront held back the advance of his lapels with heroic whiteness. "Your lordship," he repeated, as he might say *your flatulent wolfhound*. "Sir Edward will receive you in the library."

The butler didn't wait for a response. He turned his immaculate ebony back in Roland's face and walked on in the direction—presumably—of the library.

"Thanks awfully," Roland muttered, feeling less like the brother of the Duke of Wallingford and more like a dustman with every passing step.

"Ah! Penhallow!" Sir Edward said, as Roland stalked through the door of the library with as much sangfroid as he could muster. A considerable amount, he judged modestly: He wasn't the Duke of Wallingford's brother for nothing.

"Sir Edward."

The baronet's sturdy hand waved at the ancient wing chair before the desk. "Sit, sit. That will be all, Pankhurst. Oh, wait. Dash it, Penhallow. Have you dined?"

"Yes, at my club."

"Excellent. Good. Off you go, then, Pankhurst. We're not to be disturbed. Sit, I said, Penhallow. Don't stand on ceremony *here*, for God's sake."

Roland sprawled into the armchair with his usual negligent grace, though the nerves along the back of his neck gave off a warning jangle. Sir Edward Pennington, chairman of Her Majesty's Bureau of Trade and Maritime Information, did not typically begin meetings in a stream of jocular pleasantries.

The door closed behind him with a defiant thump.

Sir Edward's eyes rolled upward. "Pankhurst. I daresay I ought to sack him, but on the other hand he's frightfully discreet. A drop of something, perhaps?" He rose and went to the demilune table against the far wall, on which a tray of crystal decanters flashed invitingly. "Sherry? Whiskey? I've a noble port at the moment, last of the ought-nines my father put down for me on the occasion of my birth, ha-ha."

"I shouldn't wish to deprive you," said Roland, who felt the loss of noble ports keenly, even in his present disturbed spirits.

"Nonsense. If one waits for the right occasion, one never drinks it at all." Sir Edward picked up a decanter and lifted the stopper. "Ah! There we are, you damned beauty."

"I say, you're a good deal more generous than my brother," Roland said. He watched with narrowed eyes as Sir Edward poured out one glass and then another, filling each one nearly to the rim with thick ruby port. In the silent, book-filled room, the liquid swished against crystal like an Amazonian waterfall. "He never lets me near his vintage."

"Ah, well. Dukes, you know." Sir Edward handed him the glass. "To the Queen."

"The Queen."

The clink of glasses rang amiably in the air, and Sir Edward, instead of returning to his desk, moved to the window overlooking the rear garden. With one hand he lifted aside the heavy burgundy curtains and peered out into the foggy darkness. He took a drink of port. "I suppose," he said, "you're wondering why I've called you here tonight."

"It came as something of a surprise."

"Ah! Circumspect." Sir Edward swirled the port in his glass. "You've come along damned well these past few years, Penhallow. Damned well. I thought, when they first foisted you on me, you'd be nothing but an aristocratic millstone around my neck, with your flashy looks and your matchless damned pedigree. But I was quite wrong about that, to my considerable pleasure. Quite wrong." He turned to face Roland, and all the painfully contrived jollity had faded from his expression, leaving its lean angles even more austere than usual.

"I'm grateful to have been of service, sir," said Roland. "Queen and country and all that. Dashed good fun." He gripped the narrow bowl of his glass until the facets cut hard and cold against his fingertips.

"Of course you are. I don't doubt that for an instant." Sir Edward stared down into the ruby depths of his port.

"Sir?" Roland said, because his dry mouth would not permit anything more fluent. Then he remembered the port, and raised it to his lips for a hearty, seamanlike swallow.

Sir Edward cleared his throat. "Here's the trouble. As I suspect you're aware, we're not the only organization in Her Majesty's government charged with gathering intelligence."

"Of course not. Tripping on each other's toes all the time."
Roland offered a winning smile, his most charismatic younger-
brother effort. "Why, just last month I nearly came to a bad
end myself. Stumbled directly into a setup by some damned
chaps from the Navy office. The bloodiest balls-up you've ever
seen."

"Yes, I read your report." Sir Edward returned to the desk
and sat down in his chair. A trace of what might be called a
smile lifted one corner of his mouth. "Rather well written, your
reports, except perhaps for an excess of descriptive phrase."

Roland shrugged modestly. "Reports would be so dull otherwise."

"In any case, it appears those—er—damned chaps from the
Navy office, as you put it, aren't taking things in quite the same
spirit of brotherhood."

"No? Hardly sporting of them. They were all quite on their
feet again within a week or two." Roland flicked a speck of dust
from his jacket sleeve.

"Ah. Still. Despite your tender care, which no doubt met the
very highest standards of the service . . ."

"Naturally."

". . . there's talk"—Sir Edward set down his glass and fid-
dled with the neat rectangle of papers in the center of the
leather-trimmed blotter—"that our involvement represented a
deliberate attempt to undermine the efforts of a long and pres-
tigious investigation."

Roland lifted his eyebrows. Despite hours of concerted
effort, he'd never yet managed to raise one by itself. "You can't
be serious. Does the Navy office really think I've nothing better
to do with my time than to plot its downfall? For God's sake, my
source gave me every reason to think . . ."

"Your source." Sir Edward lifted the topmost paper from the
stack and scanned it. "Johnson, to be precise."

"Yes, sir. You know the man. Thoroughly reliable, well-
placed at the Russian mission."

"And as of this morning, aboard a steamer to Argentina with
a number of small, heavy trunks, inhabiting a first-class star-
board cabin." Sir Edward looked up. "Surprised, are you?"

Roland slumped back in his chair. "Well, I'm dashed!"

"Dashed. Yes."

"Argentina!"

"Apparently so. Traveling under his real name, of all things."

"The cheek!"

"My counterpart at the Navy is, of course, beside himself. He's convinced you paid off Johnson, that it's all part of some plot on our part to make fools of them, at best. At worst . . ."

Roland shot forward out of the chair and pinned the paper to the blotter with his finger. "Don't say it, by God."

"Pax, you young fool. I wasn't accusing you of anything."

"But someone is." Roland's voice was low, deadly, quite unlike its usual self.

Sir Edward tilted his lean face to one side and considered Roland for a long moment. "Someone is."

"Who?"

"I don't know." Sir Edward frowned. "Look, Penhallow. I shall speak as freely as I can, because I consider myself a fair judge of men, and I know no man more disinterestedly devoted to the welfare of the British nation as you."

Roland's arrow-straight body relaxed an infinitesimal degree.

"Something's up, Penhallow. I don't know what it is. Rumblings, currents. There's always been rivalry, of course; bitter, at times. One expects that, in this line of work, with no great financial benefit, no hero's reception at St. Paul's and whatnot. Power's the only currency. But the things I hear now, the things I sense, odd instances of this and that . . . I can't put it into words, exactly. But something's off."

Roland eased back into his chair, every sense alert. "What sort of thing?"

Sir Edward tented his fingers together atop the fine white paper, fingertip against fingertip. "If I knew that, Penhallow, I'd have taken action by now."

"Then how can I help?"

"That, you see, is the trouble." He drummed his fingertips together; hard, sturdy, peasantlike fingers that matched his hard, sturdy body and made the gentleman-like cut of his superfine jacket seem like racing silks on a destrier. "Tell me, Penhallow," he said, in an even voice, "have you any enemies? Besides, of course, those damned chaps you put out of action a few weeks ago."

"Oh, any number. One doesn't construct a reputation like mine without putting a few noses out of joint."

"Anyone who might wish to ruin you?"

"There are all sorts of ruin to wish upon a man who's beaten you at cards, or stolen your mistress."

"I mean total ruin. Moral, physical. A man, perhaps, who might wish to have you condemned for treason."

Treason.

The word rang about the room, ricocheted off the books and objects, settling at last between them with an ugly clank.

"None that I can call to mind," Roland said quietly.

"And yet," Sir Edward said, just as quietly, "I can say, with near certainty, that such a man exists."

"Name the man, and he is dead within the hour."

"I don't know his name. That, you see, is the mystery." Sir Edward rose and went to the middle of a row of bookshelves near the window, where a small globe interrupted the even flow of leather-bound volumes. He placed one hand, spiderlike, over the Atlantic Ocean. "Have you anywhere you can retire for a month or two? Perhaps more? Somewhere discreet?"

"What, *hide*? Oh, I say . . ."

"Not hide. Not at all. Only retire, as I said, from the limelight for a bit."

"Damn it all, sir, I won't turn tail and slink away."

"Discretion, in this case, is much the better part of valor." Sir Edward turned and skewered him with a rapier gaze from his dark eyes. "The idea is to tease the fellow out in the open. Find out what he's really after. Let him think he's won. An easy triumph breeds overconfidence."

"And I should meanwhile sit twiddling my thumbs in some country seat . . ."

"Preferably outside of England."

"Oh, rot. Outside of England? I've no tolerance for Paris, and no friends anywhere else that . . ." He stopped. A thought began to writhe its way through the currents of his brain, like a poisonous eel.

"What is it?"

"It's . . . it's nothing, really. Only some damned idea of a friend of ours."

"What sort of idea? What sort of friend?"

"A scientific fellow. Burke's his name, a very close and trusted friend of mine and my brother's. He's got some lunatic scheme in the works, proposes to spend a year in a castle in the Tuscan mountains, fiddling with automobiles and whatnot . . . really most ineligible . . ."

"Good God! It's perfect!"

"What's that? Oh, Lord, no. Not at all. Damp, wretched things, castles. And swearing off women and drink and . . . well, everything at all that makes life bearable."

"Just the thing for you, Penhallow. Marvelous. I shall write the necessary letters at once, open up a line for communication . . ."

"What's that?"

But Sir Edward was already scribbling himself a memorandum. "Beadle, I think, in the Florence office. He shall set you up with everything you need. Tuscany, eh? The land of unending sunshine, I believe they say. Ha. You'll have a splendid time. Most indebted to this Mr. Burke of yours."

Roland watched the motion of Sir Edward's pen along the paper and began to feel queasy. "I refuse to . . ."

"What's that? Oh, rubbish, Penhallow. I shall take care of everything on this end and notify you when it's safe to return. Think of it as a kind of sabbatical. You'll return to us refreshed, renewed. Full of zest for life and all that."

Roland, who was never at a loss for words or composure, found himself devoid of both. His jaw swung helplessly below his brain.

Sir Edward folded the paper and looked up. "What's that? Oh, come, Penhallow. You look as though you've been passed a sentence of death. Think of all the advantages: sunshine, wine, decent food. Ripe young women who can't speak English."

He rose from his chair, held out the paper, and grinned like a demon.

"What could possibly go wrong?"

ONE

Thirty miles southeast of Florence
March 1890

The boy couldn't have been more than five years old. He stood square in the doorway of the inn and stared at Lord Roland Penhallow with a peculiar hostile intensity, his brow frowning into his blue eyes and his thumb stuck firmly between his teeth.

"I say, young fellow," said Roland, with a gentle cough, one foot upon the step, "might I perhaps sidle past?"

The boy removed his thumb. "My father could beat you up."

Roland felt the rain rattle down from the eaves against the crown of his hat. From there it streamed along the narrow brim and into the collar of his coat, soaking the shirt beneath until it stuck, cold and stiff, against his skin. "I daresay he could, old chap," he ventured, gathering the ends of his coat collar together with one hand. "But in the meantime, I should like very much to dry myself by that cracking hot fire directly behind you. If you don't mind, of course."

"My father," the boy said, lifting his finger and pointing it at Roland's nose, "could smash your face and arms and legs and you would cry for *ever.*" The last word was delivered with particular relish.

Roland blinked. He could glimpse, behind the boy's small figure, the inn's common room: its long tables lined with people, with plates of steaming food and bottles of local wine. An enormous fire roared away the dank March air, impossibly inviting. "Of course I should cry," Roland said. "Bitterly, in fact. No doubt about it, no doubt at all. But about that fire . . ."

"Philip! There you are!"

An exhausted female voice called from somewhere behind Roland, somewhere in the middle of that stinking mud-ridden innyard he'd just crossed. An exhausted voice, yes: strained and dry, with a suggestion of incipient hoarseness, but also perfectly familiar.

Roland's back stiffened with shock. Not here, surely. He must be mistaken. Not in the yard of a rustic Italian inn, tucked into a remote hillside, miles away from the civilized comfort of Florence and ages away from the London conservatory where he'd heard those dulcet tones last.

No, he must be imagining things.

"Philip, you're not *inconveniencing* this poor gentleman, are you?" The woman spoke in agonized tones, nearer now, coming up rapidly to his right shoulder.

Good God. He couldn't be imagining her *now*. Could he?

"Sir, I beg your pardon. The boy is dreadfully overtired and . . ." Roland turned.

"Oh." She stopped at once, two or three steps away. Her face was nearly hidden by the brim of her hat, but the lips and chin beneath curved exactly as they did in his dreams. Her plaid scarf wrapped around a neck that he knew would be long and sinuous, would melt into the delicate flesh of her chest and shoulders, covered presently and sensibly by a dark wool coat.

"Roland," she said, in a whisper.

Of course he was dreaming. She couldn't possibly be real. A mere figment of his weary imagination; the strain of the journey, taking its toll on his wits.

"Lady Somerton," he said, making a little bow, so the rain dropped from his hat in a single sheet. Since it was a dream, he might as well play his part. "What a charming surprise. I have just been making myself acquainted with your son."

Son. The word echoed in his head.

"Lord Roland," she said, dipping her head. She folded her gloved hands before her. "Indeed, a very great surprise. I should not have . . . Oh, Philip, *really*!"

Roland wheeled around, just in time to watch the tip of the boy's tongue disappear into his cherubic mouth.

"I'm so terribly sorry." She swept past him to take Philip's hand. "He's normally such a *good* boy. It's the journey, and his nursemaid was taken ill in Milan, and . . . oh, Philip, *do* be good and apologize to his lordship."

"You told me to wait where it was dry," Philip said, looking up earnestly at his mother's face.

"So I did," she said, bending next to him, "but I never told you to accost unsuspecting gentlemen in the doorway. Say you're sorry, Philip, and let his lordship pass. He's dreadfully wet."

"Sorry," Philip said.

"Philip, *really.*"

The boy sighed and turned his face to Roland. "I'm most awfully sorry, your lordship. I shall never do it again."

Roland bowed solemnly. "Quite all right, old chap. Quite all right. The heat of the moment. I've done far worse myself."

"That's very good, Philip. Very good," Lady Somerton said. "Now let his lordship pass."

Philip moved grudgingly aside.

"Thank you, sir," Roland said, still solemn, and climbed the steps. He turned in the doorway and removed his hat. "Have you just arrived, madam? I understand they're quite occupied tonight."

"Yes, just now," she said, glancing upward, so the full force of her blue eyes struck him like a most un-dreamlike blow to the noggin. "But I'm sure we shall find a room. Lady Morley is speaking to the landlord this instant, and . . . well, you know Lady Morley."

"Lady Morley, by Gad!" He smiled. "Are the two of you taking a tour? Dashed beastly time of year for it."

She straightened, her hand still clutching Philip's. She didn't return his smile. "I suppose you could call it that. And you, Lord Roland? Are you on your way to Florence, perhaps?"

"No, no. Just left it, in fact. I'm here with my brother and . . . and another fellow. We're . . ." *We're off to spend a year in a drafty Italian castle, devoting ourselves like monks to algebra and Plato and God knows what else. Smashing time.*

Her eyebrows lifted expectantly.

Roland gathered himself. "Well, never mind that. I do hope . . . That is, if I can be of any service . . ."

"No, no." Her eyes dropped. "We're quite all right."

"Are you going in just now?"

"No, I'm . . . I'm waiting for someone."

He peered into the darkness behind her. "Can't you wait inside? It's frightfully wet."

"She'll only be a minute." Her voice was quiet and resolute, just as he remembered it. Rather irritating, that: If he were taking the trouble to dream about her, mightn't she do something more dramatic? More fantastical? Tear off her dress, perhaps, and leap into his arms, and engage him in sexual congress against the wall of the inn, with the rain streaming down her body?

Oh yes. *That* would be a worthwhile dream indeed.

"Very well, then." He made a little bow. "I expect I shall see you shortly."

"Yes, I expect so." As if the prospect were about as appealing as an appointment with the tooth-drawer.

From the innyard a voice shrieked, "Lilibet, you'll never guess what I've found in the stables!" and little Philip shouted back, "Cousin Abigail, come look, the strangest fellow!"

The dream was taking a most unwanted turn.

Roland walked swiftly through the doorway and into the busy warmth of the common room, leaving Lady Elizabeth Somerton and her son under the portico.

F or God's sake, Penhallow. We've been waiting for hours," drawled the Duke of Wallingford, setting down his cup. His eyebrows shot upward at the sight of Roland's face. "What's this, then? Seen a ghost?"

"I believe I have," Roland said. He tossed his hat on the table and swung his coat from his shoulders in a shower of droplets. "You'll never guess the apparition I perceived outside, here of all the bloody godforsaken innyards of the world. Is that wine?"

"The local swill," the duke said, pouring from the pitcher into an empty cup. "I don't make guesses, as a rule, but I'd venture your ghost has something to do with Lady Alexandra Morley. Am I right?"

Roland slumped atop the chair opposite, his bones sinking gratefully into the sturdy frame. "Seen her, have you?"

"Heard her. We were endeavoring to remain unnoticed." Wallingford pushed the cup toward his brother. "Have a drink, old man. Food should be arriving shortly, God willing."

Phineas Burke leaned forward from his seat next to Wallingford. "She's been arguing with the landlord this past quarter hour," he said. "The most infernal din. They've gone upstairs to see the room."

"Mark my words," Wallingford said, "we'll be tossed out on our ears and forced to sleep in the commons."

"Surely not," Roland said, drinking deep. "You're the damned Duke of Wallingford. What the jolly use is it, being a duke, if you can't keep a room at an inn?"

"Mark my words," Wallingford repeated darkly.

Burke pressed his index finger into the worn wood before him. "For one thing, they're women," he said, "and for another, it's Lady Morley. Carries all before her, the old dragon."

"Hardly old," said Roland charitably. "I daresay she hasn't seen thirty yet. Hullo, is that our dinner?"

A girl wobbled toward them, homespun skirts twisting about her legs, bearing a large pewter tray filled with meat and thick country bread. A pretty girl, Roland thought idly, slanting her an assessing look. She caught his look and set down the tray with an awkward crash, just as the voice of Alexandra, Lady Morley erupted from the stairs, cutting through the buzzing din of the other travelers. "It isn't at all acceptable, *non possiblo*, do you hear me? We are English, *anglese*. We can't possibly . . . Oh! Your Grace!"

"Mark my words," muttered Wallingford. He threw down his napkin and rose. "Lady Morley," he said. "Good evening. I trust you're well."

Her ladyship stood on the stairs, tall and imperious, her chestnut hair pulled with unnatural neatness into a smart chignon at the nape of her neck. She'd been a handsome girl several years ago, before her marriage to the Marquess of Morley, and was now an even handsomer woman, all cheekbones and glittering brown eyes. She wasn't exactly to Roland's taste, with her strong, bold-featured face, but he could appreciate her, rather as one appreciated the classical statuary in one's formal gardens, without precisely wanting to embrace it.

"Darling Wallingford," she said, continuing down the stairs toward them, her voice shifting effortlessly from commanding to cajoling, "you're just the man I was hoping for. I can't seem to make these Italian fellows understand that English ladies, however sturdy and liberal minded, simply *cannot* be expected to sleep in a room with strangers. *Male* strangers. *Foreign* male strangers. Don't you agree, Your Grace?" She stopped in front of them.

"Are there no rooms available upstairs, madam?"

She shrugged beautifully, her tailored black shoulder making a practiced little arc through the air. "A small room, a very small room. Hardly large enough for Lady Somerton's boy to sleep in, let alone the three of us." Her gaze shifted to Roland and she started visibly, her entire body snapping backward. "Lord Roland!" she exclaimed. "I'd no idea! Have you . . . my cousin . . . Lady Somerton . . . good God!"

Roland bowed affably. Why not? It seemed the thing to do. "I had the great honor of meeting her ladyship outside on the . . . the portico, a moment ago. And her charming son, of course."

A choking noise emerged from Lady Morley's trim throat, as if a laugh were suppressing itself. "Charming! Yes, quite." Her mouth opened and closed. She cleared her throat.

Roland, watching her, felt his own shock begin to slide away, numbness replaced by awareness. You could not deny the reality of Lady Morley. She crackled with reality. And if Lady Morley were real, then . . .

His nerves took up a strange and inauspicious tingling.

It was true. He hadn't dreamt it. Lilibet was here.

Stop that, he told his nerves sternly, but it only made things worse. Only made things more real, only made Lilibet's presence—the actual existence of her living body not ten yards away—more real. He had the disturbing premonition that he was about to do something rash.

Lady Morley wrung her hands and looked back at the duke beseechingly. "Look here, Wallingford, I really must throw myself on your mercy. Surely you see our little dilemma. Your rooms are ever so much larger, palatial, really, and *two* of them! You can't possibly, in all conscience . . ." Her voice drifted, turned upward. She returned to Roland. "My dear Penhallow. Think of poor Lilibet, sleeping in . . . in a *chair*, quite possibly . . . with all these strangers."

Burke, standing next to Roland with all the good cheer of a lion disturbed from his nap, cleared his throat with an ominous rumble. "Did it not, perhaps, occur to you, Lady Morley, to reserve rooms in advance?"

Roland winced. Damn the fellow. Old scientific Burke was hardly the sort of man to endure arrogant young marchionesses with patience.

Lady Morley's cat-shaped eyes fastened on him in the famous Morley glare. "As a matter of fact, it did, Mr. . . ." She raised her eyebrows expressively. "I'm so terribly sorry, sir. I don't *quite* believe I caught your name."

"I beg your pardon, Lady Morley," said the Duke of Wallingford. "How remiss of me. I have the great honor to present to you—perhaps you may have come across his name, in your philosophical studies—Mr. Phineas Fitzwilliam Burke, of the Royal Society."

"Your servant, madam," Mr. Burke said, with a slight inclination of his head.

"Burke," she said, and then her eyes widened an instant. "Phineas Burke. Of course. The Royal Society. Yes, of course. Everybody knows of Mr. Burke. I found . . . the *Times*, last month . . . your remarks on electrical . . . that new sort of . . ." She drew in a fortifying breath, and then smiled, warmly even. "That is to say, of course we reserved rooms. I sent the wire days ago, if memory serves. But we were delayed in Milan. The boy's nursemaid took ill, you see, and I expect our message did not reach our host in time." She sent a hard look in the landlord's direction.

"Look here." Roland heard his own voice with horror. Here it was. The rash thing, unstoppable as one of Great-Aunt Julia's obscene anecdotes at the dinner table. "Enough of this rubbish. We shouldn't dream of causing any inconvenience to you and your friends, Lady Morley. Not for an instant. Should we, Wallingford?"

"No, damn it," the duke grunted, folding his arms.

"Burke?"

"Bloody hell," muttered Burke, under his breath.

"You see, Lady Morley? All quite willing and happy and so on. I daresay Burke can take the little room upstairs, as he's

such a tiresome, misanthropic old chap, and my brother and I
shall be quite happy to . . ."—he swept his arm to take in the
dark depths of the common room—"make ourselves comfortable downstairs. Will that suit?"

Lady Morley clasped her elegant gloved hands together.
"Darling Penhallow. I knew you'd oblige us. Thanks so *awfully*,
my dear; you can't imagine how thankful I am for your generosity." She turned to the landlord. "Do you understand? *Comprendo?* You may remove His Grace's luggage from the rooms
upstairs and bring up our trunks at once. Ah! Cousin Lilibet!
There you are at last. Have you sorted out the trunks?"

Roland couldn't help himself. He swiveled to the doorway,
desperate to see her, now that he'd recovered his wits; desperate
for even a glimpse of her, without all the rain and darkness and
bloody damned *hats* in the way. He wanted to know everything.
Had she changed? Grown cynical and world-weary? Had her
fresh-faced beauty faded under the blight of marriage to the
legendarily dissolute Earl of Somerton?

Did he wish that it had?

She was kneeling by the door, unbuttoning her son's coat.
Typical of her, that she would make the boy comfortable first,
the little martyr. She turned her head to answer her cousin, her
voice as even and well-modulated as ever, despite the raspy edge
Roland had noticed before. "Yes, they've all been unloaded. The
fellow's coming in the back." She straightened and handed the
boy his coat and began unbuttoning her own.

Roland held his breath. Her gloved fingers found the buttons
expertly and slid them through the holes, exposing inch after
inch of a practical dark blue traveling suit with a high white
collar, pristine and ladylike, her bosom (fuller now, or was that
his imagination?) curving tidily beneath the perfect tailoring of
her jacket.

He felt a sharp poke in his ribs. "Keep your tongue in your
mouth, you dog," hissed his brother.

The landlord hurried down the steps to assist her. She had
that effect, Roland thought crossly. "I take the coat, milady," he
said, dipping obsequiously, folding the wet wool over his arm as
if it were cloth of gold. "And the hat. The hat. Ah, *mia donna*,
it is so wet. You come to the fire, you dry. *Mia povera donna.*"

"Thank you," she said. "*Grazie.*" She allowed herself to be drawn to the fire, smoothing her dark hair with one hand, pulling young Philip with the other. The light gleamed gold against her pale skin, casting shadows beneath her cheekbones. She looked tired, Roland thought, taking an involuntary step in her direction before he remembered himself. Concern! For Lady Somerton! As if she couldn't take perfectly good care of herself without him. She'd proven that well enough.

Roland looked around and found that both Burke and Wallingford had resumed their seats, and he was standing there like the village idiot, staring after her ladyship's decorously clothed backside.